You're Not You

You're Not You

Michelle Wildgen

THOMAS DUNNE BOOKS
ST. MARTIN'S PRESS ❧ NEW YORK

THOMAS DUNNE BOOKS.
An imprint of St. Martin's Press.

www.stmartins.com

Library of Congress Cataloging-in-Publication Data

Wildgen, Michelle.
    You're not you : a novel / Michelle Wildgen.—1st ed.
       p. cm.
    ISBN 0-312-35229-8
    EAN 978-0-312-35229-5
    1. Women college students—Fiction. 2. Caregivers—Fiction. 3. Amyotrophic
lateral sclerosis—Patients—Fiction.

PS3623.I542 Y68 2006
813'.6—dc22

                                                          2006040200

10 9 8 7 6 5 4 3 2

For my family

acknowledgments

I'M VERY GRATEFUL TO *Prairie Schooner* for publishing the short story "You're Not You" and to the Hall Farm Center for Arts and Education for providing a beautiful and welcoming work space to expand the story into a novel.

Bay Anapol, Jenn Epstein, Krista Landers, Steve O'Brien, Jon Raymond, and Claudia Zuluaga were insightful and encouraging readers who rarely resorted to outright mockery. Emily Dickmann, Tom Kuplic, Melissa Irr, Alison Weatherby, and the Wildgen and Rootes families all listened graciously to each report on the whole project, which I shared in excruciating detail.

Emilie Stewart's energy and enthusiasm are boundless. I'm extremely grateful for everything she did for this book, which was a lot. A big thank-you to Anne Merrow at Thomas Dunne Books/St. Martin's Press for her guidance and zeal, perceptive edits to the book, and zipping back to the office on a Friday evening to find out how it ends.

Thanks to the staff of *Tin House* magazine for the practical advice, indulging my bitter streak, and getting me out of the house a few times a week.

I feel immense compassion for all who miss out on being an aunt to the following incomparable small people: Justin! Taylor! Christopher! Caroline!

Last and most important, thanks to those who have provided the most gracious hospitality both at home and abroad, the wittiest commentary on the stupidest movies, and the loveliest solstice dinners. You know who you are.

You're Not You

one

I WOULD BEGIN ON Thursday morning. The idea was for me to arrive early, by seven thirty, so Evan could show me what he did for his wife before he left for work, and afterward I'd follow him and Kate through a typical morning and afternoon. I had one day to observe and then training was over.

I began the morning by smacking the snooze button in a single well-aimed flail at six fifteen. I then lay immobile, arm outstretched and palm still flat against the warm grooves of the clock, enumerating my regrets over the switch from a night job to a morning one, until the alarm resumed.

After a pot of coffee, however, I began to change my mind. It turned out our living room windows faced east and sunlight flooded the room, something I had not had the opportunity to note in the nine months I had lived here. I settled myself before the television, coffee cup a pleasingly warm weight on my stomach, careful not to un-balance the couch (a green and gold yard-sale affair we had to treat gingerly, since Jill and I had hacked off one of the legs to get it in the front door, then propped it back on the splintered stump). I even opened a window to let in the breeze. You really could hear birds chirping in the morning—that wasn't just in folk songs. I sipped my coffee and listened to the anchors' chitchat. Things were happening in the world. For once I knew what some of them were.

By the time I arrived at the Norrises' house, I felt downright hale. My lungs, I thought, breathing deeply as I rang the bell, seemed to be of genuinely admirable capacity.

Evan opened the front door. "Bec," he said, smiling. "I guess this is the official welcome. Come on back to the bedroom." He was wearing dark pants, a neatly ironed white shirt.

I watched his hands swing as we walked to the back of the house, liking him. Something in Evan's gait seemed familiar, but then lately I had detected a bizarre habit of trying to associate every person I liked with Liam: If Jill made me laugh I listened to the tone of her voice to see if it was like Liam's when he told a story; if a guy on the street gave me a certain kind of smile I searched his face for Liam's thick eyebrows or his straight white teeth.

In the bedroom Kate was in her wheelchair, already dressed in a khaki skirt and blue T-shirt. Her damp hair left dark patches on the shoulders of her top. Her face was pale and bare, her eyes soft. Without makeup she seemed soft-fleshed, vulnerable as an open mollusk. When she spoke to me, her voice was low, the words slurred and indistinct though it was clear she was trying to enunciate. Evan translated after each phrase, switching pronouns and glancing back and forth between us.

"So we let Evan . . . do everything today . . . and you watch, okay? Sometime I'll have you dress me . . . just so you know how, but . . . we can do that later."

When this last part was repeated, Kate gave me a sheepish smile. I said, "Oh, don't worry. I'll learn soon enough, right?" Maybe at the beginning she always gave herself a little grace period before she showed a total stranger everything. Frankly, I was grateful for the wait. I might not stay at this job beyond the summer. Perhaps I would never have to deal with dressing, period.

But I was resolved to put in the three months till September. Look at Jill—back in high school she'd stuck it out, for no money, volunteering at an ugly nursing home for almost a year. By contrast, I'd found a pretty easy deal (I allowed myself a moment of superiority), and presumably I had a bit more fortitude at twenty-one than Jill had had at seventeen.

"So," said Evan, clasping his hands, "let's get to it."

The three of us went into the bathroom, which was palatial. There was room for three chairs, Kate and Evan facing each other next to the counter and me standing perpendicular to them, opposite the mirror. On the counter was a neatly divided compartment case of makeup and a few pricey hair products lined up near the sink: bottles of creams and mousse and a vial of something syrupy and clear.

Evan held up a bottle and said, "First you take a little of this and rub it on your hands and put it through her hair."

She let her head tip back as he combed his fingers through her hair, which looked silky and heavy, and rubbed his palms over the crown of her skull. The cream smelled of limes and coconut. That was just fine. I knew how to do that. He combed her hair back from her face, parting it to one side. I made a mental note that it was the left side. Her skin was pale, flushed through the cheeks and dusted with freckles I hadn't noticed the day before. Her eyes, a light, clear tortoiseshell amber, bore a burst of gold around the pupils. It was not a girlish face, but built of firm lines instead, her eyebrows slanted rather than blandly curving, her nose long and straight, the tip slightly angled toward her lips, her mouth wide but not especially full. It was the face maybe not of a model but of a tall woman, its scale too bold to be comfortable on a petite frame. How tall had she been? Five eight, five nine? Not just the chair but her thinness made it difficult to guess. The proportions were off.

When he finished she said through Evan, "How are you with makeup?"

My hand darted up to my face. Then I knew I should have put on a little, out of deference to the job. I hated makeup—my eyelashes felt stiff when I wore mascara, and I always forgot powder. I never understood how Jill could go out on a hot summer morning with her eyes smoky and dark and her mouth covered in a coat of burgundy lipstick. Yesterday at the interview Kate hadn't seemed to be wearing much, but now I guessed it was the kind of expertly blended makeup that only looks like nothing.

"I can learn," I hedged.

"Evan learned," Kate said.

"Oh, then no problem," I said. I took out some mints and offered the tin around. It was as though we were just girls hanging out. Except for the husband it felt like junior high. Of course, if I had paid better attention in junior high makeup sessions I might have known what I was doing by now. "This is going to be good for me," I said, through a mouthful of mints. "My roommate's been bugging me to wear some mascara since we were thirteen."

Kate smiled as she lifted her face to Evan. He dotted her skin with foundation and smoothed the makeup out, covering the freckles across the bridge of her nose, which I thought was too bad. Then he dusted her cheeks with blush and held up two compacts of eye shadow. She looked them over for a moment and then nodded at one, saying in that low voice something that sounded like "just a little." Evan went to work like a pro, whisking taupe shadow over her closed eyelids and feathering a stiff brush, tipped with brown powder, against the grain of her eyebrows and then brushing them back into place.

It was a brisk, impressive procedure, and as I watched I wondered if I would ever go through anything like it myself if I were her. She didn't have to go out every day, yet she did her hair and put on a full face of makeup? It seemed silly, so precious, to go through all these motions for nothing. But perhaps she simply liked to feel polished.

Evan lifted her face with a knuckle beneath her chin and caught her eyelashes in a curler. "If I ever get sick of the marketing game I'm going to go pro as a makeup artist," he said, then wiped extra mascara off a wand and started brushing it up and down Kate's lashes.

"I'd pay you," I said. He laughed and held up a couple of lipsticks. Kate nodded at one in his right hand. As he finished with her lips, the two of us looked her over. It was the same face I'd seen yesterday, her but intensified, her eyes darkened slightly and her mouth rosy. Now that I'd seen him do it, makeup didn't seem so mysterious.

Evan leaned down and used the tip of his thumb to brush away a bit of powder, his face intent. He smiled at her. Maybe the makeup was for him.

Finished, they turned to look at me. I glimpsed us all in the mirror, the backs of their tawny heads gleaming in the reflection as they faced me, and between them the pale oval of my face. After looking at Kate, whose coloring was faintly golden, my own skin seemed whiter, my nose a formless little button and my cheeks more rounded than I'd ever noticed, my naked eyes a wolfish gray.

"Think you can do this tomorrow?" she said.

"Sure," I told her. I considered practicing on Jill tonight but decided I wouldn't need to. Tomorrow I would just remember that all I had to do was enhance what was there and I'd be fine.

THEIR AD HAD CAUGHT my eye because it was so calm, free of suspicious overenthusiasm and exclamation points. Very few jobs deserved that kind of punctuation, and I appreciated an employer who recognized that. They were seeking a helper for the wife, who had Lou Gehrig's disease. When I phoned, I was imagining reading books to her, serving tea that smelled of something crisp and bracing, like mint. Even after Evan said Kate was only thirty-six, I persisted in imagining someone tremulous and elderly, someone you take one look at and know she needs your help—your humor, your height, your muscled arms.

I may have been inventing everything else, but I knew the most important thing: The salary was fifteen dollars an hour, assuming I turned out to be a caregiving sort of person and got the job. I had no idea if I was this sort of person or not—it's my belief that sometimes you just let the experts decide. They weren't even looking for a nurse, or a true home health care worker. Helping out, Evan said on the phone. Driving her around, making phone calls, lending a hand around the house. How hard could it be?

He hadn't seemed overly concerned with my lack of prior experience, which was a plus. I was so unfamiliar with the details of the disease that I wasn't even certain who Lou Gehrig was—a baseball player, I eventually recalled, and I pictured a woman slowly transformed into a thick mannish figure, growing daily more meaty and sad, until I realized I was thinking of Babe Ruth.

Instead I found a slim woman with dark gold hair that fell past her shoulders and bright amber eyes. When I arrived for the interview the French doors had swung open of their own accord as soon as I rang the bell, revealing a woman in a wheelchair, her hands folded in her lap, and a man standing behind her. His hand was resting on her shoulder. The two of them were positioned a few feet back from the front doors. They were the very first thing I saw when I entered the house.

She smiled at me. Between her shining hair and her dangling gold earrings, she looked even younger than I had expected. Her prettiness and her berry-red dress were a relief and a surprise to me, so much so that I had to admit I must have been steeling myself for this moment. Even as I was pleased to see what she looked like, I was ashamed to think how I might have responded if she had been homely and lumpy, in a pilled but comfortable polyester jumpsuit. I'd been picturing an older couple, a smaller house.

Kate mouthed hello. She shifted her knee slightly to one side, so that it pressed something, a switch or a button of some kind, on the chair. The big French doors swung shut behind me.

"Hi there," I said. I nodded to both of them. I wanted to address Kate, even though it was tempting to go toward Evan, since I had already talked to him. He'd turned out to be tall, maybe a bit gangly, with thinning blond hair and a handsome, lean face, long-nosed and etched with lines around the lips and eyes. He wore round wire glasses and rubbed at the back of his neck in the manner of someone who recently cut his hair shorter than he'd meant to.

"Becky, right?" Evan said. There was something bookish and friendly about him.

"Everyone just calls me Bec, actually," I said. "Don't ask me why."

I took a step toward them, wondering how to greet her. The movement of her leg had thrown me off. Evan had told me she was almost totally paralyzed, but clearly she could do some things, so I held out my hand for her to shake. Her glance alighted on my outstretched hand and then on her own hands, thin and attenuated with oval unpolished nails. The hands lay in her lap, motionless. She gave me a little shrug and a smile. Suddenly I was sure I'd made a terrible decision coming here—what did I know about this job besides the money they offered? I hadn't thought this through at all.

"I'm kind of an idiot," I said.

She spoke, glancing toward Evan and grinning, and I took another step forward, straining to hear her. Had he mentioned this part, that I would not understand a word this woman said? Unsure if I was supposed to be answering, I watched Evan watch her and then say to me, smiling rather kindly, quoting his wife, "The important thing is that you feel at home enough to say so."

Evan set Kate's hand on the armrest, her fingers placed over the wheelchair buttons, and they led me through the living room toward the kitchen. The living room was cool and pearl gray, the sort of place that looks as if no one ever sits down. On a table by the wall near the kitchen door was a statue of a girl, and as we walked past it—Evan first, then me, then Kate, the chair's gears whirring softly—I slowed to look at it. One arm hung at her side and the other curled over her head. Her stomach muscles were molded clearly, and so was the muscle at the top of one thigh as she stepped forward. The breasts curved out from her rib cage and came to a smooth undifferentiated point at the tips. Someone had hung a spider plant too close to her, so she had a mermaidish mop of green hair.

Kate saw me looking at the statue and rolled her eyes. With a tolerant smile, she tipped her head toward the kitchen, where Evan was waiting for us. I took it to mean the statue was his taste and not hers.

In the kitchen she stopped her chair at the table and Evan gestured for me to sit down as well. He stood, leaning against a butcher-block island in the center of the room. Behind him half a dozen battered copper pans hung from hooks in the ceiling. A row of cookbooks slanted against the refrigerator. If I'd had a kitchen this beautiful, I thought, I'd know how to cook by now. As it was, I mostly microwaved butter and poured it on things.

Sitting across from Kate gave me a chance to get a better look at her. The back of her head was cradled in the padded half-moon attached to the back of the wheelchair. When she brought her head forward, to swallow or take a breath, it fell a little too far, so that I could see her pale side part. She had the kind of hair, straight and heavy, that I'd always coveted. I was very aware that my own hair was a dark frizz around my face and stuck to the back of my neck. I set my forearms on the table and realized my button-down shirt had a tiny stain on the cuff. I felt incredibly out of place: fuzzy, damp, badly dressed. You think you're showing up to help people out, but there they were, cool and sleek and regarding me with an air of friendly curiosity, as though I were a Girl Scout or a Mormon.

If I got through this without embarrassing myself, I decided, I'd go home and call Liam. Let that be my little carrot to draw me through. I hadn't seen him in days, which was typical, if unpleasant. Sometimes I wandered aimlessly around his part of campus just to glimpse him, though we were smart enough not to be seen strolling the lawns together. When he did see me, sitting in the Rathskeller on rainy days, a book and beer on the table before me, or when we passed one another trudging up the steep sidewalk of Bascom Hill, we nodded and smiled pleasantly, leaving our sunglasses on. Sometimes we stopped and spoke—no lingering, no idle touches—just long enough to plan a meeting at my house.

I made an effort to apply myself and listen as Kate started to talk about what she needed. Her voice was soft, the sound coming from low in her throat. I had to watch her mouth carefully. Kate would speak, and then pause, and then Evan repeated what she'd said. Evan seemed to understand her, though sometimes he had to double-check a word or two.

She was almost impossible for me to comprehend without his translation. I was becoming very worried. Would he be here all the time? Because I didn't see how I would ever understand her. I darted back and forth between looking at her and then at him. It seemed very important to pay attention to Kate, even when Evan was the one speaking. After all, I reasoned, they were her words. So I watched Kate as Evan said he would generally get Kate up and dressed, and usually help her to bed as well. Without seeming to realize it, Evan sometimes referred to himself in the third person when he quoted her.

She had pockets of movement left, he explained—she could muster some strength in her legs, enough to press a button on her motorized wheelchair with one side of her knee to open and close the front door, or to kick if she were in a swimming pool. Her fingers were strong enough to manipulate a remote control or a simple switch if it was placed beneath her hand. She could hold her head up and turn her neck, but when the muscles grew tired she often let the back of her skull rest in the padded cushion on her chair.

"We're not talking about something excessively clinical," Evan had said. "Obviously you're not monitoring her heart rate or giving her injections or something. More the general business of keeping her mobile and communicative. But I don't want to misrepresent it—she does need help bathing, for example, and using the bathroom, and as long as you're here we'd expect that to be part of it." Evan paused and looked toward his wife. "So if you're really uncomfortable with that, say so now."

"I don't think I am," I said. "But I don't know for sure till I try."

"That's honest," he said approvingly. "I take it you haven't done anything like this before? Or maybe you knew someone who did?"

"Not me, no. My roommate's grandmother needed a caregiver for a while before she died, but I think her mom did most of that."

"Uh-huh," he said, sounding as though he was waiting for more.

"I guess it made an impression on me," I said. Had it? I remembered it still, years later, so perhaps it had. Certainly it had made an impression on Jill, who was very vocal about her plans to die in some strategically timed manner. "How much they could have used some help."

In fact, there had been a home health care nurse who was supposed to be doing the heavy lifting, as it were, but Jill's grandmother had insisted her mother and Jill help her instead. "But no, I personally don't have a lot of experience." I paused. "May I ask why you aren't going through an agency?"

Kate spoke first. Then Evan nodded and said, "We have before. They're fine, but they seem to deal with Kate as sort of a generalized patient instead of as an individual." He cleared his throat. "They were never that willing to do things her way instead of what they'd always done. So we train each person ourselves. Fewer channels for things to get lost in.

"We've been using friends of friends, and now, of course, an ad, just to see who turns up," Evan was saying. "We had two, Hillary and Anna, but Anna left for graduate school in New Haven. So Kate wants to choose her own and make sure it's someone she has fun with."

"Well," I said to Kate, "that makes sense."

It was awkward, staring at this person who simply looked back at me. I nodded a lot. Sometimes she gave me a quick, understanding smile, the lines around her eyes deepening for a moment, and other times she only sat quietly and let me watch her. She was so small: her neck only a stem, her shoulders narrow and bony beneath the fabric of her dress. I tried to picture Evan dressing her. It must be such a delicate operation. On her wrists a prominent knob of bone bore outward, pressing white against the skin. If someone wasn't careful they'd bruise her against the hard metal of the wheelchair, or the walls of their widened doorways.

"I think I mentioned references on the phone, right?" Evan said, startling me out of my thoughts.

References? He hadn't mentioned references. I didn't think so, anyway, and in the absence of a job application asking for them, I hadn't even thought about it. The setup had seemed so casual on the phone.

"I'm sure you did," I lied. "I can write them down for you now, if you want." He handed me a notebook and pen that had been sitting on the table. I stared hard at the empty paper, then wrote down my boss at the steak house where I waitressed, as well as my boss from last summer, when I'd worked at a temp agency. Maybe I should have written down a professor or someone who could attest to my intellect, but I didn't know my professors very well. Liam was faculty, but I hadn't exactly taken a class with him—he'd taught Jill's class.

I pushed the notebook back toward Evan, who set it aside without looking at it. Maybe it was just a formality. No—they were looking for someone to come in and have the run of their house and be responsible for Kate. They'd call, and my steak house boss would know I was looking. I'd just have to tell her I needed daytime work. Which I did—my parents paid my tuition, but I had next year's living expenses to think about.

References dispatched, we returned to discussing what they needed.

As we got up to tour the rest of the house, I wondered how much of this they'd done before. Evan hadn't said how long she had been ill, but they seemed comfortable enough, their explanations practiced enough, that I thought it must have been some time. Five years, ten years? I was struck by the feeling—both pleasing and ominous—that they were wooing me a little, showing me how normal and easy it all was.

They led me down the hall, gesturing as we passed the den, the family room, the dining room, the sunroom. That cool living room at the front seemed strange now that I had seen the rest of the house, which was comfortable and bright. The kitchen walls were the color of buttercups, and in the other rooms there were vases of tulips and bowls of pears, big comfy chairs and end tables piled with books. As they showed me around I took in the miscellaneous details of a stranger's home: an old-fashioned shaving brush in the bathroom, a pair of dumbbells on a chair in the den. After ten minutes I knew more of their home than Liam's, though I had been seeing him for almost five months. I knew he lived in a small yellow house walking distance from campus, in a neighborhood known as a good place for big dogs and small children. Once I had made Jill drive me past the house late at night, but I had definitely never been inside. Were there bowls of fruit on the tables and vacuum tracks on the rugs? Or was it messier, with half-empty coffee cups in the living room, damp panty hose draped over the towel rack?

"I love your house," I called out, from behind them. Kate turned her head as far as she could toward me. I saw her lips move and decided she was saying thank you.

"You're welcome," I hazarded.

"Kate should have been a decorator," Evan said, as we turned left at the end of the hall. "She chose almost everything here. I helped on a couple rooms, too, but mainly it's all her."

It made sense: Her clothes were a similar palette of bright colors. Only her black wheelchair seemed out of place. I wondered if they made wheelchairs in other colors or out of other metals. She would have looked very nice in copper.

"What were you?" I asked gracelessly. The past tense sounded worse than I'd meant it to, but Kate either didn't notice or chose to ignore it. She answered, glancing at me and then at Evan, who said, "She was in advertising, too. That's how we met."

"Really?" I said. "That's my major. When I talked to you yesterday I was on my way to my final in 'Stoking Desire: Consumer Trends 341.' "

Kate smiled. "Is that what they call it these days?" Evan said, sounding faintly appalled. "We should talk about that too, maybe. What are you hoping to do after college?"

I froze. I had only mentioned it to establish a little rapport. Quite frankly I thought I'd gotten a C on the final. My choice of major was mainly borne of panic and an unproven suspicion that I might have a flair for writing catchy slogans. If pressed, I would be forced to admit I found the whole thing rather shady and manipulative. Yet these two seemed fairly straightforward, and suddenly I was unwilling to make up something interview-y.

"I honestly don't know," I said.

Kate nodded, her eyes closing briefly as if in emphatic agreement with something I had said. She spoke, and Evan watched her and then repeated: "We both totally fell into it. My major was literature and Kate's was business."

We were at the bedroom by then. They had a bed in the center of the room. Just a regular king size with a blue spread and a few extra pillows, flanked by nightstands but no railings or machinery that I could see. When I turned toward them, they were both watching me stare at their bed. Our eyes met for a moment, and then Evan began opening closets to show me how her clothes were organized, pointing out the remotes to the television, the lights, the fan. Next to what I guessed was her side of the bed was a nightstand, on which sat a small box with a lit green button. An electric cord ran from the box behind the table. He picked it up and showed it to me.

"I go out of town sometimes, and when I do we leave the lifeline under Kate's finger at night. If she has any emergency she presses it and that calls the fire department, the police, the ambulance, and a caregiver."

I pictured Kate surrounded by a swarm of dark uniforms, red lights flashing in the windows. "Wow," I said lamely. "Have you ever had to use it?"

Evan set it back down. Kate shook her head. "Not yet," she said, Evan translating. "We just got it in the past few months."

Kate said something else, but instead of repeating it right away, Evan looked back at her and shook his head. She raised her eyebrows at him. He sighed. Turning back to me, he said, "She wants me to tell you—assuming this all works out, of course—that if you're ever here and there's a problem, not to call nine-one-one or press the button without her permission. You should know that going in."

I thought maybe it was a joke, except that Evan seemed serious, even vexed. His brows were knit, and he crossed and hurriedly uncrossed his arms as he spoke. "What if it's an emergency?" I asked. "What if there's no time?" Kate spoke, looking at me and then more intently at Evan. He fiddled with the window latch as he said: "Kate feels very strongly about this. Once she goes into a hospital, say, if she were put on a respirator, it might be hard to get her off it." He stood up and put the button back on the table.

"I don't understand why you'd want to," I said, baffled. Was this some Byzantine role-playing game designed to ferret out the nutjobs? Surely anyone would press the button without asking. It seemed as if it would be a black mark if I said I might try to help her, but what did this woman want if not help?

"I wouldn't. *We* wouldn't."

Kate spoke again, more loudly this time, lifting her chin to project as well as she could. She watched him closely as he translated. "People can end up stuck on a respirator, in an institution, with no options. I know it seems odd, but it's important." He turned to me, his back to Kate, and said, in a much lighter, faster tone, "God, this is a heavy-duty way to kick off an interview. Really, Bec, don't worry. It's the kind of thing you need to have on the table and then forget about. It'll probably never come up. If it does, she just needs to sign off on it is all."

I looked to Kate to follow up on this, but she said nothing this time. Her lips were taut. She didn't seem to like something about what he'd said, but I didn't know what. She felt me looking at her and let her expression relax.

"Sure," I agreed. I paused, then decided to be honest. "I think it might be tough to remember that in an emergency, but I'd do my best." That was straightforward. I was feeling almost reckless now. I could be perfectly honest, I could be myself, because I could see now that I ran almost no risk of getting the job. They wanted someone with cooking skills, makeup skills, actual life skills, not just the ability to trounce one's best friend in handstand contests.

"I bet that way you don't risk creating an emergency if there isn't one," I suggested. They looked at each other but nodded. "I didn't even know they had anything like this," I said conversationally, tapping the cord. "Did it just come out?"

Kate said something with a tilt of her head, her eyes cast briefly heavenward. Evan repeated: "A few years back. But she was fine without it up till a couple months ago."

"Lou Gehrig's moves that fast?" I asked. So maybe even in January, for example, she had been moving well enough to reach a phone, speaking clearly enough to be understood? Looking at her now, her body carefully held in place in her chair, it seemed impossibly recent.

I thought someone in Kate's condition would have become immobilized through either one quick trauma or else years and years of slow deterioration, the sort that gave you time to prepare for each new loss. A year ago, she was probably in a wheelchair but didn't need Evan to translate. Maybe not long before that she only used a walker.

Kate spoke, and Evan waited and then said, "It depends on the person. Some people are fine for years. Kate's has moved faster than we'd like. We'd hoped she would just have tremors, or maybe use a walker for a few years, but she needed the chair after a few months. Lately she's been losing a bit more ground."

"I see," I said. I liked that measured way of talking about it, as though it were a burned cake or a vacation over too soon. Their calm seemed brave. I tried to imagine Kate walking into a doctor's office in a dress and sandals—no, a suit, high heels—nodding at the receptionist, sitting in a straight-backed orange chair with her purse in her lap while a doctor held up brightly colored charts.

I stood there, fingering the embroidered edge of a pillowcase. They were bright people, literally so: their blond hair and the vivid colors in their clothes, the light shining on their picture frames and paintings. I found them admirable, maybe for no other reason than that they had said nothing overtly angry or weepy.

"Well," I said. Suddenly we were all smiling shiny interview smiles again. Kate nodded at Evan and he said, "Thank you for coming, Bec. We have a few more people to meet to see who's the best fit with us, but we'll be in touch."

"Sounds good," I said heartily. "Of course." I shook Evan's proffered hand. Looking for a way to do something similar with Kate, I let my hand hover a foot above her shoulder, then thought better of it and lifted it into a wave. "Thanks. Thank you." I started to leave but then turned back and said, "Listen, can you recommend a book on this for me? On the disease? Either way, I might want to read up a little."

Kate's expression sharpened, her eyes focusing more tightly on me, and a faint smile touched the corners of her mouth. She wheeled the chair over to the bookcase, indicating with her head for me to follow, and nodded at one shelf.

"The one at the end, I assume?" Evan asked her. *"Living with ALS?"* She nodded, and Evan reached past us and tapped the spine of a thick blue book. I didn't know if they meant for me to borrow it or only to note the author, so I studied the spine intently, repeating the title. "I'll put a hold on it at the library," I said. I was embarrassed to have asked. I'd been sincere but now seemed disingenuous. "Thanks again."

I walked out to my car, still thinking about the notion of fit. It was a nicety of interviewing I never failed to appreciate. It comforted me to think that any job I wasn't offered was not because I was totally unqualified but simply due to a vague notion of attraction. Fit, that's what it was: fit, not failure, like a date you kiss good-bye without feeling a thing, except an unfocused sense of goodwill and the knowledge that you won't ever see each other again.

MAKEUP APPLIED AND HAIR dressed, Kate led the way into the kitchen. She pulled up next to the table but not facing it while Evan poured himself a cup of coffee. He held up another mug to me.

"Thanks," I said.

"Milk's in the fridge," he said, nudging a sugar bowl toward me. I found the milk, sloshed a bit in, and dropped a spoonful of sugar into my mug.

Evan opened a pantry door and gestured to me to follow, which I did, sipping contentedly at my coffee. It was a big walk-in, stocked with blue and yellow tin gallons of French olive oil, jars of tomatoes and peaches and pears. Beneath that was a neat shelf of bottles. They had spices I knew but had rarely seen people really use: jars filled with piles of crimson threads of saffron or bright gold powdered turmeric; tiny reddish pellets that looked like the centers of flowers; little curls of cinnamon like stubby brown cigarettes; something I first thought was a jar of almonds but that turned out to be whole nutmeg.

"This is really something," I said. I looked over my shoulder at Kate, who was sitting just outside the pantry door. "Did you cook?"

She nodded and said something. " 'I used to love to cook,' " Evan's voice translated near my ear, startling me. I'd forgotten he was in the pantry too.

I touched a plastic bag filled with desiccated burgundy peppers, like long, shriveled hearts. "What did you like to make?"

She tipped her head, with a look on her face that was half-wistful and half-proud. "All kinds of stuff."

I turned back to the pantry, eyeing a jar stacked with coins of sliced cucumbers and starbursts of some green herb and wondering who had put these up last summer. Could it have been Kate? Evan was still standing where he'd been when he first motioned for me to come over to the pantry: next to a whole wall stacked with the same brown boxes on each shelf. He reached into one of the open boxes and held up a can a little smaller than a soda. A nutrition shake. He handed it to me and then grabbed another.

"Breakfast," he said.

He took a white plastic funnel and a long clear tube from where they were sitting by the sink and held them up for me to see. "I'm going to do this today, but tomorrow I'll let you do it." He and Kate exchanged a look. "Unless you want to do it now."

"You'd let me do this before makeup?" I asked, eyeing the tube. Where exactly was that supposed to go?

Kate said something and Evan translated: " 'Well, the makeup. That's important. This is just sticking a tube into my digestive tract.' "

I laughed, but I had no intention of getting ahead of myself on the first day of training. If they offered me the option, I was watching.

Evan showed me how to attach the tube and funnel to each other.

"If you lift her shirt on the right side, you'll see a little valve." He did this, gesturing with the funnel for me to come closer. I went to the other side of her chair and bent at the waist, bracing myself on her wheelchair. I saw Kate give my hand on her armrest the briefest of glances. I took my hand off of it, bracing myself against my knees.

But I didn't see anything, just her pale skin, the faint marks from her waistband, and a freckle on her rib.

"You may have to lower her waistband a little," Evan said. He pushed her waistband down.

"Is that it?" I asked her, glancing up. I was so close to her I could smell the faint powdered fragrance of the makeup on her cheeks. When she nodded and said yes I smelled the toothpaste in her mouth, a mix of mint and something like clove. Next to me Evan was warm and very close. I could smell the clean, laundry scent of his clothes.

He pointed at a round white plastic ring inside her skin, with a plug in the center, attached at one side by a tiny plastic arm. Evan glanced at me and said, "That's the valve. We call it the button a lot, I don't know why. So now I go ahead and open it."

Kate said something and I leaned back a little to watch her lips move. Her bottom teeth overlapped slightly. "Don't be nervous because of the valve," she said. "It freaks out everyone."

This was a relief—I could hardly take my eyes off it. The valve was embedded in Kate's flesh, a few inches above her navel, and the plug that closed it was the kind that holds air inside water wings. Evan took the plug by the little nubby tab and opened it gently.

"It's—she's—lined with plastic. It doesn't hurt. Now I need to insert the tube into the valve." He steadied one hand against Kate's belly and eased the tube in with the other. She sat silent and composed, and I tried to be as still as she was. Evan stopped inserting the tube. "You'll feel a little click when it's in right," he said.

"Now you give the can a good shake and then just pour it into the funnel." He did both and then straightened up.

This posture was hurting my back, so I stood up too, accidentally brushing against him. Evan moved a step away without saying anything, holding the full funnel in the air like a cocktail glass.

"The first few days are the hard part," Kate, and then he, said. "Once you actually start the hands-on stuff. But after a few days you get familiar."

"It doesn't seem so terrible," I said. Even to myself I sounded relieved. "It seems kind of straightforward, actually."

They exchanged a glance, and Evan went on, in the faster, more relaxed tone that I now realized meant he was speaking for himself and not Kate: "You can always give me a call at work if you need anything." He glanced at Kate. I wondered if they said this to everyone, or if they sensed that I would really need it. I didn't think I would. So far it seemed easy enough: You put makeup on; you fit a simple if weirdly intimate apparatus together. Really, except for the feeding tube, I wouldn't do much for her that I couldn't do for myself.

"Or you can call Hillary, who's the other caregiver, or one of Kate's other friends. A lot of them are old caregivers." He smiled at no one in particular. "No one wants to lose touch with her."

Kate grinned at me and said something, glancing at Evan and then back at me. I smiled uncertainly. Evan laughed and said, " 'They come to worship me.' "

"Something about the wound in my side," added Kate. For a moment I gazed, smiling uncomprehendingly, at her lips even after they had stopped moving. Then Evan repeated it, and I laughed. I laughed more loudly than it warranted, because I caught Kate's pleased expression when she saw the joke was still funny secondhand, and because I knew she was making an effort for me.

It was really very difficult getting to know someone like this. The more Evan translated, the more he spoke to me about what he was doing, the more I felt as though he and I were in conversation and Kate was off in the background. I made the effort to make eye contact with her and keep my attention on her, but really I wanted to focus on Evan. It was so much easier. And though I wouldn't have thought a woman who could do so little for herself would need humanizing, I realized I had been reading her relative silence as aloofness. I turned slightly away from Evan now, focusing my attention on her.

AFTER THAT THE DAY continued a lot like any other first day on the job: them showing me things and me nodding and realizing I should have brought something to write on. But I figured it would come back to me as I needed it.

I'd been wondering how Kate spent her days. It turned out the pile of books I'd seen by the table was hers, and on her computer there was a list of folders on ALS research and fund-raising. Evan had his own computer in another room, and this one was set up for Kate, with a small round silver sensor we could stick to her forehead. She moved her head and the sensor somehow clicked what she wanted on the screen the same way a mouse would.

"Do you do a lot of fund-raising?" I asked. She nodded and left it at that. I didn't need to ask how she'd become interested and I guessed I would be making a lot of phone calls on her behalf. I hated that sort of thing.

"A lot of times we have people over, and if Evan can't get home I might ask you to help me get ready," she said, pausing to let Evan repeat. "Do you have any interest in cooking? There's caterers and Evan too, if you don't, of course."

Why not? If someone was teaching me it might be fun. Maybe someday I'd even give a dinner party, for which I'd be flawlessly made-up. This job was going to be great for me. "I'll definitely give it a shot if we start very slowly," I said. There was a pause. "Like, salad-slow," I added. She was probably the sort who thought fresh pasta was simple too.

They were showing me around the office, which was largely devoted to filing cabinets filled with medical insurance and records, when Kate said, "I'd like to use the bathroom."

"Okay," Evan said. He nodded at me to let me know I should follow, and the three of us made our way in a single-file line.

Back in the bathroom I perched voyeuristically on the edge of the counter, as Kate stopped the wheelchair next to the toilet. Evan took her by the arms and drew her to her feet. "If you work quickly," he said, "she can stand. Not for very long, but long enough." Her head fell forward but she was upright, her arms still draped over Evan's shoulders, her knees locked and legs trembling slightly. My hand reached out involuntarily toward her.

Evan was fast—he lifted her skirt to her waist and pulled her pink bikinis to her knees in practically one motion, then gripped her beneath her arms and lowered her slowly to the toilet seat. I looked all over the place as he did this, not sure where it was best to be staring: Her face, as though I were waiting for her to show embarrassment? Her pelvis, where all of Evan's motion was, motions that I guessed I should be learning? I had a glimpse of a light brown triangle of pubic hair, the little mouth of the valve above a sharp hip bone. I'd seen a few photos around the house of her when she was healthier, and she'd been average-thin before, but now her pelvis was an empty bowl, her thighs almost straight lines from hip to knee.

The three of us, Evan and me standing with our hands in our pockets, Kate sitting, had a moment of awkward silence. I could hear the sound of urine trickling beneath her.

"You have to be ready to grab her if she can't stand," Evan said, breaking the stillness. I nodded. "She'll tell you, and if that's the case, then forget about what you're doing, her pants or whatever, and just grab her and help her sit and then you can go from there."

"Okay," I said. The bathroom floor was cold black-and-white tile.

"Be very careful never to drop her," Evan said.

"I won't." I thought I would be okay. You pulled her up, held her, set her down. It was doable.

Kate nodded at Evan as the sound of trickling stopped. As he lifted her, grabbing a tuft of toilet paper first, she told me, "Just hold on to me with one hand the whole time I'm standing. Under my arm." Evan repeated what she said as he wiped between her legs and dropped the tissue into the toilet. He pulled her underwear back up and tugged down her skirt so he could pivot her back to the chair again. Then he flushed the toilet and I stepped out of his way so he could wash his hands.

When he was done, I turned on the tap and wet my hands, squirting some soap into my palm and lathering up. I was scrubbing away unthinkingly at my wrists when I glanced up and realized Evan was toweling his hands a little more slowly than one normally does, and I glanced down at my wet hands and then at my face, now beet-red, in the mirror.

"I don't know why I just did that," I said. Kate had moved to just outside the door, in the hall. She said something. I watched her mouth and caught the word "weird."

Evan hung up the towel and repeated, "This is weird, but mostly for you. I'm accustomed to it."

I wiped my hands on my jeans, my cheeks still hot. "I was feeling pretty relaxed till now. Probably makes you wish you had some old hand of a caregiver from an agency."

Kate shrugged. She was very eloquent with her shrugs. This one consisted of one shoulder lifted toward her ear, her head tilting just a little, an eyebrow raised. She had a mischievous grin. "You learn to make your own fun," she said.

AT THREE THE OTHER caregiver, Hillary, arrived. She was a tall, sturdy, blond nursing student with tiny octagonal glasses and a Teutonic briskness next to which I felt the urge to be rather frantic and talkative, my jokes sounding as though they ought to be punctuated with a clown horn. Nurses didn't wear those little folded white hats anymore, but Hillary carried herself as though one sat upon her head at all times, crisp as a starched linen napkin.

"How was your first day?" she asked me seriously. She wore her hair in a short, feathery cut, her downy earlobes unpierced and her body covered in a shapeless dun-colored T-shirt. We were all in the living room. Evan was seated on the arm of the couch. Kate was pulled up next to him, his hand on her shoulder.

"It was great," I said. I looked at Kate and Evan, who nodded briefly and in unison, their expressions unchanged. Were those diplomatic nods? "I watched today," I went on. "But Evan did a fine job."

Evan and Hillary laughed, but Kate just smiled briefly. She said something, her expression serious. Evan asked her to repeat it, then nodded and turned to me.

"Tomorrow you'll get hands-on experience," Evan said. "We try to make the first day kind of easy, but the second day we start to throw you in." He looked apologetic.

Hillary nodded. "They tried going really slow for one girl." She glanced at Kate for approval. Kate nodded. "But after a month she still didn't get some pretty basic stuff. So I got the boot camp, and so do you."

I laughed. "Oh, I doubt it's really boot camp. I'm ready to get started."

Hillary smiled skeptically. "Great," she said. She hung her bag over a chair and then looked to Kate. "Well."

It was my cue to go. I said good-bye and jogged out to my car.

two

AT HOME I SURVEYED the magazines on the coffee table, the turned-off television. There were no messages on the machine, which was odd. Liam almost always called on Thursdays. I picked up the phone to check the dial tone. Of course it was fine.

I may as well call someone. I dialed my parents' house.

"Bec," my mother said. "How's your semester finishing up?" My parents lived in the same house in Oconomowoc where I'd grown up, an hour away from Madison. My mother was off from the doctor's office on Thursdays in order to make up for the Saturday hours she worked instead. She would be at the kitchen table, sipping the decaf she switched to after nine A.M., and going over the bills, her long graying hair gathered neatly into a ponytail, her sweater sleeves—always too short, my mother was five ten—pushed up to her elbows.

"All right," I said. I put my bare feet up on the table. My heel stuck in something. Dried coffee was my guess, sticky with sugar and milk.

I changed the subject and told her about my new job instead.

"Well, it would just be a summer job," my mother said. "You might not want to stay forever, but for the time being it might turn out you have a knack. Remember when you were eight and Kelly Jervis had that operation? You went over to see her every day after school while she recovered." A note of satisfaction sounded in her voice. She had always been rather proud of me for that, because she hadn't had to prompt me. My mother loved to see initiative.

It was true that I had trooped through the yards each afternoon for a month while Kelly was in a body cast, her legs encased in plaster from hip to toe, a metal bar holding the knees apart, but in fact we spent much of those visits bickering. I could still picture the cast—and the red swell of scars that laddered up the outsides of her legs when it came off—but I couldn't remember Kelly herself very well. The visits weren't really on par with Jill's visits to the nursing home. I think I always knew how nice it looked that I was watching over my friend. And truth be told, she had gotten a lot of new toys to keep her occupied as she recuperated.

"I don't think it's very similar," I said. I licked my hand and rubbed at the sticky spot on my heel, grimacing. Jill and I had been locked in an unspoken battle over whose turn it was to clean. I was the one who drank sweet milky coffee, so I may as well concede her victory and straighten up this afternoon.

"Maybe not," my mother agreed. "But that's a point in its favor, if you ask me. Branch out. I wanted you to join Jill at some of her volunteer stuff but you always balk."

"This isn't charity," I retorted. "It's an actual job."

"Oh, Bec. Don't be so snappish," my mother said calmly. I heard papers rustling.

After we hung up I went into Jill's room and took her guitar from its case. It was just an inexpensive acoustic from a store we loved because the owners' golden retrievers greeted all the customers. Jill had gotten it with her Christmas money, and after a few months' painful strumming had let it sit. But I liked to play it, though I had no apparent talent or training. I just liked the posture of it, one foot braced on the bed frame, hunched rather bohemianly over the curved wood and strumming tunelessly while I sang the lyrics to an old Pretenders song. Liam had tried to teach me a few of the chords, but I could never remember them. I remembered sitting with him well enough, though, his hands positioning my fingers and the soft tap of his palm at the small of my back. *Sit up straight.* I pulled my shoulders back and kept playing. Jill wouldn't have minded, but for some reason I never asked her. Part of the reason we lived together fairly harmoniously was that we let each other's eccentricities go unremarked. Who wanted to explain every silly thing you felt like doing? I had a carved mahogany box on my dresser filled with keepsakes from a great-uncle who had died years ago, the contents of which—chunks of uncut amethyst, a few odd seashells, some Russian coins, a Swiss army knife—Jill loved looking at for no better reason than I liked holding her guitar. I had caught glimpses of her hefting the stones in her hand and flicking open the knife to test each tool, but I never said anything about that, either.

I strummed for a few minutes, idly singing under my breath, but I was too restless to enjoy it. What was Liam up to, anyway? I kept thinking of Evan's hand on Kate's cheekbone, those careful strokes of the brush. I'd never just dropped in to Liam's office, though I knew where it was. We'd agreed it was wiser not to.

I put the guitar away and left the apartment again. I took a few textbooks with me, thinking I might sell them back today, and drove to campus. Wisely or not.

A FEW OF THE food carts were still open on library mall, selling North African chicken stew or plastic clamshell boxes of pad thai or curry and rice to the stragglers who'd missed lunch. I was headed past the fountain toward the English building. Finals were almost over, and people were still lolling on the lawn with their books open and eyes closed, or hitching their bags over their shoulders and heading to the Union for a beer. The University of Wisconsin was a great school for studying by the lake while drinking a pitcher of beer. Deep down we all thought an excess of both balanced out.

I crammed myself into an elevator with a group who all seemed to know one another. They were mostly very pale girls with rings in their noses and tattoos looped around their skinny biceps.

On the top floor there was a communal office near the bathrooms. I peered in before knocking to be sure he was alone, and he was. He was at his desk, glasses on, reading papers. His head was propped on one fist. As I watched he reached out blindly for the coffee cup near the edge of his desk. I waited to see if he'd knock it over, but his hand closed around it and he took a sip.

He glanced up when I knocked, looked happy and then almost instantly shocked to see me there. I hadn't thought it was so daring to drop by without calling first. I could always say, quite truthfully, that I was a student. Not his student. But I was enrolled.

As he came to meet me at the door he glanced out into the hallway. When he saw it was empty he drew me in and to the side, where you couldn't see through the window, and kissed me. He pushed me back against the wall, his fingertips on my neck, glancing over my jawline, my earlobes, my collarbone. I have a weakness for men who use their hands when they kiss, and he had figured this out pretty fast. His beard was coming in, and it rasped against my chin. He smelled of soap, and, I realized, skeptically, something sweet. I stopped kissing him and pressed my nose behind his ear.

"Don't say it," he warned me. "My manly axle-grease shampoo was out so I used Alison's designer stuff. I think it's vanilla. Or ginger. Something muffiny."

I stepped back and looked at him. I didn't think it was as funny as I was supposed to, but how could I? What I disliked wasn't the fact that he used his wife's shampoo but the specificity of his wife, whom I forced myself to perceive as a vague, cloudy presence of no reality, like someone who has always just left the room. We rarely spoke of her, so I could usually ignore her existence.

"You've ruined muffins for me," I told him. I was half-joking.

He raised his eyebrows apologetically and sat down behind his desk, gesturing for me to take the chair before it. "What brings you here? I thought you were working tonight."

" 'What brings me here?' " I repeated incredulously. I couldn't tell if he was jokingly acting like my professor or if he just slipped into the habit in this environment. So I sat in the chair and said, "I haven't talked to you in a few days. I'm quitting the restaurant. I'm working for a woman with ALS."

"Lou Gehrig's?" he asked. Show-off, I thought. "That was fast."

"Yeah, I know. It was a lot quicker than I was expecting. I only interviewed the other day. I made sure all my shifts were covered at the restaurant so I get an okay reference, though."

"Good idea," Liam said, absently. He was peering down at a paper on his desk. I decided not to answer. Finally he realized he'd been silent for several seconds and looked up again. "What do you do?"

I gestured helplessly. "I didn't do anything today," I said. "But tomorrow I start doing just about anything and everything. It should be pretty simple. Her husband does a lot of the hard stuff."

He nodded at me. "Oh," he said, "she's married."

"Yup," I said.

"Do you like her?"

"I like him," I answered truthfully. "I haven't decided how I feel about her quite yet. She's very funny, and very self-possessed . . . but she's hard to know, I guess." I felt uncomfortable admitting that I wasn't sure how much I liked a woman who was in a wheelchair—I felt I ought to love her right away. But I knew I wasn't looking forward to being around her again, knowing I'd feel so inadequate as I tried to figure out her speech, even though she would try to keep things light.

There was another long pause. This wasn't going right; it was awkward and intrusive and he smelled of his wife's shampoo. I clapped my hands on my knees, trying to be brisk, and then stood up. "I just stopped by," I told him. "I should be going."

He got up and took my hand. "I feel odd seeing you here," he said. "It's risky." He sighed. "It's no riskier than anything else, though. You want an early dinner?"

We went to a Middle Eastern place down the street from my apartment. It was as safe as any other place, since no one else was eating at four in the afternoon. We went in, shook hands with the proprietor, who knew us by now, and were led to the dewan. The proprietor held the curtain open for us and then let it slide shut when he went to get water.

The dewan was a low round private table curtained off from the rest of the dining room by rosy damask. Liam always wanted to sit there, and I didn't mind that it was probably more for the subterfuge than the romance. I still loved ducking behind the heavy fabric. I didn't care that it was a little uncomfortable, the tabletop so low you had to splay your knees beneath it, hunching over your food.

We sipped at the pitcher of water on the table—it was scented with orange blossom and I always ended up knocking back most of it—and Liam slid across the cushions and kissed me. After a while he touched my neck and smiled at me. A silly grin flashed across my face though I tried to stifle it.

"Every restaurant needs one of these," I said. It was our running joke. We also thought grocery stores should have them, bars, pharmacies.

"My office needs one of these," he said.

We ordered chicken with olives and lamb stew, then leaned back against each other in the cushions. He ran a fingertip beneath the hem of my shorts and watched me.

"What'd you do today?" I asked.

He pushed his fingertip further beneath the denim and stroked it along a curve of skin before answering me. "Begged my officemate not to use the word *hermeneutic* ever again. Spent my lunch hour haggling over the cost of a transmission." He removed his hand, sat up, and took a sip of water. "Well, hearing about haggling. Actually Alison does the negotiating."

I sat up, too, briskly tearing off a piece of pita bread. At times Liam seemed to forget I had never met her, and would say, in the offhand tone that assumed I knew Alison's inability to let an argument die or her disastrous love of salted cashews, "Well, you know her."

I did not know her. During the first couple months with him, I confessed it all to Jill but added that I could never have slept with Liam if I had ever met his wife. I would have drawn the line, I insisted, with a woman I knew and had spoken to. Yet during that period I often lay in bed, considering him, and with a terrible certainty I understood that I was the strumpet of the piece. Occasionally I tried to tell myself that his having a wife actually made it better, that it was that much more he had to walk through to get to me. All that lying and effort. It was unsettling, the ease with which I had slipped into this.

Jill didn't offer much, though I prodded her endlessly at first, unable to keep it a secret and desperate to know what she thought—provided she thought it was exciting. Jill may have done her share of good works, but she was no prude. She'd had plenty of make-outs at parties with guys whose girlfriends had gone home early. She was non-committal when she knew I wanted her opinion, saying nothing when she knew I wanted reassurance. Her reticence only made me bug her more. When and if she did tell me I was being a bitch and to knock it off, the remorse would set in and I'd get my morals back. Sometimes I thought I had only misplaced them, set them on top of the fridge or some other spot I never thought to look.

But really guilt didn't change anything. I still liked it, and liked him, and I didn't want to stop sleeping with him. Simple as that. I knew, tangibly as a stone dropped in my lap, that Liam's wife could have been my friend or my roommate—maybe even a sister if I had had one—and I would have done this anyway. I was, I suspected, inches from becoming a rifler of purses, neglecter of children, and smacker of dogs. Who knew what else I would turn out to be capable of?

WHEN I MET HIM, back in February, I glanced at Liam's ring and wrote him off immediately. Or rather, I never wrote him in. So I shook his hand and smiled with nothing more than politeness when Jill introduced him as the teaching assistant who taught her class. I didn't flirt or present myself to any great advantage, and so it was all the more flattering when his interest became clear anyway. Had I been wasting my time trying to be sexy since I was fourteen? Was it really this effortless?

Anyway, the day I met him, I saw Jill and this stranger walking toward me on library mall, where I had stopped to buy a cup of coffee from a cart. From a distance, with their red hair and fast strides, they looked like siblings. I threw together an image of him as they approached, one with freckles and a snub nose, a charming gap between the front teeth. Someone a little immature and hyper.

But up close I saw I was wrong. His eyebrows were nearly horizontal lines, red-brown shot through with the same blond that tipped his lashes. His nose was not remotely snubbed. His hair was a mess from the wind that blew off the lake. He looked as though he should have freckles but he didn't. His eyes were dark green. He shook my hand and settled his gaze on me.

"A redhead named Liam," I'd said. "Not much ancestral mystery there, huh?"

He smiled. "I'm not Irish."

"Oh. Well. Shut my mouth."

Jill laughed.

A few days later I saw him again. He was coming out of the library, flipping through a sheaf of papers, a frown on his face that dropped away when I stepped in front of him. Later I went to meet a friend in the English building and glimpsed him through the window of a class-room door, standing at a chalkboard in a red flannel shirt, laughing. I was jealous of the class in there, getting that kind of response from him. I'd treasured the way I could make him laugh the few times I had spoken with him, the way he gave in to it so completely he let his head tip all the way back, and I stood out in the hallway with my winter hat yanked down around my ears, watching him talk to a bunch of under-grads like me.

After that I ran into him on campus several more times, often enough that I wondered if I had been crossing his path for years and only now noticed. We would walk on together in the same direction, picking our way over the ice and packed snow. Once I noticed him turn a corner after we parted, heading back the way we'd come, and I stood there and watched him go, wondering how far out of his way he'd gone to talk to me.

I never remembered what we had talked about afterward, only that there were never silences, that we both had a tendency to leap into each other's stories, embellishing as we went, encouraged by the other per-son's amusement. We didn't have much background in common, but we had the same sense of humor. He'd lived all over as a child, and I had never even moved from my old room until I left for the dorms. He was fascinated by the sheer Americana of my childhood, its parades and drive-ins and football games. "I didn't realize that wasn't just an old stereotype," he said once. "It sounds so fun. You really had bonfires?"

"You really lived in Thailand?" I countered.

He nodded. "I developed a real taste for dried shrimp," he said. "But why does every single bar in Wisconsin offer a Friday-night fish fry?"

You think you're just being terribly friendly until one day you start to catch on. Because it was always near zero we stopped for coffee, tug-ging our gloves off with our teeth and peering at each other through the steam. The weather made it easier; we were always inviting each other into some kind of shelter: the bowl of chili at the pub, the foggy windows in a café.

"It was a lot of fun for a while," he told me one day. This was in January, a few weeks after we met, and we had run into each other on State Street (at that point our "unexpected" meetings had been happening in the same place, Mondays and Wednesdays, around two o'clock) and ducked out of the cold for some coffee. He was telling me about the job he'd had before he moved here. He'd written about music for *Chicago* magazine, freelanced around town, and basically cobbled together a living. "You actually *have* to go to clubs and see bands," he continued, "and it's not goofing off. The rest of the time you're at home writing in your sweatpants."

"You didn't have an office at the magazine?" I'd always imagined writers sprawled in a break room, wearing blue jeans and funky glasses, popping outside every now and again for a joint or a pizza.

"Not the freelancers. I barely saw the editor for the first year I wrote for them. Frankly, after three years of it, I was getting a little hungover. Just in general. Your friends start buying apartments and cars with mufflers, and you still smell like smoke and old beer all the time. It gets in your skin."

"Oh yeah, I know," I said, nodding enthusiastically. Here at last, something I could relate to. "Jill tries to guess the daily special by the smell of my hair." In truth I was exaggerating my impatience with this kind of job. A few months later I would be ready to move on, but waiting tables was still fun to me back then. I liked bumming cigarettes off the bartender and getting a decent buzz after my shift on employee-discounted drinks. Yet as I talked to Liam I began to nurture the first seeds of discontent with the late hours, the potatoey-smelling aprons, and the way I came home from work not clean and rumpled, as a teacher would, but literally filmed with grease. This sort of thing was a kid's job, was what I heard him say, and I was all set to agree.

"I figured I could still go see bands and write about music or whatever, just make it a hobby like normal people. Plus by then Alison was ready to move somewhere quieter, a smaller firm." He peered into his mug, swirling the coffee around.

"You miss it, though," I said. He looked up at me, startled, and then started laughing.

"Yeah," he said, "I do. Thanks for giving the lie to my ready-to-grow-up routine."

"I never believe people when they say that."

We watched each other, smiling. He leaned back in his chair, stretching out his legs, and crossed his ankles. Our feet were propped against each other, but neither of us moved them away. "The job sounded a lot better when I told people what I did than when I was actually doing it. You know."

I didn't know, actually. I had never had a job description that elicited anything but a tactful nod. The best you could say about my various means of employment was that they were usually over quickly. But Liam didn't seem to know that, and I had the bizarre feeling he truly assumed I knew what it was like to have a great job you just didn't love anymore. I wasn't going to disabuse him of the notion, so I nodded sagely and made noises of agreement.

"A Ph.D., though," I said. I shook my head. "I can't imagine being able to handle that."

"Why not? You ought to be thinking about something beyond undergrad."

"I guess so." Both Jill and I had watched our grades slide downward since we had moved in together, regretful but uninvolved, as though their deterioration were divorced from us and our apartment with its freezer full of gin and vodka, and the games of rummy and poker we were continually offering to each other.

He looked exasperated. "I'm sorry," he said. "Alison tells me I do this sometimes—you don't need me to guide you. You know what you're doing."

"Oh yeah," I agreed. "I know exactly what I'm doing."

We watched each other silently, and I didn't look away. I was testing him. At the time I thought he might be amusing himself by putting out the occasional signal—the eye contact, the hug hello to the kid who was too naïve to know better—and I thought I'd call his bluff.

The silence continued. He could have done a lot of things right then—touch my hand, brush my hair out of my face. It was that sort of moment. Instead he stayed still, holding my gaze so intently I had to know it was purposeful, and said, "Do you need a ride home?"

At that point, I was almost more curious than anything, still in that bluffing mood to see how far he'd go. I didn't really think we'd sleep together. He was married, though that condition seemed to me a lot like his peripatetic childhood, something relevant to him but also far away and not very real to me. I thought he might kiss me in the car, apologize, and leave.

On the way to my house I wondered whether Jill would be there, hoping she was at class. Liam and I talked, but I was distracted, dredging up some reason to invite him in. I had always used a pretext, and so had everyone I knew. We were always mentioning specific, obscure books or CDs not just to impress but in the hopes of being asked into the apartment for the necessary loan or return. But that day I couldn't think of a thing to offer. Musically the furthest afield I had gone was late-era Beatles. I couldn't offer him unknown blues bootlegs, as I would later learn his wife had. He was earning a Ph.D. in literature, and though I sometimes read several books a week, they were the sort with a bloody handprint on the cover. I didn't know wine or even beer, so I had nothing there. The heater in the car was a little sluggish. Maybe I could ask him if he needed to get warm.

Or better yet, just ask him to come in. I didn't have to explain myself. He didn't seem to realize I had no idea what I was doing.

"Bec?" he'd said. I realized I'd gone silent. He had turned onto my street, and I pointed at our house. The driveway was empty.

I'd turned to look at him. I loved being in a car with a guy, the way the air could change as soon as you were alone. That closeness, his hand on the gearshift an inch from my knee. He had long fingers that bulged at the knuckles. I was holding my backpack in my lap. On either side of us, the driveway was piled so high with shoveled snow that it felt as though no one could see us. I was gearing myself up to say something about coming in, for a hot drink or whatever inane suggestion I could think of, when I met his eyes. He gave me a slight smile and said, "Take that backpack off your lap."

I just looked at him in surprise for a moment, and he answered me by picking it up by one strap and laying it at my feet as he reached toward me with the other hand, saying, "It's in my way."

I wish I could remember more about that kiss. Our mouths, the scrape of his chin. But mainly what I remember is his hand on my neck and then along my cheek, his fingertips pushing my hair from my face.

"Do you want to come in?" I said. It was out before I'd even thought it through, and for a second I winced, regretting it. I'd handed myself over now.

"Yeah, I do," he said.

I preceded him into the house. The living room was somewhat clean, at least, and there were no old beer bottles on the floor. I took my coat off without facing him and laid it over a chair. What was I going to do now? He was probably able to tell I was nervous just from the way I'd turned my back on him. So much for calling his bluff. Perhaps he did this sort of thing all the time. Maybe married life was like that, but no one had told me. Maybe no one ever told you until you got married, too, and then they started taking you aside at parties, drawing you into the corner to give you the lowdown on how it really was. *Everybody has these moments,* they'd whisper, slurping at a martini, *these experiences, with other people, and it's no big deal.*

But I began thinking about his wife anyway. Until Liam and I did something overtly out of line she had remained wispy. But once we were in my house together, our intentions suffusing the air like humidity, she thickened into being. We ignored the fact of her so deliberately then—and ignored the fact that we were doing so—that everything we did took on more weight. It felt as though she was there in the room, standing a few feet behind us, as I laid my bag down on the table, but we wouldn't turn and acknowledge her. I was impressed, even frightened, by the gravity of sex right then. This wasn't playful at all.

I should back down, I thought. I should make cups of tea and sit on the opposite end of the couch. I turned back to him. He was standing where I'd left him, just inside the front door, hands in his coat pockets. "You can take your coat off," I said.

"Oh, right. Sorry." He draped his coat over mine. Then we looked at each other. He took a deep breath, and I got a little calmer then, once I saw he wasn't. I gave the wife one more chance to speak inside my head so I could choose a side—was she real to me or filmy as the ghost in a movie; was this the done thing or were we really crossing a line?—but all that came to me was the silence inside the whole house, the occasional oblivious car passing by on the street, to remind me that no one was watching.

"Come on," I said, and I led him into my room. The bed was unmade and there were clothes on the floor.

"I take a stand against making beds," I told him. "It just seems like busywork to me."

"I want to say some sexy comment about rumpling it," Liam said, coming closer to me. "But I'm drawing a blank, honey."

The endearment caught me out, and I paused by the bed. He said it so easily, as though it had been waiting in his mouth for days. I still had a few condoms in my bedside drawer, left unused by my last boyfriend the previous fall, and I took them out and set them on the table. Since I was being so relaxed and up-front. He kissed me, and I reached beneath his sweater to pull his T-shirt from his waistband. He drew back when I did that, looking surprised. I gave him what felt like a mocking smile, unbuttoned his jeans, and then didn't undress him any further. After a few minutes he did it for me.

My room was the warmest in the house, thanks to the sun that pooled in there all day. Even that afternoon, cold as it was outdoors, we kicked the covers away. Once we were in bed I debated whether to relax for a moment and see what he would do. I loved this part of sleeping with someone for the first time—the second when you just waited to see what they liked, what they wanted to do to you. Most of the time in my limited experience it turned out they were fast and clumsy, but I never stopped being optimistic. He was stretched out on his back, my hand pressed flat on his abdomen. The sun cast a sheen on his skin, showing faint pearly ridges of a faded stretch mark on one hip, the coppery filaments of his pubic hair.

I thought he'd go down on me, but after a little while he unwrapped a condom and put it on. You're kidding me, I thought. Aren't older guys supposed to have taken a few courses in foreplay? He hauled me on top of him, but when I tried to turn around to face him, wrap my legs around his waist, he put his hands on my hips and guided me so I lay facing the ceiling, confused and disappointed, on top of him as though he were a mattress. My head hung down on one side of his neck, our hips lined up, and my legs fell on either side of his. His hands glanced over me and nudged my fingers down to touch myself. His fingers stroked my breasts, his tongue touched my neck, and he slid a hand down over my wrist to be sure I was still stroking myself, and then he was inside me. It was like being fucked by someone you couldn't see, only feel, and after a while I was pushing back against him with my hips, my knees raised up and my hand cramping as I moved my fingers as fast as I could, until I came.

When I turned around and looked at him, and his expression was so blurred, so rapt, that I felt my breath catch all over again, I pushed his legs apart and lay between them, reached around to cup his ass in my hands, and instead of doing any circular, seductive figure-eights like I thought you were supposed to do but which most guys seemed to grow bored with pretty quickly, I pumped up and down on him. The hell with slow gyrations—I was aware that this was a man's motion rather than a woman's, which must be why it had a strange edge of playacting and excitement to it.

After he'd left, I remained in bed, having retrieved the covers from the floor. I would never have admitted this to Liam, or even to Jill, but the encounter made me feel very adult. I didn't own perfume or pricey lingerie, but right then I felt as if I'd earned the right to both, like getting a license or turning twenty-one.

Yet at the same time, in the humid cloister of the room with the waning daylight and oniony scent of drying sweat, I had a sudden, insatiable urge for salt and something creamy—melted cheese on something, on anything—the same way I once had in high school after coming home from a long night with someone. I had the sense that I'd moved up a level, like the period just after my friends and I all started sleeping with our boyfriends as a matter of course rather than debate. (In retrospect, we seemed to have done this en masse, as if by silent vote.) Except now I seemed to have gotten some idea of what I was doing. Maybe this was why people had affairs—to reexperience all the novelty once you'd actually learned how to have sex.

I really did feel as if I got it now, the same heady realization I'd felt when I realized I had done a handspring in gymnastics before I'd even taken time to think it through. It wasn't as though I was a virgin, but I was never as confident as I had always tried to present myself. As I lay there I thought perhaps I should never see him again, because I didn't know if I could duplicate it. But I dismissed the notion almost instantly out of greed and excitement, certain that I'd climbed into a new body, a fresh skin, and there was no slipping out of it now.

BY THE TIME LIAM and I clambered out of the dewan and left the restaurant it was almost five thirty. "Shouldn't you be getting home?" I asked. "And what will you do, eat another full dinner?"

He linked his arm through mine as we headed up the walk to my front door. The windows were dark; Jill was still at work.

"I'm at a department meeting," he said. "I've ordered the Californian sub to eat at my desk. Besides, I have the cell phone on in case she calls."

"Oh." I was feeling strange; too much spice, too many protein-rich mashes of chickpeas and eggplant. We were at my front door. "Well," I said, "no more time to spend on chitchat." He pushed up against me while I unlocked the door. I had reached to take in the mail, but then he lifted my hair up, leisurely twisting it off my skin, and ran the tip of his tongue up my neck.

I left the mail. "Come on," I said. "Let's keep these meetings running on time."

I had to enjoy this while I could, since it was such a tenuous arrangement, dependent on the whims of his wife. He was not in the game of pushing her to notice what he was doing. If she seemed particularly attentive for a few days, or asked an extra question or two, I always knew it. He'd become remote, our conversations as chaste as if I were a student in his poetry class.

All that would have to happen to end it was for that detachment to last a little longer than usual, an extra week or two in which she happened to be affectionate or needy, and that would be it. Our relation-

ship was a temperamental little pet, some delicate, vivid tropical crea-
ture blinking at us inside its glass tank, requiring precisely calibrated
humidity and temperature and food in tiny frequent doses and lots of
pure water. No loud noises, no startling prods of its scaly belly.

three

ON FRIDAY, DAY TWO, I arrived and found Kate lying beneath a quilt on her bed. Evan was in the easy chair. She smiled at me and mouthed what I guessed was "Good morning."

"Hi, Kate. Hey, Evan."

"Morning," Evan said. "I'm not here."

"And yet?"

He smiled. "And yet I am, if you need me, but we thought we'd let you take over today and I'll just be backup. I'm sure you remember what I did yesterday, and if you don't Kate can tell you." He snapped open the real estate section of the newspaper. "Is that all right?"

"No problem," I said. I turned to Kate.

"Okay," she said. She glanced at the remote as I went to her side of the bed, and I took it from her and set it on the table.

Her nightgown was ivory with thick lace straps and a plain bodice, from what I could see above the quilt. The room was a little too warm for a quilt. I wondered if she was ever too hot or too cold during the periods when she was alone. She wouldn't be able to do anything about it—just wait.

I brought her chair over next to the bed and lifted her arms by the wrists while I pushed the quilt aside. Her skin was cool and dry, and I kept my fingers wrapped around the knobby bones of her wrist, thinking that this was the first time I had touched her. The white silk gleamed at the crest of her hip bones and the swell of her breasts. Her collarbone was a sharp ledge; when she swallowed the movement fluttered at the dip in her throat. I'd laid her arms at her sides when I removed the quilt, and there was something so acquiescent about her, her blond hair and white silk, neat as a doll.

I took a deep breath and planned how I would do this. When I watched Evan lift Kate, it seemed almost elegant: pull-and-turn, bend at the knees, and then stand up. I started by taking hold of her ankles and pulling her feet over the edge of the mattress, and then I brought her into a sitting position by her wrists. Her head dropped forward, her hair falling in two sheets around her face. But her feet didn't end up neatly on the ground like they were supposed to. Instead her knees were curved coyly to one side, and I tried to hold her upright while I aligned her. Evan crossed one ankle over his knee, then shifted again. Our eyes met and I looked away. He opened his newspaper. He could probably do this with his eyes closed, and he had to mind seeing his wife tugged around by some college student. I was working in silence, refusing to meet Kate's eyes in case she tried to talk to me.

My hair fell into my eyes and I swiped it away. I wanted to ask him to open a window.

I placed my hands beneath Kate's arms and stood, lifting her. But then, anxious to set her down, I lowered her into the wheelchair too fast, and left her sitting awkwardly on one buttock, leaning against the arm. Then I tripped over the footrest.

Kate said something.

"I'm sorry," I said. I watched her closely as she dipped her head to swallow and repeated herself. Evan watched over the corner of the paper. He looked poised to get up and come over, but he didn't.

" 'Ray'?" I asked. "Uh, 'rate my . . .' "

Kate shook her head. She seemed somewhat impatient, and I felt on the verge of impatience myself. For chrissakes, I thought, if you're going to throw me in like this, accept the fact that I'll be awkward. I caught a glimpse of Evan giving me an encouraging smile and I took a deep breath. Kate glanced pointedly down at her feet, which were tucked one over the other; I'd managed to make her look like a parody of a shy little girl.

"Your feet?" I guessed. Kate nodded. "Oh, straighten them." I set her feet neatly side by side. I realized that to straighten her hips I would have to cup either side of her buttocks. Well, I had to. As I loomed toward her, I couldn't shake the sense that I was about to kiss her and grab her ass like a high school boy, and I stopped and stood back.

"I don't think I'm . . ." I trailed off. Kate smiled and shook her head again. She swallowed carefully before she said something. I stared at her lips.

" 'Just lift me up'?" I repeated. Kate nodded. Again I grasped her under the arms and lifted her into a standing position, paused to be sure the position was right, pivoted her so she was in front of the wheelchair again, and finally, finally, set her down in the chair.

Evan applauded. "I know it's a lot harder than it looks," he said. "You'll be good at this, though; I can tell. I bet you'll be better than me."

He was only being nice. I knew I'd botched the very first thing I'd done for her, and I didn't ever want to try it again. I made some sort of grimace that was meant to evoke a smile, and preceded Kate to the bathroom.

She asked me to start by brushing her teeth. With her head tipped back, her mouth open, I set to work with an electric toothbrush, concentrating on not touching her gums with the whirring bristles. Her teeth were very straight on top, the middle bottom teeth overlapping, and the glistening peaks of her molars stippled with dark pools of fillings. I counted six. Her head trembled a little with the movement of the brush, and I put a hand at the back of her skull to steady it. Her hair was warm and a little tangled from being slept on. I watched her tongue move from side to side away from the brush and the toothpaste foam, and finally she let it lie in the center of her mouth so I could run the brush over it. I had to be careful not to use too much water or she could choke on it—Evan had told me that her throat no longer closed off efficiently.

The dental part went well, at least. I tried to make it last a little, just as a respite from the chair and the shower that was coming, but you can only brush someone's teeth for so long. Finally I gave up and rinsed the brush. I wiped her mouth off with my hand, but even as I did it I knew that was wrong. Of course I should have used a washcloth. I froze for a moment, and I could see in her face that she had decided to let it slide. Instead she said something else, but I didn't get what it was—

something about the shower. I nodded and smiled, but I was looking at the huge walk-in shower with its sliding door and trying rather desperately to remember what Evan had told me the day before. Fine, I thought, it's common sense. I turned on the water, the handheld attachment spraying away toward the wall, and started to put her into the plastic chair inside the shower. She looked pointedly at my leather sandals and said, moving her lips carefully for me, "You'll want them off." I kicked off the shoes.

"So, remind me: I lift you to a standing position, take off your nightgown, and then move you? Or put you in the shower chair and take it from there?"

"The chair is more stable," she said. I repeated it after her and she nodded, so I put her into position in the white plastic lawn chair, which had suction cups attached to the feet, and then I lifted her nightgown up. I lifted each leg to free it and then pulled the back of the gown up from beneath her buttocks. Then I lifted one arm at a time and took the whole thing off over her head, her hair catching for a moment in the straps before falling again, and I slung the gown over to the counter.

I looked around for a sponge or brush, and found an oversize one dangling on a hook. Thank God, I thought. Even with babies I felt like a pervert washing them with my bare hands. I wanted a nice huge sponge with lots of surface area. If they'd had shower gloves I might have liked those too.

I reached for the showerhead and turned back to her. Her head was down, her arms set on each arm of the chair where I'd placed them, her feet straight in front of her. The ridges of her ribs were faintly visible. Her breasts were small and set far apart, the peach-colored nipples contracted. Her thighs spread slightly against the chair seat, the triangle of pubic hair darkening against the spray of water as I washed it over her shoulders and chest and legs. I leaned her forward slightly and sent the water down the string of vertebrae. Her hair grew dark at the ends, and when she laid her head back for me to wet it I saw that her cheeks had flushed slightly from the heat of the water.

I turned away as I squeezed soap on the sponge. I didn't want to see her just then, the naked wings of her collarbone and her small puckered nipples and blush spreading up her chest. As I lathered up the sponge I thought about her saying when I interviewed that she'd had ALS for two years. It wasn't that long. Who knew how long it had taken her to get used to being bathed by other people? At least a few months.

She hadn't said a word since we got in the shower, and her eyes were still shut, her brows slightly knit against the spray. I sudsed her shoulders and the thin columns of her neck and arms, keeping my fingertips behind the sponge and away from her wet skin. The warm water sprayed my clothes and my legs, and once you got in there and started washing her, the shower was not as big as it had seemed. Still, I was doing okay. I almost started to believe in my own skills. This was just something we caregivers did.

I lifted her arms to wash her armpits, which bore a little patch of dark stubble. I saw a razor on the shelf but decided not to do anything unless she asked. I had washed her limbs and her torso, letting the sponge glance over her breasts as though they were no more private than elbows. Now, I realized, I would have to run it between her legs. People did that in the shower.

It was a strange time to think about my mother. But as I drew the sponge between Kate's thighs and then washed her back all the way down to the cleft of her buttocks, I was recalling washing with my mom. I suppose when I was very young it was easier than bathing me separately. But it had always seemed an arbitrary and bold thing for her to do, and I still remembered standing in the shower, looking up the landscape of her body, its wide hips and the sturdy muscle at the front of her thighs and the moon-colored curve of the bottoms of her breasts, the brisk slapping sound of her cupped hand—my mother did not believe in washcloths—mittened in lather as she rubbed at the gray-shadowed skin of her armpits and the flat curls of pubic hair. Her breasts and the flesh of her upper arms trembled as she reached, businesslike, into the dark hollow between her legs, and I had watched her and thought, *Oh, I'd better do that too.* It embarrassed me to wash myself in front of my mother, so I'd turned silently away toward the green-tiled corner of the shower and done it, one fast scrub as though I were brushing something away. I didn't look at my mother's face when I turned back. I looked at the crease across her belly instead.

I did the same thing with Kate now, a brief wipe with the sponge and then a rinse. I hung the sponge up on its hook, turned off the water, and turned back to her. Without the hot spray it felt chilly in the shower, but her cheeks were flushed even more deeply than they had been before, her neck blotched red. She had said nothing, not even a directive, since we had gotten in the shower. She dropped her chin a little farther and looked away, toward an empty corner of the shower.

I wanted to make a little comment about something inane and conversational, something to open the way for her to reassure me I had done an okay job of it. I was about to do this, had actually taken the breath to speak, when I understood that blotchy flush over her skin, her uncharacteristic gaze at the wall.

She wasn't used to this at all. She was as embarrassed as I was, maybe more so. The thought was so distressing that I stopped what I was doing for a moment, one arm reaching for the towel rack, and considered what it was like to open yourself up in this way, to whoever came along and was halfway decent enough to hire. It wasn't like sex, where you could simply refuse and put off intimacy and nakedness until someone more intriguing came along. (Unbidden, I pictured Liam auditioning a series of women in the same café we'd sat in, and I pushed the image aside.) Kate just had to let herself be handled and undressed even if it was by someone as unsure and clumsy as I was.

But why put herself through it? She was married; Evan could do it. If he had to leave town she could skip a bath for a day and avoid having a stranger do it. I could have figured this out if it were ever necessary, but I didn't see why we'd needed to do it on my second day. Why would you choose the caregiver to bathe you instead of your husband? Maybe it was only to get to the inevitable and face the prospect head-on.

Had I done anything well yet, even one thing? I wondered whether they'd pay me for the days I'd already worked if I quit the next day. She'd be all right if I did. She had Evan. I draped the towel over her breasts and belly, hoping it wouldn't offend her if I were too uncomfortable. I grabbed a second one to dry the rest of her. She glanced down at herself while I toweled her arms, and then up at me. I waited for her to say something rather arch, or amused, but instead she said, almost clearly, "Thank you."

EVAN LEFT BEFORE NOON and already I was exhausted. It was more mental than physical, from all the scenarios in my head: Kate falling, me dropping her, me mortifying her in some original way. I kept stretching my neck and massaging my face, which was stiff from smiling expectantly.

All jobs were stressful at first. All the social awkwardness, my own relentless display of ignorance. This nervousness would go away, I hoped. I didn't want to dread going to work, but if I didn't get better at it, I might have a nerve-wracking summer ahead. I couldn't leave this job too soon; the setup was too personal. I couldn't walk out after seeing her naked, like some one-night stand. I hated this about myself, my tendency to try something new and, as soon as I had begun, to wonder how to get out of it. The fact that yesterday I had been so chirpy and optimistic only made it worse. They had tried to give me some sense of what it would be like, but I'd been too dumb to recognize a grace period when they gave me one.

Even doing her makeup was harder than it seemed. After a few tries at the eye makeup, she had faked a smile of satisfaction and we decided it was done. But the eyeliner was too thick—it seemed to thicken of its own accord every time I looked at it—and I had accidentally added a tiny elongated line at the outer corner of one eye but not the other. This bothered me even more than the difficulty of getting her out of bed and more even than the shower. It made her look a little foolish and undignified, the very opposite of what I was supposed to be helping her achieve. It seemed that for her to look perfect was the very least I could do.

Around the time Kate had suggested we have lunch, Evan appeared at the door of the kitchen, briefcase in hand, and said, "Bec, you don't need me today."

I fought the urge to say that I did indeed need him, that yesterday's confidence had proved so misguided it was almost funny, would be funny if it weren't for the fact that he seemed to have believed it and was now leaving his wife at my mercy. I had been staying a few feet away from her whenever I could, nervous about touching her unnecessarily. Her kneecaps and elbows seemed brittle and easily bruised. Instead I hovered nearby, keeping a loose orbit around her, just close enough that I could smell the cream in her hair.

"You're doing fine," he continued. "I'm just running to the office to catch up a little."

"Okay," I said. I had no choice. I smiled brightly and falsely at them and turned back to the sandwich I was making. Behind me I heard the sound of a kiss and Kate's faint, warm murmur.

It seemed to me I spent a fair amount of time glancing in the other direction so he could kiss her. After he left we sat quietly together in the kitchen, the house seeming very empty. Had I paid as little attention to her directly as it suddenly seemed, now that there was no third party to focus on?

Now she and I were in the study, organizing various papers, insurance, financial stuff. I wasn't exactly privy to any major information, but I had figured out where the money came from. I saw from a photo that Kate's family had a huge house near Chicago—it made this house look almost as small as the one I grew up in—thanks to her grandfather's early patents on a chemical compound that had something to do with oranges. I hadn't quite gotten it straight, but suffice it to say her family was deep in trust-fund territory. I'd never met anyone who actually came from money. It wasn't very common in Wisconsin.

I thought I'd like this part of the job, the neat piles of triplicate copies and rational system of filing. She even had her own copy machine. It was efficient and absorbing, easily accomplished. Too bad it wasn't all like this.

"He's a grad assistant. And a writer," I was telling her. "He used to have a music column." This was also how he'd met his wife, who'd been a friend of the editor's.

Kate grinned and looked away toward the wall for a moment while she took a swallow. She had a way of shifting her gaze while she prepared to speak, and I'd learned to give her a moment, not to follow her every glance around. I wondered what she would say if I went ahead and told her the rest of it.

"Sounds like a keeper," she said. I understood her a little better now. I was forced to, like an immersion program. You had to watch her lips; half the cues lay in the familiar shapes you saw people form every day but never noticed. The sound she made was almost less important than the way she shaped the air.

She said, "You should bring him by sometime."

"Soon," I said vaguely. I wanted her to meet him. Or, more accurately, I wanted him to meet someone, to be able to introduce him for once, like a regular boyfriend. But you couldn't be sure who knew whom. The only reason I had indulged myself by talking about him was that I thought she was safely distant from my life and his, so completely secure and contentedly married. But I regretted it now—it only reminded me how sleazy it would have felt, bringing my adulterous boyfriend over for coffee, wedding ring stashed in his pocket. I tried to change the subject. "Anyway, you probably could care less about boyfriends and stuff. It must be nice to be done with all that."

Kate made a face: raised her eyebrows, turned the corners of her mouth down.

"It's not perfect," she said.

I STOPPED AT THE library on my way home, where *Living with ALS* was waiting for me. I took the book to a café near my house and sat down with a giant iced coffee, into which I had put an extra spoonful of sugar. For a few minutes I just sat there, sipping steadily, my eyes closed. I was drained. The coffee helped a bit, the caffeine making my muscles seem less tight, my head a bit clearer. Gradually I realized my shoulders were relaxing and my neck straightening out. I lifted my head. I must have been holding my head practically drawn to my chest, like a turtle.

I was thoroughly chastened. Perhaps it was something like motherhood, where you can't imagine how hard it can possibly be to carry that little baby, who sleeps all the time anyway, and whose needs are so simple, until the day comes when it's just you alone with the infant. Watching Evan, who had not only been doing this for some time but had known her so well before, hadn't given me the sense of how awkward it was to step into Kate's life and try to do it all for her, to almost impersonate her without even knowing her. It amazed me now to think how gracious she and Evan had been yesterday, though it must have taken all their willpower not to roll their eyes each time I popped a mint in my mouth as if I were watching a movie, or glibly assured them I could do anything they needed. I really had thought I could, too. But getting her out of bed seemed to have taken all morning, and while giving her lunch I blushed at the startling softness of her skin, the sickening tug of her flesh when I opened the valve. I'd slopped nutrition shake onto her skirt, and as I dabbed at the spot, our eyes had met. I didn't even have the wherewithal to fake a smile right then. I'd had a glimpse of the rest of my employ here, and it was one long plain of humiliation, punctuated by moments in which we froze and watched my latest mishap barrel down upon us.

But although I'd had no clue what I was really promising them, I wanted to make good on it. It would be a great salve to my pride to become skilled at this job, and fast, so that they'd think my confidence had actually been justified. I would go home and practice my eye makeup skills on Jill. Maybe I could even practice lifting her. Having Jill on board—I'd phoned her from the library to see if she would be my rag doll, makeup, and hair model, afraid she'd want to keep the virtuous caregiver mantle to herself—made the whole prospect feel more manageable. I would treat this like a final exam I actually cared about. I would cram for this job.

I was halfway through my coffee and feeling so much better I went back to the counter and got a cinnamon scone to nibble while I read. As I opened the book, flipping around to see where I felt like starting, I felt purposeful, even powerful. At least now I knew what was required of me. I'd had one bad day, but from here on out, it'd be better. I took a bite of pastry, set my feet on the empty chair opposite me, and began to read.

A lot of the writing was geared toward people who actually had the disease, so I skipped around a bit. I read portions of a few case histories, which tried to give you the sense of the person but did it awkwardly: *The petite brunette was known for her love of jogging and romantic comedies.* I was trying to match up Kate with the case studies, get a sense of where she was on the continuum. She'd had it for two years and had been in a wheelchair for most of that, but she had no trouble breathing that I could see. It seemed to me that she was fine at home as long as she had help. Someone could probably live that way for years—didn't you always hear stories of people who had lived forty vigorous years in their wheelchairs? I knew no such people myself, but I believed in the general stereotype. As a caregiver, I thought, I would be a maintenance worker of sorts, lending a hand well after the first shock of diagnosis, long before the palliative care at the end.

An hour later, I had finished the iced coffee and was shivering. I moved to a table near the window to enjoy the sun, losing my page in the process. I leafed through the chapter headings and was thinking offhandedly about another scone when I came to a section on prognosis. *Long-term prognosis varies for each patient,* the print read, *but the average time span from diagnosis to death is approximately two to five years.*

I sat there, perfectly still, and read it again, and still again. The sun coming in through the glass was broiling. I felt the sheen of sweat on my face, prickling in my armpits.

Around me, people were chatting, tapping their fingers on the tables, tearing into oversize cookies and pastries, spooning the whipped cream off iced drinks. I watched them, dropping napkins as they went, slopping liquid on the tabletops, shielding their eyes with sunglasses as they went out the front door.

WHEN I GOT HOME, I could hear our stereo from the driveway. The window frames were trembling slightly. Jill was in the mood to go out.

She heard me come in and walked out of her bedroom in a short robe, a towel around her head. "Hey!" she exclaimed. The prospect of going out often excited her more than the actual evening. She liked sipping the celebratory beer while she dressed, the festive announcement of the loud music.

She was holding an eye pencil. As I got closer I saw that one of her eyes was made-up, the other undone. I set *Living with ALS* on the coffee table, gazed at the plain block letters on the blue cover for a moment, then turned it facedown.

"I forgot and did one eye, but you can do the other if you want," Jill said, holding out the eyeliner. I shook my head. My resolve was flattened.

"Don't worry about it," I said. "Just go ahead and do your makeup tonight."

She shrugged, set the pencil down, and took the towel off of her head, running her fingers through her hair. "How was work?"

For a moment I couldn't even remember. Then it all came back to me.

"What are you wincing at?" Jill paused with her hands still tangled in her damp hair, staring at me.

"Nothing," I said. I stretched out on the couch and closed my eyes. "It was a hard day. I got her up and showered her and that was maybe the worst part. I don't think you told me it was this hard." I fanned myself with my shirt, giving it up after a moment. It wasn't doing any good anyway.

"Didn't I? I don't remember it being so hard. I remember it more as weird at first," she said.

"Oh come on," I said. "Just say it was hard, Jill. You always talked about how nice they all were but I'm on to it now, you know. You didn't want to admit it just sucked."

Looking at her now I felt as though the whole thing was her fault: She was the one who used to say that volunteering at the home had been such an amazing experience, so fulfilling. I never would have thought I could do this if it weren't for her. I would have volunteered with Greenpeace if I wanted to make a difference so badly, become one of the people who accosted you with their notepads at the bottom of Bascom Hill.

"It didn't suck," she protested. She looked at me and sighed, then sat down at the end of the couch, moving my feet out of the way. "It kind of sucked. At first. But it got better. I didn't want to complain."

This only made me feel surlier. I wanted to complain. Jill was always trying to put the best face on things, which right now seemed like pure fraud to me. The thing about Jill, which it had taken me some time to realize after she started piercing her ears all the way up into the cartilage and dyeing her hair pink in high school, was that she looked rebellious, but her upbringing, our town's characteristic churchgoing and community-centered activities, had left their mark on her. Hence the volunteer work, the glossing of what I now thought must have been a truly hellish job into something sweet and edifying.

"How did you feel about all those people?" I asked. "You knew they might die any time, right?"

She paused, tapping her eyeliner thoughtfully against her front teeth. "Deep down, for some of them, you know it might be best. And then I felt really arrogant to think that I could judge somebody's life like that, to basically say they're better off dead. But some I really kind of loved, and even if they were miserable I wanted to keep them around." She shrugged. "Don't forget I didn't work there very long. Not even a year. My parents made me."

"They did? I thought you chose it. You know, because of your grandmother."

"Well, it was that or take part in some repellent Pro-Life church campaign. Not much of a choice. It wasn't like I was on fire to be with the elderly instead of out smoking pot with you and Steve Brearly."

"Huh. I remembered it totally differently. Well, let's forget I brought it up," I said. I closed my eyes. "You know, it's really freaking hot in here."

"I know. I think I saw another roach in the kitchen too." She peered into the blank television screen and lined her other eye. "They really threw you in today, huh?"

"Supposedly it's better this way."

"You know, at least she's married," Jill said. Her voice was a monotone with concentration, the skin of her eyelids stretched between the V of her fingertips. How was I ever going to do that to Kate? "I'm sure you won't have to shower her too often, so don't ditch this job too because of one hard day."

"I'm not ditching anything," I said, stung. Apparently I had a pattern. "Anyway, showering is the least of it. It's worse for her than me, I bet. Let's just forget it. How was temping?"

"Vile. I read the same issue of *People* three times and someone called me 'doll.'" She straightened up and turned to look at me. "We're meeting Heather and those guys at the Union in an hour and a half, by the way."

"Who's driving?"

Jill rolled her eyes. "After today? I'm calling a cab. We're getting loaded."

She went back in her room to get dressed, closing the door behind her. I stayed on the couch, staring up at the ceiling. I was thinking that, without even trying—in fact, while actively fighting off the influence—I had adopted some of my mother's vocabulary of horizon expansion and branching out. That fetish was really hers more than mine. She signed me up for gymnastics and acting lessons when I was younger, later pointing out courses in the UW catalog that I would never have thought to take. Over the years I had indeed learned to balance on a narrow beam and leap over pommel horses, joined the freshman cast of *The Sisters Montague* as the flighty sister, and taken the occasional class in "Goddesses and Feminine Powers" and ended up enjoying it. In fact, I had been very good at gymnastics, though at first I had hated it on sheer principle (as a child I insisted on hating everything my mother pushed me into for the first several weeks) and faked a series of injuries my parents wisely ignored. After being forced to go for a month I had discovered that my usual lack of care for speed and objects around me, which translated into clumsiness everywhere else, transformed on the mats into sheer fearlessness. I was devoted to gymnastics until I was sixteen. My high school didn't have a team, and I could tell the cost of the private lessons was taking a toll, so I gave it up. Not all my attempts were so successful. Singing lessons were an exercise in humiliation from the start, and, more recently, my brief foray into churchgoing had died off as soon as it began.

I reached over and adjusted the fan so it blew right at me. I was sweating but hadn't quite gathered the energy to shower yet. I gave myself another five minutes and closed my eyes.

Church would not have been so bad except that I had told my mom I was going to attend St. Patrick's every week. I had this idea that if I went to church I'd get involved in a group of some sort, or volunteer a bit. And maybe I just liked the idea of starting each Sunday with something welcoming and uplifting. When I informed my mother, she paused for what seemed to me an inordinately long time and then responded, "Well. That's nice. Is there any particular reason why you chose to do this through church?"

My reasons seemed too vague to enumerate, plus I knew she'd suggest I volunteer at Planned Parenthood like she did if I really felt the urge, and I only wanted to try something different from what my mother would have done. But instead of saying so, I found myself on a minor tirade about the enigma that is faith. She responded skeptically. I admit the resolution struck me soon after Christmas, around the time or just after I had met Liam (my parents did not know that part), and the urge waned almost by the end of the first sermon, but out of sheer stubbornness I went every week for a month. It soon became clear I didn't really want to join the Bible study groups or volunteer in the cry room, my atheist mother was scrupulously silent on the topic, and Liam often had free time on Sunday mornings while his wife met her book club. Lent came, the season for sacrifice, and I gave up church.

The whole thing had left me unsettled. My visits to Kelly Jervis notwithstanding, kindness and concern for my fellow man seemed to be playing a pretty minor role in my life. Jill, who probably should have been my mother's daughter, not only had volunteered at the nursing home but voted Democratic and was forever forwarding me informative e-mails from NOW. Everyone else on campus seemed energetically outraged by any number of causes, papering the walls with flyers and meeting announcements and petitions. All those causes always mattered to me when I thought about them, but they didn't light a fire in me as they did in other people. I had always thought of myself as aware and thoughtful, but since January it had begun to occur to me that most people believed this of themselves, even as they cheated on their lovers and averted their eyes from the homeless. You could ask a wife beater if he was a good person, and he'd probably say yes. What if I was really one of them, convinced I had sound reasons for everything I did? The fact was, I could have worked at a soup kitchen whether I went to church or not, yet I didn't. And I could have dated plenty—at least a few—available guys my own age, but instead I sneaked around with Liam, and what was more, I liked it. I wanted to think there was goodness in me, some tough silvery cord of it like a second spine— hidden in its furrow, but resilient.

From behind Jill's door I heard her opening and closing drawers, humming, the whine of the blow dryer. She and I had lived together for more than a year, but we closed our doors carefully. If we were wrapped in towels after a shower, we darted from room to room. We knew so much about each other that at times, beers in our hands and the television on in the background, we looked at one another and realized we had told all the stories already. We had trotted out each of our Regretted Boyfriends as many times as we could, had teased one another about our families as far as it could go without offending. We had grown up together; our parents were friends, and we knew the same people. When we needed a rest from each other the air in our apartment became prickly with static and awareness. We might each be closed in our bedrooms, but we were still alert to the other person there, as though we could hear each other's voices in our heads as we puttered, naked, in our rooms or unzipped our boyfriends' jeans. That hadn't bothered me so much in the past, but now, since Liam, I sometimes felt her disapproval move through the place like a chill breeze, even if she wasn't there.

THE TERRACE BY LAKE Mendota was packed. There were families with toddlers, people with puppies, college students, couples in their sixties. A band was setting up onstage, and the air smelled of grilling bratwurst, hamburgers, and a yeasty waft of beer. There were three extra bars set up around the terrace every night in the summer, since the indoor bar could barely deal with the students alone. Plus this was the wildest week of the year: Everyone had finished finals but hadn't left town for the summer yet. There were groups of students sprawled out over picnic tables, their feet in each other's laps, and it seemed like a lot of people were blowing leisurely plumes of smoke up at the sky. The occasional cheer erupted from various tables. I waved to a couple of my professors as they strolled past, holding hands with their little-seen and much-imagined spouses. They looked as happy to be done with us as we were with them—maybe even more so. Personally, I had a tendency to develop a sudden rush of affection for a professor once the semester ended.

We picked our way through the crowded metal tables and throngs of people. The lake water smelled rich and a little fetid near the edge, where the algae coated the surface in a mossy sludge. I had borrowed one of Jill's thin dresses, which was long on me but felt good anyway in the breeze off the water. Now that we were here, my skirt blowing around my legs and my hair pushed off my neck, everything—*Living with ALS*, the next morning, when I would have to get up and go back to Kate's all over again—seemed very far away. I didn't have to think of any of that right now.

Next to me Jill slowed her usual stride to a lazy stroll. She stood a good five inches taller, nearing six feet where I was five six, and as a result her broad shoulders and rounded arms seemed powerful instead of plump, which they might have on a shorter girl. Beneath her chin was a firm little pad of flesh. To work she wore thin dark dresses, short-sleeved or sleeveless, hitting mid-thigh, that showed the curve of her belly and the nick of her bra in her sides. Right now she was wearing a red sleeveless shirt and faded jeans, earrings dangling near her shoulders. She kept her scarlet hair, which sometimes bore a sharply delineated gold-brown growth at the roots, in ponytails and upsweeps stabbed with carved sticks. She was vivid, solid, both muscular and soft-fleshed, and next to her I often felt boyish and pallid—my skin pale and freckled, my hair a plain brown instead of, say, raven. I probably fell under the "natural" category, and most of the time I was fine with that. I looked more like I'd hike than shop, but at least I was tall and slim enough to wear what I wanted, if I ever wanted to try something besides denim. Sometimes I looked at my face, the pale eyes and rounded nose with a sprinkle of freckles, and thought I was genuinely pretty. But for some reason I never did much to heighten or shape it—I found it preferable to believe I had a certain amount of raw material, if only I attended to it someday.

We stopped to buy beers at one of the outdoor bars. Jill paid for the first round. I would get the next—this was our system. Earlier that week I had worked one last shift at the restaurant before starting at Kate's, yielding about fifty dollars. It didn't seem like enough to bother putting in savings, so I'd brought it all with me.

I set aside money each summer, meant to cushion me so I could work only part-time during school. When my mother had presented me with this plan three years ago, at the end of high school—that my parents would pay for tuition and maybe one other major expense, leaving the rest up to me—it seemed foolproof. In high school I got twenty dollars a week for an allowance and worked at a drugstore Monday night and Saturday afternoon and believed myself to be swimming in money. And every summer since then I thought I could save enough. I banked cash smugly, swinging by the drive-through every Saturday morning. But each year my savings cushion began a little limper than I meant it to, and this year I was determined to save up at least a thousand more than I usually did. Jill wasn't going to take it well if she had to spot me for utilities again.

I could have picked up more hours at the restaurant instead of job hunting, but it was so oppressive and dark, all clattering silverware and swearing line cooks. Each shift I blinked as the gloom and cigarette smoke descended on me at the door, my hands thrust blindly toward the flickering television suspended above the bar. Jill said I came home smelling of Kools, beef blood, and a collective item she referred to only as "the fried." Plus I hated the bar crowd, all menthol cigarettes and cheap tap beer, several hours a night, five nights a week. At first that didn't seem so awful. They were just people getting out there and chatting with the bartender. We all want a social life. For a time I had hung out at the bar after work, too, drinking half-price brandy old-fashioneds and spooning out the mashed fruit and sugar from the slushy bottom of each glass as though they were vitamins. If I had upped my hours at the steak house for the summer, Labor Day would probably have found me wheezing and cirrhotic, my meals reduced to the occasional glob of ketchup licked from a spoon.

What had really gotten me reading want ads was when I had to take dinner orders from one of the regulars, a widower in his early seventies with a shock of white hair and thin, long hands. He always asked for a hot dog or grilled cheese with french fries and ketchup. These items came off the kids' menu. He invariably sat in the same seat at the bar, taking careful bites of pickle and dipping the corner of his sandwich into a pool of ketchup on the rim of his plate.

I don't know why that bothered me the way it did. So he wanted grilled cheese and fries. So what. And why shouldn't I see his request for an extra dill pickle (I made the kitchen give him two, then three, then four) as a tiny, simple pleasure rather than the only one he had? Jill thought I was reading too much into it, and I probably was, but I started looking through the paper anyway.

On Tuesday I had taken an odd pleasure in serving carafes of red wine and reciting salad dressings and potato preparations, marching underdone steaks back to the kitchen for another searing. It was my last night, for a while anyway, at something I knew how to do so well, joking with the customers, knowing by instinct when to check on which tables. Till today I'd forgotten how hard it was to start from nothing at a new job, how much time you spent with your hands clasped behind your back, the avalanche of details to memorize.

We were supposed to be looking for our group but were walking along the lake instead. We'd been quiet for a while, looking around, getting our bearings, and settling into the prospect of an evening out. I was feeling all right again.

"Hey, how was your date?" I asked.

She fished a lemon wedge out of her paper cup of weiss beer and sucked on it thoughtfully. "I think when you ask someone out you should prime yourself first," she said. "By watching the news or, say, leaving your fraternity house once a week."

"Another frat guy?"

She nodded, laughing, and dropped the lemon back into her cup. "I should stop agreeing in the first place, but they seem to like me, for some reason."

"You seem adventurous," I suggested. We passed a table full of tanned, wiry guys in ratty T-shirts and shorts, the shaggy kind who always have carabiners hooked to their backpacks. One of them gave us a big grin and raised a glass. I smiled back but kept walking. "You hold the promise of tattoos."

"Maybe. But every sorority girl has a clover on her ankle or her ass, so maybe not. Anyway, we just had nothing to work with together, you know? It was like trying to crochet with your feet."

We were just past the stage, heading toward the concessions stand and pondering a bratwurst, when Jill made a little noise, a soft *Oh*, and then she said instantly, "Did I tell you what the intern did today?" She turned to look me in the face, her lips slightly pursed and her eyes open a shade too wide. As I looked past her I saw what she'd been trying to distract me from: a table full of people, several pitchers of beer in the center, including Liam and a dark-haired woman I knew had to be his wife.

"At least put on your sunglasses," Jill murmured. I did, still watching. Their chairs were close to each other, Liam's arm draped over the back of hers. His hand was moving thoughtlessly through her hair, which was dark and gleaming, one of those expensive cuts that's designed to look effortless. She was in a red top and black skirt, and to me her gestures seemed definitive and assured, her earrings showing through her hair. She was large-breasted and curvy, a few inches shorter than Liam. I would have towered over her.

She was totally different from what I'd imagined. Maybe wives always are. I had had two conflicting but equally fanciful images of her—either tall and slim and sleek-haired, always in a suit, or an English Rose in chintz dresses with dropped waists and tortoiseshell headbands. In truth she looked sweet, confident rather than tough. I was thinner, but she had breasts, real breasts, a trim upturned nose, and a small red mouth. Who knew what Liam saw in me? Maybe he liked frizzy dark curls and light blue eyes. Maybe he saw me as willowy instead of gangly.

I knew, from little things Liam had mentioned, that his wife liked the blues and drank Guinness. She was a lawyer, and she was putting him through graduate school. None of this fit with my preconceptions about a wounded wife. *But she sounds cool*, I once protested to Liam. *Shouldn't she be the sort who likes peonies and spritzers?*

What the hell are you talking about? he answered. *Who drinks spritzers?*

You know what I mean, I'd mumbled and he sighed and said, *It's complicated.*

I can't believe you trotted that one out, I told him.

Jill and I were still walking, though I had slowed down, and as they passed out of my sight I finished my beer and pushed back my sunglasses again. She was quiet.

"It's not like I didn't expect it to happen at some point," I said defensively. I didn't sound very convincing.

Jill nodded and looked away again as we walked. "I saw her once or twice," she said. "I didn't want to tell you."

"Why not?" I asked. I hated the idea of being protected.

"Oh, did you want me to mention it every time I saw her?" Jill retorted. "I thought you were still pretending she didn't exist." She picked up her pace, the impact of her heels on the concrete sounding in her voice. Her earrings swung, a tag of hair loosened from her twist flapping up and down.

I sped up too. "This isn't some big drama. It's just going on, and at some point it'll quit and no one will know. It happens all the time." In truth, for all our careful planning, I could never quite believe it counted. I didn't think we were old enough, Liam and I, to make adultery a meaningful transgression. Deep down I thought it only mattered if you had been together for twenty years, or had a child. They had not even been married all that long—five years? four? Who knew how long it took for marriage to really take?—and if this affair was so dreadful our meetings should all feel worse than they did, tougher and more ominous.

"Okay," said Jill. "I know I'm being a pain. It's up to you." She glanced back over her shoulder at their table. I did too. They were barely visible now: just the tops of their heads, a hand on a shoulder. "She's pretty," Jill said neutrally. I didn't answer. If I had thought I would get a sympathetic distraction from her, I was wrong. I knew I had no room to push it. I knew what this woman's hair smelled like, I was thinking. If I were to guess from Liam's plain gold band, I'd bet her wedding ring was smooth and thick, her engagement ring a plain round solitaire.

Jill saw someone and waved. A few of our friends had found a table on the upper part of the terrace and we started making our way back to them. She glanced over her shoulder at me, held out a hand, and said, "Come on, Becklet."

I OUGHT TO HAVE gotten a good six hours of sleep that night, but after the Union we went to a bar where I pilfered from a communal basket of

2

cheese curds and watched Jill play pool with Nathan, a kid who'd been
in our dorm freshman year. The four-beer urge to phone Liam hit me
around eleven, but Jill, reliably, shamed me out of it. I resisted the
temptation but felt anxious and disconnected from everyone anyway.

They all said the same thing when I told them about the new job,
feeling modest and quietly virtuous as I did, as if I were reading to the
blind in my spare time. "Ah," they'd said, nodding. Then, "At least
she's married."

Phrases from the ALS book kept coming back to me: *It is a mistake to let
one partner take on too much caregiving responsibility.* Who else was going to do
it? I could imagine how that dictum would be hard to violate. How did
the healthy person force herself to look the other one straight in the
face and say, "I'm restless. I think I'll go play some tennis"?

By midnight it was obvious that the night had gathered steam into a
genuine bender. I wasn't sure anymore if I was really having fun or just
simulating it, but either way I was glad to be out of a quiet house,
among people and loud music. Sometime around one, as I watched Jill
and Nathan play a game of pool, Nathan reminded me I had to get up
early for work. I just snorted. Even I could hear it was a hateful sound.
Don't be afraid to make your needs clear to a caregiver. Now is not the time for shyness.
Something bitter that had edged around me all night took hold, and I
gave up my virtuous pretense and said, "Look, I basically just live this
woman's life with her. For her, whatever. And fuck it, I can do that
with a hangover."

"I thought you liked her," Jill said. She took a shot and missed. The
end of their pool game had been going on for half an hour.

"I think I do," I said, leaning against the table. "As far as I know,
anyway. She seems pretty nice."

"So what's the problem?"

I watched Nathan's cue ball sail smoothly into the corner pocket
near my hand. I didn't know quite what to say to that. *I don't know what
will happen to this woman,* I could have explained. *I don't know what I've agreed
to.* Instead I told Jill we had to get out of there before I had anything
else to drink.

But news of our departure was received as an invitation. People
trailed along after our cab, and a moment after we'd walked into our

apartment and turned on the fans to cool it down, we heard the familiar roar of our friends' decrepit cars in the driveway. They came in with
fresh packs of cigarettes and a new case of beer they'd gone to Maple
Bluff to buy since the Madison liquor stores closed at nine, and when
someone has gone to that sort of trouble you have to let them in for at
least a token beer. A pizza delivery was set in motion. The television
and the stereo were turned on; Jill moved the trash can to the middle of
the room for empties, and scattered around tin ashtrays stolen from a
fast-food joint. We were settling in, and I had no intention of removing myself to get some sleep. The last thing I remembered was Jill coming out of the kitchen toward where I lay sprawled across three people
on the couch. She was holding out a vodka tonic in a red plaid thermos
in one ringed hand and smiling kindly down at me.

four

WHEN MY ALARM WENT off I prayed it was early but it wasn't. In the shower I leaned my head against the wall and wondered if I could call it off. The smell of stale cigarettes came off my wet hair. I was in terrible shape, nauseated, with a headache that felt like white sheets of light flashing behind my eyes. It was either drink a beer, which Kate might smell, or throw up before I left. I chose to throw up. It helped a little. Then I managed to brush my teeth and shuffle out to my car. On the way out I saw that Nate was sleeping on the couch, sprawled with one foot still on the ground. The trash can stood in the middle of the room, filled with beer cans, and the ashtrays had overflowed onto the coffee table.

As I drove I tried to remember if I had called Liam. I didn't think I had—Jill wouldn't have let me, but then I might have sneaked away to do it. No. She had bullied me out of it. For a moment I was awash with gratitude for her, almost weepy at the way she looked out for me sometimes. You were always better off not calling. Why did I never remember that?

It felt okay, even appropriate, being hungover on the east side, but the farther west I drove toward Kate's house, the more overtly respectable the city became. My Honda puttered along next to gleaming minivans and BMWs and if I had been able to lift my head I would have noted how expensive and sleek everyone was. You could bet that no one else on this side of town had wet hair knotted in a rubber band they'd taken off the neighbor's newspaper. I turned into their neighborhood, wondering as I drove how long she and Evan had been in their house, or in Madison, for that matter.

It really was a pretty neighborhood, even if it did lack funk. I didn't think anyone with the kind of money they had would want a neighborhood like mine anyway. Especially not if you were trying to maneuver a wheelchair around steep staircases and honey-colored but uneven floorboards. Everyone kept saying how lucky it was that Kate was married, but I thought it was lucky that she had all that money. Who knew what the equipment and caregivers cost? At least they had no kids to worry about. Maybe they'd meant to, till they'd found out, or maybe they'd never wanted any. *It is important, though certainly not easy, not to let children take a backseat to the needs of the patient.*

I parked the car and left the windows down. Nothing was going to happen to my car in a neighborhood of BMWs. I sat there in the driver's seat for a second, finding the warmth soothing for my headache. I didn't have to stay. I wasn't locked into this. They hadn't said a word about the facts of her illness, what I was really signing on for, so they couldn't blame me if I left now that I knew. I could deal with their disappointment, if they had any. I wouldn't see them anywhere, any more than I would run into Liam's wife at Bar Association meetings.

I walked slowly up their driveway, my head pounding with each step. I thought it would be better once I got in there: I'd sit in one of their big armchairs, breathing the cool air that smelled faintly of lemons or the bowl of pears. I'd file some papers and sit very still. What a relief to walk into their living room. It was so calm and still that I thought I might even try and spend a little time in here today, lay my cheek against the cold belly of the stone girl.

Kate was in the kitchen. She had a book on a tray affixed to her chair. A frame held the book open, and there was a little mechanical hook along the bottom of the pages. There was some sort of sensor involved, so that when she moved her head a certain way, the hook turned the page. She'd shown me the device the day before. Kate glanced up and seemed about to smile, but then she looked a little stricken. Obviously I looked worse than I'd thought.

She said something, what I thought was, "Are you okay?"

Embarrassed to admit I wasn't fighting my way through the flu or malaria, I nodded. The nod hurt.

"You look jaundiced," she went on. It took me a second to get that word. Then I smiled a little when I picked up on it. It wasn't the easiest word in the world.

"I'm okay," I said. She nodded toward the cupboard and when I opened it I saw a big bottle of ibuprofen. I tipped out two and she raised her eyebrows at me, so I shook out another and took them with a glass of Coke. She shook her hair out of her face and nodded toward the book apparatus and said something.

"Should I take it off?" I asked. I was stalling. I knew perfectly well she'd asked me to remove it. "Or maybe you'd like to read for a while and give me something to do in the meantime." A nice easy day around the house would be a godsend.

"For starters, I was planning on the farmers' market," she said apologetically. "We're having people over tonight."

Before I could stifle it I looked at her in horror: It was unspeakably sunny and hot and the market would be crammed with people. Why the hell did she need me so early on weekends? Nothing truly needed to be done right then. And where was Evan, anyway? Wasn't the farmers' market a couples kind of thing?

"Oh, the market," I said. "Uh-huh. Hey, what about that filing and insurance stuff? I could do that first."

Kate gave me an appraising look before she spoke. "No," she said. "We'll do this, please." She backed up the chair and rotated, turning it toward the bathroom. Just before she turned the chair away from me she said, "Late night, huh."

"Yeah," I admitted.

"Okay. Fine. But I'm not rearranging my day around your parties, Bec."

My first thought was pure, pissy defensiveness. I could have walked out right then and there. What business was it of hers what I did when I left? I wasn't so bad off that I couldn't slap some pointless blusher on and hand over money for a bunch of parsley at the market. I watched her roll down the hallway toward the bathroom and stayed where I was, thinking seriously about whether I wanted to deal with her anymore. I thought I liked her, maybe even quite a bit, but she seemed imperious right now. I wondered if she was like this a lot.

I took another gulp of my Coke and glanced at my purse slung over the back of the chair. She hadn't made up her mind about me either, it suddenly dawned on me, and I could tell that if I was going to leave, today was probably the day to do it and get it over with. But I was too ashamed to act on it—her expression had had none of its usual humor when she told me to get it together. I pictured that shiny, unreadable fall of blond hair as she'd rolled out of the kitchen. She was waiting in the bathroom, calm and detached, idly wondering if she had to interview people all over again.

She was probably debating whether to fire me. My awkwardness around her, my total lack of experience and confidence, seemed all the more vivid through my hangover: After several tries yesterday I still wasn't very good at helping her in the bathroom—she had to tell me to wipe her harder, which seemed to cost her as much to say as it did me to hear. Twice I had lifted her so badly that she had had to tell me, her voice urgent and unintelligibly fast, to put her down before I dropped her. I splashed nutrition shake on her clothes because I looked the other way when I poured it. No doubt when she compared me to Hillary, who'd been with her over a year, I seemed even worse than I was.

I went to the end of the hall. She was at the door to the bathroom, her chair pivoted so she could back in. When she saw me still standing several yards away she spoke, knowing, I was sure, that I would have to come to her to hear her. So I did. I started walking, interested to know what she was saying, before I even thought about it. As I came closer, fighting down another lurch of nausea, I saw her break into a grin.

"It's just a hangover," she said. "I used to run races with hangovers."

"Races?" I clarified, repeating after her.

She nodded, her face softening. "But you can take your time with the makeup until the meds kick in."

"Thank god," I said, and she laughed for real this time, sending a rush of relief through me so fast it startled me.

As I did her mascara I looked at her face, at the tiny lines that bracketed her wide mouth, and the freckles that showed across her nose. After a while she began to talk, and I paused and watched her so I could understand.

"I kind of envy you," she admitted sheepishly. "I'm too old for it now anyway, but I miss just going out to a bunch of places, having a drink, and going to the next." I tried to imagine a night out with the Kate of ten years ago, knocking back shots and shouting in noisy bars, and for a second something plummeted in me. I had never been very good at facing up to the fact that some things were unfixable.

Her eyebrows were a little mussed from when I'd taken off the book turner, and I smoothed them, one at a time, with my fingertip.

"I don't know if it's as fun as you're imagining," I said.

I FELT A LOT better by the time we reached the market. The stands circled the grounds of the state capitol, and people joined the throng moving counterclockwise along the sidewalk, ducking in and out of the horde to stop at the vendors. The tables were piled with food: orange carrots with plumes of thready green leaves; yellow, purple, and green beans; early scarlet strawberries piled in wooden boxes; blocks of white cheese and butter. I'd catch the scent of basil from one table, smoked trout from the next. I leaned over a stack of spinach and realized I could still smell the dirt on the roots.

We kept near the lawn, so that Kate could pause her chair easily while I darted across to the tables. My arms were weighed down with plastic bags of radishes, strawberries, and bundles of skinny, blushing rhubarb stalks, fresh herbs, soft-skinned garlic. After a while I gave in to the slowness of the crowd and it was kind of fun. For one thing, it wasn't my money, so if she pointed me toward a stand for goat cheese in herbed olive oil or venison sausage, I never had to count the bills in my pocket. I looked over quarts of strawberries much more carefully than I ever would have for myself. At home I usually ate them standing over the trash can and spitting any bad parts out, but now it seemed extremely important that each berry be perfect.

The other perk was the samples, which I made it my business to research. Cheese, sausage, sweet peas, smoked fish. At a stand that sold beeswax candles, I took a spoonful of honey and then glanced over my shoulder at her. My constant nibbling was rude, I realized, and I held up the plastic spoon to her. She shook her head, but she was smiling.

Halfway around the capitol Kate slowed her chair and nodded toward a little café. There was nothing on the list that corresponded so I bent down to see what she wanted.

"Pastry," she said. "You really need one."

I watched her from across the street as I waited in line for a chocolate croissant. I felt I shouldn't look away from her, as though she were a toddler in a stroller. It was probably safe. No one was going to harass her, and I had her purse with all the money in it. She was sitting near the street, just out of range of most of the people, with big tortoise-shell sunglasses covering her eyes. She was dressed in a crisp blue shirt, a light skirt and sandals, and a silver bracelet that flashed in the sun. Her head was tilted to one side as she watched people go past. They glanced at her and then away, their body language showing that they didn't want to stare, or else they smiled at her to show some kind of solidarity. I watched the smilers to see how they came off. I knew that's what I would be, grinning away. Even from here they seemed a little fatuous.

When we got back to Kate's house it was still empty. "What's Evan up to today?" I asked. I was getting her into her wheelchair in the driveway. I had to reach into the car, bumping my head several times and making her wince each time, and position her as when I got her out of bed: situate her legs and feet, bring her up to her feet, and then pivot.

She blew at a wisp of hair in her eyes and I brushed it out of her face. "Just some errands," she told me. She didn't elaborate, so I got my hands beneath her arms and said: "Ready?" She nodded. As soon as I lifted her I knew by the pain across my back that I was in the wrong posture. Her head tapped the door frame.

"Shit," I said.

"It was nothing," she told me.

Back in the kitchen we looked at everything piled on the counter. I'd been an idiot not to go to the market every week. We had little buttons of white cheese floating in herb-speckled oil, sheaves of spinach, trout that was faintly rosy at the edges from the smoke. I thought of the bags of wet, pre-peeled carrots I ate most of the time.

"Would you believe this is the first time I got something besides pastry?" I asked her.

Kate was looking fondly at some radishes, their roots ice-white.
"Are you a convert?" she asked.

I started to put the smoked trout and cheese away. "I think I am," I
called from inside the refrigerator. "What's Evan going to do with all
this?"

She didn't answer, and so I stashed the food on a shelf in the fridge
and turned to look at her. She was giving me a big smile. "We," she
said.

" 'We'?"

She nodded.

"I can't cook," I reminded her.

"Don't worry. This is mainly assembling."

I looked at all the food and back at her. I decided that as far as a
day's work went, making a meal might not be so bad. It all seemed terribly healthy, too. It occurred to me that my headache had been gone
for a long time, possibly since the croissant. I'd have to remember that.

Before we cooked I followed her to the stereo and looked over her
CDs. She was into folk, it seemed, the kind of thing that relied on a
good voice and an acoustic guitar. There was a shelf full of jazz and
classical. As we contemplated it, me crouched next to her chair, I said,
"Do you two have similar taste in music? Or are some of these Evan's
and some yours?" I thought of Liam and his wife meeting at a concert.
I couldn't tell what he would have thought of her music, but I thought
he might have liked it, if only because I knew none of the names, which
was frequently a positive sign.

I turned to watch Kate answer. She was looking thoughtfully at the
CD cases. "It's hard to remember," she said slowly. "I think our taste
has merged."

"That's kind of nice," I said. I put in the CDs she nodded at. "It's
romantic."

She smiled faintly. "Yeah, I guess."

She looked at me sideways, said something I missed. She repeated it
for me: She was asking what I liked.

"Oh, I don't know," I told her. We headed back to the kitchen. "I
tend to really love a song I hear once on the radio, then I play it into

the ground and hate it in three weeks. I don't think I actually have taste. I have flings." Liam often brought me CDs, scratchy old recordings or bright Latin guitars. I'd fallen in love with one of them as soon as he played the first track. The band was a trio of saxophone, bass, and drum, with a singer whose voice was low and dark. His women were the sort who had daddies and drank whiskey and met in pool halls in the afternoon. "I like Morphine," I told her. "Did you ever hear them?"

She shook her head. "Bring it next time," she said. "I could use some new music."

I sat down with Kate and we made a list of what to do. She was right; it wasn't much actual cooking. Most likely she'd planned it that way on purpose.

I taped the list to a copper pot that hung over the island so I could glance at it as I worked. Kate sat with her book apparatus on, a magazine in front of her, but after a while she didn't read at all, but watched me and told me what to do for each thing—to tear the stems from the big pieces of spinach, to scrub the radishes but leave the tops on. First I washed almost everything and spread it on towels to dry. Then I trimmed and peeled and chopped. Some vegetables I cooked in a big pot of salted water, and other things I just sliced. Kate listened to the music as I dumped things into boiling water and fished them out again, cooled them in a bath of ice water, and drained them and wrapped them in towels.

Everything was so bright in the kitchen, the gleaming copper, the skinny green beans, and the white dish of red berries. I fell into a rhythm of cutting and dipping and draining, sweeping the trimmings into the garbage as I worked to keep everything clean. I felt warm and bright and purposeful. I felt as if the things in my hands, the fruit and fish and cheese, had started off rough, but I was refining them. There was something elemental and simple about the piles of chopped vegetables in their dishes, the deep green hue of cooked things, the fat heft of the eggplant. I poured olive oil from a tin gallon with French writing on it and cracked peppercorns from a weathered wooden mill. Even the salt she told me to use was special: big sticky crystals spooned out of a linen bag.

Kate moved her chair over when it was time to make vinaigrette.

"Didn't people used to have their own secret vinaigrette recipes?" I asked. "I think that that used to be a special thing." I mashed garlic ponderously. "Or maybe it was just an old commercial."

Kate laughed and I watched her answer. "I know what you mean," she said, nodding. I repeated it to be sure I had it and she nodded again. "Like pie crust," she went on. "Classic kitchen skills."

I mashed a little harder. My wrist was getting sore. "Yeah. Aren't French women all supposed to know some special vinaigrette recipe?"

Kate looked bemused. "French women are supposed to know everything."

"I know. Sex secrets and how to tie a scarf, right?"

Kate laughed. "Are you up on those?"

I flushed. "Hardly. I just read it somewhere. Something about a tea that, uh . . ." I trailed off. Why had I brought this up? Kate was look-ing at me expectantly. "It supposedly perfumes . . . how to put this? The nether regions."

She chuckled. "Very delicately put. What attention to detail," she said. "You know what it is about French women?" I watched her speak, nodding and repeating. "The stereotype, anyway. *Competence.* At every-thing. You'd think it'd be more mysterious than that."

At Kate's suggestion I dipped a green bean in the olive oil before I whisked it into the vinaigrette. It seemed to me I tasted the olive oil all through my head: I felt its sheen on my lower lip and a peppery hit in the back of my throat and my nostrils. It tasted rich and warm and dark, dark green.

At the end of the afternoon, shortly before people were supposed to arrive, she told me to arrange everything on big enameled plates. I had nothing like them at home, where all our dishes were secondhand china painted with tiny chive blossoms and petrified ducks. These were rich, saturated colors, and just to amuse myself I arranged by contrast: radishes and carrots on a blue plate, roasted eggplant and basil on a platter the color of a sunflower, the goat cheese in a bright cherry bowl. I put out wineglasses I'd found in the cupboard in the dining room. I heard myself humming.

"What else do you need?" I asked, looking around the kitchen. "What about drinks?"

She thought for a second and then slumped in exasperation. "I forgot ice."

"Oh, well, no big deal. I can just run out and get it, unless you want to come along."

I got the keys from their polished wooden bowl on the table near the front door. The bowl sat at the feet of the naked girl, who was still where Evan had moved her, far enough away from the spider plant that a tendril only curled over her shoulder. She looked rather nice, for such a Barbie doll. I flicked the vine off her shoulder and went out for ice.

When I came back Evan's car was in the garage and Kate wasn't in the kitchen. As I loaded the bags of ice into a big copper tub near the door to the deck I heard his voice from the back of the house. I couldn't hear Kate from here and didn't expect to—I had been unable to hear her from a foot away in the crowded market—but I could hear Evan laughing, the fast tempo of his words. The music we'd put on had been turned up, the food on the table glistening in the late afternoon sun. I ate another green bean dipped in olive oil and headed back toward the bedroom, wiping my mouth and then calling hello as I went.

They were in the bathroom, the makeup kit spread out on the counter next to two glasses of cold pink wine. Evan was leaning back against the counter, Kate facing him so I could see her profile in the mirror. She'd been laughing about something hard enough that Evan was wiping a tear away from the corner of each of her eyes. They were still grinning about something as I came in.

"Hey, Bec," Evan said. "Sorry, we got a little slap-happy for a second." Kate, still grinning, cast her eyes meaningfully at the wine.

"For me?" I asked. In the mirror I caught a glimpse of myself, face pale and shiny, my dark hair diffused by the light from the window, a hand laid coquettishly to my breast. In the course of the day I'd forgotten how bad off I'd been that morning. I felt a lot better, but I wasn't looking very good. My eyes peered, tiny and rabbity, out of a white face, circles beneath them.

"Thanks. You know, I can give the makeup a shot if you want to relax, Evan." Evan had moved behind Kate and was twisting her hair into a ponytail.

"That's okay," he said. "I'm strangely in the mood to do it tonight."

As he spoke his hand traced the curve of Kate's neck and up her jaw-line to her ear. She leaned her head slightly into the cup of his palm, her eyes closing slowly and luxuriously, like a cat's.

"You're on till about six, right?" Evan said.

"Do you need me later?" I asked. I had been planning to go home and sleep in penance for the night before. "Because I can stay if you want; it's no problem."

"You could meet some of our friends," Kate said. "You'll see a lot of them, so . . ."

I drank some of the wine, expecting it to be sweet and fizzy. At the Italian restaurant we had served white zinfandel with a spritz of soda. But the wine was stony and light and there was no sweetness in it. It was such a surprise that I stood there, holding a pool of it on my tongue, and didn't answer. When I looked back up Evan was doing Kate's eyebrows.

"Like it?" he asked, smiling at me. "It's nice with tomatoes."

"It's really good," I said. "And I can stay awhile." I settled myself on the bathroom counter and watched them finish up the makeup. When it was done Kate's eyes were darkened again, her mouth red and shiny. Evan removed the band from her hair. As she let her head fall back, Kate said, "Bec, would you mind grabbing the silver beaded hoops?"

Her jewelry box was on top of the dresser, with diamond studs and gold and silver hoops in compartments on the top, and below it a clutch of small velvet drawstring bags. I found the hoops and went back toward the bathroom, my wine in one hand and the earrings clicking in my palms, and caught a glimpse of Evan bending down to kiss her, one hand splayed against the pale skin of her neck, the top of his head showing the thinness of his light hair. How had I ever searched for Liam in Evan's face and gestures? Evan straightened up, glancing over at me and smiling as easily as if I'd seen him shaking someone's hand. How odd that I knew as much as I did about him—how he'd kiss, where he'd touch you. I flushed, imagining a hand on my neck, the laundered smell of a clean white shirt.

WHEN PEOPLE BEGAN ARRIVING, I stayed out on the deck with Kate. I loitered just behind and to the right of her until she told me she found it difficult to talk to me from there. I stepped beside her. At least I knew I looked better than I had that morning. I had borrowed Kate's lipstick and taken my hair down, using some of her serum to smooth it.

She introduced me to each couple as they came through the kitchen and out onto the deck, exclaiming over the food. They must have been familiar with the caregiver routine—they introduced themselves to me right after kissing Kate on the cheek. A tall, black-haired woman with big silver earrings nodded toward the laden table and said, "That's you, right?" The wine I had had while we were getting ready must have had an effect; I found myself blushing when I agreed. The table did look beautiful. It had a look of vivid, cheerful excess. The whole deck seemed pretty and crowded, the light the syrupy yellow that falls at the end of the afternoon in summertime.

I forgot the names of most of their friends as soon as they were introduced, suspecting it might be weeks before I could get them straight. They were mostly couples in their thirties and early forties, wearing jeans or khakis. The women wore bright knit tops that showed their gleaming shoulders, except for one redhead in a crisp linen blouse and a chunky turquoise necklace.

I stayed near Kate. The redhead in the linen shirt bent down to kiss her cheek. I glanced at Kate, who flicked her eyes toward the bar we'd set up on one table.

"Would you like a drink?" I asked the woman. "There's beer and wine on the picnic table." She turned to look at me, lifting her eyebrows until she figured out who I might be. "I'm Bec," I added. "I'm helping Kate."

She held out a hand. "Nancy." She brushed her bangs off her face and glanced down at Kate and then back at me. "I think I will. Anyone else?" We shook our heads. Kate said something to me, glancing at Nancy to show it concerned her.

"Oh. She says to try the goat cheese," I added. "It's that herby kind I guess you like." Nancy smiled and headed off to the bar. Kate and I spoke to the next couple to arrive, and again I acted as a sort of shadow hostess, glancing at her for cues.

Some of the friends could understand her better than I could, and others glanced at me for help. Even the ones who understood her must have realized that translating was part of what I had to practice, and they waited, sipping their drinks or chewing salad, as Kate spoke and I watched and repeated it. It was a little like reading aloud. They watched Kate, then me as I repeated her words. I tried to match the tone she used, so I didn't sound monotonous, but that felt odder still. I was reminded of my one acting experience, when I'd had a single line ("Yes! Truly, Lucy, what must Senator Gladwell think?") that had rung out of me like a proclamation instead of welling up naturally the way the better actors' lines did.

Someone lit a joint, the peppery smell mixing with the petroleum-and-lemon scent of the citronella candles. People were scattered around the chairs, balancing plates of food on their knees and talking loudly. Kate was at the round glass-topped table near the door, and I seated myself in the empty chair next to her. All around her conversation was going on. Kate watched a woman with cropped white-blond hair saying, "This bulldog was the most repulsive animal I've ever seen. I'd rather get a Komodo dragon." Kate laughed, then shifted her attention to the woman's husband, a good-looking bearded black guy. He was defending the bulldog, whose name was Posy.

How many other caregivers had her friends met at parties like this over the past couple years? At first there probably weren't any except for a few hours in the daytime. Then there'd be someone lurking in the background in the evening; then closer and closer, edging into conversations and occasionally repeating dialogue and explanations. Now, I'd guess, someone was always there.

Evan walked past, pausing between me and Kate. "How's everything?" he asked. He had rolled his sleeves up and was holding a bottle of water. He looked at me. "Any questions?" I shook my head, smiling. He kissed the top of Kate's head and moved on.

Kate began to speak, glancing from me to the group at large. The effect was instantaneous: As soon as she began to talk they quieted and watched, waiting for me to repeat it. It was the same each time she said something, and it was admirable in a way, how quickly they perked up, but it was tiring, too, even for me, and soon Kate went back to listening, a small grin fixed on her lips.

I ENDED UP STAYING the whole time. Each time I thought I should go, someone would draw me into a conversation and next thing I knew I was eating another cracker with smoked trout and telling them all about myself: the town I grew up in, my parents, my major, waitressing.

They began to clear out around midnight, and we stood near the door, saying good-bye, Kate being kissed and me shaking hands, Evan hugging people good-bye. After the last few I retreated and began clearing up cups, waiting to be dismissed but not wanting to ask just yet. I left Kate and Evan in the living room and went out to the back porch, slowly stacking the last of the naked enamel dishes that gleamed with oil and bore hardened white smears of goat cheese. It was peaceful on the porch, the breeze cooling off my face and the music still playing softly, and I took my time, finally blowing out the molten candles as I went back in.

Kate and Evan weren't in the kitchen. I went slowly through to the living room, suddenly aware that it was dark and quiet and twelve thirty in the morning in someone else's home. Then their voices, mainly Evan's, drifted out to me from the bedroom. I headed down the hall, trying to walk loudly.

"Look. We agreed on this," Evan was saying. The door to their room was open. "We made the compromise, so can we please just leave it alone?" I stopped in the hall and stood there. I knew I should say something, or make a noise, but I didn't want him to know I'd heard him this way, his voice so pleading and uneven. Kate's was an undifferentiated murmur, rising at the end. I pictured Kate sitting there, the narrow plane of her shoulders, her feet and hands still stubbornly where I'd laid them as we got ready for the party. I took a heavy step in the hallway and called out, "Well, I should be heading out." Then I stepped into the doorway.

The room was half-dark. Only the bedside lamp was on, casting a wan oval of light on the pillowcase. They both turned to look at me. Evan was standing by the side of the bed, holding a checkbook in one hand. He ran the other hand through his hair when he saw me. Kate looked over her shoulder. A blush crept up my neck. I hadn't much considered the room before except as a place where I worked, but it struck me now how intimate it was to come upon a couple in their bed-room. I pictured him on top of her in the bed, her unable to move. Maybe they found some compromise, somehow. Or maybe they had just given up.

"Sorry to interrupt," I said, pushing the image out of my head. I touched the light switch on the wall. "Do you want some light?"

They both looked around the dim room, startled, as though they had been in here since the sun had set and hadn't even noticed. Kate swallowed and said, "Please."

I hit the light, illuminating the wide blue bed. Kate turned her chair away from Evan and toward me. She gave me a brilliant smile, her eyes squinting against the light. Evan passed a hand over his eyes. Their faces were flushed.

"Thank you so much for staying," Kate said. She tilted her head back toward Evan. "Evan's just writing out your check." Evan had been staring out the window, and at the mention of the checkbook he started and bent over the nightstand to write it out.

"I'm giving you a little extra since you stayed on short notice," he said as he wrote. "And for such a wonderful job cooking." He signed the check with a flourish and tore it out. He wouldn't look at Kate.

I took it from him and looked at her. "Do you need any help getting to bed?" She shook her head. "Okay then." I felt uncomfortable leav-ing, though I couldn't have explained it to them. I had no pretext for staying. So what if they had argued? People always fought after parties; you either had sex, hashed over who you thought was going to have sex, or told him how he'd pissed you off. My last two relationships had broken up in the aftermath of the best parties I'd ever been to, the biggest, noisiest, and most high-spirited. Sometimes I felt I had to find some way of continuing the intensity of the evening and then it backfired on me: The resentments came out, or it turned out he'd been in a closet with some girl while I thought he was in the bathroom.

"I'll see you Tuesday," I said.

"I'll walk you out," Evan said. "It's late."

As we passed the kitchen he said, "There's wine left. Did you get a chance to try the sauvignon blanc?" He opened the fridge, reached down to the bottom shelf, and handed me a bottle.

"You don't have to do that," I said.

"You didn't have to stay," he pointed out. I conceded the point and thanked him. He held the front door open for me and looked out to see where my car was. Then he waited as I walked down the driveway. It touched me, that caution and attention. Or maybe I just wanted to sympathize with him after hearing him that way. I hated hearing a tremble in a man's voice, especially since after that morning I knew how it felt to have Kate looking at you with that uncompromising gaze. It made me pity him. Maybe he'd known that, hence the extra money and the wine. When I got to my car I waved and I saw his silhouette wave back. I got in, setting the bottle on the passenger seat, and watched the porch light flash off.

five

"TOO BARE," SAID KATE.

"If you say so." I hung the dress, which had spaghetti straps and a low-dipping neckline, back on the rack. In the mirror I saw the saleswoman watching us from behind the cash register.

"Trust me," said Kate. "I couldn't even wear a strapless bra with that. You know me pretty well by now, but I'll avoid making you tape my breasts if I can."

"Gee, thanks."

She grinned. I held a blue sleeveless turtleneck beneath Kate's chin and we considered it. A tiny, trim woman in her fifties strode past us to another rack. As she caught a glimpse of me pushing Kate's hair off her shoulders, she turned. Still holding a dress to her collarbone, the woman said to me: "It's so kind of you to help your friend." She gave us both a smile.

"Mmm, thanks," I murmured. "I'm in it for the money."

The woman looked perplexed, though her smile remained. "Oh, I see. Well, still." She started to say something else but then turned away toward the rack. Kate lowered her face a bit but I could still see her grinning.

In these first two months we'd settled into a schedule of four days a week. I arrived in the mornings to find Kate dressed but not made-up, her hair still damp from the shower. I gave her two cans of the nutritional shakes, some water, then rinsed the funnel and tube and wiped her side with a paper towel. Then we sat at the kitchen table to read a list of tasks in Evan's scratchy handwriting, which slanted up at the ends, the lines drifting toward the edges of the page.

I so rarely saw her outside her chair that for a long time I tended to forget she ever left it. Then I walked in one day to find her stretched out on the couch, her legs crossed at the ankles. She turned her head to look at me and for one irrational moment I knew that she was, suddenly, inexplicably, well. I could imagine her sitting up, swinging her feet to the floor, and striding my way so clearly that when she did not move I wondered what was wrong. It was the casualness of the posture that gave me that sensation, the arm resting on her abdomen, one leg tucked over the other.

Everyone has those dreams, the type in which the man who's just dumped you comes back, and you're laughing and sweet together again, but then you wake up and all that sweetness falls away. He's still gone; he's still moved on to a fashion design student. That was kind of what it felt like when that second ended and I went over to help Kate to her wheelchair. Later, Kate told me Evan crossed her feet so one leg didn't fall off the edge of the cushion.

To Liam I speculated that her illness had made them closer. Perhaps when you faced death, I had decided, immediate or eventual, you put aside the really silly differences. They dealt with what was truly important, or so I felt it must be. When I mentioned this one afternoon in my room, his face grew rather still, as it always did when he was pausing before disagreeing with me. That pause had irritated me, as though he had to be sure I could bear to be contradicted. At moments like this I felt the age difference between us, and with some strange satisfaction I thought that he and his wife would never make it through anything really difficult. What paltry problem had driven him to me?

Maybe I was being patronizing, or naïve, when I was so delighted for Evan and Kate merely for living normal lives. And maybe I gave Evan too much credit for simply doing what had to be done. Friends were in and out all day and in the evenings, with varying degrees of formality. Sometimes this lessened my workload and sometimes it increased it. It depended on the visitor: With some I could absent myself and make fund-raising calls or file insurance forms while they exercised her limbs. They might not even need my help getting her to the bed. But I had also learned not to assume I could head off to the front of the house any time a friend arrived with a loaf of bread. Certainly when Lisa swept in, her black hair pushed off her face by her sunglasses and silver earrings swinging, I could run errands to the library or the grocery store. She was so well-versed in helping Kate that she was even backup for the caregivers. As Kate's paralysis had progressed, Lisa had learned the physical therapy, how to move her or feed her, and she was almost as good at it as Evan. Her voice would fill the back of the house as she talked about her art supply store or her succession of boyfriends, Kate's foot braced in her hand as she moved her knee back toward Kate's chest, stretching the muscle, and pulled it forward again.

Another friend, Helen, had originally been married to a close friend of Evan's. She and the friend divorced, he moved to Oregon, and Helen, who was rail-thin and tentative, with an indistinct pink mouth and dark eyes that seemed forever on the verge of wincing, remained. When she arrived the first time while I was there I edged toward the door with a questioning glance at Kate, who waited till Helen had her head in the fridge to put away the fruit salad she had brought, and then shook her head almost imperceptibly.

Helen needed slightly more help understanding Kate than I thought an old friend should. They stayed out in the kitchen rather than using the time for therapy, talking lightly about books and movies. I hovered nearby and repeated Kate's words while Helen made tea. She always poured a cup for me. I was frequently the recipient of the extra muffin or cups from a full pot of tea. I believed visitors found it intrusive to walk into their friend's house and make themselves a snack, so they made enough for two and placed the extras in front of me instead of her. I accepted them all, understanding that, generous as Kate's friends were to me, I was only a stand-in for the person who was sitting right there.

"I'VE BEEN THINKING ABOUT your job," my mother said one Sunday morning in July, "and I would like you to take first-aid lessons. And this woman ought to pay for them."

"I'm planning on it," I told her. I had the phone cradled between my jaw and collarbone while I peeled a carrot. Ribbons of carrot skin surrounded the wastebasket and I made a mental note to clean them up before Jill woke up. I'd repudiated the pre-peeled baby carrots, but these had their drawbacks. "I need to know how to do CPR and things like that. Though I'm pretty sure I could perform CPR just from television."

"I'm not going to dignify that with a response," my mother said. "Anyway, I'm glad you'll be schooled in it. Who knows what these people had planned?"

"Who are 'these people'?" I asked, the carrot peeler inactive for the moment, a bit of vegetable flesh dangling off its blade. "And what would they *plan*? What, do you think they were hiring a dupe to commit insurance fraud?"

"Don't be so sensitive, Bec. They don't want agency people, so I want to be sure they have you thoroughly trained."

My mother made me sound like a terrier, which was typical of her. She had had a series of beautifully behaved dogs over the years.

"Well, don't worry," I said, denuding the carrot completely and tossing the peeler in the sink. I chomped a bite off the tip. "I am trained within an inch of my life. Love to Dad. See you."

Actually I was learning quite a lot, though not in the way my mother would imagine. I had to learn the basics of moving Kate and helping her in the shower, of course, but the majority of my energy was spent learning her life.

In some ways I settled in more quickly with Kate than I had at other jobs. But occasionally I felt certain I would never quite fit in. I was too gangly and uneducated, forever jarring figs from their bowls when I ran into the edge of the table with my hip, correcting the eyeliner I smudged beneath her eye.

She seemed not to notice these things. When she saw me looking over a copy of *A Passage to India*, which I had picked up idly and didn't particularly wish to read, she said, "Ooh, read that. But let me know what you think of it." If she could have, she would have pressed it into my hand.

I did take it, because I didn't know how to refuse. Also because she'd implied I would enjoy this one more than *Howards End*, and I didn't want to admit I hadn't read that, either. I was afraid she would try to draw me into a discussion of literary theory, which I found incomprehensible when Liam talked about it. Instead she waited till I'd finished the novel and said, "What did you think of Miss Quested? I always want to hit her."

These conversations, in which I had far more to say than I'd have guessed but still had to ask a thousand questions just for background, had the effect of reminding me how much I still had to learn as well as how much I had figured out without trying.

I realized even then that her approach to me was really very simple, even calculated. If I were writing a manual on how to win people over I would have made sure to recommend that attention and flattering presumption. It was that effective, all the more so because I had realized it might even be genuine. She adored her friends, but I had begun to see that Kate didn't have a great deal of patience with people she couldn't relate to. When my shifts overlapped with Hillary's, Kate was as friendly with her as she was with me, but Hillary's seriousness seemed to irk her, and sometimes when she left Kate breathed a deep sigh. Hillary never arrived returning books, or commenting on a borrowed video. It left me flattered and proud, as though Kate had shown me a secret door at the back of a closet, the safe behind the painting.

ONE SATURDAY TOWARD THE end of July, I worked until two. I had been with Kate just about two months at this point, and I knew what to expect of a Saturday: the market, cooking, maybe a nap, dinner, and then I went home. It was just starting to hit the brutally hot period of the summer, even first thing in the morning, but I didn't mind so much when I thought about the heat in terms of produce. (It was brought to my attention by Jill that this was unbearably geeky, but I stood by it.) The sun was relentless, but the tomatoes were ripening, the corn was bending its stalks. I bought so much at the markets that I could barely finish cooking it all. I tore basil and scattered it over everything, marinated eggplant and ate it as a snack, popped cherry tomatoes in my mouth like grapes. This must be the best part of the year for the lazy cook, requiring almost nothing to make a meal beyond salt and olive oil, a torn crust of bread to scoop goat cheese.

We had stocked up that day on the first cherries and raspberries of midsummer, and then I followed Kate through the wine store and held bottles up for her to choose. I was hoping she and Evan would be generous with the wine again. I kept meaning to buy the same kind they'd given me at the party, but I hated going into liquor stores by myself. I thought my ignorance was obvious, so instead I always ended up with beer.

Back at the house I put food away and readied a few things for dinner, but we weren't talking. Kate was in a quiet mood, not even cheered up by the farmers' market. We had little to say to each other. She was like this sometimes, maybe three or four times since I had known her. She was never rude or short-tempered—I would call it contemplative except that her expression lacked serenity. I could never tell the reason behind the mood, though the first time it had happened I assumed I had done something. Later I realized that if I had, she'd let me know. If it was something between her and Evan, I didn't want to ask. When they had fought, or at least the one or two times when I believed they had, I could sense it in the house when I arrived in the mornings. The remnants of tension hung about like wisps of smoke. On those days I had suggested we go out, to shop or run errands, as though we could air out the house in our absence.

That day I just cooked quietly while Kate observed. One of Evan's coworkers was coming to dinner that night, and I'd lobbied to do most of the prep work, which was not as difficult as it sounded: fava and mint spread; fresh tagliatelle with basil, mozzarella, and sugar snap peas; sour cherry crisp. The house was warm to keep Kate comfortable, but the heat left me indolent and shiny. When Evan arrived I was doing an apathetic job of straightening the kitchen and Kate was staring out the window at her garden. Whatever it was she and Evan had disagreed about, I didn't want to get hooked into it.

I was looking forward to going home that afternoon anyway. Liam had promised he'd come over for an hour or two. I didn't recall the excuse he'd planned. It was probably something school-related, a meeting with a student, something like that. I preferred him not to detail the machinations.

Evan came in the front door calling greetings and entered the kitchen with his arms full of the library books I'd set in the living room and forgotten. He also had picked up a stray sock that had been in the hallway, and a pair of shoes that had been near the front door. Kate turned to him as he entered. He paused in the doorway and gave her a tentative smile, raising his eyebrows questioningly. She smiled back, a sweet, genuine grin, and shook her head slightly, as if to wave away whatever he was asking. Evan set his things on the table and took her face in his hands. As he kissed her, I looked away, wiping nonexistent crumbs off the countertop. Whatever the disagreement, it was apparently resolved.

I always averted my eyes when they did this. It seemed unbearably public to me, these kisses he pressed into the hollow of her throat and the hand he laid on her cheek. It was as though they didn't even care that I was there. I wrung out the sponge and glanced back at them. He was gathering up the books again, waving hello to me, and as I watched, it came to me. They weren't excessive. They could even be called reserved. But after a few months with Liam and our cool hellos and good-byes, our feigned surprise at seeing each other and careful disinterest at leaving, that kiss hello seemed theatrical. I stood before the sink, the sponge still clenched in my hand beneath the cold running water. Was this what being with him was doing to me, then? Making simple affection seem rehearsed?

The realization gnawed at me, and I ducked out soon after. Kate was lying on the bed for a nap when I left, while Evan told her stories about someone they knew whom he'd seen downtown.

At home I poured myself a soda and sat down to wait for Liam. I picked up a book I had borrowed from Kate, but I didn't open the cover. Our living room was a mess, still smelling of smoke from another party we'd had a few days before. There were bags from the sub shop piled in the trash, ashes strewn in the hollows of the crumpled paper. I was walking around sweeping things into the trash can when the doorbell rang.

I let him in and kissed him. "How long do you have?"

I liked to get that out on the table first thing. It changed the way we spent our time.

"Two hours or so," he said. He wrapped his arms around me and lifted me a few inches off the floor. "Maybe less."

"YOU LOOK ROMANTIC TODAY," he informed me, a little while later. "I think it's something about your hair. And because your cheeks are flushed."

We were in my room, sipping from a pitcher of iced tea. My T-shirt and shorts were in a heap on the floor. His clothes were folded at the foot of the bed.

"That's me being mistressy," I told him. "Romance is what we illicit lovers are good for."

He smiled in the direction of the floor, a smile as private as if he were alone. "You're good for more than that," he said. He pulled on a T-shirt and lay back to put on his shorts. "Do you think of yourself as my mistress?"

"I think of myself as your guilty pleasure. I think mistresses have to wear garter belts."

Liam perked up. "Every girl needs a garter belt," he crooned, stretching out next to me. "A nice, lacy, wispy garter belt to wear underneath your jeans."

I laughed. "I have any number of sexy dresses, for the record. Not that you'll ever see them."

We paused.

"I will," he said wanly. We looked at each other, and Liam sighed. He tried to salvage it by adding bravely, "Someday I'll come over and we'll dress up and have a candlelit dinner."

I sat up, reaching down for my shirt. Earlier that week I'd set up the table for Kate and Evan's ninth anniversary, with the silver and crystal at one seat, and the smooth linen tablecloth at the other.

"You don't have to say that," I told him as I put it on. I didn't even feel angry, I just felt sad that he'd even tried to envision it. What was he supposed to say to get away at night? Evening office hours? "You know we never will."

"ARE YOU STILL SEEING the same guy?" Kate asked. "You could bring him to dinner sometime if you like."

I froze in the middle of typing. We were at the computer, placing holds on the library Web site.

"I would love to," I said. I cast about for an excuse. How could I have been so stupid as to tell her about him? She was not a confidant, I reminded myself. "But he's . . . he's kind of out of the picture." This was not really true. We had smoothed over the awkwardness of our last date with a meeting in the park and making out behind a tree. I was still nursing a scrape on the small of my back.

"That's too bad," she said, sounding genuinely disappointed. She looked up from a catalog of tools for the disabled—reachers and shower bars and feeding tubes. "Was it recent?"

I glanced back down at the list of titles she'd dictated to me. *The Professor of Desire. Open Secrets.* "Kind of. It was just the usual."

Kate nodded and tactfully dropped the subject.

"Do you need me to cook when I'm done here?" I asked. "You've already placed fifteen holds on library books, by the way. It won't let me do any more."

"Damn," Kate said. "And actually I don't need cooking today. Thanks."

I was disappointed. I had been making only simple things—a roast chicken stuffed with lemons, tomato sauce with butter and onion, a fruit crisp. (I would have liked to make a tart but was still afraid of tackling a pastry shell.) I screwed up a dish at least once a week, burning butter I'd forgotten to temper with a drop of olive oil, or forgetting the shallot. If I redid the dish at home for Jill, however, I usually got it right. The night before, I'd redone the chicken and lemon, this time getting the skin crisp and brown. "This is so cool," Jill said, helping herself to a drumstick and pouring lemony drippings over it. "I wish I had a job that taught me how to cook." She was still temping, and seemed to take pleasure in denigrating it as creatively as possible. "Though I don't need that, now that you do. You're never moving out, by the way."

Maybe this sort of cooking could have been approximated by, say, buying a roast chicken or ordering red sauce in a restaurant, but I didn't think so. For one thing, I was becoming a good cook. I even liked to think I was a natural: The transformation was so satisfying, from white flabby chicken skin to a golden, crisp shell over the meat; cool, starchy vegetables I could coax into satiny translucence. Who wouldn't want to have a hand in this? I switched from chicken breasts to whole birds, from canned vegetables to fresh, trying to get in as early as possible on the whole process. I had come to believe that cooking gave ingredients all their context. It was the difference between a photo of a painting in a book and the real, textured thing.

I enjoyed it enough that I didn't question whom I was cooking for. Other guests, for Evan, for me. Sometimes Kate was so vague about who would eat it—suggesting she just wanted "to have things on hand"—that I realized she was letting me cook mainly because I liked it, and because she enjoyed directing me to new recipes. But I guess it was mostly for Evan in the end, who reheated dishes when he came home. I left food wrapped up in the refrigerator and in the morning it was gone, as though I'd left cookies for Santa. I stayed with Kate until eight many nights, giving her the last two nutrition shakes and some water an hour before I left, but as often as not Evan wasn't home by the time I drove away.

"The wheelchair people are going to be here soon," Kate said. She sighed. "I'll warn you now this guy is an idiot. But he's the only distributor in this area so I'm stuck with him."

When the wheelchair man arrived he strolled past me to Kate. His assistant followed, clutching a catalog. The wheelchair guy greeted Kate like an old friend, grabbing her by the shoulder and giving her a hearty jostle. "How are we?" he boomed. His assistant cringed.

"We're great," Kate said, deadpan. I repeated it.

Now he shook my hand. "Name's Ted. Now what can we do for you?"

I told him which headrest we wanted to see. He stood next to me, retucking his aqua polo shirt into his waistband, nodding thoughtfully.

"Well sure," he said. He cocked one hip. "But you know what the problem with that is?" Then he stared at me expectantly.

I glanced at Kate, who was watching with a long-suffering look on her face. "What's the problem with that?" I asked.

He made a little half-moon with his hands, holding the base of the palms together and curling his fingers outward. "I don't have to tell you, Rebecca, that different headrests are made for different chairs." He clasped his hands. "If your chair isn't working for your needs, then we should look at a new chair that will keep us more comfortable."

I looked at Kate and said, "No, we really don't need to do that."

Ted made eye contact with his assistant, who nodded and headed out the door. Kate and I watched him disappear toward the driveway.

"Trust me," said Ted.

Kate said wearily, clearly knowing she would be ignored, "That's not necessary."

"That's not necessary!" I called after the assistant, who pretended not to hear.

When the assistant returned, Ted bustled over to Kate. He hefted her up from her chair as though she were a grocery sack, then staggered and started to set her back and start over. "Heavier than I remember," he huffed. "That's good. Gotta keep that weight up."

Her eyes met mine over his shoulder.

"All right," I said. I nudged Ted out of the way and gave his arms a good shove to get his hands out from under Kate's armpits. Kate gave me a warning look.

"Wouldn't be earning my money if I didn't do this for her," I chortled to Ted. Kate's face was impassive as I lifted her into the chair she didn't want, then we hemmed and hawed and said no thank you, just the headrest.

"Well, if you have any other needs I hope you know who to call," Ted said. I watched Kate answer and repeated, "Fine. Thanks."

When they were gone, Kate and I looked at each other. "There has got to be someone else we can call," I told her. "Someone who doesn't try to haul you around without even asking. He's the enemy."

She sighed and rolled her head back and forth. I went over and rubbed her neck and shoulders. "Thanks," she said, then added, "they really are the only distributor around here. And unless I want to wait ten years for everything I need, I have to deal with him."

"We could go to someone near Milwaukee," I suggested. I rubbed my thumbs against the silky warm hair at the base of her skull. "Capitalism is made for just these situations."

"Bec," she said, "it was nice of capitalism to think of me. And you know I'd like to, but it only makes it harder on me in the end. I just can't do everything I want to do."

"If you had use of your arms for just a minute you could give him a good smack," I told her. She snorted.

"I don't," she said.

I finished rubbing her neck and smoothed her hair back down. "Well, I do," I said.

EACH WEEKEND EVAN CAME home from wherever it was he spent his Saturdays and wrote me a check. Saturday nights began with cocktail hour, as I made whatever dish we had decided on at the market, a glass of wine on the counter next to me, and music on the stereo. Evan would join us in the kitchen. Then we had a cocktail and sat around the table while the pasta water heated up or the frittata baked. Sometimes I stayed; Evan and I ate dinner after Kate had had her nutrition shake, the three of us lingering until Evan got up to clean the kitchen. I much preferred this arrangement to leaving her alone as I did the rest of the time.

One night, we were talking about the first time we got caught really screwing up. This was near the end of July. I had called my friend Brian an asshole at his parents' dinner table, over salmon loaf, and was sent home with a note. Kate had been nabbed walking out of Ben Franklin wearing a stolen plastic ring, its fake ruby turned inward toward her palm.

"My friend Pete and I were supposed to be vacuuming the church aisles," Evan said. He was sitting next to Kate, periodically reaching over to touch her hand. I was at the counter kneading bread dough, preparing to roll it out. It wasn't second nature to me yet. I had to keep reminding myself to punch, fold, quarter turn.

Evan continued, "We were already being punished for something; that's how dumb we were. Anyway, we started pretending to preach, you know, using the priest's microphone and trying to outdo each other. We were listing every possible activity that might be bettered through prayer: screwing your wife or someone else's, going to the bathroom—"

"The bathroom?" Kate interrupted, incredulous.

"Baby, we were eleven."

"Oh."

"Anyway, it was pretty fun until we heard the basement stairs sort of start to rumble. And the Ladies' Auxiliary just *blasted* in. They'd been holding Bible study in the basement and the mike was wired to the speakers downstairs."

Kate and I were both laughing too hard to speak. Evan sipped his wine and looked satisfied. "Supposedly we caused some fainting but I think it was exaggerated. I mean, we're talking the Dutch Reform church, and they, if you'll pardon the term, are some tough sons of bitches."

I laughed. "I wouldn't know," I said, the effort of kneading sounding in my voice. "Not being Dutch Reform." I took a deep breath, inhaling the yeasty, tangy scent of the dough.

"Nobody is anymore, hardly. They went for an easy ride and became strict Catholics." He chuckled to himself, rubbing Kate's hand. "What were you raised, Bec?"

"Skeptical," I said. They laughed. "Seriously. My parents are your classic Midwestern folk except that they're the only ones in town whose social life doesn't revolve around church. In high school I was the only kid who didn't have to do some kind of candy striping or join a church group. So naturally I had to try going on my own, since they'd failed me in that respect. I went to church every Sunday for like three weeks last January."

"How'd that go?" Evan asked, exchanging a glance with Kate.

"Bored out of my skull. Which wouldn't have been so bad except that I'd made this big announcement to my mom about it, and she knew damn well I'd never stay with it. I just hate it when she's so sure of this stuff."

Kate said something and we paused and listened. "You're lucky," she was saying. "My family still calls me up to say they're having healing prayer services for me and do I want to come?"

"Have you ever?" I asked. They both shook their heads.

"They think of it all in terms of deserving and not deserving," Kate said slowly, "even though they don't mean to. But that's what their logic boils down to. And I just don't think—" She paused and swallowed carefully. Evan leaned forward slightly, then sat back as she

started again. "I don't think there is a reason for this. I think this"—
and she moved her chin and glanced down to indicate her whole body,
its stem-legs and unmoving arms—"is just horrible luck. And I don't
want to pretend to accept this shit and call it happy."

"I think the term is 'God's will,' " Evan put in.

Kate didn't laugh. "I call it shit," she said.

"I know," he said. "I'm sorry."

We were all quiet for a moment, except for the sticky sound of my
hands in the dough, the soft swallow in Evan's throat as he took a sip. I
had never heard Kate be this frank, or this bitter. I had believed she
was fairly accepting, if caustic, about her situation, but now I suspected
she just kept it to herself.

And I understood why people wanted more of an explanation
than this. In a way she was being confrontational rather than placat-
ing, to say it was terrible luck, like the naysayer who insists the tunnel of white light people see near death is just a trick of brain cells
dying.

I stretched out the dough. It wasn't quite square, but I was hoping
no one would notice once it was rolled up. The plan was to spread it
flat, cover it with butter, cinnamon, and sugar, and roll it back up into
an oblong loaf. I dipped my fingertips in a dish of butter that had been
sitting out on the counter, getting soft and shiny in the sunlight, and
spread it over the bread dough. With my clean hand I sprinkled a
handful of cinnamon and sugar over the butter, regretting that I
hadn't thought to chop walnuts.

"Well," I began, wiping my hands on a towel. It was seven thirty. I
waited to see if I would stay long enough for the bread to bake. It was a
half hour past the time I should have left, but I wanted to stay in their
kitchen, finishing my wine while the light grew more yellow and the
smell of yeast and cinnamon filled the room.

"Why don't you stay?" Kate said.

Evan glanced at his watch. "If you guys want to eat without me you
can," he said. "But I have to run out for a little while." Kate looked at
him. "I'm getting that movie," he told her. "And then I have to do a
few other things."

She watched him for another long moment. I turned away and covered the dough with plastic wrap. "You don't have to do anything on a Saturday night," I heard her say.

When I turned back Evan was writing my check. "No, but it would be nice to get it done and relax," he said offhandedly.

I went and got my purse from the hall table. "Fine," I heard him say as I came back in. "I won't, okay? Let's not worry about it." He looked up at me and handed me the check, the light flashing off his glasses. "Thanks, Bec, as always. You're the alpha and omega."

IT WOULD NOT BE right to say that I didn't see what was happening between them. I tried not to. I reminded myself how little I knew, and that much of their relationship took place offstage for me. I busied myself straightening the counters when I saw a frown pass between them, paused a minute before I entered the room if I had caught a contentious tone of voice. I told myself that it was not my place to guess what might happen to their marriage, but I didn't have to guess; I saw it anyway.

six

"YOU KNOW MY OWN mom never even tried to bribe me," I told Kate. "It was really frustrating."

"I'll bet," she said dryly. "You drove here and hardly broke a sweat, so I stand by my bribe. Look for something cute."

We were in a boutique in Chicago. I'd arrived at Kate's that morning to find her restless and irritable, swearing at the loud music from the ice cream truck. After I'd put on her makeup she'd said, "Is there any reason not to take a road trip?"

In twenty minutes I had put together a bag for her and left a message for Evan at work. "Won't he want to come?" I'd asked, the phone wedged between my neck and shoulder. "What if we stay overnight?"

An odd look flashed across her face. "I'm sure he'll be fine," she had said. "He's got a lot of work to do anyway."

Now I draped a huge necklace of gold discs over my clavicle and peered at myself in the mirror. "The traffic wasn't so bad. I'm glad I had to do it. What do you think?"

"Your style is a bit subtler than that," Kate said. "Try the choker, the one with the jade."

I handed the discs back to the saleswoman, who set the necklace in the case and stroked it lovingly back into place, as if to comfort it for meeting my unrefined skin. The choker was a silver ring of wire with a carved jade oval dangling from it. I put it on and stared at myself. The sterling and jade made my eyes seem a silvery green rather than plain gray. I smoothed my hair back into a ponytail and turned to Kate.

"Is it a worthy bribe?" she asked.

"Definitely," I admitted. "It's too worthy."

"Well, we don't have all day to debate," she said lightly. "Hurry up and dig out my credit card so we can get to the museum." She glanced down at her watch. "Eventually I suppose we have to plan for real life again."

I handed over her American Express and signed Kate's name. The saleswoman observed us closely, probably debating whether I was defrauding Kate. This made me glad, as if someone else were watching out for Kate as well. Most times salespeople barely registered who was signing and whose purse it came out of. To make it easier Kate often had me carry her wallet in my bag, so it looked as if I were paying with my own card. One of those little adjustments to ease our way.

After the museum we went to an Italian restaurant Kate knew, where she insisted I order a half-bottle of wine with each course, saying they were better than the glass offerings. I couldn't finish them and didn't even try, but I didn't complain. The car was safely parked at the hotel a few blocks away. I didn't know why she was so extravagant today, but she seemed as happy as I'd ever seen her.

"Sure you want to go back tomorrow?" Kate asked me.

I had just finished getting her to bed and was sitting cross-legged on the end of mine, flossing and watching television. "Huh?" I turned to watch her as she repeated it. "Oh, I guess we can stay," I said. "I don't have a whole lot going on in Madison anyway. There's you, but you're here."

Kate shifted her head slightly, stretching her neck.

"Are you comfortable? Need to move?"

She shook her head. "Uh-uh. I feel pretty good." She smiled at me. "Thanks for coming along today. I needed something different."

"My pleasure." I yawned. "You want to call Evan? I'm sure he's home by now." I was reaching for the phone, but she shook her head.

"No."

I stopped, one hand still outstretched, then changed position. I waited for her to elaborate, but she began flipping through channels with the remote I'd set beneath one hand, her gaze on the screen. Better not to pry. I headed to the bathroom instead to wash my face.

I scrubbed my face with the hotel's warm, mineral-smelling water.

As I did I had a brief vision of the two of us just living here, in the Marriott double room, wandering Chicago as we pleased and not returning for months. If ever. We'd go hear blues singers, shop, see a few plays. I supposed Liam would be the man to call to find out the best clubs, but he seemed so far away just then. I pondered him, hours away in Madison in his yellow house, feeling as detached as if he were someone I barely knew. In the other room a series of voices scurried through the television's speakers until Kate stopped flipping and settled on a channel.

THE NEXT WEEKEND I brought Jill to work with me, at Kate's request. We let ourselves in the front door, calling hello, and found Kate at her computer, the stereo on. I glanced around for Evan. We waited while she backed up and turned the chair toward us. Her hair was down around her shoulders. She was wearing a white peasant blouse and turquoise earrings.

"So Kate, this is Jill," I said. I was carrying a pizza we'd picked up on the way over. I wanted to get it into the oven, but I thought I should give them a moment before I left them together without a translator.

Kate smiled and said hello, welcome, and for a moment as I repeated her words to Jill I felt an absurd pride in Kate, her beauty and the flash of her grin and this pretty house. I set the pizza down and straightened a few magazines on the coffee table, putting a coaster back in its holder. I realized I'd felt freer when Kate's friends were there instead of one of mine. They knew me only as the person lifting and aiding her, and for some reason that was helpful; it made me perceive myself in terms of mere action. But I was afraid that doing these things in front of Jill would feel showy. Or that she, having done something remotely similar to it but in a completely different place, would see that I was doing it all wrong.

"I've been reading all your books and eating your recipes," Jill informed her. "So I'll thank you now for culturing up Bec and making our apartment a better place."

Kate laughed and answered her. Jill watched her speak, concentrating, but gave up and turned to me for the explanation. " 'She was cultured up already,' " I repeated. "Yeah, Jill." I watched Kate speak to her again and then asked Jill, " 'Which ones did you read?' "

Jill started listing her lendings from the Kate library and I took the opportunity to duck into the kitchen and put the pizza in the oven. I had expected to find Evan in here, tearing up a salad or pouring the wine, but the kitchen was dark, the wineglasses still in the cupboard. I looked in the refrigerator and found the salad makings, untouched: a head of romaine, a flat bulb of fennel from the market, and a lemon.

Back in the family room Jill was still talking, slightly nervous, clearly worried about having Kate try to answer her before I was back. I knew I'd stayed away a little too long, but Jill was too polite to show that. I felt a little stab of satisfaction that she wasn't totally at ease. I'd worked with Kate almost as long as she had volunteered, after all.

"Yeah, you know . . ." she was saying. "I liked *Jane Eyre* too. Not *Wuthering Heights,* I read it in junior high and I think I didn't get it. I tried it again later and kinda got it that time. . . ." She had obviously been trailing on for a few minutes when she turned to look at me.

"Did you get the movie?" I asked Kate. She nodded, and I said to Jill, "We've been watching those movies from the thirties where they drink a lot of martinis and wear fur-trimmed evening gowns." I handed Jill a glass of wine and said to Kate, "Where's Evan tonight? I thought he'd be here."

"No," she said smoothly, "he had a poker game. How long do you think the pizza will take?"

After dinner we sat around the kitchen table. Jill had had a third glass of wine with dinner and was flushed and charming. She was telling stories about me.

"Once Bec ruined my brand-new Little Bo Peep doll. She waited till I went downstairs for Pecan Sandies and *took the hair net off.* She actually had to tear it out of this poor doll's skull. It was stapled on."

Kate was chuckling, her cheeks pink. Jill had been in rare form all through dinner. I toyed with a crust of pizza, then tossed it onto Jill's plate. She looked at me in surprise. "You always hork the crust," I said. She ignored me, gave the crust a dismissive glance, and opened her mouth to continue.

Jill had a knack for recalling the stories that really needled me, even after all these years. Next she'd tell Kate about the time I accidentally laughed at a girl who fell in gymnastics, before I realized she'd broken her wrist.

"Do you need anything, Kate?" I said. They both looked at me, startled. "Readjust your chair, or go to the bathroom?"

Kate's eyes clouded for a moment. Jill looked into her wineglass as she took a sip. Then Kate simply nodded and we left Jill at the table while I took her down the hall. The whole way back to the bathroom I wanted to kick myself. I could tell she was embarrassed to have me bring it up so baldly, and at the table too, and I was preparing myself for a reprimand. But she said nothing. It made me feel worse.

When the door was shut and I was lifting her to her feet, she said, "Do you suppose you could take care of getting me to bed tonight? Jill can have another glass of wine and watch TV while we finish up."

I turned to face her. She was sitting on the toilet with her hands on her thighs, where I had put them.

"Of course," I said. I had never known Evan not to be home in time to put her to bed. She seemed to have an idea what I was thinking because she closed her eyes briefly and then said, "Thank you. We can talk tomorrow if that's okay."

"Of course," I said again.

When I left her an hour later she was in bed, the light off but the television on. I set the remote on her abdomen, beneath her hand, and made sure each finger was on the right button. Beneath the other hand I put the lifeline. I was worried I'd forgotten something. Normally I felt secure in the knowledge that Evan would take care of anything I had overlooked, but now I kept checking the oven, the lock on the door to the garage.

"Anything else?" I asked, peeking in on her in bed for the third time. Jill was waiting for me by the front door, and had been for the past fifteen minutes. "Whatever you need."

Kate gave me a tolerant smile and shook her head. "Really, no. This is great."

"Okay, well, I'll see you tomorrow. We can talk then."

Back out in the living room Jill was looking out the window. She heard me come in and said, "This neighborhood is eerily quiet. Are you sure other people live here?"

"THANKS FOR BRINGING JILL over," Kate said the next afternoon. We were at her kitchen table. "It was fun."

"Yeah, we had a good time." All that morning I'd been waiting for her to tell me where Evan was. The jealousy I'd felt the night before seemed very far away. I thought she would continue, but she seemed uncomfortable, glancing around the room and out the windows. "So," I said finally. "Is anything up?"

Finally she looked at me. "I wanted to ask you about your schedule. I know school is starting and you already work so much. But is there any chance you could extend your hours a bit? Come by in the mornings and get me up, or help me to bed?"

"Sure," I said. "Just for a while? Is Evan going out of town?"

Kate shook her head. "No," she said, "he's moving out."

There was a long pause. I realized my mouth was open. Of all the things I had suspected might happen—more arguments, maybe, counseling—I had never thought he would leave.

"You're kidding," I said. I busied myself with my purse, pretending to look for something. Kate just observed me. How did she do it, not being able to fidget when she was nervous?

"No," she answered simply.

I didn't say anything for a few seconds. I was trying not to put my foot in my mouth. If this had been Jill telling me about a boyfriend, I would have indulged myself in some inventive name-calling. What could he possibly be thinking? This wasn't the usual situation where you could move out and pop back in and everything would be fine. He could have gone to counseling. He could have made up a bed in the guest room. He could have just kept doing what he was doing and left well enough alone. It had never occurred to me that he would leave her alone, sitting inside that house, with no one to help her.

"I'm sorry to put you in this position," Kate was saying. "I'll hire another caregiver right away, and I know I should have hired one before this. You probably had an idea there was trouble." I watched her lips carefully, repeating as she spoke. It seemed especially important I understand clearly. She paused and took a breath. "But I had to ask him to leave."

"I DON'T WANT TO PRY," I said the next morning. Kate's eyes were closed. I brushed on shadow, watching the soft coins of her corneas shifting beneath her eyelids. Cosmetics were spread out over the bathroom counter. "But do you think this is temporary?"

Kate opened her eyes. "No," she said, "it's probably permanent."

I stopped sharpening the eyeliner and watched Kate's lips carefully. "'Permanent'?"

Kate nodded. She shut her eyes again so I could smudge the gray eyeliner near her lashes. I drew her eyelid taut, bracing my fingers against her temple, and dotted the liner on, smudging it with a Q-Tip. She opened her eyes and peered into a mirror I held up. "More blending," she said. I flicked a stiff brush over her eyelids.

"He thinks," Kate said, "he should have another outlet."

"You mean a woman?"

"And my family acts like I should be grateful . . ."

I nodded to show I was following, but I could feel my cheeks stinging. In the mirror I saw the flush creep up my neck, and I saw Kate's eyes alight on me and then shift tactfully away. I swirled a wide sable brush in a jar of powder and then swept it over her face. It left a gleam on the smooth apples of her cheeks, the high slope of her cheekbones.

". . . Grateful he wants to live with me, and just accept it."

"You talk about this with your family?" I held up three lip liners. Kate nodded at the Tawny Rose.

"Not willingly. But I got fed up and let it slip." She let her mouth relax. I cupped her jaw in one hand and with the other feathered the pencil over the rounded wings of her upper lip. I switched to broader strokes over the pillow of the lower one. Kate rubbed her lips together.

"They think I'm being unreasonable," she continued.

"I guess you know what you need," I said. I was trying to avoid offending her, but it all seemed so fast to me. Shouldn't it take longer than this to end a marriage? They had seemed so happy when I met them, and still did at times. It frightened me, though, the fact that whatever Evan had done, an affair or two, or whatever, had had such consequences. I realized that I had assumed all along, without ever stating it to myself, that he probably did something of this kind and no one felt the need to deal with it directly.

I dredged the stiff short bristles of an eyebrow brush in a light brown shadow and then blew away the extra powder in one puff. I brushed it against the grain of Kate's fine eyebrows. Their arch emphasized the almond shape of her eyes and the high dome of her lids.

"Thanks."

"And you can't work it out?" I asked. Was this affair really deserving of the name—encounters, perhaps—or was it more the satisfaction of a petty necessity? But not the kind of thing you ended a marriage for. Not in this case.

And yet how had Kate found out? Maybe it wasn't the offense itself so much as the manner. At least Liam never let his wife know. At least he was considerate enough to deal with it on his own time. Kate, of course, would clearly disagree. Yet the more I thought about an affair for Evan as something like clinical relief, like the occasional visit to a chiropractor or the Shiatsu guy, the more I felt a prickle of shame and belittlement sweep over me as well. Perhaps Liam was only moved to call me after grading a stack of especially clunky term papers, or a class that hadn't had a word to say about Andrew Marvell.

"I did try," Kate said. "I even thought I could handle it, but he didn't end up just having a little . . . encounter on the side. It ended up a whole affair. I can't just sit here while he *dates*. I need to have some say in something. Why does everyone think I don't deserve to mind?"

I thought about Evan meeting a parade of women for brunch, bringing them back to the house on Saturdays while Kate and I went to the market. I thought about his ingratiating smile, which always won me over, his extra bottles of wine and hundred-dollar bonuses for staying an extra hour or two when he was late. I not only never complained about staying late, I thought guiltily, I'd often hoped for it. I liked the wine, and I liked the extra cash.

"I understand," I said.

"I don't know how I thought it would work," she said meditatively, looking off toward the wall. "He couldn't just proposition some woman and get laid. He wouldn't go to a prostitute. So, of course, he would have to establish a relationship first."

I was too surprised to say anything. I closed the powder box and began to clean the makeup brushes.

"For a while I told him he should have an option, so to speak. I was so fucked up and sad it seemed like it might work better than anything else we'd tried. But I couldn't handle it," she said, more briskly. "I had this compulsion to ask for details."

She was quiet for a moment. Then she added, "If someone else told me this, you know, if I were just a bystander, I might sympathize with him. I don't think I'm moralistic. Everyone's marriage is different, blah blah. But from here it feels like shit, this on top of everything else. And he *knows* it makes me feel like shit, and he refuses to acknowledge that." Kate took a breath and looked away. "I just think, I won't be here forever, maybe not even that long. He can't just *wait*?"

I was running hot water over the eyeliner brush and scrubbing at the bristles. I stopped moving. Kate and I looked at each other in the mirror. She searched my face, calculating my response to this, and then said: "I'm sorry. You don't want to know this."

"No, I do," I said. That sounded creepy. "You should be able to tell me whatever you want."

"That's nice of you," she said.

"My love life isn't exactly a clear road either," I said. "So don't think I'll be shocked."

She looked faintly amused. "You're too nice to have a fucked-up love life," she said.

"No I'm not. I've been with a couple people I should have left alone. People who were involved already," I said. I imagined Liam on my doorstep, holding a suitcase, a car screeching out of my driveway with a dark blur of hair in the driver's side window.

Kate nodded. Her eyebrows had lost their high arch; they were knit together in a straight line.

I went on, not really sure why. "Or one, anyway. But it's different from this."

She looked down at the bottles and jars on the counter. I reached over and closed the lid on some eye shadow, recapped a lipstick.

"Let's drop it, okay?" she said. "Maybe we should let this lie for now."

"Okay," I heard myself say. She gave me a brief, stiff smile and turned to leave the bathroom.

I'd blown it. So much for confidences.

I finished cleaning the brushes, closed the door, and lowered the toilet lid so I could sit down. For a moment I felt on the verge of tears, but I took a few deep breaths and got ahold of myself. What, I wondered, would Evan have told her? I pictured them sitting opposite each other at the kitchen table, Evan rumpled and still in yesterday's suit, coffee steaming between them, an untouched cup in front of Kate, set there out of ten years' habit. *We met at work,* I imagined him saying. *I liked her eyes, her intelligence. She had the client in the palm of her hand. We had a drink. We had lunch. She asked about you. She's taller than you, heavier. It was sweet; it wasn't wild. She has a tiny, faded scar below one eye from a car wreck, long toes with the nails painted red. She was very quiet all through and afterward she grinned at the ceiling and got up to shower. It's not an issue of better. She wasn't better. She was someone I didn't know. She was someone who—if we're being brutally honest—could run a hand over the back of my neck, who could lift her hips beneath me and push back against me. She wasn't better; she wasn't worse. But she was nothing like you.*

KATE AND I HAD one more conversation about Liam. I had been the one to bring it up. I felt so wretched for having told her about him that I couldn't imagine why I had thought the confession would make her feel better. So the day after that I worked up my courage and said, "I'm sorry about . . . what I told you yesterday."

I sort of hoped she would need reminding, that she'd already forgotten. But she nodded and said, "It's none of my business, Bec. I can't tell you what to do. I'm sure the circumstances are different." There seemed nothing else to say to that, so I just nodded back. She gave me a little peace-offering smile, which shamed me so much I blurted out, "I think it's ending anyway." Maybe she'd forgotten that I'd already said that, weeks ago.

"Well," she said, "everyone has their breaking point."

Maybe if I had been there when Evan came to get his things, I would have felt the finality of it. But he had been around less and less anyway, so to me the house without him seemed expectant, as though he just stepped out for a haircut. His side of the closet wasn't empty, and I glanced through the clothes, guiltily, one day while Kate was in the bathroom. She'd had a bout of constipation and was hoping it was almost over. At moments like this, when I had some privacy in their house, it was so hard not to rifle through their bedroom and look for clues to what had happened. He had left his heavy winter clothes in the closet, a few densely knit sweaters and an overcoat. Maybe he didn't plan to be gone all winter. I closed the closet door silently.

I wanted to go through their bedside drawers and see if there were videos or erotic books, or if they were just empty pine boards. I wanted to look for a letter that explained the details. I wanted to know how long it had all been going on. Had he asked her permission before the first time? Or had she somehow found out, or he confessed, and then they reached a short-lived agreement? How did she know he was having an affair and not just brief encounters? He must have let it slip somehow, I decided.

I was trying to be supportive, but I couldn't suppress the feeling that what he was doing wasn't as bad as she thought. It was and it wasn't—it sounded terrible, but what if he had just never said a word about it? Evan's life, I rationalized, had taken a big turn with her illness too, and for the most part I never saw him complain. And I liked him. Or at least I remembered liking him—I hadn't seen him in weeks. I knew in his position I might have done the same, pretty much already had, and I wanted to defend it somehow. But then I remembered Kate saying simply, *Can't he wait?* and it didn't seem so much to ask.

I turned away from the nightstand and looked around at the photos that were still on the shelves: Kate, Evan, Lisa, and a dark-haired man with a beard, somewhere in Italy holding flutes of straw-colored wine; Kate with her arm thrown around an old friend from college, whose head was tilted, and mouth in midsentence. The photo of their wedding, however, which had showed her in a long, slim, blue column of a dress because she disliked white, and Evan in a charcoal suit, was gone. I peered behind the other frames for one turned facedown but found nothing. Maybe Evan had taken it with him. He probably had set it near the television in his new hotel room, something to comfort him a little, perhaps. I pictured him in a hotel bar, perched on a vinyl stool cushion, sipping at a half-inch of whisky.

Kate called to me from the bathroom and I went to get her, glancing around to be sure I'd moved it all back. The bed was slightly rumpled from the bad job I'd done of making it when I got Kate up that morning, and I thought of them, Kate and Evan, sitting up beneath the covers on the last night he'd been there, watching each other.

LIAM ARRIVED A FEW minutes early on a Thursday two weeks before school was to begin. I greeted him at the door, still wearing the shorts and T-shirt I'd slept in. He kissed me as he came in, looked over my outfit, and then glanced around the apartment. "Is Jill here?" he asked.

"You know she always leaves," I reminded him. He made a sorrowful face, which for some reason grated on me. Jill's discomfort wasn't new; it was time to stop reacting to it as though he was pained each time he confronted it. By now I found it difficult to imagine that Jill had originally introduced us. Once, she'd been running late, and was still putting on her makeup when he'd arrived. She went into her room when the doorbell rang and shut the door. A few minutes later, from my bed, where we lay without touching or speaking as we waited for the house to empty, we heard the front door open and close, a car start on the street.

We closed my bedroom door after us, a habit just in case Jill arrived early.

Later, I pulled my T-shirt back on and drew the sheet up to my waist. Liam settled himself against the pillow, crossing his ankles, as if all he'd ever come here for was conversation. He looked so relaxed and at home that I found myself blurting, "Kate kicked Evan out," just to jolt him.

It worked. Liam's eyebrows rose sharply, and he sat up straighter, crossing his legs and settling himself into a posture that looked a lot more attentive. I shouldn't have used Kate for effect that way, but it was so satisfying to catch him off guard. When was the last time I'd managed to do that? By necessity we had worked out this routine, and now I felt its disadvantages. I was always here, waiting for him. On our next day, I decided then, I'd stand him up, or at least be late. Just something to needle him, so he wouldn't look so comfy in my house.

"How can she?" he said. "Doesn't she need him? Or someone?"

I'd been worrying about that myself, because guess who would be filling in for the errant husband? Instead of admitting that part of it I stared into my mug of tea and said, "I'll take on some more hours for now. She'll hire another caregiver too."

He nodded slowly, and I felt his gaze on me.

"Did she tell you what happened?"

"A bunch of stuff," I muttered, suddenly unwilling to give him details, realizing I should have kept it to myself. This had nothing to do with him. "Sex. Other things."

"Ah. I guess that's not too surprising," he mused. He reached over and took my mug from me and sipped from it, then handed it back. I set it on the rug.

"I guess not," I told him. There had to be things I didn't know, and though I sympathized with Evan, my first loyalty was invariably to Kate. For a while, back when I first started at the job, I'd really liked him more, but somewhere along the line he seemed to have displaced himself, slipping from the room while I was busy with Kate, and it took me some time to recognize the shift. Kate was getting the short end of a lot of sticks: She was the one with the disease; she was the one who couldn't physically get up and just go fuck someone else, who, even her family seemed to believe, should take what she could get. It seemed to add insult to injury.

"Was he . . . indiscreet?" Liam asked. His voice was casual. "Did you know?"

I shook my head. "Not really. And she knew, so I don't know how much discretion was involved. But I never ran into him on State Street with a redhead in a garter belt, if that's what you mean. Maybe he just sneaked over to some girl's house every Thursday."

There was a long silence.

"Do you want me to stop coming over?" he asked.

Though I'd goaded him into asking, actually hearing the suggestion—in a voice that was horribly calm—frightened me.

"Of course not," I backtracked. "I'm just worried." I stretched out next to him, hooking a leg over his.

"I don't know what you want me to say," he said finally. "I hope it works out. I do think you have to cut him some slack."

"I am," I said. He craned his neck to look at me where my head was tucked beneath his chin, and I shook my head and went on. "Why do you just assume you know my reaction to it? Anyway, what does it matter what I think? If he wants to sleep with someone, that's none of my business. Maybe he's crazy about her."

I waited for him to respond. My head was resting on his chest, rising and falling as he breathed. He smelled of lime-scented deodorant and the slightly ferrous scent of warm skin. Go ahead, I thought, afraid to look at him, give me all the good reasons. But he didn't enumerate my sexy virtues, my mistress's tactics that drew him disastrously back to me every time.

"Or," I said, "maybe he thinks he gets a free pass on that particular vow."

Liam looked me over, forced a laugh, and said, "You sound like Rush Limbaugh."

"Well, you sound like some boys-will-be-boys . . . *excuser*."

" 'Excuser'?"

"Apologist." Goddamn it. You could never just forget a word with an English professor. "You know what I mean."

If I were watching from above, I realized, I'd have seen my leg hooked hopefully around his knees as though I might go in for a tackle—I wore unsexy clothes, but I'd shaved, moisturized, and put on matching underwear—and a hand clutching him around the ribs. Liam stirred, sitting up, and looked around for his clothes. They were on the floor by the bedroom door.

"Don't go away angry," I said.

He reached for his water glass and drank, giving me a look over the glass. "Oh good," he said, "the passive-aggressive part of the encounter."

"I'm not passive-aggressive. I'm trying to be honest."

"Fine. You're honest," Liam said. He glanced at his watch. "And I'm out of time."

"Oh yes," I said. "The glancing-at-the-watch portion of the afternoon."

He had put on his jeans and now he stopped, the zipper still undone and the flaps hanging down over his hip bones. His boxer shorts were bunched up above the waistband.

He said, "Why are we doing this now? How come we never have a good time anymore without you poisoning the water?"

"I don't," I said, startled. I'd forgotten that he noticed if I was being snippy. I was too busy thinking about how I felt.

He put his shirt on and looked me in the eye as he buttoned it.

"Yes, you do," he said. "In the past couple weeks I notice you chipping away every time I come over."

"Please," I said. "I let a little reality creep in and you're all aflutter."

"Right. Last week I was fifteen minutes late and you practically started calling me names."

I sighed and stared at the ceiling. "Everything was fine till you started telling me your vacation plans."

"I thought you'd want to know I'd be out of town. Would you prefer I just disappear for two weeks?"

I let that float out there and didn't answer. I just wanted to punish him a little right then. I would have preferred to be dressed at that moment, but I stayed where I was, my legs crossed at the ankles. "You know, there's something very disconcerting about a guy who can compartmentalize like you can."

"Compartmentalize," he repeated flatly.

"Yup." I set down my glass and climbed up on my knees. He was sitting on the edge of the bed tying his shoes, and he stopped and stared at the laces. For a second, out of the habit of being near him, I wanted to touch his hair, which had grown down over his collar in the months that I had known him. It had gotten less curly as it grew, rumpled into waves.

"It's not even all that tough on you to have this little double life, is it?" I asked.

"Believe me," he said, "it's getting tougher."

———

"I'LL TELL YOU THIS," Jill informed me, "I think I'm going to really plow through school this year. I mean it. I'm sick of all this part-time crap. I'm sick of Cs. I'm just going to do it."

She nodded to herself and sipped her coffee, handing it back to me to hold as she drove. Jill had been hit with enthusiasm a few days before, actually going out and buying new notebooks, which she labeled with her course titles, as though we were in grade school. I accompanied her to the bookstore to get our textbooks but couldn't begin to match her enthusiasm as I looked for *Creating Demand: Marketing in the Twenty-first Century*.

"I think we should make a pact," she went on. She turned into the campus parking ramp and got her ticket, shoving it into the visor. "Because it's very easy for us to influence each other. All one of us has to do is open a beer and the whole studying atmosphere is blown."

"By 'one of us,' you clearly mean 'me.'"

"Frequently, yes. But I'm guilty too." We swung around a corner to the lower level of the ramp, which had plenty of open spaces. Jill chuckled evilly. "Don't ever tell anyone about the lower level," she reminded me. "People never think to try it first.

"Anyway," she said. We got out of the car and took our bags from the backseat. "You have a good thing with Kate; she'll work with you on your classes and all. Have you figured out your new schedule yet?"

"Yeah. It'll be like five days a week," I said. Jill stopped and looked at me. I looked away and took a drink of her coffee.

"How will you keep up?" She took her coffee back from me. "I thought she was hiring a new caregiver."

"She did, but she's still being trained. And I trimmed my course load a little. Just stuff I didn't really want anyway." I started walking again, hoping to get her moving. As we went up the stairs and out toward library mall Jill was quiet and so was I, hoping to avoid a lecture. No one had asked me to drop the courses. I just thought it was the simplest way to handle it until the caregiver situation was settled.

"Well," Jill said doubtfully, "if you think so."

I wasn't sure I did think so, but I'd gone ahead and done it. At the time it felt like I had to. Hillary's schedule was already crazy, and I couldn't ask Kate to rely on the new girl full-time. I was stuck with it now, for the semester at least, and I hadn't regretted it till I saw Jill happily ticking off her course requirements and dropping in to the student employment office.

At least I had been prepared for her to be taken aback. My mother had been none too pleased either, but Kate paid me enough that my parents lacked a bargaining chip. They paid for my tuition, and all I had done was reduce their bill. "This woman is asking an awful lot of you," my mother had sniffed. "This is why people *unionized*, Becky."

"She's not asking me anything," I told her. "If you met her you'd see why I like working for her. Why don't you come to town sometime? We could have dinner."

"It's just a bit much for a part-time job that's not a career," she went on, ignoring the invitation.

"Well, I don't even know what I'm doing in half my classes. And I don't give a damn about marketing in the twenty-first century."

"Is that all this is about? So change your major!" she cried, as though I had remarked, *You know, with this plastic over my face it's really hard to breathe.*

Jill and I parted at the bottom of Bascom Hill, and I headed to my first class, heaving a sigh as I walked past the English building. The students looked even younger than usual this year. You could spot a freshman at twenty yards. I always pitied them at the beginning of the fall semester, when they emerged from the dorms sheathed in new sunglasses and pristine scarlet UW jackets though it was still too warm to wear them, panting up Bascom Hill and then facing the tougher teachers like Liam through a layer of sweat. He liked to be a hard-ass at the beginning of the semester, just to set the tone. Once he'd told me he modeled the act after a Shakespeare professor from ten years ago, from whom he'd been grateful just for a B minus. Liam was probably in a classroom right now, amusing himself by writing phrases like *"fin de siècle weltschmerz"* on the board because it intrigued the bright students and put a good scare into the lazy ones. Then he'd warn his students that if they sold back their *Norton Anthology of English Poetry* at the end of the semester, they'd be simpletons, one and all.

seven

I WAS NOT A fan of the new caregiver. She was a friend of Hillary's, which was the tiniest of black marks in my book. I had wanted to like Hillary at first, but she was almost perfectly expressionless. Until I realized in what short supply good caregivers were, I had wondered what happened to Kate's policy of hiring people she liked. When I worked with Hillary the first few times I had kept up a running patter of jokes and chitchat, much of which she simply ignored. Occasionally she gave me a mirthless smile.

The friend Kate had hired, Simone, was not a nursing student but a part-time waitress who spent her free time sculpting. She was tiny and chirpy, with a fey habit of tilting her head when she gazed at Kate. We, Kate and I, were baffled at the prospect of a friendship between Hillary and Simone, and speculated that Simone's general sprightliness perked up Hillary a bit. "Like fairy dust," said Kate. "Like a horsefly," I remarked, and Kate laughed in spite of herself before composing herself. She didn't like to say anything about the other caregivers.

When I was called upon to train Simone she frequently took out the band that held her ponytail and then stood there, thoughtfully braiding her dark hair, while Kate and I spoke to her. She had wanted to try caregiving because it was a new experience, she said, and she was always trying to "broaden."

With Kate she vacillated between overfamiliar and standoffish. When we went shopping during her training and paused to look at a sweater, she stood behind Kate's chair and fondled the tips of her hair, but in the bathroom she often tried to handle Kate with one hand and had come close to dropping her.

When we left Kate on the toilet for a moment Simone and I stood in the kitchen and stared at each other. "You really need to be more careful," I told her finally. "Two hands. A real grip. That bathroom floor isn't cotton balls."

She watched me for a moment, then gave a tinkling laugh. "I know! I'm such a klutz. Which is weird because in my art my hands are very sensitive." She held up her fingertips to demonstrate.

She was supposed to take five shifts a week, as Hillary and I did. Every time I arrived at the end of Simone's shifts, however, Kate seemed frazzled and irritable, and Simone oblivious. She was supposed to order the nutrition shakes, and I watched the supply dwindle for two weeks before I finally gave in and called myself. Hillary seemed unaware of her friend's incompetence, and rather than bring it up I asked Simone if I could have a couple of her shifts. I said I needed the money. It was just simpler for me not to worry, and though I tried to think of duties to foist off on her, I didn't trust her with many of them. With Ted the wheelchair distributor, for instance, she'd be completely useless. She'd let him lift Kate clumsily and peremptorily without getting in his way, never jabbing even one accidental heel onto his instep.

"YOU'RE OUT OF GROCERIES," I told Kate. "I can get you some things if you need them." I poured nutrition shake into her tube and held the funnel up, waiting. I reached back to the counter and took a sip of my coffee. I had to leave for class in a minute, but I had come over early to get her up and eating. Simone, who was supposed to be there, had had some sort of yoga emergency. She'd called me at seven, sounding freakishly alert for someone who wouldn't touch caffeine.

Kate looked up at me and nodded, raising her brows briefly to let me know to go on.

"Oh, I just thought you might want something," I said. "Just something to cook and keep around."

"You don't have to cook so much," said Kate.

"It's okay, I like to," I told her.

"Bec," she said. "Evan isn't here to eat anymore. Who's eating all these beautiful meals?"

I said nothing, embarrassed. I was so in the habit, so pleasantly pre-occupied with what I'd buy and what I'd cook, that I wasn't considering how it made Kate feel to have a refrigerator full of food she couldn't eat. I nibbled away at whatever I made, told the others it was there, but it was getting awkward, I had to admit. Finally I ventured, "The other caregivers?"

She observed me for a second, then shrugged. "Well," she said, "why don't we try to eat together when the evening shifts overlap? Then you have someone to cook for, and I get to taste something be-sides shakes."

I was torn, but only for a moment, before I agreed. I didn't really want to eat with Hillary and Simone, but I could. I'd get to know them. And it was a chance to keep up the cooking, which seemed like too important a part of our time together to stop. The house being empty of food, no smells of baking or simmering—it would have been another reminder of everything that wasn't going very well. Just be-cause Evan left, suddenly we should stop enjoying ourselves?

He had rented an apartment downtown, according to Kate, and throughout that fall I found myself scanning passing cars and pedes-trians for his face. I saw him only once, a few weeks after Kate and I decided I'd cook for all of us. I'd been walking around the Wednesday farmers' market at the capitol when I should have been in class.

I was holding a quart of ground-cherries and wondering whether Kate would know what to do with them. They looked like tiny Japanese lanterns, each greenish-gold berry encased in a papery shell, crisp as an insect's wing. I peeled back the translucent casing and tasted the fruit thoughtfully: It was barely sweet, tasted faintly of apples, and its seeds popped between my teeth like the seeds of a fig. I ate another and glanced around, considering how they'd be cooked with butter, when I saw Evan at another table across the lawn, his gray suit jacket flapping in the cold wind. The mild fall temperatures had dropped down to a real chill in the past week, and he ought to have been wearing a heavy winter coat, but I had seen his charcoal wool overcoat still hanging in Kate's closet. I watched Evan buy a single pear, the wind blowing his hair into a sunny haze around his skull. He patted it down and walked away, tucking the pear in his pocket. When he was gone I shook my head apologetically at the farmer and left without buying anything. I'd strolled up to the market because I knew Liam was meeting a colleague at a restaurant near the capitol for lunch. When he mentioned the lunch, I'd known I'd skip class that day. I couldn't resist the opportunity to see him unawares, but instead I'd gotten Evan. It was just as well. Liam wasn't dumb. He'd know if he glimpsed me what I was doing there. It was too humiliating to think about.

I headed east beyond the capitol and toward Lake Monona to walk home. As I passed the restaurants I glanced in the windows, but I didn't see Liam, just my own hair blowing around my face, the red blur of my wool peacoat. Since when had I regressed to sneaking after him? It was not a good sign. It wasn't that I thought he would be having lunch with yet another woman—in fact, I felt strangely complacent about that; a Ph.D. program simply didn't allow the time for more than two—but we had been so distant lately that I was curious. What did he do these days, when he wasn't with me and wasn't with her? Did he retreat to diners and out of the way coffee shops just to be alone? I pictured him jogging furtively down the back streets, head down, beleaguered by women.

We seemed to be stopping and starting every time we met. We'd made up after our last argument, and for a few weeks in a row everything was effortless. Then, for no reason I could quite discern, one date had been weirdly passionless, awkward, and stilted. It threw me off completely. As I'd walked him to the door, exchanging cocktail party chatter about the weather and our jobs, I steeled myself to say something lighthearted but pointed about moving on to other things.

Yet in the space of a few seconds as we turned to one another, I lost the nerve to end it altogether, and instead tried to think of something to say that would only nudge us apart, just to try it out, instead of something irrevocable. The gentlest little elbow to the ribs, perhaps, a white lie or an excuse for skipping our next date. I thought I wanted a little distance, though to achieve what I wasn't certain. He stopped at the front door, cupped my face in his hands, and kissed my mouth, my cheeks, my forehead. I lifted my face to let him kiss me wherever he liked and didn't say a thing.

The following Thursday I got a break anyway. His wife suggested they go away for a long weekend, and so by the next time I saw him after a two-week interval, I felt as though I'd been isolated in a glass cube for months. I met him at the door, took in the strip of windburn across the bridge of his nose, the gold tips of his eyelashes and eyebrows. I could have sworn his eyes were darker green than they had been two weeks ago. I wrapped my arms around his rib cage, hooked my legs around his ankles, just wanting that sensation of his bulk, to feel the give when I locked my fingers at the small of his back, and squeezed, as though I were testing my own strength. He'd lifted me when he came in the front door, as easily as if I were half his height, resting my butt on the table and weaving his fingers through my hair when he pressed his mouth to my neck, my ear. Why would I give up someone who mirrored me this way; who, when I pushed up against him, pushed back just as firmly as I wanted him to? I had once thought if we avoided each other for an extra week or so our relationship would dissipate before we'd even realized it, but it had proved more elastic than I had thought. If I didn't call him on a day when I usually phoned, I'd come home to find a message from him on my machine. That extra week between dates hadn't weakened a thing.

Now I was walking the long way to my house, so I could see the lake. A few ducks, fat and sleek, picked their way determinedly through the grass by the water and into someone's lawn. Did anyone ever poach ducks from their own backyard? I slowed down and observed one of the birds. How did hunters do it, once it was dead? You must pluck it first, I guessed, then cut out the intestines, and maybe take off the head too. I'd had duck at a friend's house in high school, someone whose father hunted. It was stringy, tasted rather muddy. I'd taken a few bites and then felt the smooth metal ball of buckshot with my tongue. I'd laid it on my place mat, hidden beneath the plate's edge.

There must be a better way to cook them—with some tart fruit, or a thick glaze of cooked-down wine and smoky bacon. The duck looked at me with one shining eye and took a wide-legged step away. After a moment it occurred to me that I was pondering eating random animals on my way home from school. Maybe the whole cooking thing was getting out of hand. I kept walking, leaving the duck oblivious to its reprieve.

I still wanted to tell Liam every stupid thing. So why was I pondering any break at all? Because of Kate? I was fine before I met Kate. I was sleeping with a married man, admittedly, but it seemed a paltry issue sometimes. Just because I was a huge part of Kate's life now didn't mean I had to rearrange every single thing to match her. So she and Evan couldn't find a good middle ground. For all I knew Liam's wife knew all about us and took a magnanimous, worldly view of it. And Kate knew so little about Liam anyway. She didn't know I was still seeing him.

I walked faster, feeling defiant. I was giving Kate—the idea of Kate, her voice in my head—way too much power. She was the one who needed me. I strode the last block home, feeling chill and heartless, as light and glinting as a silver wire. I didn't have to wedge her into every single crevice of my own life.

NOT LONG AFTER I saw Evan at the farmers' market, he called. Kate and I were in the kitchen making a list of people to call for the ALS Society's phone drive. I still disliked making these calls, and when her telephone rang I was relieved to have a moment's reprieve before I had to phone strangers and explain myself through a chain of prepositions: *My name is Rebecca, and I am calling for Kate Norris on behalf of . . .* Sometimes I found myself speaking to another caregiver, and with Kate at my side and the other employer on the other end, we two caregivers would carry on a conversation by proxy.

I was looking over my list of potential donors for ones I recognized when the phone rang. I looked at Kate, who shook her head. Lately she had been screening calls. Her parents, upset about the split, had been leaving long tremulous messages on the machine, reminding Kate that she had "the future" to worry about. "Your father and I are not as strong as you might think, Kathy," one message had said. "Our house has so many stairs."

We heard the answering machine pick up and Kate's voice come on. It was always startling. No matter how many times I heard this greeting, recorded three years ago and never updated, I always stopped and listened. So that was her voice, her true voice: a lower pitch than it was now that her breath was forced into a higher register as her muscles froze up. A tendency to elide the digits of the phone number into each other. She lacked the Wisconsin accent that showed itself in the vowels, like the exaggerated and almost glottal *O* you heard in smaller towns, like mine. Kate's voice had been accentless, Midwestern, and fast, a little impatient to finish the message and move on. In a way she hated to hear the old greeting, she'd once admitted, but she couldn't bring herself to erase it.

When the greeting ended there was a beep and then Evan's voice came through the machine, saying, "Katie? Hi, it's me." Kate and I looked at each other. Then she closed her eyes for a moment and wheeled over to the phone, gesturing with her head for me to follow. I picked up the receiver and clicked off the answering machine.

When I answered he said, "Bec, how are you? It's nice to hear you."

"I'm fine, thanks," I said. There was a silence. I had no idea how to speak to him with Kate present, so I said, "Kate's right here."

Kate said hello and I repeated it, relieved to be back in the familiar pattern. She raised her eyebrows at me and I remembered to flip on the speakerphone. Evan's voice floated out from the speaker, sounding flat and ghostly. I imagined his voice emanating from an empty room.

"I, uh. How are you, Kate?"

"Great, thanks," she said. There was a pause. I waited to see if he could hear her well enough, but in the silence I knew he hadn't. Or else he couldn't understand her. I repeated it.

"Look, sweetie, I'll just get to the point. I'm calling about what I mentioned before," he said. He cleared his throat. "About home."

Kate said he could come back—at this I shot her a look of surprise, but she wasn't looking at me, staring intently instead at the speaker—if he ended it with Cynthia.

Cynthia?

Kate still didn't look at me.

"Um, you . . . you have to end it with Cynthia," I repeated into the speakerphone.

"I know I need to," he said slowly. Kate rolled her eyes and looked out the window. "But I'm not sure what it solves."

"Jesus," I muttered. Suddenly I felt fed up with it all, with the talking around it for my sake, as if I didn't know. I was the interpreter; it was time to quit pretending I would never piece it together.

Kate cleared her throat so loudly Evan said, "Pardon?" She did it again, and I realized it was to get my attention. I looked over at her.

"This is me," Kate said. She ignored Evan's voice and focused solely on me. I'd never had her look at me this way: no humor, no softening the blow. She let each word sink in and added, "You're not you right now."

We looked at each other. Her lips were set, but after a moment she raised her eyebrows, as if to check that I got it; we were done with it. I felt my head nodding of its own accord as the truth of what she said sank in. The air around me seemed warmer, closer, as if the edge of my skin were softening and blurring into it.

"Kate." Evan's hollow voice rang from the speaker. "I wish you would listen to me for a minute. I know I sound like a complete asshole saying this, so please don't point it out, but I need some help here too."

"We're not talking about forever," she said. I repeated it, word for word, intonation for intonation.

"You're so pessimistic," he said. "People live for years."

"In a bed, staring at the ceiling, on a respirator," she said.

"That isn't your life."

"No," she agreed. "Right now my life is good. You know I'm talking about the future."

"Even then, there are therapists, activities . . ."

Kate shook her head. She nodded at the receiver. I looked at her, but she didn't say anything or meet my eyes. I let my hand hover over the button, hoping she would at least say good-bye, but she nodded again and I hung up.

Kate and I sat there for a moment. I was hoping she might shake her head in exasperation or say something snide about Evan, anything to redirect attention from me.

She said, "Remember it's me talking, that's all. Okay?"

"I know. I apologize. I didn't realize you could get such volume."

I'd thought she'd smile at that, but she turned her face toward the window again. I felt like I'd greeted someone with a big hug and they wouldn't even shake my hand.

I had to watch that, I realized. Sometimes I thought we were closer than we were—actually, I'd thought I knew everything—yet here I didn't even know who Cynthia was. And why would I? I was paid help, after all. Kate probably was sick of me easing my way into her life, reading her books, looking around her bedroom. Sometimes I tried to get her to laugh or crack a joke and she just shook her head and said, *I don't think I have it in me to be charming right now.*

We sat there, Kate looking away and me trying not to show that I was humiliated and worried. Maybe she'd tell me to find a new job so she could hire someone who did the work briskly and then left her alone. It was true I didn't work that way, but that was what I thought she wanted.

"I'll go make a few calls in the other room," I said. Kate nodded thoughtfully, still gazing toward the window.

In the study I seated myself at the desk with the list of names and numbers. I would quit dreading it, I decided, and just take care of this task for her like an adult. I knew no better motivator than the picture I had in my mind right then, of Kate looking at me across the kitchen table, saying the sort of thing that takes a moment to sink in as a dismissal. I'd nod stupidly until I realized the reason she was suggesting I should, say, devote more time to school was because I was out of a job. Just picturing it gave me the same kind of stinging embarrassment I remembered from being dumped in junior high—the cold plummet in your stomach, the quiver at the corners of the mouth. Because what else was worth doing? Selling food, convincing people they needed a black car or a red lipstick? Answering phones at a place where I didn't know or care what happened inside the offices? Anyone could do those things. Anyone.

"CYNTHIA?" SAID JILL.

She peered at me over the side of her bed, her eyes still swollen and her lips colorless. No doubt I looked as pretty as she did right now. I was lying on her floor with my feet propped on the edge of her mattress. It was ten on Saturday morning, and we both were nursing slight headaches from the night before. Hillary was working this morning, and in honor of my rare free Saturday, Jill and I had stayed out till two. Pretty soon I would shamble off to the kitchen to make coffee—I always made the coffee. Jill, for some reason even she could not define, loved having coffee made for her. I usually assumed it was the least I could do.

"Cynthia," I agreed. "Throw me a pillow."

Jill tossed one at me. It landed on my face. As I was tucking it beneath my head she said, "So there's just one."

"I guess. I was picturing sort of a series of mature, world-weary one-nighters with divorcées," I admitted. "All very up-front. And I thought that was kind of okay. I thought maybe Kate was overreacting."

Jill nodded, her chin propped in her hands. "I did too. I guess because you did. This seems worse, though, doesn't it? The other way was like, imperfect solution in an imperfect world, et cetera, et cetera. But this is just a chick on the side." Our eyes met and Jill looked away. I lifted a hand and let it fall to show there was nothing to be done about it. The shoe fit.

We lay there in silence. After a minute I hauled myself up.

"I'll go make coffee," I said. "Do we have milk left?"

"I think so."

While I waited for the coffee to brew I ate an apple and stared at the red light on the machine. In the other room I heard Jill moving around. It wasn't good timing, but I had to tell her at some point that Liam was coming over today. It was his wife's book club day. I poured her a cup of coffee and took it into her room.

"Listen," I began.

Jill took the cup from me, holding up her other hand, palm-forward. "Yeah," she said. "What time?"

"Noon."

She sipped her coffee. "Fine. I'll be gone by eleven. I have to study anyway."

"I thought you were getting As so far."

"I am," she said. "I bet I make the honor roll."

"Oh. Well, good," I said. Sometimes I forgot I still took classes, between Kate and Liam and Evan. School seemed a bit distant. Jill had sworn to buckle down before, but she was actually following through this time. "Thanks. Really. I'm sorry if it breaks up your Saturday."

Jill met my eyes. "Well, what else am I going to do, Bec?" she said. "You're a big girl. I can't boss you around."

"I know," I said. It came out sounding forlorn, as if I wanted nothing more.

LIAM WAS EARLY. HE came in, blanketed in cold air, his mouth chilly and dry when he kissed me. I hugged him until he warmed up.

"You want some tea or something?" I murmured into the shoulder of his jacket. It smelled like wood smoke.

He shook his head. "Let's go get under the covers and warm up there."

My room, as always, was cozy, the light filling it through the curtains. We undressed and climbed into bed, but once in it we wrapped each other up and lay there, our skin touching but strangely chaste. My breasts seemed small and cool, and he was soft beneath my hand. Liam kissed my hair, and I turned to face him. We lay on our sides, arms draped around each other's waists.

"It's almost November," I said. He nodded.

"Coming up on a year now," he said.

"Who'd've guessed."

Liam smiled. "I would," he said. He tucked my hair back behind my ear and let his hand rest for a moment, heavy against the pulse in my neck. I kissed his mouth, breathing in the faint scent of mint on his breath, something like spice or citrus that clung to his skin.

"How did you feel when you met me?" I asked him. "I mean, when you knew we were going to . . ." I trailed off.

"Humbled," he said.

He must have seen the surprise, the flattery, in my face. Humbled by what? By my beauty? At his helplessness in the face of it? He stroked my shoulder and my arm, and he didn't look away.

"You don't go into a marriage thinking you'll just branch out if you have a rough time," he said. "Or I didn't. I know Alli didn't. You really don't even notice other people except sort of aesthetically, like art, for a long time, and you can't even imagine what it would feel like to want someone else." He ran a fingertip along the curl of my ear. "And you feel kind of smug about it."

I felt a burning sensation opening up inside my chest. Liam was always more honest than I would have expected a man in his position to be, but this hurt, and it had the feeling of finality that comes when you've made a few decisions. A long time ago, I would have been flattered to hear this, hearing only that he'd wanted me, not that he also regretted it.

We said nothing for several minutes. I touched his chest, the curls of coppery hair, the ledge of his collarbone. "Do you think you'll ever do this again? With someone else?" I laid my palm flat against his chest, feeling for the thump of his heart.

"I hope not," he said softly. "I never thought I was this person."

Outside we heard geese overhead, approaching and then fading into the distance. We watched one another. I thought of all the days when we had lain here making jokes or talking about inconsequential things or not talking at all, as though silence were the mission we were on.

"You never told me that," I said.

"I never knew you wanted to know."

"I didn't."

When we kissed after that it felt solemn and quiet, but we continued anyway, because it would have felt worse to stop now. If you're going to end something, you should do it properly.

The sounds of the neighborhood were in our ears, the cars revving and the dogs barking and the kids hollering, all distant and somehow welcoming, as though we were just another couple in this neighborhood, who belonged here the same as everyone else.

After a while he pulled me up on top of him, and it felt like it used to, his arms wrapped around my rib cage so tightly it hurt, his eyes closed. Lately, I had been reaching for some kind of revulsion, trying to look at him with distaste enough that I would want him to leave, but then I knew it wasn't working and would never work—he looked beautiful and intent, his eyebrows knit with concentration, a line of white flesh where his lips pressed together. A smile hovered near the corner of his mouth as I moved over him.

For a moment I watched him, but then I gave up. It felt too sad, too hopeless, to try and commit his face, his expression, to memory. Better not to attempt it at all. So I eased myself off him and got next to him on my hands and knees, pulling his wrist to bring him up from the bed. He didn't say a thing. I felt the mattress shift as he moved, the roughness of his knees settling themselves between my own. I looked at the pillow and the headboard, my hands splayed against the blue sheets, and closed my eyes. He got behind me and entered me again, one hand braced on my hip and one arm wrapped around my waist, and we ended it that way.

eight

JILL HANDED ME A bottle of wine after holding it up for Kate to view. Then she leaned over the chair to kiss her cheek. Kate smiled, closing her eyes briefly. I got out the corkscrew.

Jill had said to me once, *I always want to kiss her hello or hug her or something, but I don't want to be in her face. She can't exactly get away from me if she doesn't want me to, you know?*

I'd seen Jill's point at first, because people were always trying to touch Kate in puppylike ways, petting her knee and her hands, stroking her hair. But later I'd realized few touched her who weren't paid help. I felt terrible for missing that, but since Evan had left this was the truth. Hillary, Simone, and I all touched her and tried to keep it brisk and unintrusive, but only Lisa and a few of her other friends kissed her hello, or put their hands around her shoulders in a modified hug.

She stepped back and surveyed the makings of dinner. A platter of silky white mushrooms was waiting to be sliced next to a pile of parsley and a bunch of carrots. Pearl onions and stock were simmering in one pan, and another was filled with cubes of beef and two bottles of red wine. The kitchen smelled so rich—all wine and meat and thyme and onion—it seemed we should be able to taste the air. Jill poked at the onions with a spoon. "Did you get this stuff at the market?"

"Not today," I hedged. Kate and I looked at each other. I said, "We had another errand." The market would close in winter: Even now it was mainly apples and root vegetables, bunches of shallots and tough, faintly sweet greens with cold-weather heft and chew, thick ribs running down their centers. The vegetable piles on the tables around the capitol took on the knobby, russet feel of a grandparent's house: everything serviceable and warming, the air smelling of the earth that clung to potatoes and onions and yams.

"Anything fun?" Jill asked absentmindedly.

"We'll tell you all about it later," Kate said.

"Cool." Jill knotted her hair and skewered it with three sticks so they poked out from her hair like spokes on a wheel. She breathed deeply and said, "It's so cozy here. I can see my *breath* in our apartment."

"You've got to be kidding," I said. I poured her a glass of the wine she'd brought. She rubbed her hands gleefully and breathed it in. "Are they trying to drive us out?"

"Why?" she said, swallowing a sip. "We never have those big bashes anymore. It's been like four months since the landlord found Nate sleeping on top of your car."

Kate chuckled and Jill turned to explain. "It was so late there was dew on the car and he thought it would be refreshing. He's a total idiot. Come to think of it we haven't seen him in a while. I barely even see Bec."

"I'm sorry," Kate said. "I monopolize her."

Jill shook her head so vigorously I thought she'd dislodge one of her sticks. "Oh, I don't mean that. I just meant our place is so much cleaner lately."

When Lisa arrived, swooping in wearing a huge cape of some sort, we had a fire going and some music on. While she was greeting Kate, Jill sidled up to me where we stood at the counter, her slicing mushrooms and me chopping parsley. She murmured, "Liam called."

"It's twenty degrees out there!" Lisa cried. She took her cape off and threw herself in a chair next to Kate, running her fingers through her hair. "Winter is going to be a nightmare."

"When?" I whispered.

"He called right before I left to come here," Jill was saying. She moved a few slices to the edge of the cutting board with the blade of her knife. "He kind of tried to be chummy and ask what classes I was taking. He's such a sleaze." She watched my face and added, "Sorry." I glanced over at Kate and Lisa.

"Is that a leather poncho?" Kate was asking. She nodded at the coat Lisa had laid on an empty chair. It looked like a deflated cow.

Lisa picked it up and held it against her. "You don't like it? I thought it was original."

I turned back to Jill. "He's not a sleaze," I muttered. "And what did he say, anyway?"

"It *is* original," I heard Kate say. Lisa tossed the cape back over her chair. "You will definitely be the only one wearing it."

I poked Jill again, but she was watching Kate speak, her brows slightly knit, unconsciously mouthing along as she tried to decipher it. I sighed and repeated, " 'Lisa will definitely be the only one wearing it.' " Jill smiled, but the joke lost something in the repetition. "Jill, what did he *say*?"

"Oh, he said he saw you somewhere or something and just wanted to say hello."

That would be today. I hadn't realized I was driving Kate through his neighborhood till it was too late. At least I had an excuse. If he saw me, he'd see Kate. I was just working. Stalking him was an unexpected bonus.

It had been almost a month since I had talked to him. There were days I thought he'd been a massive waste of time, others when I convinced myself he'd been a learning experience, and still others when it was clear to me that I would never feel about anyone the way I'd felt about him, and certainly I would never have sex again. I let Jill crow about how I had dumped him and how he'd had a Pygmalion complex and an early midlife crisis because she seemed so glad to do it, and because it sounded better than the reality. She was joking, slightly, but her version hurt anyway. It didn't even matter that I knew she was wrong—he'd never tried to make me over. Was I really so hopeless that she thought I needed a guy to take me in hand?

Nevertheless I let her take me out a lot during those weeks. She was delighted and relieved to finally take part in this relationship in the proper best-friend way, by celebrating its demise in the form of comforting me. She was so upbeat that I began to think I really was well rid of him. Of course I was. But I felt raw inside, perpetually on the verge of either weeping or kissing a stranger.

I thought I saw him at every food cart, every corner, and every bench on campus—a glimpse of reddish hair across a collar, a battered brown leather bag—and it left me perpetually startled, darting glances about library mall like a robin. When I realized how close I really was that afternoon, a wash of prickling excitement had moved over me.

"He called to say hello? I don't get that," I said. "I never call to say hi. I call to say, *Come over, I miss you,* or *I never officially won the argument about the Christmas card.*"

"He just doesn't want you to get over it," Jill hissed. She finished the mushrooms and set the plate with a clunk on the counter next to me. They were ragged-looking—some thick and some paper-thin, with tags of mushroom skin hanging off their edges. "He wants to remind you in case you've forgotten one single thing."

"Well, I haven't." I laughed a little and said, "He probably just misses me desperately."

His wife had been in the driveway, getting out of the car. Maybe he'd been looking out the window. He was probably having twice as much sex with her now. She was probably reminding him of what a woman his own age could do. I minded her more now than I ever had before.

"Oh, right. Sure." Jill gave a snort of laughter. She picked up a fork and began mixing a bowl of seasoned flour. She said to the flour, "Don't call him."

I reached over and took the bowl from her.

"I already mixed that," I said shortly. "How about if you just slice the bread."

She stood there, looking at me and holding the fork. Behind her Kate was saying something to Lisa and Lisa was repeating it, nodding to show she understood. Kate saw me look her way and gave me a quick smile.

It was supposed to be a fun night. I didn't want to ruin it. What was I really going to get angry at her for? I had no moral high ground. I wasn't above being petty, but I preferred to be able to hide it.

We sat down to dinner and passed the salad and wine. For a moment as I looked over the table I didn't care about Liam or Jill hating him or any of it: We had a deep bowl filled with beef burgundy studded with translucent onions and soft carrots and mushrooms, a crisp green salad glistening with vinaigrette, butter softening in its blue dish. It was beautiful, and I'd made every bit of it. Well, except for baking the bread. I'd learn that next.

There was a pause while they waited to see who would toast and Kate and I exchanged glances. She nodded at me and I held up my glass. Jill and Lisa looked expectantly at us, their faces flushed from the warmth of the house. Jill's ornamented sticks stuck up from behind her head like antennae. Her eyes shone brightly, and something about that pad of flesh that softened her square jaw and chin like a child's, and the silliness of the hair ornaments, made me forgive her.

"To moving," I translated. Kate spoke again and I repeated: " 'I've made a bid on a house.' "

A layer of silence dropped over us. She had told them she was house hunting, but I saw now that Lisa had assumed Kate was just amusing herself, fantasizing rather idly. Even I had thought so, and it may have been true, but the place we saw that morning was a small brick house that seemed like a cottage until you realized how far back the rooms extended. It had window boxes and working shutters, two bedrooms and a study and a nice, though small, kitchen. The kitchen would expand: Kate had cast an appraising look at the wall that separated it from the front room, and I knew it would be knocked out if she had anything to say about it. Kate maintained that most houses had at least two walls too many.

Jill broke the quiet with a little cheer and we drank. I swirled my glass beneath Kate's nose so she could smell it. Lisa took a sustained sip, her long throat working, and set her glass down carefully on the red tablecloth. After a moment she said, "Congratulations, Katie. You'll have a lot of fun getting it ready." She kept on that way through dinner, asking questions and mentioning curtains and paint, but I had seen a look flicker across her face.

Kate and I looked at each other. I'd been hoping her friends were supporting this all along, even though I loved her house and wasn't looking forward to moving her either. Yet as soon as I saw Lisa's expression I had the cantankerous urge to contradict her. If Kate wanted to move, she was moving. My job was just to help make it easy.

HELEN ARRIVED AT NINE, bearing a chocolate cake. I took a little of its frosting on the edge of a spoon and put it in Kate's mouth to melt on her tongue.

"Are you going to tell Helen?" I whispered. I took the smeared spoon from her mouth. Kate looked meaningfully through the kitchen door to Lisa and Helen, who were curled up on opposite ends of the couch by the fire. Jill was sitting cross-legged in a big easy chair, a coffee cup balanced on one blue-jeaned knee.

"I don't know," Kate sighed. Annoyance crossed her face and she said, "Lisa was pretty lukewarm."

"You think so?" I asked. I was hoping she hadn't noticed, or I'd misinterpreted. "I thought she seemed happy for you."

Kate wasn't buying it. "You saw the look," she reminded me.

"Maybe I misunderstood. Maybe she thought the beef was tough."

I put slices of cake on plates and brought them in. I could see Lisa's and Helen's heads together, Jill listening to them intently. Helen's eyebrows were raised so high they disappeared beneath the flat fringe of her bangs. She turned to us as we entered the room, her fingers resting on her collarbone, and said, "Kate, really?"

I was walking behind Kate, so I couldn't see her expression, but I could guess at it: the steely one—chin lifted, eyelids lowered almost imperceptibly—which she often wore while she was on the phone with her mother, saying, *No, I don't need any money. Tell Dad I'm fine.*

I moved around in front of Kate so I could translate for Helen when Kate replied, "Yeah. It's on Chambers Street."

"I just didn't think you were . . . at that point," Helen said delicately. She sipped her coffee and shook her head at the cake I offered her. I set it down on the table in front of her.

Kate stopped her chair in front of the fire. She said something, but I couldn't understand her when her face was backlit. I turned on the lamp and she spoke again. "He knows what I want," she said slowly. "And I know what he wants. And we aren't making any progress." She paused after each statement, looking back and forth at Helen and at Lisa, and let me repeat it. "There are things I can't count on him for."

Lisa took a bite of cake and chewed, staring down at her plate. "Are you sure you're not doing something really impulsive just to show Evan you aren't paralyzed?"

Kate laughed. Lisa blushed. "Emotionally paralyzed," she corrected herself, smiling thinly. "You know what I'm saying. It's such a big thing to ditch a marriage."

"Why are you saying this to *me*?" Kate asked. Her eyebrows were knit, her head tilted incredulously.

" 'Why are you saying this to me?' " I repeated. It came out sounding flat and odd, as though I were reading from a cue card. I shot her a look of apology, but she didn't notice. Lisa glared into the fire. Helen picked up her plate, took a miniscule bite of cake, and set it back down. I wished I could have crossed Kate's arms for her; she looked as if that was what she would have liked to do right then. Pointlessly, I crossed my own.

"Chambers Street is one of my favorite streets in Madison," Jill announced.

AFTER JILL AND HELEN left, I got Kate to bed and left her with Lisa while I did the dishes. When I left them Lisa was sitting in a chair next to the bed with her stockinged feet up on the mattress, Kate's face turned toward her. Around eleven Lisa came back out and got her cape from the back of the chair where she'd left it. She stood there for a second in the doorway to the kitchen, hefting the leather lightly with one hand, as though she were testing its weight, and then she said, "So how do you like this new house?"

I turned around and faced her, drying my hands on a towel. "It's very cozy," I said. "And it'll be beautiful. She's really going to make it over."

Lisa nodded. "I'm sorry I didn't act as enthusiastically as I could have," she began.

"You don't have to apologize to me."

"I know. I've been hoping she and Evan could work this out, though, and this just feels like the ax falling."

"Have you said that to Evan?" I asked.

She lifted her hands and dropped them to the tabletop. "Yeah," she admitted. "I'm not making excuses for him. But I've seen this Cynthia woman. She's just a replacement."

"Obviously."

"No, I mean she's very much like Kate."

"But that's worse!" I glanced toward the back of the house and low-ered my voice. "Kate's not exactly *gone*. He's trying to replace her and she's still here. You know, when I think that we used to sit around here and have a really good time together—and we *did*; they were *fun*—and he was saying he was going to the store or something and really going off . . . it just, it humiliates me that I believed him. I know it's dumb; it wasn't my marriage." It was a huge relief to say this. Maybe I had had too much wine, but it had always bothered me, to be so close to them, in proximity, anyway, and to have misunderstood or missed the biggest undercurrents. It was humiliating to have been so clueless, especially when I'd thought I was picking up on everything.

Lisa was watching me, expressionless. "You didn't know them years ago," she said, as if that explained it all. "For a while I was living with this professor and the four of us were together all the time. We went on vacations; we rented beach houses. I really thought all of us could have bought a house and lived together till we got old and feeble, that's how close we were."

I didn't see the point. "So what happened?"

"The guy and I broke up, Kate got sick . . ." She stood up and put her poncho on. "There's no moral or anything. I miss it, is all. I want her to be happy and if a new house does it, fine." She paused, chewing her lower lip. "I've known her for almost twenty years. I love her more than my own family. But I worry about how fast she's moving. She doesn't like waiting for people to catch up, you know? It's not like I don't understand why. Evan has a hard time with change in general, but especially with the ALS. It took him forever just to accept what was happening to her, and she didn't have the luxury of kidding herself like he did. He was way behind the acceptance curve, you know? Talk-ing about orthopedic shoes when she was trying to write a will. I don't think she's ever forgotten having to prop him up."

She rubbed her eyes and sighed, leaning back against the wall. "You really can't imagine how strange those first several months were, espe-cially. Your default mode when your best friend tells you she's trem-bling all the time is that it's nothing. I said it would be nothing so

YOU'RE NOT YOU 131

many times I felt guilty when it was *something*, like I deceived her. And it moved really fast. It wasn't like these last few months. We kept trying to do things, you know—plan to walk downtown, try to handle the stairs at Le Champignon. We just didn't get it; we didn't get that this stuff was over and done with. She had to keep telling us it was."

LIAM CALLED ONE MORE time, later that week. I was at home, flipping through a magazine. I was stretched out on my stomach on the couch, the phone on the floor next to me. I remember touching the receiver, the vibration ringing through my hand. When his voice came on the answering machine I felt a charge go right through me, a flash of heat range over my skin. Two calls in one week. Maybe he really did have something to say. Maybe I shouldn't be so quick to end everything.

"Hi, Bec," he said to the machine. "It's been a while. I thought we could catch up. Just to talk. Nothing, um . . . nothing else."

There was a long pause, while I listened to the staticky answering-machine tape running in the living room. My hand was still on the phone. I thought, He is right there.

"Coffee, maybe," he continued. "Or lunch, if you want. It seems really odd not to be talking to you these days, that's all."

I almost picked up the phone. What could coffee hurt? I started to pick up the receiver and it made a loud clicking noise over the machine. But then I put it back.

Liam sighed. "You're right," he said. "You're right, I know. Don't pick up."

nine

WE WERE GOING TO have the windows, doorways, and shower widened in the new house. Kate also made plans to tear down a kitchen wall and add ramps to the front door and off the back porch. I had to learn a whole new set of terms when talking to the architect. She gave me a book to read so I would understand her when she said words like "load-bearing." Our conversation was filled with references to treatments and fabrics and weird objects: *swags, sconces, andirons.*

After a while I would have simply closed my eyes and pointed, and if I ended up with celadon instead of sage, I probably wouldn't even know. I blamed my upbringing. My own mother's decorating had consisted of replacing the carpet each time I made the final, irreparable spill and sticking with wire-haired dogs that didn't shed. But Kate could file away every visual permutation, recalling each gradation of flame into scarlet, navy into indigo. (The names of the various hues turned out to have oddly political leanings: Many of the reds, for instance, referred obliquely or directly to Russia or China. I hoped against hope to encounter a true Commie Red.)

I had never had the urge to paint a room in my life until one day I saw a gallon of saffron and went for it, and now my bedroom walls glowed cozily. Kate gave me one of her copper pans, a little shallow one for omelets, and I kept it in my room, where it reflected the burnish of the saffron paint, and where Jill knew it was off-limits.

We drove over to the new place about once a week, watching as the workers set the ramps in place and reinforced them, installed the mechanical doors, and tore up the carpet of the front room, uncovering a honey-colored maple floor. ("I knew it," said Kate.) The two bed-rooms at the back of the house were now a sunny yellow and a robin's egg blue. The kitchen, though it wouldn't fit an island, had vast ex-panses of counter space and a skylight. I tried not to add up the bills as I wrote checks for them, but the whole project was astronomical. The numbers, in fact, no longer meant anything to me. I found myself making very blasé statements about "what quality costs." It was enough to let me forget that my own money managing had its drawbacks—last month I had bought a new leather jacket and then bounced a check for ramen noodles and frozen corn.

But I was enjoying myself, and as the days passed I didn't even notice Thanksgiving was on its way until my mother called. I hadn't planned on going home this year. Thanksgiving never changed at my house and I had offered to be with Kate that day. My mother wasn't pleased.

"If you say," she began, "as I have a creeping sense you just might, that this woman you work for needs you on a holiday, then I am assum-ing the next thing I hear will be the astronomical sum she'll pay you."

I'd evoked my mother's angry scholar tone: the twisting syntax she navigated effortlessly, the clipped pronunciation and long words. You would never guess, when she got going this way, that she had never even finished college. I admired her for it, when it wasn't directed at me.

"I offered, as a matter of fact," I informed her. "And she said she'd pay time and a half."

"I'd ask for double." My mother sighed. "What about your father and your grandmother?"

"I can see everyone at Christmas."

"What does she need you for on Thanksgiving?"

"Just to go to a friend's house for dinner."

"No one else can do this for her?"

I held the phone to my chin while I took off my jeans. Actually, Si-mone had offered to do it. *Thanksgiving means nothing to me,* she had said. *Al-though I sometimes find that sculpting on holidays leads me to some very intriguing conceptuals.* I was about to agree to let her take a long shift that day when I saw Kate close her eyes. I knew she wanted to say innocently, *What's a con-ceptual?* I didn't think she wanted to be with Simone on a holiday, not when they'd be at Lisa's house and it could be pure fun. There had been a long pause while I mulled it over. I almost never minded taking on extra shifts, and it was true that Kate hadn't asked me outright. But sometimes I thought it would be better if she did. I could read her so well that I never got to just be oblivious anymore, even when I wanted to be. Sometimes she let me intuit what she wanted me to do without asking, and when that meant, *Offer to leave me alone in the bathroom for a while,* it was fine. But when it was, *Don't stick me with Simone on Thanksgiving,* I wished I were blind to her, like someone who doesn't waste time on household chores because she doesn't notice the crack in the window or the dusty picture frames. Still. It was her first holiday without Evan and I wanted her to have fun, so I said to Simone, *No, no, I'll do it; you sculpt.*

"Look, Mom, I'll be there for Christmas," I began, but she interrupted.

"You know your grandmother is looking forward to showing you how to make her pie crust," she informed me. "Now that you've taken such an interest. She switched to frozen crusts years ago, Bec, but the woman has me buying lard so she can show you the old-fashioned way—"

"I'll come!" I blurted. "God! I'll call Simone."

I RETURNED FROM THANKSGIVING bloated with apple pie and beer and faintly ashamed for having flown the coop and even having a little fun. I'd gone out a couple nights while I was there, having run into some girls I knew from high school at the grocery store, where we were both in line with cans of cranberry sauce and bags of sliced almonds. I always wondered if the people who still lived there felt as regressed as I did, notebook paper with shopping lists in our mothers' writing stuffed in the pockets of our winter coats, waving outside our parents' cars.

I still had a few old boyfriends strewn around town, but I no longer appraised them as a possibility for an evening or a few weeks. Even my favorite high school boyfriend, Mike, now greeted me like a cousin. You'd never guess that over Christmas break our freshman year in college we'd spent every night together, right back to eating fish fry at the Gasthaus and going to movies just to have something to do, trying to show off new maneuvers to bluff each other into believing we'd slept with hordes of people in the first four months of college. (Maybe he had. I chose the tactic of referring endlessly to unnamed "guys," all of whom were actually a single boy in our dorm who, Jill still delighted in reminding me, had gone by the newly adopted name of Dylan.) It had been a depressing exercise in the end—suddenly we were calling each other when our families weren't home, driving out of town to buy condoms. I found myself bumming clove cigarettes, chattering in his ear at bars, and stealing up behind him to wrap my arms around his waist as though I was hoping to borrow his letterman's jacket. By New Year's Eve of that winter break I had regressed so far I almost teased my bangs.

This visit was better. For once I enjoyed telling people what I was doing these days. It sounded so much better than waitressing.

"So, how was it?" I asked Kate the next week. I was helping her back into the car after we had driven by Chambers Street. I tried to move quickly and get her out of the cold as fast as possible, or else it took her forever to warm up again. She was so thin that she was always cold, so I took to carrying a chocolate-colored cashmere shawl everywhere we went. She looked beautiful in that shawl; it brought out her eyes and made her cheeks pinker.

It was amazing how few people noticed how lovely she was. They glanced at us and instantly turned in the other direction, as though it would be rude to linger. Two years ago, I was certain, people had gazed appreciatively at her all the time. I tried to make up for it with incessant compliments. I told her her eyes looked especially bright with the shawl on, that her hair color, recently dyed a slightly darker, richer tawny blond, flattered her skin tone. I said she didn't need lipstick, just gloss, because her lips had such color. I said her new earrings looked lovely when her hair was up. I said, *You look so pretty today,* and I said it a lot.

"We had a great time," she said, and she seemed to mean it. "I ate a little apple filling."

"Really?" I said. "Simone was cool?"

Kate nodded. "She was great. It was nice of you to offer, though, Bec."

"Sure," I said. I went around to the other door and got in. "Is Simone getting ever so slightly better or is it just me? Much less about conceptuals, for one thing." I couldn't resist adding that.

Kate looked pained. "I've been feeling guilty about a couple things," she began. She looked at me to be sure I'd caught it. I nodded and she went on. "Simone is really improving, and I haven't always been fair to her."

I sighed. "I do the same thing," I admitted. I turned the key in the ignition, and though it was in the single digits outside the car started right up. I never stopped appreciating that, compared to my Honda.

"I drew you into it," she said firmly. "And I let you do too much for me. We get along so well that it's easy to let you handle everything, and it isn't fair. To you."

"It's not like I mind," I said. She was looking at me carefully. "I don't, really. It's just the job, that's all. I'm just being you."

"Say no to me sometimes," she replied. "You can, you know."

"I know." I turned the radio to a rock station, glancing at her to see if she liked it. She nodded.

"What are you doing for Christmas?" I asked. I didn't want her alone, Evan off across town drinking champagne with The Replacement.

"I think I'm going to my parents'," she said. "They'll come and get me." She smiled grimly. "This is like eighth grade." Then she kept talking, but I couldn't get the words.

"Sorry?" I had been glancing behind us for traffic and now I stopped and concentrated on watching her.

She said it again. I thought maybe she'd said "pretend," which baffled me. Patiently, she repeated herself for a third time.

"Am I going to my parents'?" Finally, she nodded. "Oh, yeah," I said, "I always do. They'd freak if I didn't come home for that."

We drove in silence for a few minutes, and then she said, as we stopped at a light, "Is it harder for you to understand me lately?"

I shook my head. "No, I think that was just me being thick. Why?"

She looked away. "Because it's harder for me," she said. "I'm really working to talk lately."

I stared at her. "I'm sure it's just that you're tired," I began. "The house, and—"

She shook her head and interrupted me. "No," she said. "I held steady, for a few months, but I know this feeling. My legs are harder to work too."

I didn't know what to say. The truth was I had noticed some changes, but I'd thought maybe I was mistaken.

"Is there anything you need me to do?" I asked. "What about Christmas? Or New Year's? Are you positive you won't need me then?"

"WHAT'S KATE DOING FOR Christmas?" Jill asked. We were sitting on a couch beneath a huge fake oak tree festooned with little white lights. The bar, which had opened recently, was beset with university people here to check out the new place: guys in rugby shirts, sorority girls, and a squealing group we knew was a bachelorette party because of a girl wearing a veil with her jeans and a fake penis pinned to her shoulder. It dangled, limply, over one breast.

Jill and I were here for the jukebox. The rest of our friends liked it for the tree. Every time Nathan passed by it he touched the bark like he thought it might be made of velvet.

Jill took a sip of her beer, a cloudy amber from somewhere in northern Wisconsin. She made a face.

"That's what you get for ordering pumpkin beer," I told her.

"I thought it would be Christmasy. Sam kept going on and on about how it was like drinking pumpkin pie."

"That was a point in its favor?" A Neil Diamond song came on the jukebox and a general cheer went up among our friends, who had recently decided to find him cool. I watched Samantha raise her beer in the air and do a little shimmy.

"We have to quit listening to our friends," I told Jill. The bachelorette was perched on a stool, being kissed on the cheek, one by one, by a bunch of guys in cable sweaters and hair gel. "Although I can't quite decide if I like this place or think it sucks."

"I know. Is it possible I'm too mature to enjoy it?" Jill sipped her beer resolutely. We were not of the mind that you threw away a bad beer once you'd paid for it, and it would never have occurred to us that we could ask for a new one.

"Oh," I said, recalling Jill's question. "Kate's going to her parents' house."

"Is she close to them?"

"Not really. I met her mom a couple times and she thinks Kate's about twelve. I don't think she was like that before she got sick, but she just is all over her now."

"What do you mean? It's not like Kate can do that much for herself," Jill pointed out.

"No, but there's an attitude to it. You know what I mean—like she's a toddler, not a grown woman who needs help."

"Oh."

The bachelorette was in tears. One of her friends hugged her.

"They better be careful," Jill noted, watching them. "They're gonna squish that nice penis."

"Want to hear something weird?"

Jill's eyebrows darted up. "What?"

"It's nothing crazy. It just happened when her mom was there last time and she'd had all these home movies put together on videotape. So they were watching them, while I was doing some filing, and her mom called me in to watch part of it."

Before they called me over I had been nearby but not watching, when I caught the unmistakable sounds of a wedding reception, people talking to the camera about marriage and offering honeymoon advice. I heard Kate's mother say, "I feel like an idiot. I'd already ordered the tape," so I walked a little closer in case they needed a translator. Kate had replied, "That's okay, Mom; it was nice of you." Her mother had looked my way, an apologetic smile on her face. She had had a difficult time comprehending Kate during this visit, apparently worse than usual. I pitied her, so I gave her an exact repeat instead of paraphrasing. " 'That's okay, Mom,' " I said. " 'It was nice of you.' " Her mother had looked relieved after a moment, but I saw that the exact repetition hadn't had the right effect: I'd wanted to let her hear Kate as clearly as possible, and keep my voice out of it, but instead what Kate's mother saw was a total stranger turning to her with a little grin and calling her Mom.

Anyway, I had gone to the study to file some insurance forms, but Kate's mom called me back a few minutes later. I sat next to Kate on the couch. Her mother was on her other side, Kate's empty wheelchair pushed away near the table. Kate nodded toward the television. Before the segment there was a computer generated placard saying 34TH BIRTHDAY. The screen lit up on a kitchen filled with people. It must have been an office kitchen, too white and plain to be in someone's house. The camera was focused on a door. The sounds were all disembodied conversations from the people milling around. Someone peered out into the hallway and turned back to the room, flapping her hands and shushing, and everyone got quiet.

In Kate's living room, her mother and I were quiet too. The three of us sat there on Kate's couch, Kate in the middle. Her mother stroked her hair. Kate leaned her head back against her hand.

In the video the door opened and Kate came in. It had taken me a moment to realize what was different: She was walking. She had this fast, bouncy stride, and she was turned halfway around, talking to another woman as she walked, and when people yelled, "Happy birthday," she gasped, her hands flying up toward her face and her whole body leaping in a flutter of surprise, and then she leaned against the woman next to her and laughed. When they raised their cups in a toast, you could see just the slightest tremor in her hands. And in the video you could tell she saw it too. As her cup gave a tiny lurch, a shadow of confusion flickered over her face, and she looked around to see if anyone else had noticed.

I had put the remote beneath Kate's fingertips, and now she hit the pause button and turned her face to me. On the screen the image flickered of her and her cup.

"That," she said, "is when I started to wonder." She made a face, as though she disagreed with herself, and then said, "To know."

JILL HAD FINISHED THE pumpkin beer. Mine was still pretty full.

"It's amazing to think her own mom can't understand her," she said finally.

"It might not be her fault," I said. "Kate thinks she's getting worse."

"God," said Jill. "In a way I want to say how could she?" She blushed. "I'm sorry; that was awful. I didn't mean it that way."

"I know what you mean," I told her. "You'd think it's almost as bad as it could get."

"Doesn't it make you paranoid?" she mused. "Every time you have a cramp or tremble or something?"

"It kind of does," I said. "Except that the odds of the caregiver and givee with the same disease are pretty slim. If I did get sick I'd just glom onto her and we'd boss the other caregivers around, share a forked feeding tube."

"Don't joke about that," Jill said.

"Oh come on," I said. Kate would have laughed. "What if it's a good joke?"

WE GOT KATE INTO the new house shortly after New Year's. I reeled a little at how quickly it had all been accomplished: Even as close as Christmas Eve, when I'd told my family about the move as we nibbled on herring and rye bread and boiled shrimp at my grandmother's house, I hadn't really believed we'd pull it off. But it turned out this was one of those problems that responded briskly to a shower of money. The movers did everything for us, even putting books on shelves and dishes in cupboards. The house was almost completely in place when we walked in. Kate had painted the kitchen the same butter color as her old one, but the other rooms she did in a series of bright colors: a crimson wall in one room, azure in another, a rich grassy green in the living room. As you walked through them they looked like a series of jewel boxes, with that air of surprise.

"It's like those myths where fairies do everything," Simone had said, gazing around at the paintings on the walls and the fruit bowl on the end table.

"I'm sure the moving men would appreciate that image," Kate said. But she was grinning. The house looked perfect.

A few days later, as I got her into bed, I said, "What else do you need? Do you want the remote?"

She shook her head. "I didn't want to ask you this," she began. I turned aside, laying a blouse on a hanger, to hide a flare of annoyance. What could there be that I couldn't do?

"But . . . it's in that drawer," Kate said, turning her chin toward the bedside table. I opened it and saw a blue butterfly, modeled out of some smooth, cushiony rubber. Its wings were attached on either side to two loops of black elastic. When I picked it up I saw there was a compartment for batteries. I turned it over a few times, looking at it.

"The loops go around your legs, like underwear," Kate said.

"My legs?" I said. I had realized what the butterfly was for, and I had a terrifying flash of myself standing at the foot of Kate's bed, stark naked except for black straps slung over my hip bones and a butterfly buzzing brightly between my legs.

She started to laugh. "No, mine," she said. She blushed, and looked away, then said, "I need something, you know?" There was another pause. "You just put it on me and put me on my stomach and go out for an hour or so and that's it."

I was blushing too. I thought I had gotten over this. Wiping away urine or shit was just cleaning. Even with bathing her I just relied on briskness, and my hands stayed safely behind a sponge or a removable showerhead. But now I was as mortified as on my first day.

I hadn't dealt with this yet and frankly I'd thought I'd never have to. That there was a clitoris tucked behind the lips of her vagina was something I knew but had been pretty careful not to consider. I had never even considered how sensitive she might still be—I'd imagined her rather numb, her flesh inert as clay, from knees to waist. I'd always assumed she was angry at Evan for getting the sex she couldn't have, but now I realized she was capable at least of some things. He just wouldn't give it.

I brushed my hair behind my shoulders.

"No problem," I said. I laid the covers to one side and reached beneath her nightgown. I drew her underwear down, trying to be gentle and less businesslike than usual, folded them, and set them on the chair. She was still blushing a little, gazing firmly at the lamp as I came back to the bed. I put the two loops around her ankles and eased the butterfly up, lifting her legs as I went to make it easier.

I settled the butterfly on the soft brown curls between her legs. I was thinking of my own body and I tried to put it low enough that it would touch her clitoris. I adjusted the straps over her hip bones. "Is that all right?"

Kate nodded. "Thanks," she said. I nudged the tiny switch on with my fingernail, and the butterfly began buzzing. We both ignored it, and the sound was muted by her body when I turned her onto her stomach, making sure her head was comfortably to one side and her hair out of her face. I started to leave, but then I stopped at the door, one hand on the light switch.

"Do you need anything else?" I looked back over my shoulder at the headboard of the bed. I focused just above her blond hair.

"No, thanks," Kate said, and I nodded and took a deep breath. I turned out the light.

OUT IN THE LIVING room I turned on the television. The volume was too high, and a laugh track burst out. I lowered it and flipped through the channels. I didn't know what Kate could hear from her bedroom, but I didn't want her to have to hear canned laughter or the screams from a cop show. I had switched the lights off earlier and now I reached over and turned on a lamp as I searched the channels. There was nothing—wildlife shows, the Food Network, football games. Nothing at all romantic. Finally I tried the stereo. There was a jazz CD in it from dinner, and I raised the volume enough so that Kate could probably hear it, but I couldn't hear anything from the bedroom.

AFTER AN HOUR I thought I should knock. I got up, but then paused. If this were a crucial moment it would be the worst possible time to interrupt. I wandered around the living room instead, paged through a book of photographs: a breast, a river, the stem of a lily. An unmade bed, the sheets glowing white. A willow.

FINALLY I DECIDED IT was time. I knocked and she said, "Okay," like I was coming in to collect her tea tray.

I pushed her hair behind her ear again, revealing a cheek flushed pink as a geranium. I tried to keep my hands off her thighs as I reached beneath her gown. I slid a hand between her heated skin and the bedsheets, cupped it beneath her hip, and lifted her pelvis, tugging the butterfly down by its strap. Then I took it into the bathroom, ran it under warm water, and dried it off. I put it back in its box in the nightstand drawer and turned Kate over to her back so her neck wouldn't cramp from being turned to one side. I didn't say anything, and she kept her eyes closed the whole time.

ten

I WAS ON MY way to hand in a paper, the first big assignment of the spring semester, when I saw Liam again.

I was looking through my paper—a study on the representations of demons in medieval painting—as I headed up Bascom, thinking it was slight but that at least it was on time, when Liam came jogging up next to me and touched my arm. I wasn't even startled. I'd been waiting for this for months. I hadn't seen him since October. It was February now.

He was wearing a jacket I'd never seen before. His hair seemed redder, as though the winter sun had intensified it.

"Hey, Bec," he said. We stopped on the hill and stood there awkwardly for a moment. He took off his headphones and then he kissed my cheek. Just a friendly, public, my-wife-knows-you kind of kiss, but—and here it struck me so clearly I didn't know how I had managed to avoid thinking about it for so long—no one had touched me in months, and the warmth of his mouth made me close my eyes a moment, exhale without meaning to. I was going to have to do something soon. Maybe I needed a butterfly of my own.

"Hey," I said. "How're you doing?"

He grinned. "Okay. I'm glad I saw you. I was just thinking about you a little while ago."

"Oh, yeah? What about me?" I wanted to hear how someone's perfume reminded him of me, or maybe how he'd been missing me a lot. I'd never called him back, but I'd saved the answering machine tape.

"Just how you were. Curious."

With him standing right there my resolve was thin. His hair was shaggy, his eyes greener than I remembered. I bet if I asked him he would come home with me, but standing out here I felt young and callow, bumbling. Where had all the confidence gone?

"I'm fine. I'm the same as I ever was."

"Okay." He looked skeptical, then seemed to take a breath and said in a rush, "Listen. I miss you. I think I was an ass to you."

I didn't see how I could answer that except to agree that I missed him too, and I didn't want to admit it. Instead I said, "Did you ever tell her?"

"Maybe someday." He looked off down the hill. "Things are a little precarious right now. I figure if I feel like shit, then that's my problem. I don't get to make myself feel better by foisting it off on her." He paused, and I kept watching him. Finally he admitted, "I don't want to tell her, really. I just don't want to go through all that."

He ran a hand through his hair. He rocked back and forth on the balls of his feet, stuck his hands in his pockets. I never noticed before how constantly he moved. He switched his briefcase to the other hand.

"Listen," I said. Who knew if I would run into him again? If I had anything to ask him, I knew, now was the moment. I lowered my voice as a group of girls in knit caps and gloves went by, cackling. "Why me? Or could it have been anyone, anyone pretty?"

"Of course not," he said. "You because you're funny and smart and by the way you never seemed to realize how smart you were. Are." We started walking again. "And I guess it might not have happened if Alison and I weren't going through a rough patch. But that's no reflection on you."

"You were going through a rough patch?" Why did it hurt me to know that? Was he supposed to have told me all about it?

"Yeah. With the move to Madison and this whole switch with her working and me in school . . . it's been different." He looked at me and then stopped, taking my arm. "Bec, don't look that way. I couldn't have talked to you about it. It wasn't your problem."

"Oh, no," I agreed, keeping a tremor out of my voice. It was so sordid. He should have just gone to a strip club. "The whole thing barely seems to have anything to do with me when you put it like that."

———

I'D BEEN DRIVING PAST a store called A Woman's Touch for months, but I finally decided to stop in and browse. For a minute after I parked I sat in my car and stared at the noodle shop next to it. I was debating whether I needed to detach the removable face from my new CD player if I wouldn't be gone long. Kate had given me a slightly exorbitant Christmas bonus, and after weeks of dithering I'd bought a better stereo than my car really deserved. It gleamed in its slot, all black surfaces and green lights shining softly, so sleek and out of place that I had had the car detailed just to make it seem more at home. I'd been driving the long way to and from Kate's house just for the pleasure of listening to my CDs. I was supposed to detach the face every time, leaving behind a blank rectangle of black plastic and a blinking red light marked SECURITY SYSTEM. This was a lie, but what thief would bother to test it? Finally I took the face off, put it in my bag, and got out of my car.

I'd assumed I'd stroll right in without hesitating, but as I went past the noodle place and record store, it was all I could do not to glance around to see who was watching. It was embarrassing to be embarrassed; I'd thought I was pretty straightforward. Mistress of my own erotic potential and such. But the openness of it was daunting, the way anyone could look you over and ponder what it was you needed, what you'd do with your purchases. I didn't mind, say, Liam knowing things like that about me, but I could have done without the tacit understanding of the record store clerk who was smoking a cigarette out front. I walked past him without meeting his eyes, and as I went in I turned my back to the door, relieved there were no glass windows open to the sidewalk.

Inside, there was music playing softly, and two women were looking at a silk teddy on a hanger. One woman lifted the silk and rubbed the fabric between her fingers. She grinned at the other woman, who laughed. I smiled nervously at the woman behind the counter, who was plump and blond, in a flowing skirt and muslin blouse. She looked like a waitress in an organic restaurant, which was somehow reassuring.

Along one wall were books and videos, vibrators and dildos and harnesses along the other. I glanced over my shoulder: The other two women were now examining a package of body paints. Then I faced the vibrators, glad to turn my back on the rest of the quiet store, and set about scrutinizing them as though I had some idea what I was doing. The store was so hushed that I could hear the murmur of the two women as they decided on their purchases. I thought I ought to be acting like a discerning customer, so I picked up a hot-pink vibrator with a long shaft. A pink plastic bunny head was attached to the same base as the shaft, the bunny's nose facing inward toward the plastic column, like an opposable thumb.

I turned it on. A whirring sound filled the store as the shaft rotated like a joystick and the bunny's head pattered back and forth, as loud as a woodpecker. I almost dropped it. The whole apparatus seemed extremely complicated. I turned it off, forcing myself not to look over my shoulder.

I kept browsing, sticking to the simple items now. Finally I settled on a Japanese-made purple wand, buying a tube of Silk Glide to go with it after the clerk said, "You'll want lubrication," and, to demonstrate, made me run my finger along the sticky rubber of the vibrator. As I watched her wrap the box in tissue paper, sealing it with a pink sticker bearing the name of the store, I began to feel much, much better. What had I been embarrassed about? No one else was self-conscious. This was going to be fantastic. Something new, something exciting, something whenever I wanted it. I took a catalog with me and drove home with the heat blasting, tapping the steering wheel in time with the radio, and retired to my saffron-yellow room.

eleven

EVAN MOVED BACK INTO their old house right after Kate moved out. "I know I've forgotten something," Kate warned me, and I said it didn't really matter if she had. I could make the trip over for anything she needed.

But she was more comfortable seeing him than I was, as it turned out. I was there one evening, cleaning her feeding tube after dinner, when the doorbell rang. The look on Kate's face told me right off who it was. She turned her head toward the doorbell, her lips opening slightly. Her face took on a bit of that stoniness it sometimes did when Evan's name came up, but there was something else too. Curiosity?

When I opened the door Evan had leaned toward me for a second, as if to kiss me on the cheek, but I turned around fast and called over my shoulder for him to follow me. He was flushed from the cold, snow in his hair, a blue scarf wrapped around his neck. I saw Kate eye it, and thought Cynthia had probably bought it for him. You never see a man buy his own scarf. I was dying to see this woman, to see if she really was, as Lisa had said, very much like Kate. What did that mean—well dressed, slender, a reader of books? Every now and again I thought I saw Evan downtown when Jill and I met up with people, but only once had it really been him. I saw him going into a restaurant just behind someone else. He'd been holding the door, his hand on the person's waist. It had to be Cynthia. There'd been a glimpse of gleaming dark hair, a black leather coat.

I looked him over as he took off his coat. He had gained weight. I took a perverse satisfaction in the flesh beneath his chin, the slight roundness of his sweatered belly.

He looked around for a place to hang his coat. After a good long minute I took it from him.

"I like your hair, Bec," he said. I'd splurged at Kate's salon and had it cut to shoulder length and shaped around my face.

"Thanks," I said. I pushed it behind my ears.

He looked behind me. Kate had come in. "Hi. You look beautiful," he said to her. "Really lovely."

She glanced down at her lap and said, "Hi. Well, let's go to the study." Evan didn't move. There was a long, uncomfortable stillness, and finally he broke it, his cheeks mottled, by looking my way. He didn't understand her, I realized, and out of fury I just didn't answer. Kate said it again, and he turned to watch her. She moved her head in the direction of the study, and this time he got it.

"Do you need me?" I asked. Kate smiled and shook her head. He saw her do that and then said, "Thank you, Bec, no." He shut the study door behind him.

TO WATCH EVAN IN her new house, seeing their things in this place, was enough to make me pity him. He kept casting startled glances around and recovering himself, reaching out to pick up a knickknack before realizing how presumptuous that would be. He had the tentative air and the diffident, slightly off-balance posture of a man who ought to be carrying a suitcase. I could have sworn he would move right in if Kate let him.

They had worked out a formal separation but nothing further, and Lisa still maintained he would never have left in the first place if Kate had stuck with the counseling. I hadn't realized they'd spent as much time in counseling as apparently they had, some of it before I even met them. But Kate had given up after several months, saying, *We weren't getting anywhere. I just don't have time for this.* And when he came over I saw that he still looked at her the same way, and as she moved ahead of him I'd seen him reach toward her shoulder, in the unthinking way you lay a hand on someone's neck, smooth their hair behind them, that proprietary way you pretend the other body is yours. His hand swung out toward her, paused, and then he drew it back.

———

WHILE THEY WERE IN the study I straightened up the living room. I could hear the low rumble of Evan's voice, and the occasional answer from Kate. What if they did get back together? I tried to imagine everything changing around all over again: Evan moving into this house, my schedule scaled back to part-time. Maybe I ought to have wanted that for Kate—I knew I should want them to work things out, for Evan to do as she asked for whatever amount of time was left, but the idea of accommodating him all over, just when things seemed re-settled, infuriated me. And it was terrible that I wasn't even angry on her behalf. I liked what I had here.

Besides, even if he did decide to ask to move back in, to get back to-gether, how could he do it? It shouldn't be a businesslike transaction, but that was what he would have been reduced to. What were you sup-posed to do, close your eyes and dive in for a conciliatory kiss? She couldn't give a lot of clues about how receptive she was, and I couldn't imagine Evan feeling secure enough to risk it. What signal could she give him to kiss her?

It made me think of how I used to punish Liam, turning away be-cause I knew he'd follow, if we had had an argument and I felt I was in the right. There must have been something in my posture that told him I would be receptive if he tried to touch me, even if I was ignoring him. Maybe it was my head turned slightly toward him to hear his movements, my hand curled on the bedspread, my open palm facing him—but he could always see it. He would turn me back to him, his hand a hard cradle at the back of my skull, and sometimes it made me moan in surprise before he even got to kissing me. You could not use that kind of motion with someone who couldn't signal you back with a hand on the neck, a leg slung open. You couldn't even let that force well up behind your actions, because nothing pushed back to keep the balance equal. So you'd stifle it. You could be gentle, definitely, you *had* to be gentle, but even then the options were limited. I just thought a person would get tired of a tender love scene every time.

One of the last times Liam and I were together, I tried being still and letting him make love to me as though, physically, I could not re-turn it. I did it for a moment. I did it just to see. I left my legs still draped around the backs of his knees, my arms where I'd wrapped them around his neck. My head slid up and down and shoved the pillow to one side. My hair rubbed roughly against the headboard. One arm fell to the bed as he moved, and I had let a sound escape me, because sounds were allowed. Sex changed without the resistance on my part, that push upward. It felt like—it was, of course—being fucked, the receiver of the action, and for a moment it was exciting to see what he did when he was, in a way, alone. My arm flopped out over the edge of the bed, rolling back and forth as he moved, and he'd glanced at it before pushing his mouth back against my hair. *What the hell are you doing?* he'd said. His breath was ragged and harsh in my ear. *Move. Move.*

twelve

WE WERE IN THE living room after dinner, early in March, watching the snow come down. I'd made a fire. On the coffee table was a list on which I had checked everything off, but it was satisfying to look at so I hadn't thrown it away. We had mailed packages, ordered two more cases of nutrition shakes, written letters to two state congressmen and five or six university researchers about abortion rights and funding ALS research, and placed holds on three books from the library.

Next to the list was a compact orange bong that looked like a gumball machine, with a cover that slid across the opening to hold the smoke inside it. It was packed with sticky, sage-green weed Kate kept in a little Chinese lacquer box in her bureau drawer.

I pressed the lighter button on the bong and we watched the smoke cloud up the orange globe. I held it up to Kate's mouth. She leaned her head forward while I slid the cover aside, letting the smoke out and into her mouth. She could hold it for a few seconds. We did this a few more times and then she shook her head when I offered it and gestured for me to have some if I wanted to. I took a few hits and settled back into the couch, my head buzzing softly.

The bong was my little innovation. She'd been having someone roll joints. Downtown there was a dank little head shop I'd always wanted to go to anyway. When we asked the clerk for a bong for someone with very little lung power, he actually rubbed his hands together. He might have been waiting all his life for a new pot-related conundrum to solve. He didn't seem to notice that Kate and I, in my jaunty red bucket hat and Kate's gold hoops, looked as if we had gotten lost on the way to Ann Taylor. He'd directed us to the little orange bong, fondness blazing in his eyes. It was squat and oddly cute in a benign-robot kind of way. We were in and out in ten minutes.

I was a half-hearted pot smoker, but this weed was really something. Older people must have better connections, or spend more money.

I was somewhat aware that the television was on. I gave Kate the remote, placing it on her leg beneath her forefinger, and we watched a flashing parade of bad primetime for what may have been a very long time. I was sprawled out on the couch with my feet flopped over the arm. Kate had moved her chair up next to me.

"Where does Lisa get this stuff?" I asked her. There was a long pause, in which I debated whether I had spoken.

"Oh, just some guy," Kate said vaguely. "I should grow my own, anyway. I doubt they'll raid me, or arrest me even if they did."

"The wheelchair gives and gives," I said. "You could say it was medicinal. Is it medicinal?"

"Hell, yes," Kate said. Her head was tilted back against her headrest. She gazed beneath lowered eyelids at the television, looking slightly bleary-eyed but also very tranquil. "After this video I'm going jogging."

I was still laughing when she said, slowly and seriously, "It does help. It's kind of what swimming does too. You don't feel the inside of your body so much." She looked confused, then grinned. "No. You don't feel like you're inside of your body so much. Or you don't care, anyway."

I nodded. We sat quietly for a few more minutes.

"I really want some bread and butter," I informed her. It had just occurred to me.

"Me too," said Kate.

I propped myself on one elbow and turned to look at her. Kate raised her eyebrows at the bong on the coffee table and I hit the lighter button and held it up to her lips.

"What would you eat right now?" I asked.

"Tamales," Kate added after a moment. "Tamales with pork and red chiles."

"I can't make tamales," I sighed. "You're totally out of masa and

lard." I looked at her over my shoulder. "Can you believe I knew
that?"

She gave me a long, careful nod. Down, up, down, up, grinning.
"Well," she said, "then it's all been worth it."

"Oh my god," I said, embarrassed. "You think I'm like those TV
movies where the person with the disease teaches everyone how to
live."

Kate laughed soundlessly. "It's always so *nice* of us."

We sat quietly. The fire snapped in its grate. Outside the lights
glowed hazily, snow falling past. The air smelled peppery. "This is
nice," I said after a while.

"Yeah," she said. "Pot's still fun."

"What else?" I asked recklessly.

She cocked an eyebrow at me. "How do you mean?"

"What else is fun for you? Do we have enough fun?"

She nodded. "Yeah. Movies are fun. Watching you cook is fun,
you've gotten so good at it. Hanging out with my friends. Redoing the
house." She met my eye and smiled gently. "Sometimes I can still make
it an okay life, Bec," she said. She swallowed. "I'm not in a hospital
bed. I still make my decisions."

"You don't think you would if you were in a hospital?"

She shook her head. "I know I wouldn't. You hear stories . . . you
go into the hospital, go on a respirator, and they can't just disconnect
you, you know. You're stuck. You lay there and hope someone comes
to see you. You have no control anymore, and you're there till the end,
pretty much. And the end never comes because of the respirator."

I almost protested out of sheer politeness, but what she was saying
made a grim sense. "That's awful," I said instead.

She nodded, looking into the fire.

After a time she spoke again, but I was staring out the window. I
turned back to her, faintly surprised to find her right there. "Sorry?"

"Maybe it won't happen like that," she repeated.

"Definitely not," I agreed. I was about to go on—*Nothing like that will
ever happen; don't worry*—but I stopped myself. Why be patronizing? She
knew what she was talking about.

"Listen," I said. "Can you eat bread and butter?" I'd always assumed she couldn't eat anything at all. In nine months I'd never seen solid food touch her mouth, only drops of meltable things placed on her tongue—frosting, a miniscule smear of soft cheese.

Kate nodded. "Just takes too long," she explained. She made a face. "Embarrassing."

I set the bong back on the coffee table. "You can't be embarrassed in front of me," I said. "You want some bread and butter?" Kate gave one of her tiny shrugs, nodded. "Great," I said. I gave a long sigh, pretending to be annoyed. I felt like being silly all of a sudden. "I suppose you expect *me* to get it?"

I peeked over my shoulder and saw her laughing silently.

"I keep meaning to tell you," Kate began.

I watched her intently. She was very far away from me.

"There's a chance I may be slightly paralyzed," she finished. "Do you still want to take the job?"

I got up, chuckling, and went into the kitchen, taking out a round loaf of peasant bread and some butter from the refrigerator. I cut the bread carefully, keeping my hand far away from the blade so I wouldn't have to haul myself, stoned, to an emergency room and leave Kate alone.

The bread took forever to toast. I sat on the edge of the counter while I waited.

"Don't you worry that pot's bad for you?"

"Worse than this?" Kate answered.

"Good point," I said. She wasn't being maudlin. She was right. Kate didn't care about health risks. She had had Lou Gehrig's for close to three years, and a lot of people died within two. In a way she could do anything. She took birth control pills straight through each month with no placebos, so she never had to deal with having a period. What was it going to do to her?

I carried a plate of buttered toast back to the coffee table. I broke off a small piece, held it up for her to approve, and when she nodded I placed it in her mouth. Kate chewed slowly and carefully, her head tipped forward so no crumbs went down her throat and started a coughing fit. I took a piece myself and ate it quickly, happily, enjoying the melted butter.

"I don't know if I can handle driving," I said. "I had no idea your pot would be this good."

Kate swallowed a bite of bread. "So stay here," she said. "There's an extra room."

"Okay." I held up the toast so she could take another bite. Then I sprinkled some salt over my next piece and took a big bite. I thought I could sit here by the fire and eat buttered toast for the next several days at least. Toast was one of the more available pleasures in life. I felt the way I had when I first started working for Kate, and Saturday afternoons we'd come home from the market, cook, and have drinks with Evan once he arrived. Nostalgia welled up in my chest. Just for summer, I suppose, for cold wine and the porch at the old house. I didn't like to admit it, but it had been fun when it was the three of us. Why hadn't they offered me a joint back then? Maybe it had been their little thing, a private thing.

"Do you miss Evan?" I asked. The words were out almost before I realized it, and I wished I could make them disappear. Kate didn't look angry. She smiled, her eyes swollen and bloodshot, but she looked content.

"Yes," she said.

"Sometimes I do too," I admitted. I felt I could admit this, softened by pot and companionship as we were. She watched me carefully, and nodded.

"Sometimes we all had fun," I said, and I gave Kate another bite. We sat, chewing, in companionable silence.

thirteen

L ET'S GO TO THE ZOO," Kate said.

"The zoo?" I asked. I was holding up a red sweater with a low square neckline. She looked it over and then shook her head, so I folded it up and put it in a cardboard box for the Salvation Army. I loved that sweater, but I also knew why she was giving it away. The last time she'd worn it I saw her do a double-take in the mirror at her own collarbone, which had grown more prominent in the last couple months, notched deeply at the center like a tiny cup above the shadowed hollows of her sternum. It startled me too. I'd given her an extra nutrition shake that day.

I held up a fuchsia turtleneck. No one else could possibly wear that color.

"Why the zoo? What are we, kids?" I was only teasing. Lately we had been doing things like this: jaunts to museums, the botanical gardens. She'd been talking about another trip, this time to New York. She was bored, I thought, staving off the winter monotony.

"Let's keep that one," she said. "And I like the zoo. Everybody lets the chick in the wheelchair go straight to the front."

I laughed in spite of myself and offered up a sapphire-blue blouse for her consideration. She tilted her head, then nodded toward the "keep" pile.

"You realize it's March," I said.

She was unperturbed. "We can go to the indoor exhibits. Besides, no one goes this time of year. The animals probably need validation."

"Prima donnas." I turned back to Kate and looked her over. Her eyes were a little watery, her mouth pale. She'd come down with the flu a week before and it had lingered, casting a blurring, pinkish effect around her eyes and her nostrils. It had the opposite effect on her body, paring away any softness until each rib showed even more clearly than before. It had knocked her out so badly that I'd had to sponge bathe her for a few days instead of dragging her into the shower. We usually used so many gadgets and computers that it was soothing, somehow, to be so old-fashioned: squeezing out the big natural sponge into one of those old-fashioned basins, lifting her up from the mattress and wiping it over her neck and her shoulders, down her thin arms and legs, toweling away the traces of water and soap. It wasn't easy to give someone a sponge bath in bed without getting the sheets all damp. I was good at it now.

"Are you sure you're up to this?" I asked.

She met my eyes. "It's just sitting," she said.

So we made our way into the gorilla house later that day. It was set up so that it felt as though the people were enclosed in glass and the gorillas had free reign of their hillside. The gorillas lounged around like teenagers, digging through their fur and chomping steadily at something in their mouths—bamboo, I imagined, or gum. One relaxed on a fallen log, gazing up the hill with a foot propped up on a rock. The gorilla picked up a long stick, plucked at the bark, and contemplated it, his brow low and his long, leathery lips working slowly.

"Watch," said Kate. "He'll bend it into a wheel."

I chortled. "They're probably building a barbecue pit on the other side of the hill."

I was glad we'd come, surprised to find I still enjoyed something as simple as staring at an exotic animal. Morally, I had my doubts about zoos. You could argue that some of the animals at least were alive here when they were nearly extinct elsewhere, but there was something autocratic and lordly about the whole notion of importing them here for our pleasure, or at least our intermittent interest—what were they supposed to do with their lives in the meantime? That day, however, misgivings or not, I gave in to the pleasures of the privileged, meandering alongside Kate's chair over the paved, wide paths—at a stately pace Kate called a "stroll-and-roll"—and gazing through the glass at the gibbons and elephants. It was fascinating, actually: What bored prince had been the first to have some beast paraded before him and penned nearby, out of idle curiosity?

The gorilla's walnut-brown eyes roved past me as he took up another branch. He seemed so mysterious and unknowable, even a few feet away. Kate murmured something, and I stopped pondering and saw that her hand had fallen from the control of her wheelchair and lay bent in her lap.

"Sorry," I said, fixing it. I looked her over once more to see if anything else was out of place; then we turned back toward the gorilla.

We were sitting right up at the glass. Another gorilla had come up to the edge to stare at the caged people. He looked listless.

"We ought to be entertaining him," a voice said. I smiled to myself, agreeing with the voice even before I had registered that it was one I knew. Kate turned her head. "Maybe they need more to do in there."

It was Evan. Now both of us turned to look. He was about ten yards away, standing on a deck that allowed a better view of the gorillas. I was about to exclaim at the coincidence, when I glanced at Kate and saw the expression—defiant, sheepish—on her face. Our eyes locked.

"Why didn't you tell me why we were coming?" I asked her. We had followed him here. For a moment it all seemed perfectly decipherable: She had sought him out, the first time since they separated. It had to mean a reconciliation. But I had heard the petulant note in my own voice and understood, horrified, how much the prospect upset me.

I saw Evan look at us, his face slack in surprise before he recovered and turned to one side. The crowd of people shifted, and I saw that he was leaning over, murmuring something to the woman next to him.

"Cynthia?" I murmured. Kate nodded.

"Well, my checkered past and I are here, too, so it must be adultery day at the zoo," I said lightly, refusing to acknowledge any possible reason the scene could upset Kate. She didn't respond, so I gave up that tack. "I don't get it. Did you just want to see her?"

"Sort of," Kate said.

There was a silence. I brushed her hair off her forehead and re-draped her red scarf. She resettled her shoulders, squaring them slightly, and I looked toward the exit, hoping for a clear path. She couldn't want him back, surely, I thought, but her face was a studious blank and I was uncertain. She did miss him, after all. We had followed him here. A streak of pity ran through me, almost stopping me cold. I had never, ever pitied her before.

"Let's go over," she said. I started to protest, but she gave me a look and I stopped. You're not you, I reminded myself. You're her. So I followed Kate to the base of the platform where Evan stood. By the time we got there and Kate craned her neck to look up at them, Evan and Cynthia were very still.

"Hello," Cynthia said, smiling awkwardly. She wore black pants and a blue silk shirt. I had wanted her to be cheap-looking and brassy, but she was as polished as Kate. There were pearls in her ears and her auburn hair was drawn back in a knot. "You must be Kate."

I placed myself close to Kate. It was loud in the ape house.

"Yes," Kate said. "Yes," I repeated. There was a silence. Kate looked at them, but they kept looking at me, maybe because I was the last one to have spoken.

"I guess I mentioned we'd be here today," Evan said. Kate shrugged. Without meaning to I gave a little shrug myself.

"We used to come here sometimes," Kate said to Cynthia. I translated.

"Yes, well . . . I hadn't been to a zoo since I was little," Cynthia said.

Kate lifted her chin to swallow and took a breath.

"How are you, Evan?" Kate asked.

I could see him debate how to answer without annoying either woman too much. He settled on, "Fine, thanks."

"Good," Kate said. "I'm doing well, too. Thanks." Her voice, which in its weakness always seemed to issue from some flaccid muscle low in her throat, was higher, stronger, but it shook.

We all stared at each other. Evan and Kate watched each other.

Cynthia stared at me. Finally Evan leaned over the railing at the edge of the platform.

"This is uncomfortable," he said. I stepped to one side and looked at Kate. Before she could say anything Cynthia joined Evan at the rail.

"I don't quite understand why you came here," Cynthia said. She too leaned over, holding on to the rail with both hands. Her long nails gleamed with clear polish. "It seems counterproductive, but maybe you just had to see me. I'm not a monster." She paused, flicking something off the railing, and then said, "In fact, you'll think I'm crazy, but in a way I understand why you had to separate. Evan too. Think how hard it was for him to watch you go through this."

She was crazy. It was obvious.

Kate sighed. She looked worn out. I had the sense she'd forced herself to come here and speak to them, whether she wanted to or not. I watched her profile—her long nose, the firm curve of her jaw—as she tipped her head back to contemplate Cynthia. I watched her mouth flicker into a smile, something so weary it was almost gentle. What had Kate expected of an encounter like this? I didn't understand her at all; her face suddenly seemed entirely foreign to me.

"I doubt you understand why we separated," Kate said. She looked over at Evan, then back to Cynthia. "I'm not sure Evan even does." She didn't sound bitter but resigned, even slightly indulgent, like a parent who's given up for the time being.

I repeated it for them and looked back at Kate. She turned her gaze toward the entrance, and rather than wait for her to do a three-point turn with her chair I moved it myself. It was the sort of moment you need to handle with efficiency, the equivalent of turning on your heel and striding off. So I lifted the front wheels off the ground and pivoted the chair, then stepped behind it and followed her out.

"CENTER ME," KATE SAID, later that week. "The exact center."

She was stretched out on the bare mattress. I stepped back to get a better view of her: her hair spread out around her face, her hands flat against the mattress, her legs a few inches apart, all of it bounded by the quilted white fabric of the mattress. Despite the sweater and skirt, her dark tights, she looked a bit like a sunbather. I moved her a few inches to the right. "Okay," I said, and I knelt on the bed next to her midriff and uncapped a black Sharpie. Before I touched the felt-tip to the fabric just above the crown of Kate's head, I paused. We exchanged a look, and Kate smiled and let her gaze move past me and settle serenely on the ceiling.

So I began. I kept the path of the marker as close as I dared without getting ink on her clothes or skin. I wanted the silhouette to be crisp and unmistakable.

We were in her old house, now Evan's, in the master bedroom. A royal blue comforter, sheets, and mattress pad were heaped on the floor. A box containing the last of her things sat by the bedroom door: A few minutes ago I had walked through the house, picking up the items Kate nodded her head at, putting them in an old nutrition-shake box. She chose a framed photo of herself and a friend who had since died in a plane crash, a gilt-edged copy of *Jane Eyre,* a book on dictating an effective living will, a stray makeup brush, and a big stone molcajete, its pestle set at a jaunty angle inside the huge bowl. It was time to make one last trip to the old house, Kate had informed me that morning, and get any leftovers all at once.

I'd grinned when she indicated that the molcajete, sitting on the counter next to the stove, should go into the box. The meals I made for our caregiver dinners three or four times a week were of varying complexity: Like any cook, I got overwhelmed sometimes and fell back on pasta or turkey burgers, especially once Simone admitted she ate meat. But the prospect of a new gadget excited me again, and I knew I'd be grinding cloves of garlic, pumpkin seeds, or rings of sliced onion against the rough stone bowl, while she watched and gave directions. Since the toast, I'd been able to persuade her more often to eat in front of me, and sometimes at our shared meals with other caregivers: a shred of beef, a crescent of poached pear. I'd feed her guacamole, I decided, pale green and unctuous, rich as butter.

I had situated the molcajete in the box and then paused outside the kitchen, resting the heavy box on the table that held the nude statue in the living room. The spider plant still hung above her, but the statue had been moved, yet again, a few inches to the left and out from under the vines.

"Let's take her," I said, and Kate looked at it with distaste. "For a hat rack," I went on, and Kate laughed. "We'll set her in the garden, let her get overgrown with pea vines."

Kate had looked toward the back of the house. "Maybe we'll do something else instead," she hedged.

I nudged the statue back beneath the plant and followed her back to the bedroom. Something about being back in this house, alone in the silent neighborhood on a dark winter day, had made me restless, nervy. I wanted to crack an egg behind the radiator, knock over the milk, loosen the salt shaker cap. It was the kind of diffuse mischief a teenager would feel while cutting school. Did it even matter whose house we were in? I might have felt the same impulse anywhere to chuck a rock through a stranger's window or dig my nails into the fruit at the grocery store. Maybe it was only winter, the impersonal stillness of the air outside.

"A friend of mine lived with a guy who collected board games," I told Kate. "Which should have been a clue. Anyway, when she moved out she went through and took one necessary piece from every single game."

She grinned. She was surveying the dresser top for her possessions, and I set down the box and observed the room while she wheeled around the perimeter. I sat on the bed, thinking about the first time I'd had to get her up, reaching across that expanse of sheet and comforter and blanket to where she had lain, marooned at the center.

"I wonder if he'll notice the wheelchair tracks," she mused.

"Probably. We could rub something messy on your wheels just to be sure. Why?"

She shrugged, then said, "I know him. I bet he can pretend I was never even here."

"Leave handprints on all the walls at wheelchair level."

Kate did a three-point turn in the chair. She let her head lean back against the headrest, her chin raised and her eyes slightly lowered as she looked at me, sly, imperious.

"No. We'll leave an outline on the bed," she said.

I stared at her. I'd been feeling hyper but hadn't planned to act on it. First the zoo, now this? Was this how things were going to be—

following Evan, getting at him? I thought of all the times Jill had stopped me from calling a guy, or going to see him, and wondered if Kate was just beyond worrying about all of that. It was something to imagine—what if I had just called Liam one of those times, talked to his wife as though I were a coworker, a telemarketer, to see what it led to?

"Are you sure you want to start this kind of thing?" I asked her carefully.

She was already waiting by the side of the bed. "I'm not starting a sad pattern of harassment," she said. "It's a one-time thing, I promise."

I gave in, and I had to admit that once I began the outline I enjoyed it. I loved the sneakiness of it. An outline, beneath all the bedding, drawn directly onto the bare mattress. No one would see it for weeks if Evan was the sort of sheet changer who left the mattress pad untouched. It wasn't malice, only mischief. I made the lines of ink as thick as I could.

I traced around Kate's hair, which, a day or two after the zoo, she'd had cut into thick bangs swept across her forehead, stylishly haphazard wings framing her face and neck.

I got just right the silhouette of her earlobe and the hoop earring where it peeked out from a bell of dark gold hair. Next I traced the stem of her neck, in which a tranquil pulse beat just beneath the curve of her jawline. The small shoulder was easy, then the line of the arm, so slender it tapered below the shoulder joint, swelled at the elbow, and clearly showed the bone of her wrist. On the middle finger of her right hand was a thick gold ring with a topaz set flush in the metal. I spread the fingers enough to trace the outline of its bulky band. I coveted that ring, and though Kate offered to let me wear it, the ring needed slim, neat hands like hers. Mine were long but now bore the signs of a cook: healing nicks and burns, nails a little too short. Maybe if I took more care with knives and hot pans.

I moved the marker along her rib cage, from the tuck of her waist to the arc of her hip. The outline of a slim thigh was effortless, and of the knees. Below the calves, the cool purpled skin was puffed with fluid that obscured the bones in the ankle and in the tops of her feet. Except for the feet, the silhouette would be all sweeping lines, slim bone. By now I was kneeling at her feet, one hand braced by her leg.

A few years ago Evan would have been in this same spot. I used to sit up on my elbows and look down at Liam as he knelt at the foot of the bed. Somewhere, both of them might be in this position even now, marveling at a slim body or a rounded soft one, marveling the way everyone does for a while. The way you're so determined to remember each detail that you learn it several times over, with your fingers and eyes and mouth. There's that pocket of time between people, when you're so rapt in the heat and furrow of another body and every flaw seems like just a clever variation, but then of course you start to seek out every mole and stretch mark without wanting to, and that electric skin cools and sets beneath your hands.

Kate had lifted her head and now she raised her eyebrows at me. I realized I had paused and I resumed tracing the calves, then around the soft skin of the heel, out along the swollen ankle. When I got up to her left hand, now bare of jewelry, I was glad I had been so careful to show the bulge of the ring on the other hand. I didn't want Evan thinking the ring just didn't show up. I wanted him to know it wasn't there at all, that a few days before, Kate had gestured with her chin to indicate the wedding band, and said, "Take it off." We had put it in her nightstand, in the drawer below the blue rubber butterfly.

I was back at her head again, the tangle of glossy hair and the curve of the jaw. I kept tracing until I closed the line at the crown of her head.

I steadied her in a sitting position, a hand at her back. She was so slim, the light bones of her shoulder blade sharp and warm against the palm of my hand. I would definitely make that guacamole; she no longer allowed me to give her extra nutrition shakes.

I lifted her to a standing position, pivoted, and placed her in the wheelchair. We both gazed for a second at the silhouette on the bed. It felt like it had taken forever, but it looked perfect.

"It was a good idea to do both sides of the mattress," Kate said. I laughed.

A few months ago I would have liked to do something like this in Liam's house, a house I'd never seen inside. But had I done it at all, back when I might have wished to, I would have put my figure on his side of the bed instead of in the center, the lines of my body indelible and hidden under his.

I spread the mattress pad down again, covered it with the sheets, and smoothed the quilt over everything. Before we left the house Kate told me to crack a window, and once I locked the front door I took the brass key off the ring and tossed it through the open window into the front hallway, where it ricocheted off the nude statue and landed beneath the swaying tangle of the spider plant.

fourteen

I STOOD IN THE shallow end of the pool, my hands beneath Kate's back. People swam past us, kicking up a wake that lapped over her torso, pooled in the depression of her navel beneath the navy suit. Her breasts were small cones in the shiny fabric, her hip bones peaking sharply on either side of her stomach. I kept my hand splayed against the back of her neck and head, holding her face above the water, and the other arm looped beneath her body. Her legs floated easily, straight out and slightly shapeless, like a clay sculpture whose musculature hasn't been fully detailed yet.

"How's it feel?" I asked her. She was looking up at the ceiling, the tendons in her neck tensed against the water, and she looked down her nose and cheeks at me and smiled and mouthed, *Fine.*

The doctor was the one who suggested swimming. He had listened to Kate's lungs, clucked over the most recent cold she had not been able to shake, and warned me never to let her face hit the water. *It'll help the muscles,* he said. *Those muscles are getting a little sulky, you're right. A little lazy. But the water gives them some resistance.* He had listened to her chest again, his brow furrowed. *We need to clear out those lungs,* he said. *If they're not clear in a few days, come back.* He gave me a look, to emphasize that he spoke to me as well. Then I left them alone in the exam room while I got the car. I'd offered to stay and translate, but they'd glanced at each other and Kate said, *We have a couple things to cover still. I think we'll be okay.*

I felt the muscle at the back of her neck fluttering—it tensed, or tried to tense, then went flaccid again, the cords in her neck leaping. Her ribs leapt up and down with a sharp breath.

"Relax," I said. "I have a good hold on you."

Evan had done this for her before, I knew, and I thought she must be used to being held by someone larger and stronger than I was. I shifted my arms so she'd feel the hold I had on her. It didn't matter that I didn't have a man's long arms; she was so light that it was easy to bear her up. Stretched out, though, she was surprisingly long.

She nodded, blinking rapidly as the water splashed near her temples.

"Check your legs," I said a little later, "see if you can work them a little. The doctor said you might."

I looked down again at her legs, pipe stems, pale as lilies, and watched one move. Then the other. She managed a decent kick out of each of them, and another and another, pelting my face with chlorinated water.

"Hey! I've never seen you kick that far."

I knew the water made all the difference, that without gravity it seemed as though she could do much more than she could. I shouldn't trust this display, but I fell for it completely, as though I'd watched her stand up and take a step.

Her brows had been knit in concentration, but now the tension in her face broke and she laughed. I squeezed the back of her neck just barely, lifted her a little higher, and felt the muscles along her spine loosen and soften against my palms.

AFTER WE GOT HOME from the pool, Kate said, "I have something to ask you."

I was filing insurance papers. "Shoot," I said.

"Dr. Klass thinks I need more care," she began. It felt like a blow; I heard air rush from my mouth as I turned to her. She read my expression and said, "No, not better care. But he doesn't think I should be alone at night."

I sat down on the edge of the desk. We looked at each other. I began deadheading a basil plant.

"What about the emergency button?" I asked.

She lifted her shoulders and dropped them. "We talked about that too. My lungs are not so great. It's possible it could happen very fast, too fast for people to get to me in time if I started to have trouble breathing. But maybe that's okay; I don't know." She paused and watched my face.

I pushed the basil plant away.

ALS paralyzed everything eventually, including the muscles she used to breathe. That, suffocation, was often the final, single cause of death.

"Are you really ready to think that way?" I asked her. There was a snag in my voice and I got it under control before I went on. "It doesn't seem right to me."

Kate said, "No, not really. I try it on for size sometimes. But he's been after me to have round-the-clock for a while. And lying there from ten to eight every night is not the party I thought it would be."

"Are you asking me to move in?" I asked. "Because I would, of course I would. Or do you want to get someone more qualified for nights?"

She shook her head. "If you want to, we can work out something for you." She seemed to be debating what to say for a moment, and then she said, "Don't you dare do it just because you think you have to. I need someone but it doesn't have to be you. I was planning on hiring someone. I just thought I'd ask you first."

It wasn't that I wouldn't move in. I would if I had to. Better me than Simone, who despite great improvement was still a little too sprightly to have around all the time, or Hillary, with her generally deadening effect. But Jill and I had lived together pretty happily for a couple years now, and since she no longer had to dart out of the house to avoid Liam, we were back to having fun together, sitting around when we got home from work and making fun of bad cable. I even liked her new boyfriend. The three of us hung out without awkwardness, a rare enough thing that I was reluctant to give it up. We knew I was a third wheel, but we all felt comfortable with it.

Something else occurred to me. "You're going to think this is a stupid question," I said. She watched me. I took a deep breath, unsure if I was being selfless or self-serving, and said, "What about Evan? Maybe he could live here for a while and give it a shot." She quirked an eyebrow at me. "He didn't strike me as all that happy at the zoo. And maybe he hasn't even seen the mattress yet," I added.

She shook her head and glanced away from me. "I wish I could, in a way. But I can't count on him, even if . . . we worked out the rest." She made a sound in her throat, clearing it. "Plus. I should have told you. Cynthia is moving into the old house."

I had a palm full of dead basil buds, and I got up to throw them away. It shocked me a little, the flush of disappointment I felt when she said that. I remembered the way Evan had looked at Kate, even when they were together only to figure out a separation agreement. At the zoo I'd looked back and thought, *It won't be long before this Cynthia thing just resolves itself.*

"I'm thinking," I told Kate. I sat down behind the desk and didn't look her way, staring at the blotter instead. It gave me a second of privacy. She knew I needed to see her, especially lately, to understand her words. Looking away from her was almost as effective as turning away from a deaf person signing. I tried not to do it much. It was cowardly, and even cruel, but I did it now.

This was a nice house. I could live in a really nice house, for once in my life. And Jill and I wouldn't lose touch. Nevertheless I was regretting how quickly I'd said I'd move in if Kate needed it. Kate and I had a good rhythm going. I came over after classes or first thing in the morning. We ran our errands and I made my phone calls on behalf of the ALS Society (I had given up the convoluted introductions and now I just pretended to be Kate) and I cooked dinner for the evening caregiver and me, and gave Kate her nutrition shakes. Soon the farmers' market would start up again.

But what would I really be leaving, anyway? It wasn't as though I was cutting such a swath through society on my own.

Kate had said nothing. She sat in her chair, letting me debate myself. You can't help but be flattered, to be given such a proposal and know that you're the only one who got it. It didn't matter that she told me not to take it out of guilt. She knew I would take it, because it was the lesser evil. I'd rather be inconvenienced than ashamed for refusing to help her. I was already working my way around, in my head, to the things I would like about it: that pretty house, the more frequent use of the BMW. I looked up at her and gave her what I hoped was an enthusiastic smile. But, again, and just for a moment, I regretted having left that state of unawareness, when I hadn't known much of what was going on in her marriage or her life, and I hadn't had to respond to it. I could just show up, wheel her here and lift her there, my duties as simple as a maid's.

I HAD AN EMBARRASSING compulsion to put on makeup and take particular care with my hair and clothes when I went back to Oconomowoc. It was one thing when I lived there, running errands in my sweatpants and doing little more than wiping the shine off my bare skin before I stopped at the Kiltie for a peanut butter milkshake. But in the past two years I had become a visitor.

I just hadn't come home one June, having lucked into a cheap sublet on Spaight Street, and when Jill and I drove back for a weekend that summer it was clear we no longer had the same ease with our old acquaintances, or even once-close friends. When we all ran into one another at The Main Event over dollar beers, or at the fairgrounds in line to buy cheese curds, we didn't even try to hide our appraisals: After the hug came the tilted-back head, the extraneous, contemplative nods. I felt I came up wanting in these one-offs. Some of the girls I'd been in gymnastics with, the compact muscled ones who came up to my shoulder, had gone on to compete on college teams, and I must admit that seeing them again brought out the worst in me. Just when I thought it didn't matter to me anymore I'd seen Christie Juska at a fair, her shiny black ponytail bouncing and her muscled legs in a tense, splayed-toe stance, sipping mineral water and eschewing the bratwurst as if she never knew when she might be called upon to perform an impromptu floor exercise. Next thing I knew I was doing handsprings in the backyard, out of practice and panting, my mother tapping on the window and telling me to come in before I snapped an ankle.

I no longer tried to renew old friendships beyond a night out, but that didn't mean I wouldn't put on my jade choker, mascara, and a swipe of sheer blackberry lipstick when I went back in early April. No point in handing people their gossip on a platter, as Jill liked to say.

I was going home for my mother's forty-fifth birthday. It was already dark when I arrived, after leaving Kate's at five. I was carrying a bottle of champagne and an expensive wool sweater, both of which she had helped me choose. It was extravagant, but Kate wouldn't be charging me rent, so I had been enjoying the freed money since I had agreed to move in. I'd been on a bit of a spree: stocking up on new CDs to play in my car, a sweater for Jill, a new winter coat for myself. It was much more fun shopping for my mother with some money. As I browsed I had thought of all the drugstore cologne and aftershave I had bestowed upon my parents over the years, and then I grabbed a silk tie for my father as well.

When I had gone back at Christmas the house was festooned with colored lights and wreaths—being a religious skeptic did not prevent my mother from enjoying the trappings of the holidays, including the tree which, she often noted, was really a pagan hand-me-down—but now the decorations were long gone and the snow was piled in gray heaps on either side of the door. The siding had been avocado for years, but my father had recently painted it light blue. The house was just a tiny bungalow, with a living room at the front, their bedroom and mine off to the side, and a dining room off the kitchen. The basement held my mother's sewing machine and my father's workbench.

Mom had worked at the doctor's office since I was fifteen, a job she said appealed to her organizational zeal. She took trips to Chicago every now and again, wandering around the Art Institute or visiting some library with rare manuscripts. My father accompanied her about half the time, but as far as I could tell it was not a point of contention. She seemed to like the time alone, or with a friend, and my father spent the weekend grilling steaks and doing yard work. They seemed to have reached a point in marriage at which they regarded each other's faults with no more than a roll of the eyes, my mother's brisk wave fanning it away.

I'd never thought of a tactful way to ask why and how they got married. My mother had meant to go to college but somehow never did. *Money was tight,* she'd once told me when I was in high school, and it had all seemed impractical at the time. Besides, she'd get to it one of these days. *In the meantime,* she'd add, one fingertip tapping on my untouched pile of textbooks, *you study.*

For a long time I assumed some sort of phantom pregnancy had precipitated their marriage, maybe a miscarriage or a scare that didn't pan out, since I was born more than a year after their wedding. This was when I was about fourteen, around the same time most kids decide they're adopted. My mom and dad seemed to like each other, and they rarely argued, but even to me they seemed mismatched. As a child I spent wildly divergent days with each of them, alone, every few months: a Brewers game with my father, something educational with my mother. The Brewers games, where my dad settled back comfortably in his seat, wordlessly allowing me sips of his beer, were far more fun.

For a brief period my father and I were very close. I was eight or nine, so he would have been about thirty, the same gray eyes beneath straight brows and a lot of thick, straight nutmeg-brown hair. I'd inherited the eyes and the hair color but not, unfortunately, the straight hair. Even young, he was never one of the voluble, funny dads, or the excitable ones cheering on the sidelines during my various athletic careers. He was always watching calmly, periodically calling out some specific bit of advice to me; sipping from a thermos of coffee. I remembered a lot of weekends spent with him after the matches or games, walks downtown when my father stopped in hardware stores, examining drills and sanders while I pored over the racks of seed packets for lack of anything more colorful. But I always got a little bribe, the suggestion we not tell my mother delivered straight-faced. An ice cream cone, a vanilla Coke, a book that wasn't educational. Later I realized my mother wasn't bothered by these little transgressions, but at the time it both worried and pleased me to know the mischievous side of him. I suspected my mother had no idea.

We didn't talk a lot now, but we hadn't conversed extensively back then, either. I went to my dad mainly with specific questions: I have rarely asked him something he couldn't answer. I don't know where he learned it all—carburetors, insects, electoral colleges, vegetable fertilizer, and mutual funds—but I do know he never volunteered any of the information he seemed to have picked up by osmosis and stored away. Once, last year, the Honda began to overheat as I drove back from Madison, and despite the seventy-degree day I turned on the heater and got the car home that way. When I told him this, he said mildly,

"How'd you know to do that?" I realized I wasn't sure where I'd heard it, but not from him. "It didn't occur to me to tell you that," he'd said. He was staking a tomato plant while we talked, kneeling in the dirt. I was looking down at the gray-blue top of his baseball hat, his fingernails ringed in dirt. "I should have, I guess," he continued, "but you knew somehow." Then he patted the tomato vine into place and stood up. He smiled at me, obviously proud of my quick thinking, totally oblivious to my annoyance.

Sometimes I felt I could already see the old man he'd be in thirty years, still working methodically over the house until it was almost entirely new, planting gardens until the yard was filled with greenery, mulling over all the things he knew so thoroughly it never occurred to him to mention them to me.

My mother must not have minded his reticence, or else she too already knew what to do when a car overheated. Who was to say they didn't dance in the living room when I was gone? Maybe after their weekends apart my father met her with candles and music.

My parents greeted me at the door, exclaiming over the drive and the snow. I reached up to hug my mother, realizing yet again that she was four inches taller than me and always would be. She pressed her cheek against mine. It was fuzzy and smelling of powder, with that menopausal down that I had begun to notice on her when I'd been gone for the first few months of college. She turned toward the dining room table and drew me with her. My mother was still slim and broad-hipped, her dark hair in a low ponytail streaked with white. She wore a cotton turtleneck, a sweater, and corduroys against the cold in the house. My parents were fanatical about heating bills. Heat was one thing Kate refused to stint on. I left my coat on.

"Well, come in, have something to drink," my mother said. My father ruffled my hair and gave me a rough hug.

She poured me a glass of sweet pink wine and I took a sip.

"What's this?" she said, smiling quizzically into the bag I had set on the table. She held up the champagne and swiveled it around, gazing at the label. "I haven't even opened one of these bottles in years. I'm not sure I remember how."

"I'll do it. You just turn the bottle and hold the cork still."

"Huh," she said. She tucked it into the fridge and sat down with me. My father sat down too.

"How's Jill? We saw her parents at fish fry last week."

"She's great," I said. "She decided to get down on it at school and signed up for eighteen credits."

"Good," my mother said with finality. "I hated to see her floundering. She's too bright for that."

She hadn't seemed to be floundering so badly to me, probably because I had been the one handing her the beer when she was supposed to study. I hung my jacket over the back of my chair.

"Well," my father said, "what about you? Did she inspire you to get a little more serious?"

"Sort of," I said. I examined the cracked skin of my hands and got up to get a squirt of moisturizer from the kitchen. "I'm still taking kind of a reduced load while Kate needs more help," I called to them. "But the classes I have are pretty easy." I came back in, rubbing my hands, and added, "I also branched out and took an art history course. Italian."

The redirect seemed to work. Mom nodded with satisfaction. "Don't sell the book back for seventeen dollars or whatever fraction they pay," she said, pointing at me over her glass.

"Just take a class, Mom," I said. "It would be a lot more helpful than just the book."

"One of these days," she said. "Maybe when you're done." Then she crossed her legs, leaning back in her chair, and said, "When will you make up the credits, this summer?"

"I'm not sure," I said. I had been debating whether to mention this, but they seemed fairly relaxed. I went for it. "It depends. I might be taking a trip right in the middle of the schedule."

Their eyebrows rose in unison. "Where to?" my dad asked.

"I don't know quite where yet. It's Kate's thing. She was thinking maybe Italy. She'd have to rent a house, obviously, something without steps, and maybe bring some people."

My parents exchanged a look.

"I'm going to get some water," my father said, standing. "Becky? Marianne?" My mother and I shook our heads. He nodded and disappeared into the kitchen.

Mom and I sat silently for a moment. "That's really something," she said.

"I know." I was nodding a little too heartily, I could feel it. I straightened up my posture and folded my hands on the table before me. "I'd never get the opportunity otherwise."

Something flitted across Mom's expression and disappeared. "You can save your money, of course," she said. "Open a separate savings account and set up an automatic deduction kind of thing."

"Oh, I know. But that would be like youth hostels, and backpacking. I couldn't afford to go rent a house if Kate weren't going."

My father returned, setting a big glass of ice water on the table. None of us said anything for a moment. Sensing a good moment to flee, I started to get up and put things away.

"Bec," my dad said. He held up a hand, palm toward me. I sat back down. "I think it's great you've decided to help this woman," he began.

"Kate."

"Kate," he agreed. "I'm glad to see you lending a hand—"

"It's not charity work. It's a job."

"We realize that," my mother broke in. "And I'm glad you like it. But this is supposed to be about trying something new, not abandoning school for some menial job, no matter how fun it is."

I took a deep breath. My mother made it sound as though I'd just come across a TV show I really liked. "I wouldn't call it *fun*," I said. "It's not quite that . . . light."

She raised her eyebrows so far her whole forehead furrowed. "Okay, it's not fun, per se, but you enjoy it. You get to do things with this woman's money and lifestyle you might not otherwise. But you're in college for a reason," she pointed out. She sat back in her chair and eyed me. "Are you thinking of switching majors? To nursing, maybe?"

For some reason this had never occurred to me. School and Kate seemed so separate, I never would have thought to overlap them. "No," I admitted. "I hadn't thought about it."

"Don't overreact," she began soothingly, "but are you sure you're just not letting yourself be taken advantage of?"

There was a deadly silence for a moment. I became aware of the lightness of the falling snow outside the window, the music still playing faintly through the door, from my dad's radio in the garage. Mom and Dad both observed me warily, as though I might become violent. And for a moment I would have liked to throw something, or peel out of the driveway. I'd done that once or twice in my life. It was a satisfying way to end an argument.

But instead I made an effort to think through what I was going to say. I reached over and took a deep drink from my father's glass of water. So this was what they'd been thinking. I took a breath, then drank some more.

I set the empty glass back down in front of him.

"I'm not being taken advantage of," I informed them. My voice trembled slightly, and I concentrated on steadying it, but as soon as I began talking again it rose. "She pays well. I'm learning. You can enjoy something without getting taken advantage of, you know. Anyway, I'm learning, a lot, and I can save up more money now, and I don't even need rent—" I was stringing words together without quite knowing where I was headed.

"Rent?" My mother had become very still. "Is she paying your rent?"

I folded my arms, then unfolded them. I wasn't eloping. I didn't need to get all defiant. Really, I'd gotten a promotion. "I'm moving in with her," I said simply. "She needs someone at night."

"Well," my father said gently, "honey, shouldn't she have thought of that before she left her husband?"

My brief moment of calm split open. "Oh, goddamn it. I never should have told you about that."

I stalked into the kitchen. As soon as I got there I stared around me and realized I had nothing to accomplish in there and no one to yell at, so I turned around and stomped back out and added in a rush, "Of course she has no say in anything and should cling to any jackass who'll have her or even one who won't."

They stared back at me, mouths slightly ajar. Mom recovered herself first.

"Don't oversimplify," my mother said. "Kate has a right to make her own decisions"—a pointed glance at my father—"but you're not responsible for the results."

I stood there in the doorway, glaring but unable to think of any good arguments. Their patronizing way of saying Kate's name made me crazy. The tone when they mentioned her—and only if I had mentioned her first—was one I remembered from high school, when they invariably missed the mark as they tried to connect with me, asking me about "boys" instead of guys, how "The Rems" show had been.

I used to see it as pitiable ignorance, but it struck me now as sly. That gentle emphasis they gave her name—as opposed to the easy way they asked after Jill—was purposeful. They knew whatever I liked or even loved was a passing thing, so fleeting they need not even treat it as a fact.

So I hadn't followed through on every single thing my mother had pushed me into trying. What did she want? I had tried out for the plays and taken the music lessons. For a few years I had been a talented gymnast. So what if none of that had changed my life?

"My life is really different now," I said. I wasn't certain where this was going.

"We gather," said my father.

"Look, I'm not trying to make things even harder for this poor woman," my mother said.

The words actually made me recoil—I found I had taken a step backward into the kitchen. She made Kate sound so downtrodden and helpless. I saw how they imagined it: a shabby house; me springing for groceries when a government check mysteriously failed to arrive; Kate slovenly, wheedling, mawkish.

"I haven't *fallen* for anything," I said. "Jesus, I'm not an idiot!"

I headed past them and into the living room, where my bag was still on the floor. All I could think of to do was find a task and get away for a moment before I did something to make myself look like a fool or a child. The polite and reasoned veneer of the past three years since I'd left for school had dissolved so quickly I knew it must have been only a thin shell anyway. It was so ridiculous that I laughed bitterly to myself as I threw my bag over my shoulder. My father started to speak.

"I'm just taking it to my room," I said, and paused, realizing I'd banished myself to my bedroom at the age of twenty-one.

I shut my door behind me and sat down on the bed. I'd chosen a slightly ghastly shade of lavender paint in sixth grade, evoking a sort of sprigged-cotton, stale-cookies-and-tea atmosphere. The carpet in the corner near the window still bore a stained triangle from a shelving unit that had held a bunch of knickknacks—tiny glass rabbits, unicorns, and the occasional kitten—and trophies. They were probably in a box in the basement, unless Mom had thrown them out.

I lay back against the headboard, hands crossed over my belly, and breathed deeply. This was not a calming room. It was sluggish, the embarrassment of my own bad taste acted like a weight on my diaphragm, and I could still feel my heart pumping too fast, my face hot.

I pulled a pillow from beneath my head and put it over my eyes. It smelled faintly of bleach. What had I hoped to accomplish in telling them? I should simply have given them a new phone number and said I'd moved. They didn't have to know if I was gone for a few weeks over the summer, whether I was sweating in front of a fan or off sipping champagne and checking my travel bag for passports. I didn't really have to tell them a thing, but I'd wanted to talk about it. I was proud of myself.

WHEN I SHUFFLED OUT of my room an hour later, I went to the kitchen door and found my mother lifting the bottles from the paper bag where I'd packed them: a cognac Kate had recommended, whipping cream, a jar of peppercorns. I'd bought baby green beans instead of the woody, finger-thick ones at the market. I had planned to make steak au poivre, which my mother had never tried. I'd thought it would be festive. I'd been looking forward to cooking for her, and maybe that was part of the reason I chose the steak au poivre—I had planned to flame the cognac when they weren't expecting it.

She hadn't heard me come out of my room, and a glance out the front window revealed my father shoveling the front walk of its most recent dusting of snow. I watched my mother uncork the cognac and sniff it. "My," she muttered, examined the label, then sniffed again. She rattled the peppercorns. The whipping cream she put into the refrigerator.

I went into the kitchen and she turned, startled, a hand at her throat.

"Just me," I said. I took out the beans and a bowl and began snapping off the tops and tails.

"You didn't have to bring all this," my mother said. "There's no need to be so fancy. Really, just steaks are fine."

"I know they are," I said to the beans. The soft prickle of their fuzz on my fingertips, removing the tough floss of the strings, made me feel better. The steaks, which were sitting on a plate on the counter, were beautiful too, pomegranate reddish-purple threaded delicately with snow-white fat. I'd cook anyway; they didn't have to appreciate it. "I just thought it might be fun to show off a little."

fifteen

JILL HELPED ME MOVE in exchange for—her words—"the best meal of my life thus far."

"You can make me something," Jill informed me. She hefted a box full of hair gel, brushes, my single zippered bag of makeup, and shoes. "Or you can just buy me dinner. Someplace I cannot afford."

"You're enjoying the idea of me with a little more money, aren't you?"

Jill hefted a box full of sweaters. A purple sleeve dangled over the front. "You're not?"

We filled the trunks of each of our cars and that was about all it took. I didn't have a lot of stuff, and my room at Kate's was already furnished—we'd bought furniture for it back when she was renovating. Had I known I would live there I might have taken a more active role in planning it. But it was a lovely, quiet room that drew the sunlight in the morning and faced the garden in the backyard. I would have liked to push for my saffron paint, though. Maybe I still could.

A girl from Jill's program was moving into my room. I had sold my bed and bureau to her for fifty dollars. The bed was still in the center of the emptied room, stripped to its limp pancake of a mattress.

We shut the trunks of our cars. Jill brushed off her hands and looked at me. "Okay," she said. "I'll meet you at Kate's."

"I'm going to run back for one more spot check."

The saffron paint looked a little odd without framed posters on the walls and the copper pan reflecting the glow. Too bright, too full of effort. With everything else it had seemed cozy. My bed sagged in the middle. I counted myself lucky and maybe slightly immoral for having gotten fifty dollars for it. Maybe I should have felt nostalgic to see it go—memories and all. But I thought about Kate taking item after item from her old house, remembering this and rediscovering that, and for once I was glad I had nothing. I had some new clothes and makeup, a cookbook, a vibrator, and a copper omelet pan.

MY MOVE NECESSITATED A switch in caregiver schedules. Simone took on four mornings a week. Hillary took the afternoons, and I filled in the gaps and the nights. Against the doctor's wishes, we left Kate alone for a few hours a day, which she maintained was essential for everyone's sanity.

The emergency button was backup now. We bought intercom monitors to string between our rooms instead. The first night I slept there I turned on some music as I lay in bed, reading, then wondered if it was keeping Kate awake. I couldn't recall if the noise went both ways or not, so I turned the radio off and tried not to rattle the pages. I could hear her slightly through the monitor, the staticky, liquid tremble of her breathing. After the flu, then a cold, something just lingered in her chest, bubbling and viscous. The antibiotics hadn't quite kicked in. No one really came right out and said why it mattered so much, though we all knew. If she couldn't control her coughing or if her lungs didn't clear from a routine cold, she'd be hospitalized.

I had been hovering in the background a lot with my head poised on a level with her shoulder blades as I pretended to root around for the cake pan or the Cuisinart, listening.

"I think it's a little better," I said to Simone one evening. The three of us had taken to conferring as we arrived and left our shifts—pausing outside the front door after dinner, murmuring about how she'd sounded that day. Now we stood on the front porch, Simone holding a dish towel and shivering while I searched for my keys. Kate had gone to her room to read after dinner. We'd had a homey chicken and rice dish with a side of okra, which I'd found in an old issue of *Gourmet*. Unexpected preferences had surfaced in the months I'd been cooking: Hillary adored Mexican food, corn tortillas, chicken with lime, and salsa loaded with more serrano peppers than the rest of us could handle. I gave extras to her in a little side dish. Simone had a thing for oxtail stew and all mahogany-colored, winey meat dishes. All three of us turned out to adore okra, though this was the only food I'd ever heard Kate say she disliked.

Instead of cooking our meal at the end of my afternoon shift, I made it the first duty of my evening shift. The food was better this way; I had more time to shop, felt fresher, and cooked more complicated things. It could backfire if I got overly ambitious: I made lasagna the old-fashioned way and discovered it had been simplified for good reason. By then I was too far in to quit, so over a period of two hours I prepared the tomato sauce and béchamel sauce from scratch, sautéed the sausage, cut up the wide fresh sheets of pasta, while Hillary peered in occasionally and Kate periodically glided by with a bemused expression. When we finally sat down, I was supposed to be starting my shift and I was already filmed with sweat and exhausted.

"I think you should approach the dinners with a little more healthy fear," Kate had told me.

Now I dug around my bag while Simone, who was on duty that night, glanced back inside the house to be sure Kate hadn't come out from the bedroom.

"Is that rumbly thing gone?" she asked.

"I'm not sure. It was more a rattle. But I think it's softer."

She nodded, chewing her gum loudly. "Hill said she was definitely better Tuesday night," she informed me. "So I'll keep an ear out but I think we're okay for now."

At first I hadn't taken her lung problems as seriously as I knew I ought to. It just seemed hard to believe a mere cold might do that much harm. I was almost always there, or someone was, and I think deep down I believed I had some power of persuasion, as though I could lay hands on her and stop it. But soon after I returned from my parents' house she had had a coughing fit.

These were not as minor as they sound—a real fit could last for ten minutes, in which she gave her body over to it completely because she had no other option. I was no help. For one thing, it took me far too long to realize she couldn't stop. What was worse, and what I later castigated myself for, was that I was in my bedroom, reading, tuning out the sound of her cough until I realized how long it had been going on.

By the time I came in she was half-hunched over in her chair. Her head had fallen forward from the force of the fit and the short wings of hair hid the sides of her face. From beneath her hair her eyes rolled in my direction, shining with moisture, showing the white. One of her hands had fallen from the armrest and dangled near the wheel.

I knelt by her, trying to remember what to do. Finally I bent her forward, holding on to her carefully, in the hope it would help her lungs expel fluid. I had the urge to give her the Heimlich though I knew it was unlikely she needed it. I could hear from the cough that she wasn't choking on something, and she hadn't eaten by mouth in days. But what had I been told to do? I just stood there, holding her in a bent position with her shoulders near her knees. I was casting about for the cordless phone as I held her, wondering where the fuck I had put it because I never just put it back and she hated that and now I knew why. If it didn't clear I'd leave her and call an ambulance, I told myself. I felt her lurch and shake. She sucked in a breath that sounded as tight and ragged as a tunnel in a cave. Then the coughs began to space further apart, and when it was over I wiped her mouth with a tissue and sat on the ground next to her chair, exhausted.

When she'd gained her breath back fully she said, "We have to discuss something."

I sat down on a chair opposite her. "Okay." I knew what was coming. I had done a terrible job with the coughing fit. I should have called 911 before I did anything.

"Do you remember that you *must* ask me before you call an ambulance?" she asked. *Must.* I watched her lips curve in over her teeth as she said that, thinking it was a useful word for her, so unmistakable, forceful. Then I considered what she had said. I had forgotten until then that I was supposed to check with her.

"Right. Of course."

"I need to count on you to force yourself to pause, no matter how it feels." She swallowed, grimacing slightly as she did. She caught my eye and held it. "You have to realize what happens once I'm in there," she told me.

"You make it sound as though no one would listen—"

She cut me off. "You think anyone will follow my orders? They can barely understand me." She paused to make sure I got that. I repeated it and nodded. "If I'm on a respirator I can't talk anyway. And it might take lawyers and court to disconnect it even if I told them to. I can live at home, with a lot of help, for now. After that . . ."

"There are nurses and therapists," I pointed out.

"They're busy. I'm privileged here. I have someone who takes care of only me."

"Several."

She nodded. "Several," she agreed. She swallowed again, her head dropping forward. I waited a moment to see if she could right herself and then, when she didn't, lifted her head again. "Thank you," she said. "You might ask me and I might say yes," she went on. "I won't know till then. But you cannot send me somewhere where I lose control of what happens to me. Do you understand how important this is?"

I nodded. "Okay," I said. I was thinking about how I'd panicked a minute before. I was promising her I'd do it right as though it were an incantation. If I said I would, I'd have to. I'd remember somehow. Kate was still watching me, her eyes bleary from the coughing spell. I got another tissue and pressed it to her lower lashes, watched the damp stain the tissue.

"And if I tell you not to call, and . . ." She paused, shook her head. Our eyes locked, and she raised an eyebrow, knowing I understood. "You would have to wait awhile too, afterward. If I've made that choice, I don't want some ER doctor to bring me back."

"What about Simone and Hillary?"

She left her eyes closed as I blotted the other eye. Then I sat back. "They know," she said.

THROUGHOUT MARCH I HAD been hoping uselessly for spring, but the night I took Jill to Le Champignon for her thank-you dinner, the wind was blowing wet and chilly. It whipped our hair into our eyes and mouths as we ran from the car to the door. As we ascended the stairs into the restaurant the warmth and chatter settled over us, the clink of silverware, the faint strings of violins. We glanced at each other as the maitre d' took our limp cloth coats and hung them along a row of buttery leather and fur.

I used to walk by this restaurant when I skipped class and went to the Wednesday market instead, looking over the menu they posted in a glass window and making a note to look up some of the words. One of my old notebooks had various culinary terms scratched on it over the marketing theories.

"Are you sure we shouldn't split this?" Jill whispered.

"Positive," I said.

In fact, Kate had given me her credit card. This had come after a long, troublesome week. For the first time I had said to her, "You don't need to," and meant it. Since I had moved in I often found myself wandering pointlessly around the house while Hillary or Simone helped Kate with the insurance or fund-raising phone calls.

My first morning there, Hillary was on the early shift and Kate was already reading in the front room near the window when I got up. She glanced over at me, smiling good morning, not moving her head too much so the page-turner didn't move before she was ready.

As I threw yogurt and frozen blueberries into the blender, I listened to Hillary on the phone: ". . . on behalf of Kate Norris of the ALS Society." Who would give her money when she sounded so flat? You had to sound serious but bright. I pulsed the blender, the motor shrieking, and Hillary covered the phone and glanced up at me, the light flashing off her glasses.

"Oops," I'd whispered.

She shook her head and went back to her phone call. "Also called Lou Gehrig's disease. Right."

I poured the smoothie into a glass and set the blender noiselessly in the sink. I started to walk away but then returned and washed up instead. Kate was a neat freak. I didn't want to be a slob my first week. I was still in my pajamas. I had lain in bed and listened to Hillary come in that morning and get Kate up and into the shower. I could hear the drawers opening, the toilet flush, the water running. It was like spying. So this was how Hillary did this and that, and this was how they talked when they were together. I'd lain there, thinking Hillary wasn't quite as deadening as I usually made her out to be. In the morning, I thought, and I'd bet at night too, her low steady voice seemed soothing. I'd bet her movements were all slow and careful and trustworthy.

The switch in hours, now that nights and not days were my main responsibility, meant that a lot of my old duties were taken care of. In order to keep a few nights off I had retained some mornings, and I found those a bit of a relief. I set my alarm early, got into the shower by six thirty, and was tending to Kate, my hair wet and brushed back in a headband, by seven. At those moments it felt like my old job, and I felt less like a freeloader, drinking tea I hadn't paid for and eating one orange when I wanted two. Frankly, by the time Kate and I had stocked up the kitchen to feed an additional, non-shake-drinking person in addition to our dinners, I was both pampered and pointless. (There had been some leftover condiments, baking supplies, and spices from the previous house, but a lot were items Evan enjoyed—a certain type of grainy mustard, star anise, which Kate never liked—I quietly threw them out.) I believed I was costing her far more money than my presence in the house was worth. She didn't need me most nights, except for the occasional bathroom trip, and I found it difficult to get over the idea that I should be working madly all night if she didn't call for me. So when I wasn't sleeping, I cleaned or cooked, straightened up compulsively. Finally, the morning of my dinner with Jill, Kate told me I didn't need to dust the windowsills when she paid someone else to do that. Then she added, "You're going to dinner with Jill tonight, right?"

"Yup," I'd said. "We're going to gorge ourselves. In a demure way."

She'd laughed, and said, "Get my purse, would you please?"

I stalled as I walked over to the table with her bag in my hand. "Take the American Express," she said. "Treat yourselves."

"I haven't done anything for you," I'd said. I tried to speak softly because Lisa was in the next room. I held on to Kate's purse but didn't take out her wallet. I had the money for once, and I had planned to write a check for dinner. To be honest, I was looking forward to it, to signing with a little flourish and overtipping.

"You moved," she retorted. "Jill helped you. People always give things when friends help move."

"A twelve-pack and a pizza, not a six-course French meal. It's too much. You're paying me to sleep," I told her.

Kate had given a big, rattling sigh. "Please let me give this to you," she said. "Do you realize how lucky I am that I even have the money to employ you? I'm grateful. This is me being grateful."

"But I feel like your—your kid," I said. I had almost said "mistress" but caught myself. I was thinking of kept women in old movies, all marabou and nail polish, but I knew I had teetered on the edge of invoking Cynthia instead. We tried not to talk about her. We blocked all the chinks in our conversation to prevent her slipping in.

"If you were my kid I would never send you to Le Champignon," she said. "I probably wouldn't even buy you tacos." She gave the purse another pointed look. "And I know what caviar costs," she added. "So I'd better see some on there."

THE MAITRE D' SEATED US near a window, pausing, holding the wine list up against her chest as we settled ourselves. She handed it to me and then said, "How's Ms. Norris?" I blanked for a moment, then realized she meant Kate, who at one time had been a regular.

"Oh, she's great," I said, recovering. "How did you know?"

The maitre d' gave me a mysterious smile. "She had her friend phone and ask us to take special care of you tonight," she said. "Please give her our regards."

When the maitre d' had strode away, her long skirt swishing around her legs, Jill and I looked at each other.

Jill raised her eyebrows at me.

"She and Evan used to come here a lot," I explained.

"Oh. Lucky. What do you suppose 'special treatment' means?" Jill asked.

"I'm not sure," I told her. "Maybe we get a massage."

I opened the wine list and recognized nothing, so we asked for glasses of champagne. There was a pause while we studied our menus, and then I said, "You look really good, you know. I like your hair."

Her hair was no longer scarlet but auburn, and the effect against her skin was kinder and warmer. She was wearing big silver hoops and a black silk shirt, her mouth the color of a berry.

"Thanks." Jill blushed slightly. "I toned it down for interviews. I got this internship thing and just thought I should screw them into thinking they'd hired a professional."

"Well, I love your unprofessional look too," I said. "But you're graduating soon, et cetera."

"Et cetera," Jill agreed. She sipped her champagne. How adult we seemed, dressed up and out to dinner without parents or even boyfriends along. I liked this. I could develop a real taste for it.

"What's the latest with this trip this summer?" Jill asked.

"I'm doing a little research," I said. "In a way I want to push for Turkey, you know, or Bangkok, but then I remember that I'll be the one navigating all this. So we're thinking start small. Florence, maybe. Paris. It's all new to me anyway. Think you'll come?"

She rolled her eyes. "God, I hope so. Let me know when you have a date set and I'll see what work looks like." She chewed some ice and then said, "How are classes?"

"They're not bad. I'm just taking the two, you know, the Renaissance art and then the lit class."

Jill laughed. "You're not even taking anything in your major?"

I started giggling like a fool, trying to keep it quiet so we didn't seem unsophisticated. Next to us a woman with upswept ash-blond hair glanced our way over her wineglass.

"Not one pathetic marketing course?" Jill went on.

I caught my breath. "Oh god, I hate my major," I said. I started laughing again. "I hate ad people and marketing people. I think they're all full of shit."

"SPECIAL TREATMENT" TURNED OUT to mean courses we hadn't ordered but which kept arriving nevertheless, accompanied by thumbnail descriptions. Each tiny portion was set before us with a flourish, gleaming against the black plates like jewelry or tiny works of sculpture that demanded some admiration before we even thought of touching them. There was a fat ivory-and-coral lobster claw with pale green endive browned at the edges; thick coins of gold-and-garnet beets laid with chunks of bacon; a creamy, rosy-beige disk of duck's liver atop a doll-size salad of mushrooms and greens. I kept wondering how they had done this, asking myself if they had roasted the beets or boiled them, if you could get the endive like this just by searing it or whether it needed braising first.

"Wake up," Jill whispered.

"I'm sorry," I said. "How do you think they got this olive crust to stick on the lamb?"

"They have free labor to do it for them," Jill said. "Didn't you see that article in the *Cap Times?*"

"What, like slave labor?" I paused in chewing my lamb. "I wouldn't have come here if I thought they had some dicey illegal immigrant thing going on."

Jill sipped her water. "No, it's some apprenticeship thing. People come in and work for free because it's an education or an honor or something. I think a lot of high-end restaurants do it."

Now I remembered. I'd read part of it to Kate. "Just think, some unpaid geek might be back there plating our next course even as we speak. I'm kind of jealous, actually. I bet they taste everything."

By the time we had finished coffee and cognac and agreed to call a cab and get my car in the morning, I was leaning back in my chair, hazy with goodwill and dazzlement.

"Can you imagine the people who come here all the time?" Jill said.

"Sure. Evan and Kate did. Maybe now he and Cynthia do. But they probably don't disgrace themselves quite like this. Well. Maybe Cynthia does."

I was trying to imagine taking my parents to a place like this. After I'd cooked for her birthday my mother had conceded that just steak wouldn't have been as nice. But I could just hear them: my mother asking question after careful question before she finally ordered the chicken, my father going straight for the steak and asking for a baked potato.

I took a last sip of my coffee. I really couldn't see my parents here. It embarrassed and even hurt me a little that I didn't really want to.

Jill was looking thoughtfully around the room, which had gotten darker and quieter as other people finished their meals and ours kept going on. Her lipstick was long gone and her cheeks were flushed from the wine, a faint sheen across her nose. She—and I, I bet—looked a little worn and tired out by food and wine, like we'd both been made love to instead of cooked for. The music was interrupted every now and again by laughter from the bartender, a murmur from another table.

"How's life at Kate's?" Jill asked. She poured a little cream from a silver pitcher into her coffee. She normally drank it black but had informed me a few minutes before that she believed in using everything put before her at a good restaurant. Then she had used the tiny silver tongs to drop one lump of brown sugar and one lump of white sugar into her cup.

"It's good," I said. "It takes some getting used to. Someone else's house and all."

"Well, if you ever need to move back in just let me know."

"Why would I need to do that?"

Jill looked away. "No reason. Just if you decide it wasn't such a good idea."

I felt a plum-sized knot of misgiving gather just below my diaphragm. "You don't think it was?"

She shook her head and laughed lightly. "Of course it was. I just mean if something comes up, or whatever. I don't mean anything. You feel good about it, right?"

"Sure," I said. "I feel great."

I WOULD HAVE LIKED to go back with Jill to our old apartment and just sleep on the couch. I missed being back there after a long night, drinking coffee in the morning and arguing over whose turn it was to go for scones. Since I had left, we still saw each other once a week or so, for lunch or on Friday nights for fried cod and beer. It was a shock to me how much I missed her. I didn't have these throw-away moments with Kate, sitting around between school and work in the dead time of an afternoon, and running into each other, happily tipsy, in the living room at the end of a long night. At Kate's everything was organized, right down to when one of us would leave the house to give the other some space. Jill and I always stumbled into cooling-off periods like that when we realized we were arguing over whose teacup was in the sink, who'd bought the toothpaste that tasted like cough syrup.

It wasn't that Kate and I didn't get along. It just had taken me more time to get used to this new arrangement than I had expected. I had thought it would be easy to get comfortable in a house I already knew so well, so I was doubly surprised to find myself wandering back to my room and closing the door when Hillary or Simone was there. The house, I saw, became another place when they were in it. They moved through it differently than I did; I saw them set the remote and the flower vases in different spots than I would have, and I heard by the rhythms of the showerhead that they did not bathe Kate as I did. Hillary's showers were over quickly, and I imagined her standing three feet away, hosing her down like a Chevy. I detected the same scent hovering around Kate's skin each day Simone was there, and it turned out she used a lavender oil to massage her shoulders and arms after her shower. "Do you want me to do that too?" I had asked Kate.

"Oh, you don't have to," she said. "It's just a little extra Simone always does."

I heard in her voice that faint note of surprise at having to explain something to an outsider. It was a private thing, I gathered, a little ritual Simone had devised. I cooked, Hillary took her around for the brisk and boring errands, and Simone, who'd briefly attended massage therapy classes, rubbed her shoulders. It should have pleased me the way we divided up the duties of providing Kate with little comforts and pleasures here and there, but I found it discomfiting. I'd felt I knew the most intimate things, and did the most for her, was trusted the most by her, but maybe I wasn't. Maybe I lived here because I was the least of three evils. Maybe on my nights off Kate, blushing, asked Simone to get the blue butterfly out of the nightstand. Or maybe it was understood, and she didn't even have to ask.

EVENTUALLY, AFTER A MONTH or so, I felt less like a visitor. I would stay out in the living room, reading, forcing myself not to put the book down and jump up when Kate arrived with Hillary or Simone. This is my home too, I reminded myself, staring at the print on the pages. I can sit here and read in my home, on my couch.

When Lisa showed up her presence was like a blaring stereo. It stirred us up. She jolted the quiet of the atmosphere in Kate's house, her voice hoarse and loud where Kate's was so tiny and mine—I had recently realized—had become sympathetically, unconsciously soft. She strolled into the living room with glasses of wine or beers for each of us, pausing to swirl it under Kate's nose if it was one she liked. When Lisa was around I was furthest from feeling like a visitor, or even an employee.

"How's Jill?" she asked one night. We were sitting in Kate's bedroom watching *The Godfather*. I had put Kate against a pile of pillows on her bed, and Lisa and I had dragged a couple armchairs to each side of the bed.

"I saw her downtown the other night with this hot little thing," Lisa continued.

"That's Tim," I said. "She met him at her new job. She's deeply involved. Now she wants to fix me up with all his friends."

Lisa laughed. "She looks deeply involved," she said. She glanced at Kate. "The 'Guess what I'm going to do to you in the car' look."

"I think we all remember the look," Kate answered, with a sardonic roll of her eyes. "However long it has been since we had it ourselves."

I did know the look. When Jill talked about him her face took on a secretive, voluptuous expression, her gaze cast off to the side, eyelids slightly lowered, mouth opening just enough as she considered him that it showed the whiteness of her teeth. Every now and again a smile surfaced and disappeared again. It was that face that says you're thinking of something you won't share, but you'll keep it there with you, like extra money in your pocket. It was kind of maddening. I had forgotten about that sensation, but, seeing evidence of it, I felt how it had been that first time after Liam left the house, when I kept thinking of the backpack he'd pushed to the car floor.

Well. Good for her. Jill may have exuded such general contentment that Lisa could spot it twenty yards away, but I was becoming more distanced from sex every day, like a foreign language I'd forgotten to practice. At least I tried to practice. My Japanese purple wand had gone from whimsical purchase to sexual oxygen. The problem now was the monitor we'd strung between Kate's and my rooms in case of an emergency. I couldn't, wouldn't, fire up my vibrator with those around. Mine was only a speaker, not a transmitter, but the connection was too intimate, somehow, and I couldn't shake the sense that I'd be broadcasting my lonely passions into Kate's room and all over the house. I thought of turning off the monitor and switching it back on when I was done, but when I tried it once I was sure it only telegraphed my intentions: that suggestive click off to dead air and then, eventually, the sated, quiet static.

So instead I took sybaritic showers and baths, accompanied by ever-filthier narratives in my head. The baths felt secret and hidden, like when I was eleven or twelve and had just discovered the perfect use for the warm jet of the faucet. My parents never said anything about those baths, which often took forty-five minutes, and neither did Kate. (Unlike Kate, my mother occasionally had rapped on the bathroom door when, enthralled, I had probably run the water bill into the thousands. From where I lay with my ears beneath the warm shelter of the water and my eyes shut against the bright overhead light, the knock on the door was always startling, shocking me up through the water's surface like a criminal rejected from the depths of a puritan lake.)

Half the time it wasn't even that I was so desperate for sex itself. I wanted the distraction of it, the concentration that excluded everything else. Sex with myself satisfied something completely different from what sex with Liam had done. With him, self-awareness was so much of it, the way I felt him watching me, as though I must be so irresistible. But alone, I didn't do any of the things you see in magazines, the ones that tell you to admire yourself in the mirror and revel in your beauty and what have you. Alone I was an instrument, a working tool of the simplest sort.

When Jill offered to set me up with one of Tim's friends I didn't even pretend to hesitate for form's sake. I'm sure she had in mind some nice conversation over dinner, but I was thinking about the end of the night when I and whoever this guy was would get rid of the other two. I wanted out, out of my own body and out of my quiet bedroom. Let someone else join in.

Kate, of course, was in a similar dilemma, but the only solution we'd come up with for her was structure. I put the blue butterfly vibrator on her about once a week—often Thursdays, for some reason neither of us elucidated—and then went for a walk. I told no one about this, not Hillary or Simone or even Jill, and I don't think Kate ever said anything to Lisa. No one thought to ask me anyway. As I once had, most people were content to assume that Kate had forgotten sex when she got the diagnosis. I wasn't too embarrassed to admit what I did. Had someone implied there was anything unusual or distressing about the situation I would have protested. I think I might even have meant it. But whatever my involvement in her sex life, it was, as always, not mine to reveal. It was Kate's, and it remained the one topic we did not bridge with humor or self-mockery. Everything else was fair game, which made the taboo even stronger. Even Cynthia, whose name was close to verboten in our house, came up for the occasional jab, especially if Lisa were there to spur it. But we talked around the vibrator and the nights Kate chose to use it. She cast her gaze in its direction and I followed, and we didn't have to say a word.

Eventually I had decided I was wrong in assuming Hillary and Simone did the same thing for her. Kate still seemed mortified by the whole process. I couldn't imagine her putting herself through it with more than one person. Sometimes I thought I should just say something to her to break the tension, make reference to my visit to A Woman's Touch or leave a pornographic novel lying about—not to out Kate but to out myself. I thought it might be helpful to expose, so to speak, my own habits, just so we were both out there, equally vulnerable.

One evening, I strolled around the block, waving to neighbors and checking my watch to see if the hour had gone by. I had my winter coat on but unbuttoned. April had been even slower to warm up than usual, and we'd had more than one flurry. As I walked I began thinking about the butterfly. After the first time I put it on her I'd done a little Web research—unsure if I was being a good, clinical caregiver, figuring out precisely what my employer needed and wanted, or if I was intruding: She couldn't even come without me trying to figure out the physiological functions. What there was on the ALS sites was fairly general—the nerves weren't affected, and the muscles that affected sexual function weren't either. Then the sites went on to talk a lot about the partners, and intimacy, and touching. There was only so much I could take away from it, not being Evan, or an actual lover.

When had she bought the butterfly? Maybe it had been a gift from Evan years ago, a lagniappe before it had become a necessity. Or perhaps not. Perhaps she had bought it once she felt her hands giving way, the muscles getting softer and duller. (Was there a Web site or catalog out there that specialized in sexual fulfillment for the disabled? The idea almost stopped me in my tracks—if there wasn't, there should be. I felt brilliant.)

I kept picturing Evan presenting it to her as a gift, wrapped up by her plate at dinner one evening, balanced atop the ice in a bucket of chilled champagne. But even when I tried to think kindly of him I couldn't, and I imagined this as the most backhanded of gifts, the replacement, the turning away.

Why, I thought, stumbling over a tricycle on a sidewalk, did he get to go off and find sex somewhere else? Lately I just kept coming back to it, over and over. Why was it that he lived across town, rolling around naked and sweaty on a bed or a floor or the manicured lawn with Cynthia, while Kate and now I lived in a house so overheated with suppressed sexuality that it barely needed a furnace?

I turned the corner back to Chambers Street and checked my watch. An hour already. I jogged up the drive to the front door. I wanted Evan there with us, sleeping fitfully in a little room of his own, his skin constantly stippled with a rash of excitement until he finally gave in and spirited himself away for a solitary shower of his own, desperate for romance.

sixteen

I'M SORRY. I JUST . . . I feel awful," I said. I stood beside her bed, arms crossed over my breasts. Kate, on her belly, looked back over her shoulder at me, one eyebrow arched.

"How bad is it?" she asked. "I can tell it's bad."

"It's not so bad," I said, staring down at her skin. I was stalling. It was bad, but not as severe as I had feared at first: a bruise in the middle of one of her buttocks, but no breaking of the skin. The contusion was the size of my palm, plummy and vivid, with an oval splotch in the center that would soon turn yellow, like a serpent's eye. I was more worried about a red patch I'd noticed near the base of her tailbone, which could be the beginning of a pressure sore. We moved her from her chair to her bed to a recliner several times a day, and padded everything in sight with foam and sheepskin, but with bad circulation and her bones pressing on her skin, sores were a big risk. Looking at that red spot now, which could have been a sore and could also just be a mark from the fall, I felt as if I'd just hit something with my car. My job included keeping her free of sores—and not dropping her—and I'd fucked it all up.

"It's not terrible," I said. "Really." I wasn't saying anything about the spot for a few minutes, though I would tell Hillary to look. I touched the red spot with my fingertip. It felt as cool and soft as the rest of her skin. It blanched white when I pressed lightly.

"Stop it," Kate said. Then she closed her eyes for a moment. "I'm sorry. I know it was an accident."

"I know it hurts," I said. "I don't know how I let you slip."

It had happened as I was getting her from her wheelchair to her bath chair—one moment I was lowering her right in place, and the next her skin was terribly slippery, and I felt a sickening lurch as I lost hold of her. Her buttock had hit the arm of her chair, hard enough to bruise, especially since she had no extra fat to cushion the blow. Now it hurt her to sit, and I had to keep her on her belly, in bed, for at least a day, and when I'd checked her bruise I'd seen the red spot for the first time. It was mortifying, all the attention we had to pay to a bruised ass, a bruised ass I'd caused. She was angry at me and trying not to be, humiliated and trying not to show it.

"It could've been worse," she said now as I pulled her panties back up and her nightgown down from where it had been bunched around her waist. I set a frozen gel-pack on the curve of her butt and excused myself to go to the bathroom.

I washed and dried my hands, staring at myself in the mirror. I needed a shower and a few pounds of makeup if I was going on this stupid blind date tonight. Kate had called for me at four that morning, I'd dropped her in the shower at six, and nothing had gone well since. She hated being on her stomach or her side the whole day, stuck in bed, and it was making her irritable and me guilt-ridden. I splashed water on my face and went back in.

"You want the window cracked or anything?" It was still chilly outside, but the room smelled musty and close. I'd meant to change the sheets today.

She shook her head. "I told you, I'm really too cold for that. Open a window out front, if you need to, but close my door. Please."

She was facing the television, one hand crooked up toward her shoulder with the remote beneath it. "What do you need?" I asked. I settled another blanket over her. "Can I move you, or give you a back rub, or put on some music? I can read to you, if you're bored with TV."

She shook her head. "Nothing, thanks. No, wait. Maybe a hit of the sleeping stuff."

This meant grinding up a sleeping pill, dissolving it in water, and running it through the feeding tube. It was such a production that I wished we had a liquid form, maybe dispensed with an eye dropper. Moreover, I hated the pills because she looked waxen and unreachable hours after taking them, her eyes unfocused, white strings of saliva clinging to the corners of her mouth. It frightened me how ruthlessly the medication knocked her out, the way she could barely speak as she came out of it, much less crack a joke. But it was the wrong day to suggest anything else, so I went back to the kitchen to get it ready.

I got out two of her sleeping pills and set about crushing them in a little mortar and pestle designated for this alone. Then I scraped the powder into a glass of water and stirred, watching till I didn't see any particles. I could have used some rest too. I needed to get out of the bedroom that smelled of old laundry and the heavy coconut moisturizer I anointed her with each day, away from the endless strobe and blather of the television set. I needed to get out of the house, go somewhere I wasn't a liability. How had I lost my grip on her? I kept imagining the moment, but worse: What if I'd really dropped her on that ceramic tile? I looked at the floor of the shower, its gleaming white squares. I could have knocked her out, or maybe even killed her. Her eyes had flicked open and the exclamation that flew from her mouth was made unintelligible by surprise.

I went back to her with the water glass and the feeding tube tucked under my elbow. "Ready?" I asked. She nodded, and I put another layer of foam beneath her hips, where I had to roll her over to get to the valve.

I tipped her over, careful to keep from touching the bruise directly. A muscle strained across one side of my back. I must have pulled it when I tried to catch her. Kate watched me while I pushed up the nightgown and opened the valve, fitting in the feeding tube and pouring in the medicated water. We stayed silent while the water drained into her. When it was done I removed everything, patted her belly with a towel where a bit of water had dripped off the tube, and resituated her on her side.

"Thank you," she said.

I turned off the television but left the remote beneath her hand. She closed her eyes, though I knew it hadn't put her to sleep that fast, and I turned out the light and closed the door quietly behind me.

There was still a ton of stuff to do—she had needed me so much today that I hadn't had a chance to straighten the front room, do the

YOU'RE NOT YOU 199

laundry, or eat a better lunch than a carton of yogurt. I felt filthy, my hair unwashed and my face shiny. God, maybe the bedroom smelled stale because of me.

It was five o'clock. Hillary would be here soon. I'd start the laundry; she could finish it and probably even change the sheets without waking Kate. I couldn't ask her to straighten the front room because it was all my stuff, but maybe she'd hate it so much she'd be compelled to clean. I should clean it up before I got in the shower. I had the time, and I was in the doghouse whether Kate would admit it or not. But I just couldn't face it right then, any of it. I felt like a housewife with a kid who hated me, and the kid was right.

I started to stack some magazines, but stopped. I wouldn't touch any of it, not the library books and magazines scattered over the table, the pairs of shoes beneath the couch, or the coffee mugs on the end table. I was going to shower, slap on some makeup, and go out for a drink before I met this guy, Mark, who Jill thought I'd like so much. I couldn't even recall why she thought we'd hit it off. She was probably dead wrong, just trying to steer me away from anyone with any remotely Liam-like qualities solely to make the point. As I ran the shower and dropped my dirty clothes in a limp pile on the floor, I decided I didn't care who this guy was. I was going to blow off some steam whether I liked him or not—if he was a fun, nice guy, so much the better. If not, I'd get drunk and ignore him till he went away.

AS IT HAPPENED, I didn't wait for him to go away. I followed him home instead. Mark lived in an apartment on the second floor of a house on Spaight Street. The hallway outside his door smelled of cedar.

"I think I only have beer," he said. He was struggling with the lock.

"Beer's fine." Actually I didn't think I would drink a beer. I wanted water, or better yet, caffeine, something to keep me awake and alert. Once I had known, back at the bar, that I was coming here with him, I'd switched to Coke. Who knew when I'd get this chance again? I wasn't going to waste it by ending up hazy and frustrated, my nerves dulled from drinking.

Mark got the lock open and held the door open for me. I went ahead of him into a small front room. There was a brown couch, the kind you inherit from your parents, a little television, and a fish tank that glowed in the corner. I went over to it and peered in. I could smell the odor of the water, the faintly sulfurous, fishy smell of the jar of food. Inside the tank a couple fish swam serenely in and out of fake coral, all graceful fins and bulging eyes and lips.

"They look like socialites," I said.

"Huh?"

"Nothing. Just—the facelift look." I wanted to stop talking, I had been talking all night. It wasn't doing me any favors. He came over next to me and looked into the tank, grinning.

"I see what you mean," he said. "I've been thinking of them as Goldie Hawn, but now I know why."

I felt his hands on the collar of my coat, one cold finger brushing against my neck.

I let him slide it off my shoulders. As he turned to put it in the closet, Mark said over his shoulder, "Their names are Silvio and Annette, by the way."

"Are you Italian? Or are the fish?"

He came back over, handing me a green bottle of beer. "My great-grandparents," he said. "Their names were Silvio and Annette."

"Oh. Well, that's . . . that's really odd."

Mark looked pleased. "Well, I didn't know them," he said. "Not that this exactly makes me close to them. I just liked the names."

I sprinkled a little food on the surface of the water. "I'm glad they're not those fighting fish," I said, for something to say. "I hate guys who have those."

He took a sip of his beer. I watched his fingers curl around the bottle. "No *Soldier of Fortune* subscription either," he said. He sat down on the armrest of the couch and watched me. I was only a few feet away, and it seemed to be the time to go stand between his legs and lean down to kiss him, so I did. I was nervous and brittle, trying not to be jumpy. At the bar we'd been dancing, and now I wished for that sweaty heat, the bass beat coming up through my shoes and thumping through my lungs, and the excuse to speak into each other's ears.

It was dead quiet in his apartment, and when I kissed him the only real sound in the room was a faint murmur at the back of his throat, an

intake of breath when I kissed his neck. He smelled of sweat and something green and herbal, maybe pine. How lovely to touch someone
who didn't smell of blossoms or fruit, whose limbs were thick and
whose hands dwarfed mine. His skin scraped me if I rubbed it in the
wrong direction, like a shark's. I felt his teeth against my tongue. Even
his hair was coarse.

I had been in the bar a half hour before they arrived, nursing a glass
of wine and flipping through a magazine. By the time I saw the three of
them come in the front door the light in the place seemed to have softened, the murmur of the other patrons a cozy swell around me. They
headed straight to a table, Jill glancing around as she seated herself. I
finished off the glass of wine and left the magazine and its soothing
vapidity on my chair for someone else. I was too relaxed even to regret
the brusqueness with which I'd given Hillary a rundown of the day—
though I'd made sure to tell her to check the red spot—before jogging
out of the house at six.

This guy was so polite that he actually stood up to shake my hand
when I walked up to the table. As he did, Jill had raised her eyebrows
behind his back, as if to say, *None of our friends are this nice.* He was pleasant looking in a pale-skinned way. He had a mole on his left cheek,
which is something I have always hated in a man. I seated myself on his
right side.

The four of us drank and listened to the band until I ran out of polite chatter. Mark let me sit quietly for a moment, then asked me to
dance. At first, sweaty and knocked together by the swaying hips of the
surrounding dancers, I wasn't sure how much I really wanted to be
there at all. I had glanced back at the table, where Jill and her
boyfriend were kissing. Mark took my hands and raised them up,
twirled me around. We didn't really have a clue what we were doing,
but he didn't care, he was laughing, and it made me like him more.

We had danced awhile longer, stopped trying to talk above the music. He drew me to him, just slightly, a question. Not the presumptuous arms around the waist, the shove to your pelvis that some guys
tried to bring off. His sideburns were dark with sweat, and he lifted my
hair off my neck and twisted it against my head to cool me off. I looked
him over and saw that his face was shadowed and his mouth serious. It

was this concentration in a man that I had missed so much, this attention, and I thought, I remember this.

In bed he got confident, silent but for an occasional murmur of my name, and I pushed myself up with my palms against his shoulders. I was moving faster and faster, concentrating so hard that each thrust was like striking flint. I was thinking, Oh thank God he's not a whisperer, I just want to do this, and he gripped me around my hips and pressed his head back into the pillows, and kept quiet, as though he understood.

AT THREE I JERKED awake. I was sure I'd heard something—a scrape, a thud. I sat up on my elbows, heart pounding, and looked around, trying to orient myself. After a moment the bedroom, my clothes on the floor, and the dark shape snoring lightly next to me ordered themselves again. I breathed deeply, trying to calm my pulse. I'd been waking up like this lately, ever since I moved to Kate's. Once or twice a week I tore through a layer of sleep as though I were coming up through the surface of an ocean. The sounds that woke me never turned out to be anything. Just a murmur from the intercom that revealed itself to be a dream, a car driving past.

I got up and brushed my teeth with his toothbrush, then combed my hair into a ponytail and wiped off stray mascara. I felt tired, hard-used, soreness starting to flare through me, but it felt good. I felt clear and tranquil, ready to sleep. Thank god I'd stopped drinking. I would remember everything.

He was awake when I went back into his bedroom, lying on his side and watching me.

"You're leaving?"

"I'm sorry," I said. He gave me a look of mild skepticism. "I actually am. But I work for this woman and I told her I wouldn't stay out all night."

"Oh, right," he said. "Jill said you were a caregiver."

"Some caregiver," I muttered.

"Sorry?"

"Nothing." I zipped up my jeans.

"What do you do for her at night?" he asked. "Or are you there just in case?"

I zipped up my boots. "Sometimes she has trouble breathing," I said. I stared at the pointy brown toe of my boot. I'd gone off for a one-night stand right after hurting her and drugging her. She'd asked for the drug, but still. It frightened me to think of Kate alone. Since I had moved in I had realized how quiet the house and neighborhood became after ten, which was probably why I jerked from sleep with every creak. It terrified me to think how vulnerable I had left her, only the button beneath her finger if someone broke in. A burglar, a rapist, could come in the window and she'd be as helpless as in a nightmare.

I stood up and put on my jacket, casting about for my purse. I just wanted to get home.

Mark ran his hands through his hair and sat up, reaching for his pants. "I'll walk you to your car."

"You don't have to," I said. "This is my old neighborhood."

A smile flashed up at me in the darkness. "I know."

Outside the temperature had dipped again. Here it was nearly May, and the forecasters were still assuring us this was to be the last cold spell ("I'd eat rat poison if I thought it would bring on spring," Kate had said that morning). A few snowflakes drifted by the light of the streetlamps. I could hear distant music from someone's house, laughter from the direction of the Jamaican joint I used to go to for brightly colored mixed drinks that might kill you if you had more than two. I could have walked awhile longer in this neighborhood. I wanted to go to the biker bar and play Patsy Cline on the jukebox, or take a walk and see who was on their porches sneaking in one last joint before bed. Mark held my hand, swinging it between us, and I thought about coming back sometime when I knew Kate wasn't alone, asking him to walk with me, showing him where I'd lived. I dismissed the thought a moment later. No one else was ever that interested in your old neighborhood. Especially since he still lived there.

We paused at the trunk of my car. I jingled my keys. He smoothed his straight dark hair with both hands.

"I don't suppose you want to be called," he said.

I looked at him, trying to discern if he meant it or just didn't know what else to say.

"I do like a good phone call," I said.

Then I kissed him and got into my car. I sat there a moment, watching him in the rearview mirror as he waved and headed back up the empty street, hands stuffed in the pockets of a gray flannel jacket. I couldn't have handled a trendy guy right then. No one in a bowling shirt, no one with facial hair. He was like a steak when you craved the iron. I started the engine, which rumbled ominously, and turned the heat to high. The seat was stiff and cold. It wasn't any warmer in the car than on the street. I looked around to see if I'd left a window open, and it was then I caught the scattering of hardware and glittering window glass in the seat and on the floor, the glint of a few nuts and screws in the streetlight, the empty mouth in the dashboard. Someone had stolen the stereo.

seventeen

THE NEXT MORNING KATE said she could sit again with some extra padding. She gave me a smile and said, "It's not as bad as I thought it'd be." I'd turned away, even more relieved than I'd have guessed, to get the extra sheepskin and some foam. The red mark was gone, but I'd told her about it in case she had any pain. I'd only felt guiltier since I woke up at Mark's and made my way home. It wasn't fair that I could hurt her, accidentally or not, and then debate whether to tell her what I saw on her own body. It wasn't right that I hadn't brought it up, and it wasn't right that I'd passed it off to Hillary and then dashed out to have a good night. I was so relieved to see her look at me again that I decided I wouldn't mention how late I'd gotten back. It wasn't an issue of a curfew, of course. But I didn't want to remind her of what I got to do.

I bundled her up against the lingering chill and we went to the first farmers' market of the season. We bought what we could: spikes of rhubarb and hard blocks of white butter; potatoes that had been cellared all winter; tiny, stunted greens.

We toured the capitol square slowly, me sipping on a cup of coffee and swinging a mesh bag that was disappointingly empty. The light had that fragile chalkiness mornings have in winter and early spring. I saw now that I had been too excited for the opening of the market, which, Kate had warned me, was more of a stage-setting than a true market for the first few weeks. But I had always missed out on the spring markets before, and I insisted on seeing them this year. Against all logic I had thought some sly farmer would have managed something glorious and deep green, or pried a few morels from the frosty ground. The farmers had coaxed what they could out of the mud, and it wasn't much.

"I read somewhere that you should wait to plant till after a dogwood blooms," I said. "That's how you know the frost is over."

Kate nodded. A week ago we'd tried to plan for her garden, which I had promised to plant this year, but the day we sat down to make lists had been so cold, the sun so watery, that we'd looked at each other and sighed, as hopelessly as if we wanted to plant a mango tree.

Kate was wearing a crimson knit cap with a brim that hid her face. She had to look up to me for me to understand her, and when she did I saw her cheeks bore a mottled red stain from the chill. Her eyes were teary and pink-rimmed. I reached down and wiped away the moisture that had seeped from one corner.

"Are you too cold?" I asked her. "We can go. There's not much here. I'm sorry I made you come with me."

She shook her head. "You didn't make me," she said. I shook my head once and she repeated it for me. "Let's at least go all the way around."

So we kept going, watching the farmers pile their folding tables with what little they had. We'd arrived as soon as it opened, at seven, because we were already up. I had gotten into bed at three thirty after coming home from Mark's house, and just before five I had woken to the sound of Kate wheezing, her breath sounding as though it were catching on splinters. I went in to her room and sat on the edge of the bed. I had turned her from her stomach to her side, taken her hand, and watched her face, switching on a lamp even though she squinted against it. She looked down at her hand, the finger above the emergency button, held away from it. "Did you press it?" I asked, and she shook her head vigorously, looked pointedly at it, trembling, until I offered to move it away from her hand. Her chest rose and fell in jerks, the cords in her throat leaping and going slack with each gasp. She fell from wheezing into coughing, a low liquid cough, and I sat her up against the headboard, wrapping the blanket around her shoulders, forgetting the bruise until she winced.

"Let me call a doctor, just to be safe," I kept saying, but she shook her head as she coughed, her eyes screwed shut. I replaced the blanket as it fell off her shoulders. Finally, the slack ribbon of her mouth closed and she took a cautious swallow and a slow breath. We looked at each other. She looked as wan as I had ever seen her in the light from the bedside table, her eyes swollen and damp-lashed, skin pale as her nightgown.

Neither of us could get back to sleep, so we turned on the television in her bedroom and flipped through cable until six, when she said, *Just fuck it, let's go.* Still exhausted as I drove to the capitol, I had practically sideswiped a construction barrel. The swerve had jostled Kate against her seatbelt, and my own locked tight around me, leaving me exhausted and panicky at the same time, my sluggish heart shocked into a gallop. It wasn't until we got to the market that I began to calm down.

We paused to look at planks of green onion and some jarred cherries from last year. The honey and beeswax vendors were there at least, and the guy who sold eggs, but there seemed to be long spaces between the tables. Everyone had their hoods up to shield their faces from the wind. The sky was clouding over, and what I thought might have been a cigarette ash in the wind turned out to be a stray snowflake. It landed on Kate's red hat and melted into the knit. The shawl I'd put over her hand had fallen off, and her fingers were curled like a crab claw, the skin purplish and crinkled.

"Listen," I said, depressed and, suddenly, faintly frantic. "I'll make you something tonight. You can go crazy and really eat something, for once, right?" I was tucking the blanket in tight around her hands, looking up at her face. She was watching me, looking amused and drained. If she made a joke now I couldn't handle it. If she made a joke I'd have to walk away and leave her to keep from throwing down the mesh bag so that the eggs broke and the frozen butter cracked. "I'll make something that won't give you a coughing fit," I told her. "Lobster bisque. Beef soup. Eggs and truffle oil."

Kate tipped her head forward to clear her throat. The momentum of moving her head overtook her; her chin dropped toward her chest. Her hat slipped off her head and into her lap. When I righted her, easing her head back upright with a finger beneath her chin and replacing the hat, she said, "That's nice of you. But let's just head home. I need that nap now."

FOR DINNER THAT NIGHT, Simone and I had tagliatelle with lemon and cream sauce. I'd found a little fresh tarragon in the fridge and stirred it in at the end. I wasn't really in the mood for something so heavy, but it seemed rich and silky and I hoped Kate would agree to a taste of the sauce. She let me touch a spoon filmed with the sauce to her tongue, but that was about it.

Kate looked much better than she had that morning. When we'd gotten back from the market I'd put her to bed and she was still sleeping when Simone arrived and I left for an appointment to fix the window on the Honda. Kate had pointed out I couldn't very well drive around with a plastic bag taped up around the hole, but the stereo just seemed like too much to deal with right then. I was driving the short routes again, trying to enjoy silence instead.

"Somebody already bought them the KitchenAid, the upright mixer," Simone was saying now.

Simone slurped a little on a noodle and patted her mouth delicately. I was struck anew by how lovely her manners were. She and Hillary both ate slowly and neatly, knife in their left hand, fork in their right. I was always switching hands to cut things, which in comparison was inelegant, at best. I'd begun to suspect they knew each other from finishing school.

Kate murmured something and Simone watched her and then said, "They don't cook? Why'd they register for it then, to hock it?"

"Who's getting married?"

Simone glanced at Kate for permission and then answered, "Kate's nephew. From the religious side."

I smiled into my water glass. "Have fun."

Simone twirled a thread of pasta around the tines of her fork. "It's on the eleventh. That's your Saturday. I checked." Kate laughed.

"Shit."

"How about the goose down comforter?" Kate said. "That's pointless extravagance. No one needs a goose down comforter."

We watched her, both briefly perplexed over deciphering "extravagance," then agreed.

"Of course," I said, "they might need a good set of knives."

"True," Kate said. "Okay, I'll be practical."

"I'll order them before I go," said Simone.

"I can do it; it's my turn after dinner," I said.

"Oh, we were looking at the registry site before; it's just as easy if I take care of it."

Since I had switched to nights, Simone seemed to have discovered a well of efficiency which, Kate told me, was truly impressive. The nutrition shakes were always fully stocked, the wine rack piled with bottles for guests, dry cleaning picked up, and library books dropped off on time. It wasn't unusual for me to find the daily ration of pills already crushed and labeled in individual plastic tubs. Apparently Simone had also turned into a bulldog of a fund-raiser, and a few weeks earlier I had come home to find her apologizing profusely to Ted the wheelchair distributor for accidentally elbowing him in the temple when he tried to lift Kate without asking.

Nice work, I said to her that day. We were waiting for Kate to finish in the bathroom. Simone said, *You can't believe how nice that is to hear. Especially since I was such a jackass when I started here.*

No, you weren't, I said, and I meant it. Why had I been so hard on her at first?

Now she finished the last of her pasta and turned back to us with a pleased sigh. "Fantastic, Bec. Thanks. What're you guys going to do tonight?" she asked. "Hang out? Go to a movie?"

"We should get back to travel plans," I said brightly. "You did all that research and it's just sitting there."

Kate was gazing past me. "We should," she said. "I'll get to it." She flashed a smile but it was unfocused, offhand, and more in the direction of the window than me.

eighteen

I REALLY HAVE TO get my stereo fixed," I said. I fiddled with the radio in Kate's car. "My car is just silent. It's so quiet I can hear every weird noise it makes but I'd rather just not know what's set up house inside my engine."

"It's been over a month," Kate scolded. "I thought you loved that stereo. You were insane about it when you bought it."

"I know," I said, "but it was over so fast. It's like I had a little stereo interlude and now it's finished. You look good in that dress, by the way. It shows off your hair."

We were on our way to her nephew's wedding. The dress was bright blue silk, its neckline draped over the shelf of her clavicle and loosely around her midriff. The skirt fluttered over her knees. She had a silver choker looped around her neck, and a pair of sterling earrings that dangled by her jaw. My concession to the fine weather was a bright scarlet pedicure. I kept glancing down at my feet in their sandals and admiring them.

My only complaint was that we'd missed the market today. I'd even called Jill to see if I could persuade her and Tim to go and buy me a few things, but he'd answered her phone so groggily that I knew it was a lost cause and hung up. Plus I felt a little odd talking to Tim. What had developed with his best friend and me was a little less romantic than what they—or she, in any case—had had in mind when they introduced me to him.

Mark had called a few days after I'd been over there the first time. I went to his apartment carrying a DVD we didn't watch. Instead it played like a soundtrack as I straddled him on the couch, holding on to the rough tweed upholstery, his hands hooked over my shoulders and pulling me down against him. His furniture was still college furniture, hand-me-downs he hadn't replaced yet. His patched brown couch, the twin mattress that sagged in the middle and engulfed us as we moved on it. The third time I went over I borrowed a bottle of wine from Kate's stash and brought that with me. He didn't even have wineglasses. We'd had to cadge an opener from the neighbor and drink pinot from juice glasses. The arrangement was a teenager's, pretending to go to a movie when I was heading out to have sex. I hadn't exactly hidden the wine I took, but I left when Kate and Simone were in the bathroom. I told Kate I was meeting up with friends. I didn't want to flaunt it, but if she had seen me come home she would have known in a heartbeat. Maybe she knew anyway. She probably didn't have to see me coming in with my hair a mess and my shirt untucked and my face rubbed clean of the little makeup I left with. And anyway I wanted it to be secret. I wanted it to be purposeful and neat, like a shot of whisky.

As we drove farther into the country, the air smelled better, of cut grass and drying rain. There were dogwoods and lilacs blooming in front of houses, frothy sprays climbing up against the siding and blocking windows. My parents had dogwood and lilac, and I missed the fragrance of them, so strong you'd think it must be fake. I slowed the car and rolled my window farther down to breathe it in.

THE WEDDING WAS IN a tiny church, a plain white wooden structure with a cross perched at its apex. As Kate and I made our way to our aisle seat, however, I was struck by how beautiful the building was from the inside: It was simple and unadorned, filled with light through the tall windows, a plain blue cloth over the altar.

People kept coming by and leaning down to kiss Kate, who grinned up at them, her eyes sparkling, while I translated, keeping a festive smile on the whole time. There were so many that by the time the service began I was glad for the rest.

The flower girl was about five. She scattered the petals solemnly, careful to distribute an even layer. At our row, she paused for a long, interested look at Kate, so taken she dropped her handful of petals in a clump. A bridesmaid nudged her.

Up at the altar, Kate's nephew looked even younger than I did. He was tall and gangly, a red smatter of razor burn along his jawline. As the pastor talked about the various duties of marriage, the rich and poor and sickness and health, he lifted his shoulders slightly and took a visible breath.

The couple lit a candle, and as they turned away the bride's skirt jostled the table, and the candle wobbled and fell, the flame lengthening as the pillar tilted. The whole church gasped and leaned forward, but the groom was already catching it. Still, just before he did I was tensed to move, figuring I could get Kate straight out the door before a fire took over. People would just have to get out of the way. I had it all planned in an instant. But then the candle stopped in the groom's hand. The flame had licked over the bride's satin bodice just once, harmless as a raindrop, before he righted it. There was an audible sigh throughout the congregation, followed by nervous laughter. Kate and I looked at each other, debating whether to smile with relief, but then turned back to the ceremony.

LATER, THE FLOWER GIRL summoned her nerve, slipping in beside us as we left the reception. She stared up at me, trying to figure out who I was.

She'd been in the background the whole day, darting around people and peering over at us, but I'd been too busy to care. I hadn't done one of these family gatherings with Kate, and they were killing. It wasn't only the sheer numbers of people who came over to catch up; it was the conversation: the minutiae of every life trotted out, the jobs and divorces and school choices and sciatica. The conversation was really no worse than any other family gathering; it was only boring to me, since I knew no one. Kate obviously enjoyed hearing every detail. The family also seemed to be reproducing with genuine concentration and purpose, and baby after baby was lifted up and had their round faces pressed against Kate's cheek, their startled eyes meeting mine as I smiled at the mothers. I saw Kate close her eyes briefly and breathe deeply, and I realized it must have felt delicious to her, the pure sensual pleasure of a baby: the rounded weight of them, the silky skin pressed against her cheek, the scent of powder and milk rising out of their hair.

By the time we began heading toward the car, I was exhausted. Luckily, the flower girl had a lot to say. She told us about her dress and what she planned to put in the basket that had held the flower petals (some pretty rocks, possibly a dried flower from her crown). She took every opportunity to gaze searchingly into Kate's eyes. It was clear that everything about Kate enthralled her: the strangeness of her thin blue dress and slender arms against the motorized black chair, the way Kate had to work for speech each time she said something, with a dip of her chin to swallow and carefully delineated lip movements so I could understand her and translate.

"What's your name?" the flower girl asked. Her eyes darted back and forth between Kate and me as Kate told her and I repeated it. We were at the car now. She nodded, then ducked behind me and peeked out at Kate. She balanced herself against my hip and said, almost sighing romantically at the end, "I love you."

I expected Kate to say something funny and maybe slightly admonishing. Or perhaps I only wanted her to; the bride's niece embarrassed me. My grandmother had a habit of expressing too much pleasure in the company of people of other races, people in wheelchairs, et cetera, and this felt similar. (*There's a group of Chinese people over there,* she'd murmur conspiratorially, of a table eating serenely a few feet away in The Dumpling House, *just laughing and talking and having as good a time as you can imagine.*) I'd had about enough of it for one day. Kate gave her a smile, a genuine grin, and said, "Thank you."

I thought it was nice of her not to let on that she understood that the attraction was the chair, the person who walks beside you everywhere you go. And I supposed I should cut the kid some slack. Affliction fascinates children—my friends and I used to feign fainting spells or close our eyes and pretend to be blind, swiping about with an umbrella we used as a cane.

Anyway, the girl was still clutching my dress, her knuckles digging into my hip, and as I detached myself I glanced down at the top of her head: Her part had gone crooked, and the flowers in her hair had started to wilt around their wires. Thinking, from her view, of the un-mitigated pleasure everyone took in the babies—who were tedious, really, hadn't even considered the uses of a flower basket—I felt a flash of sympathy for her.

As we drove away, the flower girl stood, waving, at the end of the driveway. I beeped the horn at her and glanced over at Kate. I had arranged her hands so they crossed demurely in her lap, her legs and feet set neatly before her. She turned to me, keeping her head against the headrest for support. As she looked up at me, her head tilted and chin lowered, her posture seemed faintly flirtatious, but it was only a trick of perspective. She waited till we were at a stop sign so I could look straight at her lips, which still bore the rose-colored lipstick I'd painted on them a few hours before.

She swallowed carefully, then lowered her chin so she could speak again. "Maybe I should have said 'I love you too,'" she mused. "But I just had no idea who that little girl was."

FOR THE REST OF the drive Kate was quiet. I concentrated on the smooth empty roads, and Kate looked out her window at the fields. Soon the outermost subdivisions would show up on each side of the road, big brown-and-white signs with pictures of pheasants and ducks, faux—English manor names.

"I can't believe that candle didn't even catch her skirt," I said.

Kate shook her head. "I still have the impulse to reach out," she said. "I thought I actually did, for a sec."

I had looked at her as it happened, seen her eyes widen and her chin jerk forward as the candle fell.

We passed the first huge subdivision on the western edge of Madison. A couple years before it had been farmland, and now it was all big houses rearing up on flat fields. The BMW's headlights flashed across a deer on the side of the road, pale brown bulk and a smear of scarlet on the concrete.

"Slow down a little," Kate said. I slowed down to fifty. "They start watching for speeders around here." We were quiet for a few moments, listening to Mozart on the radio.

When I looked at her at a stoplight, I saw that her eyes were closed. To our right was a wine store where we used to buy mixed cases for guests, a florist Kate had liked, a caterer. To our left was a road that went off toward Kate's old house, where she had lived with Evan. I peered down the road on my left, wondering what Evan and Cynthia had done with the house.

When I glanced her way again Kate was looking at me. The skin beneath her eyes looked puffy, and her mouth had lost its color.

"Are you exhausted?" I asked.

"I'm okay," she said. "Just a little tired."

The light turned and we started down the road. "Ever wonder what your old house looks like?" I asked.

"Their whole living room is probably devoted to nude statues by now." We snorted, but then she said, "Never mind. It's probably fine."

After a moment she let her eyes close again, but they opened in surprise as her head fell forward, her chin dropping toward her chest. This had been happening more lately. The next step was a new headrest on her wheelchair, more of a brace, to grip her skull and hold her up. I reached over as I drove, my palm and fingertips flat against her forehead as I tipped her head back again. She felt warm, her smooth skin leaving a faint trace of powdered slickness from her makeup on my hand.

"Thanks," she said. "I hate that. Maybe it's worse when I'm tired."

I took a left onto Chambers. "You want me to stay home tonight?"

She shook her head. "Don't be silly. Hillary will be there. Go out. You put your time in."

nineteen

HILLARY WAS WAITING AT the house when we arrived. She and Kate went into the bathroom while I changed into jeans and a jacket, called out good night, and went out to meet Jill at the Union. We got our beers and went out to the terrace, where I gave her a thumbnail sketch of the wedding. Though the air was still a shade too cold for sitting outside we did so anyway, stiff in the metal chairs.

It was a quiet night, which bore the faint air of disappointment that neither of us was terribly vivacious. Our recent stories had all been told. We drank one beer and ordered another out of habit before realizing we were tired enough already. We left them unfinished, hugged, and walked away to our cars.

I rolled the window down as I drove. I wanted it to wake me up, refresh me now that the wedding was done and the day was over. I wanted nothing more, I had realized as soon as I sat down with Jill, than to be silent. After a day of nonstop translating and speaking for Kate, I finally got to drive, just drive, to leave my mouth closed and stop looking searchingly around to find the cues that let me conduct other people's conversations for them.

At home Hillary was in the living room, the intercom monitor next to her on the couch, a cup of tea on the table. She looked up from her book as I came in, adjusting her glasses.

"I thought you'd be later," she said.

"Yeah, I was tired. Long wedding." I threw my purse on the counter and glanced at the mail: nothing for me. "How's Kate?"

Hillary was putting on a jacket. "Fine. Sleeping. I'm not sure that cold isn't coming back though. She's been a little raspy."

"I'll keep an eye out," I said.

Hillary got out her keys. "Maybe I'm wrong," she said. "I could have made myself hear it."

"Yeah," I agreed. I picked up the mail again and shuffled the envelopes. "Do you think she looks smaller? At the wedding today I looked at her and she seemed really thin."

Hillary leaned back against the door frame and sighed. "You're probably right. I can't say I've seen it myself, but we're so used to her. It would make sense, though."

We were both quiet for a moment. "Maybe we should give her an extra shake a day," I suggested.

Hillary gave me a cheerless smile and said, "If she'll let us. Couldn't hurt." She took off her glasses and rubbed the bridge of her nose. Sometimes she seemed about forty.

"Thanks for staying for a while," I said.

"Sure. Good night." She waved over her shoulder as she headed to her car.

I washed my face, used some of Kate's eye cream. It was close to midnight when I got into bed, and I stretched out, happily tired, enjoying the cool pillow and the breeze from the open window. Just to be sure I turned up the volume on the monitor.

I THOUGHT AT FIRST the sound that woke me was a scrape. Like a drawer, perhaps, a window forced along its frame. I was suddenly staring into the darkness, listening, not quite sure where I was or what was happening. I couldn't decide if I had heard nothing at all or if I had been listening to it for a long time.

Then the sound came again. It wasn't stealthy and soft, like someone breaking in, but reckless and haphazard. Desperate. This time it sounded large and echoing.

I could hear it in the hall as I ran. I could hear it still echoing through the monitors as I dashed into her room. I thought—illogically—that I'd see chaos in there, Kate on the floor in a tangle of sheets, possessions thrown everywhere.

But she was right there in bed where Hillary had left her. I could see the heave of her ribs, their lurching, and I saw her eyes shine at me in the dark, the whites showing all around. This, I knew instantly, was far worse than the coughing fits of the past weeks. I was still stopped in the doorway, hands braced inside the jamb.

I shook myself out of it. I crouched next to her.

She had the button beneath her fingers. I put my hand over her wrist. I didn't know if she'd had the strength or presence of mind to press it yet.

"Do I need to call?" I asked her. My voice sounded brisk at first, as though this were just another daily question, except that I seemed so loud.

She stared at me but didn't answer. I wasn't sure she could. "Do you want me to call?" I said again. I tightened my hand on her wrist.

In my mind I saw myself pressing down on her fingers and hitting the button. I saw it so clearly I had to take my own hand away, digging my nails into my palms, or else I knew I'd do it. I told myself I still could—I just had to make her agree and then I could mash her hand down on the button and wait for the sirens. I watched her face, waiting for her to nod and let me call them.

She was making eye contact for seconds at a time and then looking all around the room. I couldn't get her to focus on me, and the sound she was making—it was wood cracking; it was tires on wet pavement—seemed to enthrall her, so that I didn't know if she quite registered anything other than its rhythm. No matter how I listened I couldn't hear words. There was nothing of communication in it.

She couldn't talk. I tried again, my voice even louder. I didn't think she was even listening to me. I wasn't even sure if she could nod or shake her head. If she was on the verge of convulsing, then nodding or shaking her head wouldn't be accurate anyway.

"Listen to me," I said. "Kate, listen. Do you want me to call? Blink. Blink once for yes, twice for no."

I was holding her shoulders, bony and rounded in my fingers. I realized I was pressing down on her with all my weight to hold her still so I could read her face. If her body could have moved itself she would have been arched off the mattress, but only her neck did, the tendons straining, as she lifted her chin, and then lowered it, her teeth gleam-ing in the light from the streetlamp.

"I can't understand you," I said. My voice rang through the room, all over the register, high, low, cracked. The frustration made me des-perate, almost violent—suddenly I knew why people in films slapped the hysterical or uncommunicative. I got hold of myself and said, "Blink once for me to call, twice for no."

Kate's gaze had been roving all around the room again, as though looking for breath in a corner or near the window, but now she met my gaze, her eyes huge.

She squeezed her eyes shut, and opened them. She squeezed them shut again. Two blinks. Her tongue touched the roof of her mouth, just behind her teeth. Her lips curved into a circle and she shook her head.

My hand had already been moving to the lifeline. I was about to press it when I comprehended what she was saying. I stopped, my hand in midair. For a second neither of us moved. In the dark her hair was a wild mass around her small face, her skin white and opaque as a ce-ramic mask.

I turned on the lamp. In the light I could now see that her face was strangely mottled, red, bloodshot, but drained white around her nose and mouth.

"Tell me again," I said. "Once for me to call, twice for me not to."

She was still gasping, but she did it again, a blink. Another blink. It wasn't a spasm. It was *No*.

I stared at her. Her eyes, red-threaded, rimmed in tears, watched me fiercely.

I reached down to her hand on the button, took hold of her wrist, and lifted it away.

"Are you sure? Do you want me to do this?"

It was a whisper. I'd been yelling before, but suddenly now the room was still but for her attempts at breathing, that sucking in and wheezing exhale. She stared at me, down at my hand lifting hers away from the button. I paused, holding her wrist a few inches above it.

"If I move your hand you won't hit it accidentally."

She arched her neck, a great spasm of a gasp filling the room. She nodded into the pillow and gave me an exaggerated, single blink.

"Okay," I whispered. "I'm moving it then. I'll get it out of the way."

I set the button carefully on the floor, away from my foot, being certain not to hit it accidentally. I could tell I was moving slowly, so slowly it might have been maddening to her, but I wasn't capable of anything faster.

I felt us to be miles away from everyone else in the world. The room, with its one bright light and the silence outside, was like a chamber in the center of a mountain—isolated, helpless, airless.

I climbed up on the other side of the bed, next to her. I was on my knees up near her shoulders, looking for a way to hold her, to cradle her head in my lap, to wrap my arms around her. I didn't know how to do this. I was shifting around pointlessly, trying to find the right spot to lift her or touch her. Her eyes rolled as I moved, following me each moment.

"I'm not going anywhere," I said. Finally I knelt next to her on the bed, my body folded over and my face only a few inches to the side of hers. I wanted to be closer to her, closer than this. I gathered up her hands in mine, and they felt cold and clayey, the bones shifting beneath my grip. I pushed her hair, still warm and roughened from sleep, out of her face. Her lips were turning blue at the edges. They were stretched back from her teeth, her tongue. She watched me the whole time, her gaze locked with mine.

I could ignore her and push the button. It would take less than a second. I decided I would do exactly that. I didn't care if she would thank me later, or hate me for it. She could do whatever she wanted later; I just knew I couldn't watch this happen. She looked petrified.

"Please," I said. I leapt on that fear, relieved, and hoping I still had a good chance at persuading her. "Please let me call."

But she blinked and shook her head again, her eyebrows knit together. *No.* I couldn't pretend now that I hadn't understood her, and she was watching me to see if I would override her. We kept looking at one another as she struggled for breath, our gazes locked. I couldn't look right at her, when she knew what I was thinking, and disobey her. The opportunity to ignore her and hit the button had slipped away from me for good. Everything was shifting out of place, as though the disinterested earth had just shrugged us both off its crust. There was nothing she would let me do.

I stopped looking for opportunities to call for help. My job had just changed into something else. I stopped begging and stopped shifting around. I stayed next to her on the bed, facing her, but sat up, close enough so I could feel the heat of her body in the blankets pressed against the sides of my legs. I loosened the light bones of her fingers from the grip I'd had on them. I waited there, her hands damp and cold inside mine, and watched her try to breathe. The last time I'd been in a position anything like this, I'd had that stupid marker in my hand, tracing its way around her body.

How long had this been going on, how long had I been here? I was afraid to talk to her because I felt I must concentrate on letting her communicate if she wanted to. Nevertheless I became aware of soft sounds I was making without meaning to, a long shushing, a sibilant murmur. I brushed her hair off her face though it fell right back with each spasm, letting my hand linger on the curve of her skull. I wanted to be calm and comforting, but I felt my mouth trembling uncontrollably.

I laid my hand against her forehead, then her cheek, and she closed her eyes, briefly, as if in comfort, so I left it there. Her skin was chilled; a fresh sheet of moisture had risen from her pores. I stroked my hand over her forehead. I thought she might keep her eyes closed now, that that might make it easier. She was concentrating. I could tell. She was still gasping, her mouth open so wide, her chin high in the air, as if to let in as much air as possible, but I could hear her lungs letting up. Her chest beneath my hand wasn't rising and falling as hard. It felt more like a flutter, a tiny shudder of the fragile bone.

Her eyes sought me out again, her gaze darting around, as though she couldn't quite believe I still held her and needed to see me too. She was frightened, but losing the strength even to show it.

This was not how I had ever thought she'd be. I'd imagined her stoic.

Her face was genuinely blue now, her lips lavender, and finally she arched her neck, her head starting to drive farther back against the pillow as she reached for breath, and it was like the motion couldn't finish itself. She lost momentum part of the way through and relaxed.

I felt a fog of stillness fill the room. Kate's eyes were still turned in my direction but the darting, frantic energy was gone. I stared back into them even though I knew she no longer saw me. I felt myself to be a rapidly dissolving shape, a dimming shadow.

In the rest of her body, there was no sag of relief in muscles that hadn't been able to hold themselves taut in the first place. All that movement and effort had been concentrated at her neck, her mouth. I could only see the release in the way the pillow no longer creased as deeply from her pressing her skull into it. I waited for her face to relax too, but it didn't, not all the way. Instead a rush of air was released from her lungs, whatever she had kept or managed to claw into herself, and I felt its tepid warmth against my face where I still leaned in close to her. I smelled the faint must of saliva and the artificial mint of her toothpaste, the cooling heat of her breath as it returned to the air she'd snatched it from.

I WAITED THEN. I sat next to her, holding her hand, and waited for another twenty minutes. We had only discussed it in the vaguest terms: Wait. Then call. We had never talked about what I was supposed to do in the meantime.

I couldn't leave her there. I couldn't go get a drink, or put a robe on. I couldn't go about the business of comforting myself while she lay there. I didn't even want to get her papers, her will, her living will, her lawyer's contact information, from their clearly marked folder in the front top drawer of her file cabinet. But I did shut her eyes, tip her jaw up so her mouth was closed again. Outside it was still pitch dark.

I couldn't feel my body. My awareness of it went in and out: Suddenly I would realize I was holding my eyes so wide that they must have been bulging, that my lower lip was drawn away from my teeth, my shoulders hunched so far forward my back hurt. Then I would try to fix it, and a minute later I'd realize I'd tensed up again.

Finally I got up to call. I couldn't just reach across her to the phone, like reaching across a table, so I went to the kitchen and called from there. I unlocked the front door and turned the porch light on. Then I went back down the hall.

When I got to the door of her bedroom I went in slowly, as if something would have changed while I was gone. For a moment I was sure something had. Maybe I'd been wrong about everything—she was merely unconscious. I was no doctor; it was to be expected that I was too inexperienced to find a weakened pulse. I had a mighty faith in my own incompetence just then. I had misinterpreted the whole thing. What did I know? There would be a movement on the bed, a turn of the head, and she would take a breath and speak to me.

I went around the corner and peered in: the window cranked open, a filmy curtain billowing in and sucked back against the screen, the panic button on the floor, the rumpled blue bedspread drawn up off the corner of the mattress, the gleam of her hair on the pillow, her impervious profile against the white sheet.

I picked up the panic button and set it down next to her on the bed, thinking it didn't look good, so far from her. But I wasn't faking anything, I thought, suddenly fearful. I was just tidying up. I fixed the comforter, smoothing it down over her. The outline of her body showed through it, the long twin hills of her legs, the flat plain of her belly and chest. Her body had been drawing into itself all spring. She must have known this, though she had not discussed it with me. Perhaps she hadn't thought she could: The notion of making eggs and stews for her, as I had wanted to so badly a few weeks before, as though it would have helped, struck me as ruinously stupid. I'd focused on the wrong thing and let her approach this completely alone, as if she'd asked me for morphine and I'd petted the back of her hand.

twenty

THE LONG DISTANCE ACROSS my parents' backyard had lent an odd drama to certain childhood memories: I had several images of my father walking the length of the grass toward me as I sat on a swing set and watched him approach, my toes braced in the dusty hollow beneath, my fingers smelling of iron from the chains of the swing. Was I really out there so often that every time he had to tell me bad news—my grandmother had died, my kindergarten best friend was moving—that was where they found me, or did I simply race out there the moment I sensed something coming?

That would be like me, to hear one ominous murmur in the next room and zip outside to swing or do something else equally pointless until they forced me to listen to whatever they had to tell me.

I was sitting in a fraying green lawn chair on the patio behind the house, wearing a T-shirt and shorts rolled up to the tops of my legs. It wasn't really sunny enough for the outfit, but I'd slept in it. My toenails bore patches of red polish across the centers, what was left after the nails grew out and the polish flaked off. When I shifted in my chair a faint, sour scent rose up off of me. That morning my mother had promised me lunch at the Kiltie if I got myself ready. I'd made a sarcastic comment about dressing for the drive-in, but I got her point. I'd been here three weeks. It was probably time to try and get it together.

A book was facedown on my lap. After reading the same paragraph four times I had turned it over on one leg and stared out across the yard. The swing set, dome-climber, and jungle gym had all been gone for years, but I thought I could still see a slight depression in the earth, the grass sparser in the spots where the hollow metal poles had been sunk into the dirt.

You couldn't plan a truly wonderful day in the backyard, I was remembering. You never said, *Today is the day I'm going to build a town under the dome-climber.* You just went out there with an old blanket and threw it over the metal dome and got inside the tent it made and waited to see what came to you in the warm musty-smelling shade. If it was a good day, everything unfolded as you went: You lived alone in the forest beneath the blanket and ate roots and berries, and you stayed out there well into a fall evening, till your fingers were pleasantly numb from cold. Or the swing was a time-and-universe-traveling swing, operated by pressing the chain-links as buttons, and you might accidentally end up on the Viking planet and battle your way through them before launching yourself back onto your swing, belly down, clutching furiously at the links to blast off. I remembered the Viking war as taking up most of a day, but it had probably lasted twenty minutes before my mother called me in for an egg salad sandwich. I had tried to re-create it a few times, but it never worked.

I was reinstalled in my old room. For some reason Mom had wheeled in the television, though I could have come out and sat on the couch in the living room. I didn't point this out, figuring it was easier for both of us if I stayed out of her way. She brought me plates of eggs, cooked carrots, and sliced pink supermarket tomatoes. When I was sitting out in the yard, as I often was, she'd appear at my elbow bearing sweating glasses of ice water or juice with an odd, gritty texture and malty aftertaste. I suspected she dissolved some kind of protein powder into it.

I'd been out in the yard since Simone and Hillary left an hour before. They'd driven here from Madison, sat with me in the living room for half an hour or so, and then stood up and hugged me. I was embarrassed at looking the way I knew I did and kept the hugs brief and distant, averting my face.

The house on Chambers Street was empty, they'd told me. No one had heard from Evan what he would do with it. *Here,* they had said, and they each handed me their keys to the front door. There had been no advance decision that I would be in charge of it, but there was a faint air of deference in the way they dug into their pockets at the same time, each presenting me with a key on the palm of her hand.

I had set them in the crumbs on the half-empty plate of cookies my mother had put out. They both stared at the keys for a moment and then turned back to me. Hillary tore at a cuticle.

Simone cleared her throat. "The funeral was terrible," she said. "Her parents planned it, so it was all God's great plan and what did we learn from it all."

Hillary looked at me and looked away, sipping the iced tea my mother had made for them. The sunlight glinted off her glasses. It was hot in the living room, I realized; the heat baked the dark carpeting and heated the air. I shifted uncomfortably. I hadn't showered in days.

"Why didn't you come?" Hillary said. She'd set her glass down. "It was very odd that you weren't there."

"Hillary," Simone said. She turned to me. "People understood. You were there when it mattered. I wouldn't ask but . . ." She paused, then shrugged slightly, as if to say there was no gracious way to continue. But she kept her gaze on me. It was clear she wanted an answer.

I felt sick, the tannic tea on an empty stomach, the aspirin I had taken for a headache before they arrived. Simone, flushed, dropped her eyes to the cookie in her hand.

"I just . . . I woke up and it felt like I'd heard something in my sleep. I went in to check on her but—" I felt my face getting red. "She was . . . I wasn't there fast enough, I guess."

They stared at me. I shouldn't have tried to lie. They weren't amateurs—they knew what we'd been trying to prepare for, and in fact they seemed calmer about this than I was. Had everyone else understood how close we'd been to the end but me?

I could have told them the rest of the story, but suddenly it occurred to me how it would sound. How could I say I had taken away the call button, whether she had told me to or not? I had actually moved it out of the way. At the time I was sure I was preventing her from accidentally summoning someone, the same way I'd forced my own hand away from the button, but in the days since Kate had died, everything that had happened in that room seemed mysterious and malleable. I could reinterpret every part of it, second-guess each decision I had made. What if I had completely misunderstood her? In that professional, appraising way, Simone and Hillary might hear what I'd done and know I'd done it wrong. Most people had no idea what to imagine, but they did, and my worst fear was that they would find some loophole I hadn't, and say simply, *But why didn't you just—*

"And I was at the funeral," I said. "Jill and I came late and stayed toward the back. I just didn't want to make a scene."

Hillary looked at me. "Why would you make a scene?"

I was afraid of Evan. I was afraid he'd grab me and drag me off to a corner to demand I explain.

"I guess I wouldn't have."

We had arrived as they were closing the casket, unfolding a cloth over it, and as Jill and I waited to sneak in to a seat I had had the overwhelming urge to walk forward, calmly, so everyone would know I wasn't crazy, and just raise the lid, keep the coffin open. The urge didn't feel as macabre at the time as it seemed later; I'd just realized with the force of irrefutable logic that we didn't *have* to seal her inside that thing, cover her indifferent face, which I had glimpsed surrounded by pale satin. We had been standing at the back of the chapel, Jill and I, and I'd grabbed her wrist without thinking, captivated by the possibility of reprieve. I was the only one who knew we could all refuse to do this. We could still have her here. Not forever, but we could put it off. For an hour, a whole afternoon, till tomorrow.

Up toward the front of the chapel I'd seen Evan's blond head, his dark suit. I felt Jill staring at me, and shook my head without looking at her. We stood there and watched two people wheel the casket toward the front of the church, covered in a green-and-white sheet that looked like a tablecloth and that Kate would have hated. She would have hated all of this.

Jill and I had taken a seat in the last pew. I didn't run after the casket, it goes without saying. But I could not forget that I could, that we all *could,* and I marveled at the sheer willpower of what we were all doing there—not the service itself, but its aim. Step by step we'd force ourselves to cover her, layer by layer, take her body somewhere else, somewhere far from us, and leave her there.

I let go of Jill's arm then and concentrated on the back of a woman's head in the next pew—ash blond, dark roots, the smooth curled-under ends a little flat at the very back where she hadn't been able to reach. A few rows ahead of me I saw Kate's sister, the mother of the boy who'd gotten married. Where was the nephew? Already on his honeymoon, maybe. I couldn't remember where they were supposed to go. The wedding seemed like months ago.

I had the feeling that all of this, the funeral, the gathering, the ceremony, was something that had just gotten out of hand because of a single decision I had made, like fables in which one lie leads to crazy, grand consequences. If I'd come into Kate's room a few seconds sooner, would I have caught her in a less resolute moment? It would only have taken a moment to press the button and then she would, in all likelihood, still be alive.

Could she have pressed it herself? I thought so, unless she'd gotten so weak in the past several weeks that even that was beyond her. I'd managed not to comprehend how thin she'd become; it was possible I'd avoided seeing that loss of strength as well.

I had gazed toward the voice issuing from a woman singing into a microphone near the coffin, still pondering. The church smelled of sawdust and perfume. Before I moved in with Kate, I had occasionally wondered what a crisis might be like, but I had envisioned her with a certain amount of tranquillity, calmer, the certainty more understandable. And after one imagined scene like that, having discharged my duty to at least picture it once, I had put the possibility out of my mind. It still didn't seem possible that that night—her terror and her determination, the way I'd teetered on the edge of overriding everything she'd ordered me to do and nearly jammed my hand down on the button—was really what she'd wanted.

The air was stifling. As the singing reached into higher octaves I had to steady myself on the back of the pew in front of me. How had I managed not to acknowledge what it meant to promise to obey her?

There were whole days in my parents' house when I lay in bed and stewed, hating her for being so circumspect—speaking in terms of asking her permission to call, of talk about remaining in control instead of saying plainly that we were talking about death. But I couldn't stay

angry. I knew that, had I let myself, I would have faced what I'd promised to do—not that single after-school-movie image of something
quiet and dignified—but what I had really signed on for, and what, finally, I had done. Kate hadn't needed to explain more than she did. I
understood it; I just managed never to think about it.

It didn't comfort me to know that I had done what I'd promised. I
should never have told her I could do it.

JILL BROUGHT ME SOME of my things from Chambers Street, but
everything else was still in there.

"What was the house like?" I asked her. "I may have left some food
out; it'll get ants. I don't suppose you checked for ants."

She looked at me, her face blank, and said, "No. Don't worry about
the ants."

I was waiting to hear from Evan. I waited for him to send a registered letter, notarized, signed by a lawyer and telling me to remove my
effects. I waited for him to drive to Oconomowoc in the middle of the
night with my things in a trash bag and dump them on my parents'
lawn. I would have liked for him to do that, or I would have understood if he had made a bonfire of my clothes and books so I would wake
up and see it flickering through the shades.

I intimated this to Jill. Nothing direct, just a veiled indication that
I was afraid to encounter Evan. Not afraid, I amended, just worried,
sort of.

Jill had been digging around her purse for her keys as I spoke. She
was on her way to visit her parents, now that she was in Oconomowoc
anyway. She glanced up at me briefly, then reached over and squeezed
my hand. It felt strange. We were not hand squeezers. That was our
mothers. We both stared down at her hand over mine for a second;
then she took it away.

"Do you have enough to do out here?" she said. "Or maybe not.
Maybe you're just relaxing before you decide what to do."

It must look like relaxing. It felt more like inertia so heavy there was
little point in fighting it. When I let myself think of the things I ought
to do—looking for a job, an apartment—they seemed to be incredibly
intricate, detailed tasks.

"I picked up a few papers so you can look at apartments." She paused delicately. "I don't know what classes are still open but I bet you can find something."

"I'm not going back to school right now," I told her. I had been saying this in my head over and over, not in preparation for telling her but because it comforted me. How had I ever navigated the bureaucracy of the university, its deadlines and credit requirements and forms? I had, of course, and with no more difficulty than anyone else, and no doubt I would again, but I couldn't imagine dealing with that now.

She nodded, unsurprised.

"How's Mark?" I asked her. "Tim's friend," I added inanely, as though she wouldn't know.

"He's okay," she said. "He said he called you but you haven't called back."

"Yeah," I agreed. I hadn't seen the point. The notion of having the energy or even the need to bother with it all—the stairs up to his apartment, keeping my fingernails away from the condom, the adjustments, shifts, and murmurs. Was that really what I was going to do now, anyway, go out and get laid?

EVEN AFTER SEVERAL WEEKS at home, I still awoke at odd intervals in the night: yanked upward at one, at quarter after three, at four. It took a few seconds every time to figure out where I was, and that the sound that had jarred me was the clanking of pipes or my father closing the bathroom door, and not the watery gurgle of breath over an intercom. The first few times it happened I picked up the clock radio next to the bed in a haze and listened to it as though I'd hear her through it, breathing.

I never dreamed of Kate. I wanted to. Jill had dreamed of her grandmother once, shortly after she'd died, and she said it had felt like a gift. I didn't believe some spirit incarnation had come to her, or that one would really come to me, but I thought my mind might be keeping something back, one forgotten moment that could come to me like an apparition, that I could savor.

I tried to will it. At first I only thought of Kate when she had been happy: at the market, at parties, but it felt maudlin, undeserved, and self-serving: *Oh how happy she'd been, the trouper, and wasn't she happy somewhere else now too.* So instead I pictured her stretched out on Evan's bare mattress as I traced around her, smiling grimly up at the ceiling.

But I stopped after a few nights. I was afraid I wouldn't get Kate standing calmly in my doorway, or laughing. I thought she would come to me pale and pinched with anger, her arms crossed, her lips a white-rimmed line.

WHEN I HAD BEEN home about four weeks I heard my mother answer the phone in the kitchen. From the way her voice rose and then lowered, the muffle of it where she must have stood at the far wall of the kitchen where I would not hear, I knew it was Evan. She came in after a few minutes and said, "That was Kate's husband. He wondered if you'd like to get your things this week." She sat down next to me and said, "He's selling the house, so it needs to be cleared out a bit."

"I'll go," I said. "Will you drive me?"

She nodded. "He asked that you send the house keys in the mail." She stroked my hair and sighed. "Can I make you something for dinner?"

I HADN'T BEEN OUT much in the weeks I had been home, and back to Madison only for the funeral. As my mother and I walked down our driveway and got into the car to go to Chambers Street, the first thought that struck me was that it was too easy. No pause to lift and settle someone, no folding up a chair. It felt incomplete and careless to simply slide into a seat and snap the seat belt in place.

We didn't speak during the drive. When we reached the neighborhood, I peered around at the people sitting on porches and kids tearing around yards. The neighbor's dog was racing in circles around their house.

"My," my mother said. "Those kids are loud."

I knew those kids. They were always wrecking their bikes near our house.

"Remember when Jill and I lived near that elementary school?" I said. "They sound like bloody murder when they're playing. I don't know why people think it's supposed to sound nice. Liam called them hyenas."

She shot me a curious glance as she parked in the driveway. "Who's Liam?"

I was looking up at the house. It had only been a month since I had been here. There was no reason for it to be cobwebbed and decrepit, but it surprised me how neat it looked. The flowers in the window boxes were still blooming.

"What a nice little house," my mother said.

The night Kate died, my mother and father had arrived together to take me back home, one of them to drive me and the other to drive my car. I had watched them get out of the car, my mother in her old jeans and a windbreaker, my father, oddly, in neat khaki pants. How comforting it was to see them coming toward me, so grave and calm. I experienced a vestigial surge of trust from childhood, as if all were truly well now. I rarely even spoke with my father other than hello and how are your grades, and it made the sight of him that much more significant now. What did I think he could do for me, just because he was here? But it had moved me, the sight of his thinning dark hair at the top of his skull when he bent down to help me up from the couch where I'd been waiting, the wrinkled flesh around his neck and jaw, soft, loosened from age.

I had been sitting there for an hour and a half when they arrived. The ambulance was gone, Kate was gone, but my blood raced anyway, my pulse running rapid as a sparrow's heart. I think I was trembling. I was that way until my parents arrived. My father came in first. When I saw his shape in the doorway, the sloping width of his shoulders, his calm face, it tore me open.

I UNLOCKED THE FRONT door and held it open for my mother. Then I followed her inside.

It smelled like nothing at all. Not stale air, not flowers, not the last garlicky dinner I had cooked. I looked around: Nothing was out of place. The calla lilies that had been on the kitchen table were gone, the vase that had been drying upside down on a towel by the sink. Who had been here? I thought of something then, and went into the kitchen to look around. The funnel and tubing I had used to feed her was gone too, from its place beside the sink where we always left it after washing.

I opened the refrigerator: some bottled water, a jar of jam. I had had it stocked full of vegetables before I left, but of course that would have spoiled by now. I shut the door.

"This really is a lovely house," my mother said. She was standing in the middle of the living room, gazing around at the bright walls, the photographs in their frames. In her shorts and tennis shoes, her dark hair, streaked with gray, falling from its ponytail, she looked baggy and out of place. Well, she should feel that way. I wanted her to see what it had been like—that it wasn't drudgery, that I had lived in a pretty house on a welcoming street. She had never once accepted an invitation to visit us.

"Such a lovely color," she went on, looking toward the living room wall. She glanced over at me and gave me an innocuous little smile. I didn't understand how she—how anyone—could look at me as though I were still myself, or even made up of the same stuff they were. I felt as conspicuously different as if my skin had changed color overnight. Even my face looked wrong these days, my eyes stark and gray, my mouth colorless and somehow a whole new shape. I believed that Kate had sunk into me like a sunburn, rooted herself in my skin like a pelt, but everyone refused to acknowledge it.

"Let's go," I said. I turned my back on my mother and went down the hall to my room.

My room hadn't been touched. My clothes were still piled on a chair, the bed unmade. The day of the wedding had been chaos, I recalled, and I had left it a mess as I tried to finish Kate's hair and makeup.

"I'll go get the boxes," said my mother.

When she was gone I went to Kate's room. The shelves were cleared of photos and statues, the plants removed. But when I peeked into the top drawer of the bureau I saw that the cleaning had only been a surface sweep, maybe by the real estate agent, and her clothes were still in there. I moved aside the underwear and lace bras, and found the Chinese lacquer box. I put it in the pocket of my jacket.

I opened up the nightstand drawer too, and found the wedding ring we'd put in there, and the blue butterfly in its little box. I left the ring and took the butterfly. I was planning on throwing it away somewhere, or just hiding it. I didn't want Kate's mother, or Evan, turning it over in their hands and figuring out how it was used and who helped. It wasn't any of their business.

I was back in my room when my mother returned. She stood next to me, folding my things and placing them in the boxes, moving them to the floor as we filled them. She was very strong. She knew to bend her knees and not to use her back. She could carry heavier boxes than I could.

I had to keep telling her what to take and what to leave. *I just borrowed that from Kate*, I said, as she held up books stacked by the bed and a sweater draped over a chair. *That's not even mine.*

twenty-one

WHEN I AWOKE THIS time I could tell it was well after midnight. There was no sound—no cars on the street, no television on in another room. I was sitting up in bed, and suspected I had been for a while. Even in the dark I could see the shapes of clothes and towels all over the floor, some empty soda cans, and a glass I'd been drinking water from, cloudy with fingerprints. The clock said 2:43 A.M.

I sighed, rolled over, stared at the lavender wall, and then got up.

I could still walk through this house in the pitch dark and find my way. I moved through it slowly and carefully, easing open the back door and leaving it ajar.

The lawn was wet and cool. My feet picked up grass, but I kept walking out to the center of the backyard. I was in a T-shirt and shorts—dressed, at least, even if it was a little odd to be out here in the middle of the night.

I paused and looked around, wanting to sit down, or stretch out, and look up at the sky. I thought of Nathan a year ago, drunk and feverish, lying down on my car for the dew that had settled onto it.

I could see the dark windows of the houses on either side and across the backyard. I didn't know these neighbors. I saw them sometimes, on their way to cars, coming up the drive with a handful of mail. Who knew if any of them were watching me now.

I'd begun coming out here instead of trying to get back to sleep. Walking around the yard, even around the neighborhood, in the total hush of the middle of the night, was strangely exhilarating—just opening your door at this time of night was so taboo, yet once you were out here you felt the breeze and the quiet and you didn't see why anyone tried to do anything in the crowded daytime heat. The air tonight was cool and damp and smelled of cut green leaves.

I went around the house, the occasional firefly zipping past, and slipped my wet, grass-pelted feet into a pair of flip-flops I'd left on the front porch. I was about to walk down the driveway when I heard the front door open.

My mother's head, her long hair rumpled, poked out the front door. She was still tying her robe, and with one hand she motioned to me to come to her. I stood in the driveway, disappointed not to be alone any longer. She stepped out, shutting the door carefully behind her, and walked over to me. As she neared me her expression came into focus: eyebrows drawn together, lips set in annoyance.

I turned away and began to walk down the driveway. She fell into step next to me.

"Is this what you do at night?" she asked lightly. "Prowl the neighborhood?"

I glanced at her profile. She was looking straight ahead, swinging her arms, as though we were on a power walk. "It's better than staring at the ceiling," I said.

"True, I suppose," she admitted. "Though you could also read."

We walked to the end of the block and turned right onto Eucalyptus. Beneath the thin rubber soles of my flip-flops I felt the crabapple berries squashed on the sidewalk, the grit of the concrete. My mother's hair was twisted over one shoulder. Her white robe flapped as we walked. When I looked down I realized her feet were bare.

"Don't you want shoes?" I said.

She shrugged. "I'll be careful. I haven't gone barefoot in years. It's rather pleasant."

We came to the end of Eucalyptus and took another right up the hill onto Pine.

"I still think of this hill like a mountain, practically," I said. Riding a bicycle down it had been terrifying.

She smiled wryly and did not look over at me. "I remember that. You would tell me these very dramatic tales of near misses on some craggy mountain and scare the bejesus out of me. I thought you were leaving the neighborhood and riding your bike down some other hill. You got very angry with me when I realized you meant this one and I said it wasn't steep at all."

We were halfway up the hill now. I looked up at the sky to see if it was light yet, but it was still a deep cloud-streaked navy, the moon a calm yellow orb. Next to me I saw my mother's profile lift as she followed my glance. As we neared the turn to our street, she paused, one hand braced on my shoulder, and checked the bottoms of her feet, briskly brushing off the soles. I heard the sound of gravel dropping to the pavement.

When we began to walk again she said, "It's time for you to leave, Rebecca."

I listened to the sounds of my flip-flops slapping on the sidewalk.

"Do you realize how slowly you move?" she said. "You used to charge around here and now I watch you pull your shoulders up to your ears, practically. Look how you tuck in your arms."

I became aware of my elbows folded in, my hands clasped lightly below my breasts. I made to swing them easily, but it felt showy so I let them drop to my sides.

"Exactly," she said.

LATER THAT WEEK I found a cheap enough place on Jenifer Street, the top floor of a mint-green house with lavender trim. It was the kind of place that telegraphs a landlord's shoddy intentions from a mile away, the way it's not really an apartment space but can be forced to bring in money as if it were. Even the stairway changed once you reached the landing of my floor, becoming narrow and low-ceilinged, painted a uric yellow.

When the landlord opened the door for me, I smelled fresh paint and cedar. Most of the place consisted of one long room the length of the house, its walls painted basic off-white, plus a small bathroom and a sort of sleeping alcove. It didn't have a kitchen so much as it had the elements of a kitchen stashed in various places: a small stove in a corner toward the back, a sink on the opposite side of the bathroom wall, a countertop near the half-fridge beneath the window. There was a tiny clean bathroom, cheaply outfitted with a plastic shower that looked as though it had been built from a kit. The lavender carpet matched the paint on the house. As I walked across it, it made fizzy sounds beneath my feet.

I paused and looked at the landlord. She was olive-skinned and wiry, somewhere in her forties. She and her husband lived across the street.

"Is there foam or something under here?" I asked.

She took a few tentative steps, hands on her hips. "Huh," she said. "I bet Daniel laid some down and didn't tell me." She looked up at me, all delighted surprise. "This feels great," she assured me. "You won't need slippers."

I shrugged. I wasn't expecting a lot from this place anyway, and it was month-to-month. It was also the first place I looked at.

I'd hoped I might move in with Jill again, since her roommate had talked of moving out for the summer, but then it turned out Jill was moving in with her boyfriend.

No doubt there were better places out there. But this was my old neighborhood. It was hot and dusty and I sneezed just breathing the air. When I told my mother about the place that night, she asked, "Are you sure?" I felt too tired to make the case for an apartment I didn't much like, either. I just said, "Yeah."

So I bought a mattress and put it on the floor of the tiny bedroom. I bought a couch out of the newspaper, and set next to it a little maple table my father had brought home from a garage sale. Then I went to the grocery store and tried to remember what I would need. Cereal and toilet paper, shampoo, and soap. The thought of stocking up a real cooking kitchen was overwhelming, so I got a few boxes of macaroni and cheese, some frozen spinach and peas, and a couple of cans of soup.

I had some savings in the bank, and I used it to pay two months rent right off the bat, so I didn't have to bother writing more checks. I had to think about a new job. I could have lived off the savings for a while longer, but it seemed a shame to waste the money. I'd need it somewhere down the line. Kate was the one who had bugged me to open a savings account when I moved in with her. For someone who hadn't needed to worry about money, she had taken some pleasure, I often thought, in the management of it. It appealed to her organizational side.

Anyway, I didn't have Kate's financial acumen or her trust fund, so I began setting my alarm in the mornings with the belief that I would rise early and walk over to the coffee shop on Willy Street, read the paper, and circle classifieds. In actuality, I woke up indolent and baffled each morning, resetting the alarm until finally I got up at eleven instead of eight. This was probably better anyway. That way I didn't waste time or money eating breakfast, only lunch. My days were filled with these sorts of solutions: the stretchy sweatpants I could wear to bed and throughout the day as well, the knife that just stayed in the jar of peanut butter instead of being washed.

It was August before I actually got out of the house in the morning and down the block to the coffee shop as I'd planned. The summer was practically over already. I paid for my latte and scone and settled myself with the paper at a table near the window. I sipped my coffee, prepared to look at the ads, uncapped my pen, and for a shimmering second believed that I slipped back to a moment more than a year ago, when I had come to the same café, ordered the same cinnamon scone, and sat here, my pen poised above the paper and the fleshy side of my hand getting smeared with newsprint as I skimmed the ads. I stayed utterly still, the steam from the coffee rising into my face, the unchewed morsel of scone cupped in my mouth.

It would have been understandable if that feeling had made me want to crumple the paper and go back to the safe distance of waitressing, as though I could simply back up and veer around the experience of caregiving altogether. But instead I felt hopeful, and immensely relieved. Inside that little pocket of time, if nowhere else, I felt that I could do everything again. The outcome might be no different, but that seemed insignificant. The whole experience didn't have to be so finished.

Moments like this had revealed an embarrassing, previously unknown mystical side of me. I had never spent much time clarifying what I thought of an afterlife. My brief church attendance had been more about the immediate. But at times Kate seemed so near to me, her presence palpable but just beyond my field of vision, that I found myself thinking I had some inside track on finding out what happened after death—as if Kate would let me know once she got acclimated. She herself had always refused to guess. It seemed to me that whole religions were based very justifiably on this refusal to believe that your contact with a certain life, a certain person, was simply over. And I was so accustomed to ordering my life around Kate that the habit persisted.

The déjà vu passed, after what felt to be several minutes but wasn't even long enough for my coffee to stop steaming. I looked around: I was seated at an old table painted green, nicked and gouged and a pack of matches keeping the legs level. It was too early for the lunch rush, and the only other customers were a woman and her child at a table nearby, the toddler crumby and chapped around his mouth. The café window seemed filthy. How I had ended up back here?

IN THE END, HALF-HOPING nothing would come of it, I placed an ad in the paper, advertising the services of a helper. My mother perceived it as a "get-back-on-the-horse" gesture, and Jill said, "Well, if you think you want to do this, I guess you have to get used to losing people. Maybe you should go to nursing school."

It was more that I could not imagine myself doing anything else. I wasn't sure I even remembered how to do restaurant or temp work or sales.

I missed the routine of my days at Kate's, the way I could see the results of my efforts so quickly: a person fed, clean, comforted, moved. I found it hard to recall how uneasy I had been the first few weeks on the job. Surely it hadn't been that bad. Anyway, I knew what I was doing now. I could be better, smarter, quicker to respond to problems, efficient, and brisk, if someone let me.

The first call came from a man in Sun Prairie, who needed round-the-clock. Here I faltered. It was foolish to believe crises would only occur after dark, but I did, and I knew as soon as he asked that there was no chance I would try nights again.

The next one was a woman on the east side with multiple sclerosis. She needed someone to help with her physical therapy, to keep the household running decently. Her house was a one-story brick ranch with a switchback ramp going up to the front door. I parked on the street and looked it over. The neighborhood was bustling and loud, nothing like Kate and Evan's had been, with the synchronized sprinklers on the empty lawns.

I put my hair into a ponytail, anticipating a lot of bending and reaching, and went up to the door.

This woman was much older than Kate; in her late fifties was my guess. She had bright silver hair that fell in short curls around her cheekbones, cut close at the back. I noticed how tan she was, the skin around her dark green eyes notched deeply with lines, her teeth yellowed at the edges. When she spoke it startled me. How clear and loud her voice was, how perfectly she enunciated. She had a faint Southern accent.

"Come in, come in," Barbara said. "You're younger than I thought, hon, I have to tell you." She led me into her kitchen and turned her chair to face me. "But you say you have a year's experience?"

I nodded. "I worked for a woman with ALS," I said. "Live-in and visiting."

She nodded. One hand lay, clawed, in her lap, but with the other she could grip a thick pen, and with her hand curled around it she took laborious notes. "And you did that until this May, you said." She looked brightly at me over her glasses. "What prompted you to leave?"

"She died," I said.

She set her pen down. "How sad," she said. "That's a tough one."

A tough one. It sounded like such a minor setback when you put it that way, reminding me of Kate designating her illness as simple bad luck. Why did people resort to such sporting, blithe language when they should have hauled out the real words? A tough one was a math problem. A tough one was a steak. It wasn't that I wanted hyperbole. I just wanted someone to say the right words: Dreadful. Catastrophe.

I WENT TO BARBARA'S four days a week to begin. Her physical therapy was much as Kate's had been, massage and moving her limbs whether they wanted to or not. She wore brightly patterned sweaters and elastic-waisted pants, her legs still plump in the navy blue fabric.

On my first day I walked her two miniature schnauzers, watching their stumped tails quiver. I had taken an instant dislike to them. Every now and again one turned a wet-bearded face my way and yipped. "Oh shut up," I said.

It was not a good sign, directing my hostility at a couple of dogs, but I spent all my energy trying to be kinder, happier, saner than I felt, showing Barbara and my mom and Jill and Nate and Samantha and whoever Jill brought to my new place for occasional endless, awkward visits that I was just fine. So I relished this small chance at surliness, and sank into anger like a soft, cool bed. When I petted the dogs' heads and scratched their chins, which I did perversely, to see if they knew how I felt about them, their beards left viscous threads of saliva on my skin. They snorted grumpily in my direction.

What sort of dog might Kate have had? Maybe a soulful, gleaming retriever, a stately Alsatian, or a silvery wolfhound stalking silently around the room. The schnauzers woofed at me and turned away.

"I would not have let you slobber all over Kate," I crooned poisonously. "I wouldn't have let you near her."

Barbara's friends appeared most days around three, calling greetings in the door and striding into the back room with a cursory wave to me and a hug for Barbara. They talked about children and grandkids, commiserated over husbands. I tuned them out while I wiped down the counters and fetched Baggies to clean up after the schnauzers.

The job was kind of a skilled maid position, with some cooking. I made tuna or chicken casseroles and tore up iceberg lettuce, steamed rice ahead of time for stir-fry. I tidied up the bathroom, the study, whatever rooms we had used that day. Barbara never needed me to do her makeup.

I did not look forward to going to work. I didn't dread it either, but arrived and left as somnolently as if I'd never quite woken up at all. I cooked what Barbara asked me to, cleaned this and that, took Barbara's tiny feet in my hands and maneuvered her as required. Her husband was hearty and jocular. I could no more imagine him having an affair than voting Libertarian. They kissed hello and good-bye with pursed lips and resounding smacks. They were a relief to me.

AS SEPTEMBER BEGAN I realized I finally felt used to my apartment, and to the strangeness of being back in my old neighborhood. It felt different to me each time I drove home after work in my quiet car. (I had never had the stereo fixed.) I didn't know as many people here as I once had, and there seemed to be a lot more beer-littered lawns and sophomore parties.

I saw Mark once, walking to his car. He only lived a few blocks from me. Sometimes I tried to imagine myself showing up at his door with a bottle of wine or a pizza. But I could barely remember what he looked like, and when I saw him as I drove past he seemed taller than I had recalled, broader, and it was disconcerting to be reminded that I had only known him for that month.

One afternoon I came home from Barbara's and couldn't find a parking spot. I sighed, and circled the block one more time, hoping someone would leave, but I was stuck with walking a few blocks to my house.

I walked slowly, enjoying the heat after Barbara's turbo-cooled room. I never got warm there, but I thought I could lay odds it would be sweltering in the winter. Jesus, just the thought of winter in Barb's house—the darkness at four o'clock, the schnauzers pissing idly in the snow—I tried not to think about it. I didn't know what else I would do if I didn't do this.

I passed the park and turned onto my block. My favorite house was now right here on my street: a vampy-looking Victorian with a bright red door. I used to go out of my way to walk past it when I lived near here with Jill. Our old apartment was only five blocks away, right near the elementary school, whose mayhem I could still hear in my new place. I slowed down a little, looking around for something that was totally different from when I had lived in this neighborhood the first time. Sometimes the sense of displacement—or its reverse, of wondering whether I had left at all—was so powerful I had to stop and look around until it made sense again. I had only been gone about six months. I had lived in the house on Chambers Street for only four.

I was walking so slowly it must have looked like trudging. Mostly I was dreading my un-air-conditioned apartment, the fact that I had nothing to do that night, no plans, so what was there to get started on? I came to my house, started up the front walk, and then slowed to a halt. I had some cans of chicken soup, saltines, and peanut butter for dinner. I'd go buy a six-pack and a movie, I decided. It would make short work of the evening. Maybe two movies. Maybe a twelve-pack.

Once I had smoked some of Kate's marijuana, having improbably convinced myself that sitting, stoned and alone, in my attic apartment, watching a movie by myself, would be as fun as an evening with Kate. As the high set in, a glittering buzz that darted around the edges of my vision, I had felt that same isolation I had in Kate's bedroom the night she died. There was an unbridgeable distance between me and everyone else. The television's noise was tinny and overbearing, the air in the room musty, heavy as a quilt. I called Jill, some of my friends I hadn't seen in weeks, even Nathan. Jill and Nathan showed up separately, exchanged a look when they came upon me huddled in a corner of my couch and staring at the door, and hauled me out for fried chicken. *No wonder you lost it,* Jill had said. Nathan was in the men's room. *I'll smoke with you.*

You hate being high, I reminded her. She handed me a paper cup of coleslaw and said, *Oh, I'd be fine.* She was lying, but I appreciated it.

I turned around and went back to my car. It was a pretty day; I could have walked. At the video store I browsed the new releases. I finally chose a comedy I'd seen two or three times, and bought a Coke on my way out. I was at the door, opening the soda bottle, when I saw Liam walk by.

I stood there, one hand on the window, and looked at him. He hadn't seen me. I watched him turn into the Thai restaurant a few doors down, holding the door open for a couple walking out. His hair was shorter. He was wearing a blue shirt I remembered from last summer. I'd never liked it. I would never have guessed that seeing him now would feel so powerful. I felt weakened and warmed through, some current slipping palpably through me.

Head down, I walked to my car. Once inside it I peered into the windows of the restaurant. The glare of the sun made it difficult, but I caught his shape stopping at a table, bending over to kiss the woman—it was a woman; I could make out the breasts and the swing of shoulder-length hair—before sitting down. For one sickening second I thought it was a girl, yet another girl, but then I got a better look. It was his wife. I remembered the shape of her, the way she sat, even from seeing her just once at the Union and once in front of her own home. They weren't doing anything of importance, just flipping through their menus and speaking to each other as they read, deciding what to order, what they were craving, and what they were sick of.

This was his real life; this was its fabric. Not the illicit stuff, the curtained restaurant tables and bedroom shades down in the daytime, but the mediocre Thai food they both sheepishly enjoyed, the liquor store they liked for buying beer but not wine, the roads they drove because they were convenient, and because they knew them so well.

twenty-two

I HAD NEVER BEEN to Lisa's house before. She had always come over to Kate's house, saying rightly that it was easier. As I drove to her house now, watching as she had told me to for a little white one with red shutters near the capitol, I felt jumpy and sick to my stomach with nerves. I felt as though I were on a date, or going to a party at the popular girl's house.

Seeing Liam had touched something off in me. The first was some mild form of self-awareness: I did not buy the twelve-pack of beer. Self-awareness was the worst thing to happen to a person at loose ends. Without it, like someone who hasn't yet seen the ink splotch on her cheek in the mirror, I could pretend that the existence I had been slogging through for the past month was fairly normal. I could overlook the evenings I spent in front of the television set, parceling out the night half-hour by half-hour, delighted when a show I liked enough to stare at took up a whole hour. I had tried to go for walks around the neighborhood I thought I'd missed so much, but I had a tendency to make it down the block to the park, choose a bench, and stare balefully from behind my sunglasses at the kids on the playground as they hollered and knocked one another to the ground. My comfort was the fact that at least I wasn't working with children.

The other effect was nostalgia. Maybe that longing for the past year's life was connected to the understanding that my current life was shit. I could have sworn that I used to have a certain amount of comfort and even minor luxury, of amusement and challenge. That had been Kate's doing—that had been Kate's *life*—but I had fit well in it. I thought I had. I had liked her friends, and I thought they'd liked me, and I had liked her habits and her books and parties. Yet here I was, utterly severed from what had felt an awful lot like my life as well.

Lisa came to the door before I had a chance to ring the bell. She hugged me briefly, her shoulders broad beneath my hands. I squeezed her harder than I meant to, and she gave a little sound and then a nervous laugh, her shoulder hunching between us as she turned aside.

"Come on in, have a seat." She waved over her shoulder around the room, at a futon and an armchair. "I'm just getting some iced tea."

I sat in the armchair and waited, holding my purse on my knees. She came back, setting a couple glasses on the coffee table and seating herself on the futon. She drew her legs up under her.

I sipped at the tea for something to do. "You must be looking forward to poncho weather," I said, inanely.

She smiled. "I donated it," she said, and shook her head. "Kate gave me such a hard time about that thing. She liked to tell me I looked like I was drowning in Holstein."

After a moment, she asked, "How have you been?"

"Okay," I said. Then I couldn't think of anything else to say.

"It was a bit of a shock to hear from you," Lisa tried again. "I know I should have called or something, but I just—"

"That's okay," I interrupted. "You wrote." She looked startled, then recovered, as if she had forgotten all about it. Maybe she'd had to get drunk to write to me. The letter, it was true, had been short but disjointed, as though she had been plucking ideas out of the air randomly and committing them to paper. It had said Kate was lucky to have me with her, that she hoped I would be okay. It had also said something about duty and fate, and sharing good wine.

"I thought I saw you downtown the other day," I said. She looked skeptical. "Or just someone who looked like you, and I wondered how you were. I used to see you so much, and it felt strange to have no idea how you're doing."

She was nodding, but it wasn't the enthusiastic agreement I'd hoped for. It was more resigned, as though she'd known something this uncomfortable would happen.

"I really am sorry to bug you," I said wretchedly. I seemed to be watching myself talk from a great distance. "I'm living in my old neighborhood again, on Jenifer Street, and . . . I don't know, sometimes it's like I never left. It's not that I've forgotten anything, but I just—I can't believe how fast it all went."

"I understand," Lisa said.

"Oh good," I said. "I thought you would."

She didn't say anything. She sipped her tea, her brow knit.

"Um . . . how's Helen?"

"She's all right," Lisa said. "She and I were never very close, you know; she was more Kate and Evan's friend."

"Yeah, I remember. I just thought, maybe . . ." I drank from my cup. I was glad that at least she'd blown off Helen, too.

"Do you," I began. She looked up at me. "Do you ever talk to him?"

When I first went home I'd waited for him to call me, or sue me, or something. And when I came back to Madison I kept waiting, but I hadn't heard a thing. I had begun to realize that whatever he thought, I'd never know. If he hated me, if he knew what I had done, he was not planning to say so.

Lisa went still for a second, then nodded. "I do," she said. "We've managed to talk a little more these days, as a matter of fact. I still don't exactly invite Cynthia to dinner, but . . . you know. We go way back."

This surprised me. I had thought she would say something cutting about him, indicate that she would never lay eyes on him again if she could help it. I had a sudden image of Evan and Lisa embracing, of me seeing them a year from now, holding hands. "Sure," I heard myself say, my voice a little higher pitched than I'd meant it to be. "Right. How is he?"

She made a little face, a teeter-totter motion with her hand. "Better now, I think. I think he felt relieved once he sold the house, and he and Cynthia have moved too. So both those houses belong to someone else now."

"I wonder if they left the ramps," I said. "If people in wheelchairs bought them."

Lisa poked at her tea bag with the tip of her spoon. We drank our tea and looked around at the folded blankets on the back of the couch, the books of photographs on the coffee table.

"Well," she said. "It's September. Are you back in school?"

"No," I said. "I'm working as a caregiver again."

Her face did the most extraordinary thing then. It was like I'd told her I'd bought the house on Chambers Street. She was so shocked I could practically see the distance between her features increase. Her whole face just gave in, like she'd let go of every muscle. Then she recovered herself and put a hand to her mouth. She said, "I'm sorry, I don't know why I reacted that way."

I fumbled to put down my tea and it slipped and spilled some liquid on the table. I swiped it away with my hand and tried to reach over to touch her arm. "It's okay," I started to say, but she scrambled back from me, one hand held up.

We waited, and then she breathed deeply. "I'm sorry," she said definitively. "Please don't take it personally. It just shocked me, somehow, to think you can do that for someone other than Kate."

"People do," I said defensively. "People do it for a living, and they don't work for just one person."

"I know," she said, "but I didn't have that feeling about you. I just thought you might . . . I don't know. Something basic while you finished school, something just totally different, I don't know what."

"I didn't know what else to do," I admitted. "I thought it might make me feel better to work for someone else."

"Helping others?" Lisa said, a bitter edge in her voice.

I set down my teacup. "No," I sighed, worn out by her. "Another person to concentrate on, I guess." I stood up. To my satisfaction, Lisa looked chagrined and apologetic.

"I'm sorry," she began. She seemed surprised. "I'm way out of line."

She'd been indulging herself a bit, I realized, probably repeating the kinds of things she stewed about all the time. It made me feel a little better, to know she was doing just as badly.

I KEPT OFFERING TO do more of Barb's errands—getting groceries, taking the car in for an oil change. It was just an excuse to be alone. Her cheer could be downright virulent.

I spent the morning picking up little items here and there, a flashlight, some Magic Markers, toilet paper. When I ran out of excuses to be away, I headed back to the house. There was another car parked in the driveway, yet another friend.

I headed to Barb's room to let her know I was done for the day. Near the closed door to her room, I paused. I could hear a voice, tearful and tremulous, and someone making soothing sounds in response. A voice dipped to a hiss, then rose to a sob. I couldn't make out any words. I assumed it was one of Barb's friends crying, and for a moment I simply felt regretful. Who knew what problems people poured out to Barb, who believed in common sense and God and was probably comforting in a bracing way.

Another murmured exclamation came through the door. It sounded like Barb. The scene I had had in my head reversed itself: I saw Barb's friend holding her good hand, stroking it, and Barb sobbing inconsolably. I stood for a moment in the dark hall, a stunned, panicky dread overtaking me. There seemed no logical reason for this to shake me the way it did. People cried, even cheerful religious people who had the comfort of God and husbands and schnauzers.

I backed away from the door, nearly tripping over one of the dogs dozing in the hallway. It leapt to its feet and stalked away.

I hadn't realized how fragile the peace in Barbara's house was for me, how much I had relied on its stability, the pure, boring momentum of her husband and her friends, with their casseroles and their roomy tunics and jazzy earrings. I felt as if I had just come upon a bag of heroin in the desk drawer. I didn't have it in me to face that sort of anguish again. I saw what would happen if I stayed at this job. I'd be in her life more and more, till I couldn't help colliding with that Something, whatever it was I didn't know yet and that had nothing to do with me, but that I'd try to fix anyway.

"HEY!" JILL SAID. "YOU bring the wine?"

I shook my head as I came up her steps. She and Tim had moved into one half of a duplex near campus. The neighborhood wasn't like our old one. It was more like the one around Chambers Street: families, retrievers, SUVs. If anyone was smoking pot they were doing it indoors.

"Oh, right . . . I didn't quite get it together. I brought money, though." I had thought I would stop by the liquor store Kate and I used to go to on my way over, but as I had neared it I kept driving. I hadn't bought a lot of wine in the last several months, and I didn't want someone asking after Kate.

Jill looked perplexed. "All right. We'll walk over to the store around the corner, okay?" She stepped out and closed the door behind her.

We put our hands in our pockets and started down the sidewalk, kicking leaves away as we went.

"What's for dinner?" I asked.

"Oh, just pasta and some salad. Tim bought biscotti and ice cream. Nothing like you make."

I snorted. "Boy, you haven't eaten at my house in a long time," I said.

"Oh, what, are you not roasting the beef bones before you make stock?" she teased. I was eating frozen okra and white bread spread with Nutella and bananas, but I knew she wanted me to laugh, so I did.

Jill said, "So how's Barbara?"

"She's fine," I said. "She's looking for a new caregiver but fine."

"You quit?" Jill said.

"Yeah," I said. It was a relief to say it, an even sweeter one to know I didn't have to go back.

I had phoned Barbara, intending to invent something about a family emergency, or some incredibly well-paying job opportunity. The lie hadn't come out once I heard her voice. "Barb—I'm not ready to do this again," I said. "I thought I was but I'm not."

I heard her sigh. "Okay," she'd said simply. "Okay. My daughter can help out till I find someone. Good luck, hon."

"It was going all right before," I told Jill. "It was boring but it was okay. I thought I would be so glad to be caregiving again, but I can still hear that voice." I zipped up my jacket. "Maybe if I'd heard what she was saying it would have turned out to be nothing. Maybe she'd just seen a really sad movie."

Jill didn't smile. "Are you going to try another ad?" she said. I lifted a hand, let it fall. "Maybe you need to give yourself some time, you know. Get some dumb job and relax for a while. Then you can do some more caregiving and see how it goes."

I stared at my feet as we walked. "I don't think I want to," I said slowly. "I don't think it's an issue of waiting. I just don't want to dive back into someone else's life again."

Jill looked shocked. "It can be less involved than it was with Kate," she said. "And you were so good at it. I really think that's the thing for you. You're just not ready yet."

I had thought so too. There had been a period, before I moved in with Kate and once I was well settled with her, when I had felt as content and calm as I ever had, and though I hadn't articulated it, I saw now that I thought I'd found what I wanted to do, and was already doing it.

"I *was* good at it," I said. "I probably would have worked for Kate forever, but I'm not doing this anymore. I think that was my shot, and that's it."

"That's so sad." Jill sighed. "That's such a depressing way to think of it."

Maybe it was. Melancholy was a comforting, tranquil way to feel once you got used to it. But this felt to me more like being wise, like simply understanding what lay before me. I wouldn't be a caregiver anymore, but it was true: I had been so good at it, for a while.

IN THE STORE JILL looked around and then turned to me expectantly.

"Well, what do we need?" she said. A sales guy approached us and she gave him a bright smile and gestured at me as if I were on top of it. "No thanks."

He started to turn away, but I was looking around at the walls lined with bottles, the crates filled with them, the labels incomprehensible blocks of color.

"No, we need suggestions," I called to the salesman. I held up two twenties and said, "I have forty dollars and I need a couple bottles of wine. Can you just steer us in the right direction, please?"

As we walked back up to Jill's house she got quiet. Finally she turned to me and said, "Listen, don't get mad. But Tim invited Mark over."

I stopped and looked at her. "And he said *yes*?"

"Of course he said yes. He liked you."

"I haven't called him in like six months." Jill opened her mouth to protest. "Whatever, four. In dating terms, that's a lifetime. I can't believe he said yes."

"I thought you guys might like talking," she said slyly. "You know, give it a shot for once."

"Fuck off." I said it automatically, because she wanted me to respond to being teased.

She laughed, sounding pleased. Then we started walking again and she said, "I bet he doesn't mind. Or understands, or whatever. Come on. You can have a little fun."

"I look like hell. I haven't even worn makeup in months."

"You never wore it until Kate forced you to learn how to use it. You don't need it anyway. You look pretty. You have wine. On more than one occasion you fucked this guy's brains out, so I bet he has some residual fondness for you. Now come on."

WE HAD SPAGHETTI WITH tomato sauce and prosciutto scattered over the top, salad with fennel and blue cheese, and biscotti and blackberry ice cream. When Jill set the bowl in front of me I just sat and breathed it in for a second. It was the nicest food I'd seen in a long time. When I looked up, Mark was watching me. He smiled at me, but I was hoping he wouldn't ask me why I was teary over pasta, and he didn't.

We walked out to our cars after dinner.

"I should have called to see if you wanted a ride," he said. "It's stupid to drive separately when we live right near each other."

"You know I live there?" I said. Then I shook my head. "Of course you do. I'm sure Jill mentioned it."

We came to my car and I leaned back against it. "I thought maybe you'd come by sometime," he said. I didn't say anything. I just nodded.

"So, you're job hunting now, I guess?"

"Yeah," I agreed. "Or I'd better. Once I figure out what. I guess I could just get something to hold me over. Go back to waitressing."

"Oh. Well, good luck." He stuck his hands in his pockets and glanced around. "My car's down there."

I unlocked my car door and got in. He bent down, his hands on the window. "Hey," he said. "You know you have a big hole in the dashboard?"

I sighed and looked at the empty stereo niche. I'd stuffed all the wires back inside. The nuts and bolts and screws were in a plastic Baggie in the ashtray. "Yeah," I said. "I'm aware of it."

He rocked back on his heels. "Bec," he said. "Why don't you just come over for a while? It's early."

I looked up at him. One of the things I had come to like about him, or at least I had before, was that there was no roundness in his face. The streetlamp cast shadows beneath his cheekbones, at the corners of his mouth, alongside the straight line of his nose. I couldn't think of any good reason to avoid him. I wanted to go to his apartment and turn off the lights and look at the fish tank.

"Okay," I said. "I'll meet you there."

SILVIO AND ANNETTE LOOKED none the worse for wear. Mark disappeared into the kitchen. I heard the hiss of bottles being opened and then his footsteps returning as I was shaking some shrimp flakes into the water.

"Am I overfeeding them?" I asked. I stopped sprinkling. "I'm probably ruining their feeding schedule."

"Oh, they're resilient," he said. "Maybe they'll just get really huge, like tuna."

I replaced the cap and set the bottle of fish food on the table. When I turned to face him we looked at each other awkwardly. He tapped the lip of his beer bottle against mine. We drank.

I sat down on his couch and put my feet up on the table. He seated himself on the coffee table, facing me. He set down his beer and picked up my foot, unbuckling the shoe.

My heart sank. I didn't know why I had bothered to come here, but I knew I didn't have the wherewithal to soothe some guy's ego while I explained why I had no energy to fuck him. I took my foot away.

He looked surprised. "I'm not hitting on you," he said. "I thought you might be more comfortable."

I must have looked skeptical, because he chuckled as he unbuckled my other shoe. "I know it's been a while, but we do have a little history at this. I'd just kiss you if that's what I meant, Bec."

"Oh. Okay."

He set my shoes on the floor and sat down on the couch next to me, and we looked at the fish tank and drank our beers without talking. He picked up my hand and held it. He turned it over to see the palm and then turned it back, stretching the fingers out. I had a round maroon scar on one knuckle, the remnant of a burn on the side of a hot pan, and a faint pink line from an old cut. They were almost healed over.

"What are you looking for?" I asked.

"Nothing." He pressed his thumb at the center of my palm and rubbed it in circles, loosening up the muscle. He wrapped his hand around my wrist and made a gentle rolling motion with his fingers. His hands were warm and large, the fingers callused, nails ragged. "Give me the other one."

I did, turning toward him and leaning back against the arm of the couch. He pressed each knuckle lightly between his fingertips, then massaged each finger all the way out to the torn nails. He kneaded his way up my forearms and back down till they felt soft and relaxed.

"Who taught you how to do this?"

"Old girlfriend," he said, concentrating.

"What was she, a manicurist?"

"Nope. Just touchy-feely."

He pushed my sleeves back and rubbed my arms in long, oval motions. I leaned farther back, stretching out my legs while he sat on the edge of the cushion. He pushed my hair away from my face and I waited for him to try to kiss me, but he didn't. The room was dark except for the watery light from the fish tank. I watched the silver light slither over his neck and shoulders. I couldn't see his face very well. I closed my eyes. It was such a comforting couch. In my mouth lingered the bitter taste of the beer I no longer felt like finishing. I caught the waxy scent of a half-burned candle on the coffee table. Mark kept rubbing my hands, gently, matter-of-factly, saying nothing. Tears pooled beneath my eyelids, then mercifully receded, but sadness rose through me like dark water filtering up through the ground. I seemed for a moment to be all liquid, warm as seawater, a rushing, tidal sound faint in my eardrums. I let him touch my hands and then rub my feet until the skin felt as though it had been roughened up, enlivened, and then he laid my hands carefully on my midriff. I heard him walk away, heard his footsteps return, and felt the light warmth of a blanket settle over me.

twenty-three

I WOKE UP AROUND seven the next morning. I was still on the couch, a blanket wrapped around me. I looked around, startled, trying to figure out where I was. The blanket was yellow flannel. I smelled the scent of the candle a few feet away, then saw the fish tank.

Once I realized where I was, I didn't feel so frantic. It was Saturday. I was wonderfully comfortable. The blanket was soft and light, just warm enough to be cozy. The sun had come up. There were a few neighborhood sounds outside too—cars going past, a squirrel skittering along a tree branch near the window. I turned over onto my side, fluffing my pillow and wondering when I'd acquired it.

Mark was in the armchair across from me, his feet propped on the coffee table. He was still asleep, the quilt from his bed spread over him. His mouth was open, his beard shadowing his chin. His hair stuck up on one side. I watched him, the quilt rising and falling with his breath, and wondered why he hadn't slept in his bed. Maybe he'd thought I might want it. Maybe he'd just passed out. Except there weren't any more beer bottles than our two half-full ones, on the table.

I got up quietly and tiptoed into the bathroom. I splashed my face, smoothed my hair, and brushed my teeth with my finger. I looked okay, though. I looked flushed, the circles beneath my eyes diminished.

I found a notebook in a kitchen drawer and debated what to write. I didn't want to wake him up. Finally I wrote, *Good to see you. Thanks.* I thought about some reference to the massage, or whatever it had been, but I didn't know what to say about it. I didn't even know what to call it. Finally I left the note on the table, paused, and then before I could over-think it and chicken out I added one more line. Unfortunately what came out was, *Pool this week? (Billiards.)*

The first words on the lined paper looked so carefully dashed-off, and then that ridiculous billiards addendum, as if he'd think I meant a swim. He was going to tease me about this, I thought, but oh well. I realized I was smiling.

I stood near the armchair for a second, touched an experimental fingertip to his cheekbone. I had never seen Liam sleep, not even a doze. At some point, the few guys I saw sleeping had stopped seeming boyish in repose. Mark had a heavy, slightly musky scent when I leaned near him, his beard thick as wire, the shadows beneath his eyes suggesting he had not slept as soon as he had coaxed me to. Yet I liked him better for it, the faint evidence of work and worry. I anchored the note with the candle and let myself quietly out the front door.

The air felt wonderful, truly autumnal and crisp, the sun bright and the faint smell of wood smoke in the air. At first I began to walk toward my apartment. I was maybe five blocks away, and I was dying for a real breakfast. I didn't even know the last time I'd had one. I had no food at home, no eggs, muffins, oatmeal, or fruit. I didn't even have good coffee, for God's sake. I was living like an animal.

So I changed my mind, and headed toward the capitol. It was too lovely not to take the long way, so I walked past the lake. The farther downtown I went, the more people were out, already on their way to the market. As I walked up King Street I saw the trucks parked along the square, the throng of people—but not too crowded yet—moving in a slow stroll around the lawns. There would be pears, and apples, and the beginnings of winter greens and root vegetables. There would be shallots and beets, pastries, cheese, handmade butter.

I decided to buy some pears. Suddenly I was craving a pear crisp. I thought I might even make one and eat it for breakfast. I could pick up some lemon and butter, oatmeal and nutmeg, on my way home.

As I passed people I peered into their baskets. They were carrying bunches of flowers, carrots with leafy tops, fingerling potatoes still shedding dirt.

I think I wanted to be hit by the smell of pastry and coffee, the closer I got. I had realized recently that I no longer wept whenever I was driving, and the loss felt terrible to me. For so long it had happened every time I got in my car, like water running over a too-full glass. It had been a comfort, in a way.

I was at the entrance to the square now. I could smell the bittersweet chocolate from the croissants, the coffee and hot cider sold from carts.

On the other side of the capitol, I remembered, there was a woman who sold tiny Seckel pears that tasted like honey. The crowd was moving past me, and I stepped into it.

I REQUIRED AN EXPEDITION just to stock myself up on basic equipment. I had spoons, and a few cereal bowls, and of course my shallow omelet pan. I briefly wondered if I could fit a Lilliputian version of a crisp into that, like a doll's dessert, but that didn't seem in the spirit of the thing. I wanted to pile up fruit, press the topping down over it so it wouldn't fall off the sides.

I dropped off my farmers' market purchases and went back out to a kitchen supply store for bowls and a knife and hot pads. I might have found some of this at the co-op, and it would all be hand-tooled and woven by well-treated indigenous peoples, but it would also cost four times as much. Frankly, it was time to remind myself I wasn't living on Kate's bank account. I wasn't sure what my next job would be, but whatever it was, it was unlikely to pay well, so I may as well be frugal.

I bought the basics, a big plastic bowl, a vegetable peeler, a glass baking dish, and oven mitts. Then I headed over to the knife section to eye the Wüsthofs. Their chef's knife was a thing of beauty. Once I'd gotten a salesperson to let me handle it—its sleekness, its weighted, steady handle, its diamond point—there was no way I wasn't buying it. I had saved *some* money, after all. A good cook knows where to invest.

At home, I set my purchases on my two square feet of counter space and looked them over with satisfaction. The pears were beautiful, speckled and blushing, leaves still clinging to a few of their stems. They smelled of honey and of their own tough, herbal-scented skins. I'd gotten a block of sweet butter too, and a little bag of black walnuts. I hadn't had them since last winter. They were expensive—Kate had told me once it was because they were murder to shell—but they tasted intensely nutty when they were roasted. On my second trip I'd gotten some oats and brown sugar for the top. I also bought—this was the one secret I recalled Kate telling me—a little bag of small-pearled tapioca. Unlike flour, it thickened the pears without making them gluey.

I washed and dried everything, then set my ingredients and equipment out in front of me. The counter space was so tiny I had to use the top of the half-size fridge. I didn't have a recipe, except what I recalled of making it at Kate's direction. And there wasn't one in my only cookbook, so I couldn't consult that. I had always just asked her.

I ended up doing it by guesswork and memory. I used a coffee cup to measure flour and then just dumped in oats and sugar and pinches of spice, rubbing in cubes of butter with my fingertips until the mixture felt crumbly and silky with fat. I peeled pears, sliced them off the core, and left them in big chunks. I tossed the fruit with a little tapioca and sugar and lemon zest.

My hands were slick and sweet with pear juice and lemon and sugar. I put the dish in the oven and then looked around my apartment while it cooked. It was pretty much a mess. I walked around, followed by the fizzing sound of my carpet, picking things up and setting them in what I arbitrarily deemed the right place—I had never really settled when I moved in. Finally I opened the blinds all the way and sat down on my couch. My apartment began to smell of pears and lemon and browning butter.

I had looked around for Evan at the market. Though he had never come with us, back when I took Kate each week, I knew they used to go together. It was my guess that he had stopped going with her at first because it gave him time to be alone, then, later, time to be with someone. After they separated, he probably didn't want to run into us. But I had always remembered seeing him at the little Wednesday market, buying a piece of fruit. This morning as I had strolled around trying samples of goat cheese and honey, I kept glancing about, expecting to see his thin blond hair fanned by the wind, the flash of his glasses in the sun.

I checked on the crisp. Bubbles rose through the syrupy glaze around the fruit and the top was brown. I took it out and brought it

YOU'RE NOT YOU 261

back to the coffee table. Steam rose off the crust. I had a plate and fork and a square of paper towel for a napkin, and for a satisfying moment I thought I might eat the whole thing myself, plate after plate.

"BEC," EVAN SAID. HE leaned against the door frame and gazed at me. His mouth curved into a bit of a smile, a pass at one. "Come in."

"I brought you a crisp," I said. "A housewarming thing, I guess."

"That's sweet of you," Evan said, taking it from me. "Still the chef. We'll have it tonight."

Lisa had told me, the day I went to see her, what street he was on now. Maybe she was hoping I'd go see him too. Today I had driven slowly down the street, the crisp sitting on the passenger seat, until I saw Evan's car in a driveway.

I followed him into the house, looking around. It was nice enough, a little dark. I didn't see any Kate-like touches. No bright paint, no bookcases. It was just a house.

He led me up a couple steps and into a kitchen. There was a newspaper spread out on the table, the smell of coffee in the air. Through the window I could see Cynthia, kneeling in a garden. Her hair was shorter than I'd been imagining it. She wasn't as slim as I recalled either, but rounded and voluptuous.

"Have a seat," Evan said. He set a cup of coffee before me. Traces of cream still spun in its center.

"Pretty good memory," I said. Evan sipped his coffee and looked at me.

I wasn't sure what I had thought he might do, welcome me with smiles like an old friend, or tell me to get off his property. Maybe my intentions would have showed, if I had a better idea of what they were. The crisp was just an excuse. It wasn't even Evan's favorite; he preferred something more elegant: a sunburst of sliced peaches in barely sweet almond custard, baked inside a tart, crème fraiche rather than whipped cream. It was Kate who'd loved the generous chaos of crisps and cobblers, who was charmed by old American dessert names like buckles and slumps. Before me on my coffee table the crisp had steamed away, smelling gorgeous, and I couldn't believe I wasn't going to eat it. I decided I'd make the next one perfect and make this one a good excuse to see Evan and get it over with. I wasn't going to dart around town like a squirrel, afraid of seeing him any time I went somewhere pleasant. And I certainly wasn't going to stop going to the market.

Evan just kept watching me, his expression unreadable.

"I don't have a good reason to see you," I admitted. "I just thought I might . . ." I stopped. "I saw Lisa the other day."

He nodded. "Yes," he said slowly. "I heard. You seem to be making the rounds, apparently."

I stared at him. My face felt numb. You imagine these moments, but most people don't just lay it down for you like this. If I'd been less stunned I might have respected him for cutting to the chase.

Evan sat back and regarded me. His expression wasn't very neutral anymore, just hard and still. I was about to cave in and apologize— for a second I felt the onset of a tremble in my lips—but his face stopped me. Instead of saying anything I just looked back at him and waited.

I had never heard one thing from him after Kate died. Not one letter, or a questioning phone call asking for me instead of sending a message through my mother, or any of the things I would have done. He had never asked me what happened. I kept telling people the same thing, that I had woken up too late, that I'd gotten up to silence but had just missed the noise that roused me, maybe the last sound she'd made, and found her. It was what she had told me to say. But if Evan had asked I would have told him. When he didn't call, I assumed he'd believed the same thing everyone else did, that I'd simply found her too late. Looking at him now it was clear to me he knew what had happened.

"Well," I said slowly, "I seem to have to make my rounds. Since no one will call me." I took a sip from my coffee mug and set it down. "But then, I'm used to jumping into your shoes for you anyway. You should pay me for this, too."

Evan took off his glasses and wiped them with the hem of his sweater. Deep red welts were on either side of his nose.

"That was snide of me," he said. "I'm sorry."

"Well, I'm not," I said. "I meant it." My doubt had vanished—I had done exactly what she'd asked me to because none of them had done it for her, and now I had to go begging for contact, handing out desserts just to get someone to talk to me about it.

"I don't know what to tell you," he said. "You seem to think I went skipping off, when in fact she made me go. I wanted to work things out."

"Yeah, she could tell. We could all tell how much you cared while you were out on dates."

"You were there a lot," he conceded, "but not every second. And you don't know everything. Don't talk to me as if you do."

I smiled at him. "Fuck you, Evan. I know a lot more than I ever asked to."

He shook his head and got up from the table. "No offense, Bec," he said, then shook his head and gave a mirthless laugh. His back was to me as he poured coffee. "You were wonderful to Kate. But she was my wife. You were the employee. A good friend to her too, but I don't have to answer to you."

He turned around, but he didn't come back to the table. He crossed his arms and regarded me from the counter. "And I'll tell you something else," he said. "I would not have let her do what she did. That's what *I* know. I would never have let that happen, not the way you did."

I thought of Kate's face, her mouth stretched wide for air, her eyes bulging with the strain. Of course he wouldn't have done what I did. I had barely been able to do it. Evan would have taken one look at her and called the ambulance. There were times I still saw myself lifting her hand, the skin cold and dry, placing the button on the floor away from my foot, away from any impulsive or accidental contact. I remembered it as the slowest moment of my life, the most silent and determined. I knew there had been noise, her attempts at breathing, my voice, but in my memory the room was always hushed and empty as Kate and I looked at each other.

I sat there and cupped my hands around the coffee cup. I felt pure rage at her then, at her willingness to bring me into this and leave me

with it. I was as furious with her as I used to be with Evan on her behalf, when I had hated him for being outside the body of illness, just
for having the luxury of his options, that ability to walk away.

"I know you wouldn't have," I said. "So did she. Why else was I there?"

twenty-four

L E CHAMPIGNON LOOKED ALMOST modest in the daytime. Sunlight streamed into the windows at the front of the dining room. The chairs were haphazardly shoved into a corner, and the tables were bare except for blank cloths. I was sitting at the empty bar, waiting.

The woman who came out of the kitchen, Anna, was shorter than I was, broad and sturdy in her whites. She didn't have on a chef's hat as I had expected. She wore a baseball cap with a Muskie on it. We shook hands, hers rough and damp, though she'd wiped it on the towel that hung off her belt. She smelled of onion. From the kitchen floated a rich, meaty fragrance. Anna saw me sniff and gave me a brief smile, saying, "Beef bones. For demi-glace."

As I followed her into the kitchen she glanced over her shoulder at me. There were rubber pads on the floor, an open screen door at the back, steel tables everywhere. Pans of beef joints, browned dark, were balanced on every surface. "Make a lot of demi-glace?" she asked me.

"Just lots of stock," I said. Thank god I'd read enough of Kate's Julia Child books to know what I was talking about. In the hopes of showcasing this, I added nonchalantly, "I never needed to cook it down that far."

She nodded. "I think we spend about half our time making stock," she said. "It's the backbone. You bring knives?"

I shook my head. It hadn't even occurred to me. I thought they'd have them.

"Cooks bring their own knives and they watch them like hawks," she said. "You don't want them getting dull or dropped or whatever. You'll need to get a couple good basics and a knife case."

I flushed. I had told her over the phone that I had some professional cooking experience. It was not quite a bald-faced lie, since I had indeed learned to cook while on the clock, but it was clear she was going to grasp the extent of my ignorance pretty quickly. Apparently cooks brought their own knives. Who knew?

She led me to a long table near the door. There was a pile of shallots in a wooden crate sitting on it. Anna laid a hand on them and said, "These need to be peeled and trimmed. Come to me when you finish that."

IN THE TWO WEEKS since I'd seen Evan, I cooked every day. It had been months since I'd cooked regularly. I missed making the caregivers nightly meals, missed the rhythms of buying my ingredients, setting them out, and transforming them into something. I even missed the parts I'd enjoyed without wanting to admit it: I liked disjointing a chicken, seeing the construction of the animal and knowing how I'd change it. I began to cook again for the pleasure of seeing how new dishes would turn out, whether making my own sourdough starter was worth it, if squash ravioli were better with prosciutto and sage or just brown butter and parmesan.

My kitchen was ill-equipped to do any of this. I ended up dragging over the coffee table, balanced on some books for height, to get extra counter space.

Not everything turned out perfectly—I had to limber up. Jill and I gamely chewed a few bites of a lamb ragu, conversation dwindling, until I admitted it tasted like dirty wool and we went out for pizza. But others were flawless. Mark and I each ate huge platefuls of squash ravioli, unable to stop. We'd made more than we needed, yet at the first touch of the handmade pasta slick in our mouths with sage-scented butter, velvety squash on our tongues, there couldn't possibly be enough of them. "I feel *insane*," Mark had said, helping himself to another spoonful. "I think I'm going to have a big buttery aneurysm and it's going to be fantastic."

The day after that I had begun to look at classifieds in the restaurant section. There were quite a few diners hiring, and though I liked the fantasy of simple honest food, homemade pie, and freshly ground

burgers, I knew that wasn't likely. I could make burritos to order in
several locations. But the good restaurants never ran ads.

I was feeling very uncompromising. There was no point in going
into the restaurant business if it was only to thaw a preformed burger
and pour out a carton of soup into a vat. I could remain an amateur if
that was all I wanted. Still a little high on the success of the handmade
pasta for the ravioli, I decided to think it over while making my first
batch of croissants. I thought I had it right, kneaded the butter into
the dough as quickly as I could, and cut and rolled them, waiting as the
smell of pastry filled the apartment. They looked stellar until I tore
one open, only to find they were leaden, oozing butter.

I took a bite, chewed thoughtfully, and tossed the rest. I was never
going to get anywhere like this. I might stumble into a good dish 75
percent of the time, but it wasn't the same as studying. This was too
random. I needed a plan, a directed, educational plan. Somewhere in
Oconomowoc my mother was probably grinning but didn't know why.

People did these free apprenticeships, unpaid time in good restaurants, just for the experience. Though I was fairly certain I didn't
qualify even for slave labor, still it seemed worth a try. I'd bluffed
my way into jobs I didn't want, so I ought to be able to argue for one
I did.

Finally, bolstered by the sight of brown pastry in my trash can, I
called Le Champignon. I wasn't sure how the titles worked, so I asked
for the person in charge of the kitchen. This turned out to be someone
named Anna, who was distinctly unimpressed by my skills as I de-
scribed them.

"I'd like to apprentice, for free, for a week or two," I said. My voice
sounded tentative, so I sat up straighter, which seemed to help. I was
sitting cross-legged on my fizzy carpet. "I have experience," I went on.
"I was a cook for a year, a private cook. The thing is, my training was a
little . . . haphazard. You know, it went according to the client's taste."

Anna treated me to a skeptical silence, during which I blushed
though I was alone.

"Oh yeah, the article," she said. "For a while after it ran we had retired executives calling every day. I love the people who think restaurant work will be a pleasant retirement hobby."

I laughed with her, a hearty, skeptical laugh. Amateurs. "But you've done a little professional cooking, huh," she said finally. "Just privately though."

"Yes," I admitted. Then I continued, with a silent apology in case Kate was rolling her eyes at me, "I worked for a pretty demanding client though. She had very particular taste, but it was also pretty eclectic." Silence hummed over the line for a moment. In the background I heard someone hollering about a ten-top. "But I'd do this for free. I'm skilled enough to be useful, and I'm cheap labor for you. The cheapest, actually. If I get in your way you kick me out again."

"Very true," she said, "I will. Whatever. Come in tomorrow at ten."

After the first thirty shallots or so, I got into a rhythm, peeling and tossing them into a big metal bowl I'd found near the dishwasher. There seemed to be more shallots than they could possibly use in a day or probably a week, and I wondered if she was just trying to get me so bored I'd give up on the first day. When I had peeled them all I started on trimming. I was trying to remember to keep my fingers curled back and protected, but that was always my worst habit, one pinky sticking out as if it were begging to be sliced away. If that habit had driven Kate crazy, then for these people it would mark me as an even bigger amateur than I was.

Around me people kept squeezing by with trays of roasted walnuts and little salted crackers, beef joints and root vegetables that had been roasted and caramelized. After a while I stopped jumping in surprise when someone bellowed, "Behind!" and shoved past me. I just pressed into the table till my hip bones bruised and let them pass.

"Behind with sharp!" someone said, and a guy in a stained apron went by with a long knife gleaming in his hand. Earlier I had almost collided with someone when I misunderstood "Behind with hot!" and turned to see what it meant. It turned out to be a pan still sizzling with fat, clamped in a pair of tongs and carried by one of the cooks to the dish sink.

I got the occasional cold breeze from the open door, but the rest of the kitchen was sweltering. People dressed in jeans and ragged jackets stormed in the back doors carrying boxes of meat and vegetables. They asked me where to set them and before I could answer that I didn't know they put them on the nearest table, so that was what I started telling them.

No one seemed very surprised to find a stranger peeling shallots in a corner. They either ignored me completely or wiped what I hoped was beef blood off their hands and offered one to me to shake. I couldn't remember anyone's name.

When I finished the shallots I found Anna in the walk-in cooler with a clipboard and a marker. Without looking at me she nudged a box of carrots my way with her toe. "Peel them," she said. I hefted the box and went back to my corner.

The whole place was much louder than I had imagined. I think I had pictured neat rows of people dicing and sautéing quietly. Instead there was a great deal of swearing and exclamation about the state of the truffle oil. "Don't leave the fucking truffle oil on the table, people!" Anna yelled, holding up the offending bottle. "The next time I see it out here it goes in the walk-in right next to your severed head."

Around two o'clock she walked past me and set a piece of foil bearing a small chunk of blue-veined cheese next to the carrot box and said, "Eat that."

I was smart enough to keep peeling carrots while I ate the cheese. It was fantastic. Salty, pungent, a combination of something creamy and melting and little delicate grains along the blue threads. I wished I had a pear or some port to have with it. Or Sauternes. Kate would have known which was better.

One of the guys who had introduced himself came back and set a metal pan of water on the table. He cocked his head at me, so I went over and peered in. In the steaming water was a white ceramic dish, filled with something that looked like layers of mousse, a creamy beige color.

"Foie gras?" I asked, and he nodded.

"We'll put a taster out for the servers after staff meal," he said. "Fight your way in and get a smear. And I do mean fight. Fucking servers are like vultures."

By now my legs were sore and my feet throbbed. I'd been leaning over a table so long my back was aching all around my hips, and I wore the soreness like a sash tied around my waist. Under my cap my hair was damp and hot. It felt as though someone had stretched me on a rack.

"Dinner," said Anna. The foie gras guy turned and practically sprinted. Anna glanced my way and said, "You staying for staff meal?"

"If it's okay," I said.

"Fine by me," she said, "but then you have to get out so you don't get in the way of dinner service. Come back tomorrow at six A.M. You can help with the baking."

THE STAFF MEAL WAS chicken in a smoky red sauce. There was also a huge pan of rice, a metal bowl of greens and a squirt bottle of vinaigrette, a loaf of bread and a couple squares of butter. I got in line and took a white plate from a pile and served myself a little too much of everything. I was starving.

I sat down near one end, giving a mute smile to the people on either side. It was like being at a very awkward dinner party, but at least by now I'd had experience with real embarrassment. This was easier than the first time I'd tried to get Kate out of bed.

"You visiting?" a woman asked. I had a mouthful of chicken and as I chewed and swallowed she took another bite of bread, watching me the whole time. She was one of the servers, who all looked too dressy to be at a plaid tablecloth at four thirty in the afternoon, gnawing chicken legs. They wore shirts and ties or crisp blouses and skirts, hair swept up and eyes lined.

"Yeah," I said finally, swallowing. "I think Anna's letting me see if a professional kitchen will wear me down or kill me outright."

She grinned and took a sip from a can of Diet Coke. "Where'd you work before?"

"I worked for a couple, just cooking for them privately. And their friends, for parties. It was like being a caterer, sort of."

The other people near us were listening in. The foie gras guy looked surprised. "Does Madison have people rich enough to hire private chefs?" A few servers chuckled. "No, I'm serious, does it? Because I'll wear a uniform and a toque, I don't care."

"It wasn't quite like that," I told him. "She was disabled and couldn't cook, and she had very good taste. So I learned a lot from her."

"This must be different," the woman said.

"It's more chaotic. And I'm a lot more tired than I thought I would be. And I don't have a clue what anyone is doing. But I'm told I get to try the food."

The foie gras guy laughed. "We have to keep you around somehow. No restaurant lets go of free labor if they can help it." He took another bite of his chicken and said conversationally, "I saw you cutting the tips off those shallots. Remind me to give you a lesson later. Your knife skills fucking suck."

AFTER THE MEAL I went home and left them to dinner service. They were all just getting their second wind, the servers whisking away the plastic tablecloth we'd eaten off of and rearranging and resetting the dining room tables. One by one they disappeared and returned with their neckties neatened or lipstick applied. The cooks were in high gear in the back, yelling about a béarnaise someone should have prepped. I snuck out the back door. The dishwasher waved to me.

At home I drank a beer and then took a long bath. There was a message on my machine from Jill, but I didn't call her back. I was feeling virtuous. If I went out and got home late or drank too much, I'd look like a lightweight. Anyway, I felt warm and relaxed now that I'd bathed. I put on my thick terry cloth robe and lay down on my couch with a book and the menu I'd borrowed from the maitre d'. Coulis, ganache, mille-feuilles. I didn't know how to make any of this stuff yet, but I planned to learn it all.

Outdoors I heard cars go by, trailed by waves of music. I missed my car stereo. Across the street my landlord's car pulled in and rumbled to a stop. The landlords weren't so bad, actually. They liked to talk my ear off if one of them cornered me in the laundry room, mainly about the neighborhood association. I had this place for another month, longer if I wanted it, but I was trying to think ahead. I missed living with someone, or at least having neighbors to visit. I decided I'd start looking soon, just to give myself plenty of time. I could do better than this if I tried.

I set my alarm for five, and went to bed.

I WOKE UP AS the people downstairs came trudging up to their door. It was four thirty, and I lay there and watched the sky lighten for a while before I had to get up and go to work.

For a long time after Kate died, I forgot that I didn't believe the dead visited. I kept trying to picture her, a diaphanous form at the foot of my bed, in the door of my bedroom.

I glanced at the alarm clock. Almost time to get up. I had promised Jill we'd go for a drink after I finished my free-labor stint for the day. I thought I might call Mark, but I had seen him a few days ago for the ravioli. We'd had fun, but I wasn't quite sure how this was going to go. I didn't want to be all over him. We seemed to be doing a dating sort of thing now, and who knew how that was supposed to work? I had managed to avoid dating like a normal person for nearly two years.

At five I got up and showered. I put on jeans and my most comfortable tennis shoes, a T-shirt under a fleece jacket. Once I was in the hot kitchen, the T-shirt would be plenty.

Outside it was cold and still a little dark. It was almost November. I started walking toward the restaurant, figuring it would take me about half an hour to get there. I could have driven, but I thought the walk would wake me up. And it did; it felt good to be out and moving, my breath freezing in the air. The sky lightened. Around me the tree branches began to shiver as birds and squirrels moved through them. I could get up to do this every day.

When I arrived I went up the fire escape to the back door. It was unlocked. A guy in whites was dumping butter into a huge mixer. He glanced up as I came in and said, "Hey. You Bec? I'm Chris." He offered me a floury hand. "Coffee's by the door."

When I came back with my mug he had me cutting apples for pastry and measuring flour. Then I chopped hickory nuts and walnuts in a food processor, its bowl dusted with oily crumbs. I glanced at the recipe card clipped to the edge of the shelf, looked around to find the brown sugar and cinnamon. This kitchen was easy to get comfortable in, much easier than it had seemed in the chaos yesterday.

In the morning, it turned out, the kitchen was calm and peaceful. The room grew warmer and more humid as we opened and shut the oven door, filling a rolling rack with trays of chocolate tart shells and croissants. It smelled of cinnamon and baking apple, coffee and lemon zest. Even after my walk I was still stiff from my apprenticeship from the day before, so I stretched my back out and rolled my neck to shake off the soreness. I felt my joints warm up and roll smoothly.

Maybe I should be a baker. I thought I could spend my days like this forever, and maybe this week I'd learn to make a better croissant than the ones I'd tried at home. But I still wanted to know the rest of it, the roasting and stock making and pâté sieving. And this was just the French stuff. I hadn't gotten started on Indian, or Japanese, or Thai.

I went back to chopping, keeping the tip of the knife on the board and letting the blade do the work. I would have to buy more knives, and now that I had handled a really good one, even better than the ones Kate had used, I knew what to look for.

The knife edge slid right through apples and pears, quick and smooth. I kept my knuckles forward to guide the flat of the blade, my fingertips curled in toward my palm, my thumb tucked under and protected. It wasn't actually so different from the cooking I used to do for Kate—or actually, for me. It hadn't fully occurred to me till now that she had rearranged a whole section of her life just so I could have that, the dinners with caregivers, the elaborate meals for only Evan, or only me.

I finished the apples and pears. I brought a big stainless steel bowl filled with them over to Chris, who was tucking dark chocolate inside croissant dough, his fingers shining with butter. He glanced into the bowl and nodded. He stepped back, wiping his hands on the towel tucked inside his apron string.

"You want to finish these?" he said. "I can start the apple ones. Just follow what I did here. But work pretty quickly. If the butter in the dough melts it won't be flaky."

"Okay," I said. So that was why my croissants had been such doorstops.

I sounded more confident than I felt. Le Champignon's pain au chocolat was something of a city institution. I wondered if someone had given Chris the idea that I had a lot more experience than I did. On the counter lay several more trays of satiny, cream-colored dough, cut into rectangles and resting on parchment paper. I took a couple chunks of chocolate and laid them in the center of one, then folded the dough around it. I worked quickly, and tried not to handle it much to keep the heat from my hands to a minimum. It looked lopsided, so I neatened it up as best I could and went on to the next, working a little more slowly but still briskly, and tucked it—prettily, I thought—into a rectangle. This one looked neater, more professional. It wasn't that difficult, though admittedly I hadn't done the hard part, the dough-making. But I didn't want to get caught up in that yet. I'd learn it, eventually. It was better to give yourself a moment to get your bearings. You had to find that rhythm, and have your plan set out in front of you. The day I'd first cooked at Kate's house, putting together the food for the party, had felt something like this. You set your ingredients and your tools before you; you drank some cold water or some good coffee and breathed in the fragrance of tomato stems or olives or runny cheese. You fortified yourself.

I did another croissant and then another, the heady chocolate scent rising into the heat of the air. As I worked I realized I'd been hunching over the trays, my neck bent and my shoulders rounded. There was no need to be so tense about it, I thought; no need to be the crabbed figure in the corner of the kitchen. I straightened up and continued working, letting my mind drift while my hands lifted, spread, and folded. I listened to the streets starting to move with traffic, and the vendors setting up for the market. Butter and sugar were browning in the ovens. I knew how to do this. I felt the ease settle back into my muscles, and the memory of the work came back to me.